FINALLY WOKEN

FINALLYWOKEN

DEAN MOYNIHAN

The Book Guild Ltd

First published in Great Britain in 2019 by
The Book Guild Ltd
9 Priory Business Park
Wistow Road, Kibworth
Leicestershire, LE8 0RX
Freephone: 0800 999 2982
www.bookguild.co.uk
Email: info@bookguild.co.uk
Twitter: @bookguild

Typeset in Adobe Garamond Pro
Printed and bound in Great Britain by CPI Group (UK) Ltd, Croydon, CR0 4YY

ISBN 978 1912575 985

British Library Cataloguing in Publication Data.
A catalogue record for this book is available from the British Library.

1

I.

I am.

I am Max.

I am Max Hope.

Always Max. Never Maximillian. Only my mum calls me Maximillian when I've done something bad.

Wait. I need a moment.

I overheard voices saying people had been killed. There was a lot of blood, they said. Maybe I dreamt it. I'm troubled by horrifying dreams.

I haven't been myself lately.

I perceive activity taking place. Day continues to follow night. Things are happening. Society is still behaving as if stuff matters. There is a strange deliberation and a complex motivational procedure involved in life's ultimate uselessness.

Something is missing.

I vividly remember a smear of sunset along the horizon. Powdery snow covered the ground. The trees cried from cold and clawed at the bruised twilight. Claire walked beside me, her beautiful smile obscured behind intermittent clouds of vapour.

A catastrophic event happened.

It was getting dark. Claire kissed me. I didn't see it coming. Then, out of nowhere, a lifetime of enigma was set in motion.

Who can say why these things happen?

***

The darkness began to lift.

Little splashes of colour appeared amidst the Rorschach ink blots under Max's eyelids. In the distance, someone started to laugh. Or scream. It echoed along a corridor.

There was also a gentle rhythmic tapping.

Tap, tap, tap, tap, tap, tap, tap.

Max listened. Raindrops on a window. The tapping comforted him. He was lying supine with a growing awareness of aching stiffness in all of his joints. He didn't dare move a muscle.

A smell of bleach became evident.

Footsteps approached. Three sets, on linoleum. Two sets stopped. The third took a few steps closer.

Shadows passed across Max's closed eyes.

A rustle of clothes.

Click. Brightness. A small torch.

A warm finger raised Max's left eyelid up. Blinding white light filled the void. It glided from side to side, one way, then the other. His eye automatically tried to escape the glare, but there was nowhere for it to hide. The glassy black pupil shrank back into the onyx brown iris and skittishly flicked in every direction while the lid strained to protect it.

The finger retreated, releasing the lid. Relief.

Seconds later, the same thing happened to the other eye. When it was over, Max kept his eyes tightly shut.

'Look, he's pissed himself,' said a man's voice.

'Do you mind?' said another man's voice, with weary irritation. The voice belonged to the person with the torch. Max assumed him to be a doctor.

'Well?' asked a third man.

'Well what?' replied the doctor.

'Is he ready?'

'Of course not. Does he look ready to you?'

'How long?' asked the first man.

2

'Days. Weeks, possibly. It's too early to say,' said the doctor.

'That's not good enough,' said the third man.

'Dood enough,' said a slurred voice. Max recognised it, just, as being his own, but an unfamiliar, deeper version.

'What did he say?' asked the third man.

'Dood enough,' said the first man.

'You'll get nothing intelligible out of him right now,' said the doctor.

The three men moved away a little. Max could hear them consulting. Planning something. The first man and third man were quite persistent in their bargaining, but the doctor calmly and adamantly rebuffed their requests.

Max felt an itchy twinge in his nose. He tried to raise his right hand to scratch it, but the arm only lifted a few inches before a clanking metal sound stopped it going further.

He tried with his left hand. Same. Something was attached to both of his wrists.

Weird, thought Max. *This is no way to treat an eleven-year-old.*

'Nurse, can you get him cleaned up, please?' said the doctor.

Squeaky rubber shoes approached.

The swish of a curtain. A breeze of movement brought with it a waft of boiled cabbage and diarrhoea. Definitely a hospital. An instinctive recoil of vomit-inducing disgust welled up in Max, then subsided. He hoped a window would be opened to clear the stale air.

The bed sheets were swiftly removed. Then his pyjama bottoms were taken off, making him momentarily naked.

I'm stark naked! thought Max. *What if Mum and Dad see me like this? Where are Mum and Dad?*

'He'll have to be transferred to a private room,' said the doctor. 'He shouldn't be on this ward.'

The three men moved further away, muttering.

Nurse One was joined by another nurse. One used a sponge to clean Max. The other wiped him dry, then they both busily fussed around applying new bed sheets and pulling on fresh pyjama bottoms, quite roughly, Max thought.

'Do you know who this is?' said Nurse One in a low voice.

'Yeah, I know. Creepy, huh?' said Nurse Two.

'I took a selfie with him earlier,' said Nurse One.

'Really? Why?' asked Nurse Two.

'It's not often we get people like this in,' said Nurse One.

'In my country, he'd be stoned to death,' said Nurse Two. 'Not that I agree with it, but in his case I'd make an exception.'

Who are they talking about? thought Max.

'You'd never think he was capable of doing what he did, would you?' said Nurse One.

'People are capable of anything,' said Nurse Two.

'Hope he rots in hell,' said Nurse One.

Their rubber shoes squeaked as they retreated.

Rain continued tapping on the window. It began to irritate Max now, as did the persistent itch in his nose. He wiggled it to no effect.

The wrist restraints must be there to protect me, he thought. *I badly scraped my hands when I fell off my bike. I hit my head, too. Almost died. People are so rude when they don't think you're listening.*

Max wondered if his mum had gone into his bedroom yet to read the latest entries in his "Secret Journal". He deliberately left it out for her to find. Max knew she read it, so he filled each page with outrageous lies about sex and drug abuse with the intention to shock her. It never did, to his annoyance. He also wondered if she had fed his goldfish, Trumpet. And there was no way he'd finish the history essay on time about the wives of Henry VIII, (divorced, executed, died, divorced, executed, widowed) which was a shame as he'd put effort into it. Yes, he did copy most of it from a library book called *Henry VIII and His Wives*, but he'd cunningly changed some words and rearranged a few sentences to avoid accusations of plagiarism.

Mrs. McCabe would show no sympathy for it being handed in late, as usual. She wouldn't care that Max had been in hospital and nearly died. No one cared, really. The accident was his fault. Yes, he'd been going too fast and it was getting dark. He didn't see the kerbstone.

Claire was one of the few people at school who would realise Max wasn't around. She cared. They'd known each other since nursery school. He loved her endearingly slight lisp.

God, he thought, *I'd better not die here of some unforeseen sudden medical complication. I have a life to live.*

A boy had died in his form class before. They left his seat empty for weeks after, like a macabre gap in a row of rotten teeth. Then a new boy filled it and soon people forgot all about the dead boy. Max had liked the dead boy. They had been friends. What was his name? Ben? Brian? Darren? It didn't matter anymore. Such is the pitiless hand that fate deals us. Max hated the new boy. He got into a ridiculous argument when the new boy said horses didn't have brains, and Max said they did.

'If horses had brains they'd be able to talk, you moron,' said the new boy, with so much conviction even Max thought twice.

Max's sister Margot would likely show nothing but contempt for the bike accident, too. Her view would be Max did it deliberately to seek attention, or simply to get out of PE for a while. Like she had never tried that shit on before. Max imagined her hooded cynical eyes and pursed mouth. He really hated Margot.

Actually, the mutual dislike developed between them later, in their mid-teens when Margot started screwing a series of douchebag boyfriends in her bedroom. Max thought it sounded as though they were murdering her. It caused a rift. ('I have a high sex drive,' he heard her say to Mum. 'Would you rather I had sex here, or in an alley?')

At the time of the bike accident they were still close. Margot was two years older than Max, so she was thirteen. A few weeks earlier, Mum and Dad had driven them to a park miles from home, ostensibly for a day out. It must have been one of those boring Bank Holidays.

While Max and Margot were in the adventure playground (Margot was explaining to him in graphic detail about menstruation), Max saw his parents get back in the car and drive away without telling them. He panicked, but Margot told him to calm down. They waited for an hour (it seemed like a week), but their parents didn't return and no one had mobile phones back then.

Neither Max nor Margot knew the way home, but they started walking and asked people for directions. They had some money, so they got on a bus heading in the right direction.

When they got home, the car was parked on the driveway. Mum and Dad acted like nothing had happened. Max and Margot said nothing about it. The incident wasn't mentioned again for many years until Max brought it up during an argument, and both his parents claimed to have no memory of it.

Another time, after arguing with his dad, Max went upstairs to drown himself in the bath. He nearly succeeded.

Dad shouted at Max through the door to stop, but Max was now fully submerged. Dad broke the door down and dragged him out of the bath, then he smashed Max's piggy bank and took the money out of it to pay for the repair to the lock.

'Life is pain,' cried a dripping wet Max to his dad.

'Deal with it,' his dad replied.

Dad was a failed writer who became an accountant by mistake. The job bored him. He privately drank too much and lost his temper in short bursts, mostly at Max.

Mum worked as a college administrator. She often broke crockery at home in frustrated silent anger, and complained about being passed over for promotion because she was a woman.

'If I was a man I'd be on a higher pay grade,' she said.

(She had a T-shirt made with "Misogynists can suck my dick" printed on it, but she never wore it.)

They had money worries that Max didn't fully appreciate. Home was a continuous cycle of lower middle-class tension. He could only remember one time Mum and Dad invited anyone over. They were some friends from their university days. It all seemed to go well. There was lots of talking and laughing. Mum and Dad pretended to be happy. But when the guests left they said they were glad it was over and those people never returned.

Max got bullied at school by older kids because he looked puny and vulnerable. He never complained about his tormentors. He stoically figured that if they were bullying him, they were leaving others alone.

His early ambitions were to be either a veterinarian, or a top human rights lawyer. Something with morals and a social conscience.

People were approaching. Squeak, squeak went their shoes.

Max's mouth was dry. He didn't know whether to ask for water. He didn't want to talk, and didn't want to open his eyes either. He felt like he was in some sort of trouble.

Mrs. McCabe told him he'd be nothing but trouble.

'You'll never amount to anything,' she said to him in front of a class once. 'I know you, Max, you're a bad one. Children like you will be the death of me.'

What a thing to say to a child, even to one she had just caught "torturing" a pigeon in the field next to the playground. The pigeon's wing was already broken when he found it; he was trying to rescue it. Max thought what poetic justice it would be if, years later, he saw Mrs. McCabe walking down a street and deliberately ran her over and killed her, thus proving her prophecy to be uncannily prescient.

'Where to?' asked a new voice.

'Next floor up, Room 9,' said another.

'I'd like to tip him out of the window, that's all he deserves,' said the first voice.

'They want to contain him,' said the second.

The bed started to move. Max could feel eyes staring at him. He pretended to be unconscious.

The bed glided into a corridor where several people were waiting to join it. They walked alongside and behind.

Light, dark, light, dark.

Stop.

Ping. Lift doors slid open.

The bed wobbled into the lift. People crowded in around it. Max felt exposed and vulnerable.

The doors closed and a short journey up one floor commenced. No one said a word.

A few minutes later, Max was ensconced in Room 9. As the last person left, he heard them say to someone outside, 'No one enters the room unless they have clearance.'

Why the fuck did that hospital porter want to tip me out of the fucking window? he thought. *I fell off my bike. I'm only eleven fucking years old for Christ's sake! What is wrong with these people? Where are Mum and Dad?*

It suddenly started to get dark again. Sleepy time.

They injected me with something. This feels very unnatural. I've been kidnapped!

Max wanted to open his eyes, but they were now too heavy. He slid into the inky blackness of a dreamless sleep.

2

What follows? A starting point. Everything has to begin somewhere, but not necessarily at the beginning.

There was an explosion. A big bang. Carnage. The universe bled. A fissure opened. In the midst of life, a paradigm shift occurred. Somewhere here I was born. Epochmelancholiaquincunxintangibletransienteternityellipsislacunae.

Cool.

This feels like a transcendence. Or a metamorphosis. I embraced the outstretched arms of infinity. I witnessed the start of creation. I saw the initial spark. I. Max Hope.

This is confusing. I'm getting mixed up. Let me begin again.

The cat sat on the mat. The quick brown fox jumps over the lazy dog.

One, two, three, four, zebra, six, seven, nine, ten.

Can I trust myself? I'm dubious of the fiction labelled "identity". We have no idea how physical matter gives rise to consciousness, thought or feeling. We live in the gaps between dreams.

Solipsism. Dialectic. Inertia. Words, words, words.

I saw blood everywhere. The trees dripped with viscera.

Wait. Let me go back. This is something else. It needs context. I think I died, albeit momentarily. It was only a small death. Quite inconsequential. I remember profound disappointment.

Something felt odd about me. An awkward outsider. A polemical conformist. Ostracised. I failed to engage or comprehend on an adequate level.

I'm not being disingenuous or paranoid.

Is death a penalty, or a reward?

How long does death last? After a year or so it must get boring. Who knows where it will meet us, or what disguise it will wear. When and why did we decide this is the way to exist?

I clearly recall floating above a hospital bed, looking down at myself. Only I wasn't myself. People were fussing around the me who wasn't me. I felt no pain. I don't like fuss.

I swam through opiates of emotion, and bathed in the black waters of Lethe. Is this meaningful? Relevant? There are many contrived flaws in existence, but I'm intrigued to know what happens next.

A gap. Time has passed. Difficult to say how much. It's dark again. Life appears to be a mere sequence of random events and tasks. We get caught in the maelstrom. We feel obliged to connect.

Why did this happen? What does 'now' consist of?

My parents took me to see a doctor, once. They were concerned I was autistic or something because I stopped talking. I observed life as if it happened somewhere else, just out of reach. I can't remember what conclusion the tests came to.

We're all adrift on this sea of unease. Alone. Alone together. I want to wash away my ego and pretension, my need for affirmation. Kill my war. End my irreconcilable dissonance.

The arrogant patterns of our behaviour. Maybe it was a self-inflicted wound. Something fascinated me about the masochistic actuality. The unknowing horror of wakefulness; of personality and self-awareness. The vulnerability we try to ignore. I am terrified of who I am and who I am not.

How long have I been in this purgatory?

I wade across the shark-infested pus of ennui. Listless. Dreaming of some faraway freedom. Who are the desiccated mourners in the fog? Eerie forgotten lives with fatal wrong turnings. Drowsy and hypnotic, we suspire in a feverish delirium.

***

'I want to help people,' I said to the school careers advisor. 'I have a great need to save lives. I'm an empath. A humanitarian.'

The careers advisor looked at me, then burst out laughing. He thought I was joking.

***

It is ultimately a question of self-image. The determining factors one makes for oneself. The empty accomplishments and experiences. We remain unknown in life, even to ourselves. We haunt each other. The ghosts we call identities are nothing more than a necessary artificial construct of self-deception to help us function. We're creatures who wear masks to disguise our inadequacies.

I beat fifty million sperm to get here. I murdered fifty million potential people, which made me a mass murderer before I was even born. Such profligacy deserves merit.

If normality is only a concept, normal can be anything.

We remember so little. Is it any wonder that almost all of life's energy is fear and anxiety? It motivates most of our decision making. Luckily, I realised everything is nothing, which is a huge relief.

I heard screaming. The ice-cold texture of death. The silent fugue that awaits.

Oblique. Gothic. Brutalist. Quotidian. Aesthetic. A kiss.

We prefer not to admit our own ignorance. We tend to prefer certainty, however bogus, to uncertainty, however truthful.

When I woke up in the hospital, my parents and my sister were there. They had brought a big teddy bear, which I liked. It was an unusual gesture for them. I never saw the teddy bear again as they gave it to a boy in the terminal ward. I was angry when I found out, but everyone said I was being selfish. Then we heard the boy had died, and I asked if I could have the teddy, but they said no, it was going to be put on the boy's grave, and I was sad for the teddy bear but not for the boy.

When it rained, I pictured the teddy sagging and rotting in the cemetery. That made me cry. It seemed symbolic.

My exterior life looked mundane, but the interior landscape of my life was my gift, and equally my curse. It's amongst those ruins I now lie.

The pools of blood were almost black. It congealed very quickly. Why was I so shocked by all the blood?

When? Whose blood? What is this in reference to?

Mhugjowoqadkvygnlbszmhfcojjwq!

I was riding my bike. Going too fast. It was getting dark. I hit a kerb, fell off and hit my head. Nearly died. I didn't want anyone to worry.

That is absolute fact. I didn't see God, or heaven or hell, it just felt like going to sleep.

I have no desire to cling to the lifeboat of immortality. The galaxies are merely points of light in an abyss of ignorance. I am but one of the infinite legions of sick abnormalities of creation, which Nature, with an inventiveness of breath-taking ingenuity, fills every burden in her atlas.

You think you know.

You have no idea.

***

Another gap?

Something egregiously wrong has happened. I hear things. Bad things.

Echoes through the mist.

Malevolent voices. Movement.

Claire?

Time and space have been temporarily suspended. I'm falling, and I haven't hit rock bottom yet. Is this an ending? Am I dying? Did I die?

Is death not impossible?

No. It feels like a beginning. A purge. Embarking on a pilgrimage.

I reflect a warped entity. Dissolve into decay all youth.

I don't think I have an option. I close my eyes and count to ten.

***

Another gap.

Curiouser and curiouser.

***

A story begins somewhere here, beyond the bleak elliptical verbiage of unidentified abstract misanthropy.

Blood. Pools of congealed blood. Smeared in the snow.

We live our lives all wrong. The frantic attempts to outrun death. The meaningless hum of imagination.

We think of ourselves as having a "self" beyond the chemical reactions in our brain – but where's the evidence? My refusal to believe I am just a deluded automaton could be my mind deceiving me.

A life cannot be considered an end in itself, only a means to promoting the success of genetic survival. The death of the individual has always been the precondition of evolutionary progress. We knowingly trick ourselves with the endowment of a soul which aspires to immortality within the resounding emptiness of this impenetrable labyrinth. I need to go through the maze to get to where I want to go.

But where?

Nothing is what it seems.

Now is not the time or place for metaphysical assumption and theory.

I have a potentially great first line for a novel:

After a brief funeral service, which was attended by no one, they buried me in an unmarked grave. That's what they do to murderers.

Did I mention I'm only eleven? I'm very precocious. I have big plans for myself. A full life. I will make Claire love me.

Why did I only ever pretend to be me? I existed in plain sight. A lone wolf. A sniper. Someone. Loved. Suspended in delicious helplessness.

On my first morning at junior school I cried and cried with existential angst. The boy next to me gave me his carton of milk. I'm still not sure if it was an act of humane generosity, or if he just wanted to shut me up.

I presume there'll be a back-story to frame this in? Can it be explained in one sentence? Come at it from a different angle. Set out your objective early. Be clear. Stay focused. Never apologise.

A time will come when this is all long in the past. I'll have forgotten my entire life by then. I'll be forgotten. Memory wiped clean. Harsh.

Some events happened and I was there, then it was all over and other people did the same things as if for the first time. Then they died too. But you have to laugh, don't you? Death is life's great motivational tool. We are unique individual survival machines fighting against a beautifully doomed perpetual present.

What did Albert Einstein say about time? *The distinction between past, present and future is only a stubbornly persistent illusion.*

My eyes are fixed upon the crepuscular horizon. I recognise a host of death-hollowed faces. They ignore me, the holocaust-bringer. I'll soon emerge from my chrysalis and unfold delicately into becoming.

A single leg hung in the branches of a tall tree. The leg wore jeans and a black Converse high-top.

That happened later, of course.

Certain I was destined for greatness, I read Dostoyevsky's *The Idiot*, aged eight, Homer's *The Iliad*, aged nine, and Camus' *The Myth of Sisyphus*, aged ten. I waited patiently for life to live up to my high expectations in an age that despises intellect. But nothing happened.

Was my trauma the realisation of failure? Or the failure of ambition itself?

I experienced everything, even death.

Not wanting is power.

Life isn't ours to own. It's incomplete. Unfinished. It seems important when it's happening. We put so much pressure on ourselves to achieve random objectives which have no value outside those we place upon them. How appallingly trivial things are. How illogical are the insignificant triumphs and worthless victories. The game is rigged against us, yet we're compelled to keep playing. No one can win in this violent arcade – the lesson is learning how to lose with dignity.

We work towards silence. Tenants in temporary bodies, evicted at any moment without warning or explanation. Ghosts in a machine.

I can't remember the first time I saw Claire, but it must have been in junior school. She was my first kiss.

Couldn't she see it in my eyes?

She was my journey, she was my prize.

First love never dies.

The dead. Everywhere the dead, underscoring life. Reminding us of our bewildered ignorance as we stagger through each day. (Insert cliché here.)

It's useless positing huge intellectual conundrums without recourse to following them up with a reasoned explanation. According to religious teaching, we're being scrutinised by a mysterious invisible benevolent hypocrite with psychopathic tendencies. He assassinates us randomly, then demands our devotion.

My parents reminded me many times (whenever I moaned about any negligible matter) to be grateful for my First World privileges. There are millions of children starving to death in the world, they said, and I needed to appreciate my good fortune. It did make me sad to think of those legions of surplus children, unloved and disposable. It made me angry, too. And resentful. And confused. I gave my toys away to a children's charity in a guilt-ridden well-meant gesture of penance, but no one praised me for it.

It's my bike I'm most worried about. When I lost consciousness I heard the back wheel clicking round and round redundantly.

Let me get back to the first line of that novel. I have something else, but I don't think it's the correct genre:

As I watched the zombies rip my intestines through my rib cage, I began to realise my chances of survival were narrowing.

No. It's time to abandon myself in the margins of my juvenilia. It's time I woke up and faced the consequences.

'I know,' whispered Max.

There was silence for a moment. Two men on either side of the bed in Room 9 glanced at each other.

'What did he say?' asked the older man.

'I know,' said the younger.

'What does he know?'

'I don't know.'

The older man stared at dust motes floating gently in the air, then he cleared his throat.

'I'll get the doctor. Listen if he says anything else, and write it down.'

The older man exited the room.

The younger man leaned in close to Max's ear. His breath stank. Max wanted to flinch, but didn't dare.

'We've got you, you bastard,' whispered the man with the terrible oral hygiene. 'You're not going anywhere.'

They were on the cusp of another day. Life was about to bloom again, but it wasn't smiling.

Max Hope was back. But where had he been?

3

Max opened his eyes.

It took a few attempts for them to focus. He was in a private hospital room, alone. A blind, pulled halfway across a large window on his left, let hazy morning sunlight filter in. From the pillows propping up his head, Max gazed upon his body, lying before him encased in a tight sarcophagus of tucked-in bedsheets.

Through an oblong of glass in a door in front of him, a hard female face looked in. When she saw Max looking back, her face retreated, as if playing peek-a-boo.

Seconds later the door opened. A man stood at the threshold showing an identity card on a lanyard to someone just beyond the doorframe.

The man entered the room, then shut the door and stood at the foot of the bed. He wore a white coat over a blue shirt and chinos. His build and facial features were generically handsome.

'You're awake,' said the man (the doctor from before).

'Well observed,' said Max, groggily. 'I presume you're a doctor?'

'Well observed,' replied the doctor.

'I have an instinct for the obvious,' said Max.

The doctor nodded, then set about reading the chart hanging on the end of the bed.

Max's arm was attached to a drip. The doctor saw him looking at it.

'We took you off the ventilator and heart monitor a couple of days ago. You'll be kept under observation for a while.'

'Where's my bike?' asked Max.

'Your bike? I don't know.'

'It was a birthday present.'

'Oh,' said the doctor.

'How long have I been here?'

'Two weeks.'

'Really? Are you sure?'

'Quite sure,' said the doctor.

'Can you loosen the sheets, please? I can hardly move.'

Max wriggled to demonstrate his lack of movement.

The doctor seemed reluctant, but he pulled the sheets slightly out on one side, giving Max some leeway.

'Are my parents here?'

'No,' said the doctor.

'Have they visited?'

'Not that I know of.'

The doctor returned to the foot of the bed and resumed looking at the chart. Max sensed fear in him. He worried if it was because he had bad news to relay.

Max moved his arms, legs and torso. All of his limbs were intact, and he wasn't paraplegic. He felt tenderness from bruising, but apart from that everything felt normal.

Max remembered how his parents insisted he wear a crash helmet when he was finally allowed to ride the bike again, and how stupid he felt wearing it. His so-called friends had laughed at him in the park when they saw him. From then on, he only wore the helmet until he disappeared around the corner from his house, then he'd shove it into a garden hedge and ride away. On the return journey, he'd get the helmet out of the hedge, put it back on and ride around the corner to his home. One day he discovered the helmet had been stolen from the hedge and a row broke out with his parents and his dad said he was irresponsible and he couldn't ride the bike any more without the fucking helmet. But he did anyway.

No, none of that could have happened yet, thought Max. *That all come later.*

Max tried to lift his arms again, but the restraints were still on. They clanked on each side of the bed, metal on metal.

'Why do I have restraints on my wrists?' asked Max.

'For safety's sake,' said the doctor.

The doctor's eyes flicked in Max's direction, then returned to the chart.

'Do my parents even know I'm here?' asked Max.

'Yes, they do.'

'Where are those two men?'

'They'll be back shortly.'

The two men didn't like Max. No one seemed to like him right now.

'What's your name, Doctor?'

'Doctor Brooke,' said Doctor Brooke.

I must remember that name for future reference, thought Max.

Doctor.

Doctor Something.

Damn, it had already gone.

'Has no one visited me?' asked Max.

'Look, I'm not supposed to be talking to you, okay?' said Doctor Brooke.

'Why not?'

'You need to rest.'

'You shone a torch in my eyes, didn't you?'

'Yes.'

'To check for brain activity?'

'Among other things.'

'Did you find any brain activity? I don't think I have any.'

Max thought this self-deprecation would make the doctor smile. The doctor didn't smile. Their dry initial engagement seemed to be over.

The doctor finished reading the chart, then stared at Max.

Max stared back.

'You were involved in an accident,' said the doctor. 'You received a serious head trauma, and have been in an induced coma.'

'No, I only fractured my wrist and got concussion,' said Max. 'That's why they forced me to wear that stupid helmet afterwards.'

'What?' asked Doctor Brooke, confused.

'Do I look like the Elephant Man?' asked Max.

'The cranial swelling went down. Your head is normal size.'

'Do I look gross?'

'No,' said the doctor.

'Do I look like I should be on the cover of *Fangoria*?'

The doctor's lack of reaction showed he didn't get the reference.

'Got a mirror?' continued Max.

'No.'

Max noticed the hard face beadily watching him through the oblong glass in the door again.

The doctor turned, following Max's gaze. The face retreated, as before.

'Why is there security on the door?' asked Max.

Doctor Brooke went to the window and adjusted the blind needlessly.

'What do you remember of the crash?' he asked.

Max thought he must mean the bike accident.

'I'd gone over to Nigel Huxley's house to play video games, but they were rubbish ones and he kept winning. It started to get dark, so I rode home for dinner. A kerbstone was sticking out and my front wheel hit it. It threw me over the handlebars.'

Max left out the detail of Nigel Huxley showing him one of his dad's porn films. It was the first one Max had seen, and he thought it was disgusting and weird, especially when Nigel Huxley began furiously masturbating to it. All Max could remember of the porn film was lots of ugly naked people groaning in a room, and someone got fisted.

Max never went to Nigel Huxley's house again.

Doctor Brooke folded his arms and looked out of the window. 'And then?'

'I hit my head on a wall as I landed and got knocked out. I was told someone found me and called an ambulance. Paramedics came. The doctors treated me nicely. The nurses were friendly. No one wanted to tip me out of a window, or wished me to rot in hell. I even worked on my Henry VIII essay.'

Max thought it was a superfluous detail to add that Mrs. McCabe eventually only gave him a D for his Henry VIII essay. She said she recognised most of the sentences as being copied verbatim from a book.

The doctor turned and looked at Max.

'So, you don't remember the car crash?'

Car crash? thought Max.

Max could recall nothing of a car crash. An obsidian wall obscured any memory of such an event.

'Are my parents okay?' he asked.

'Your parents aren't involved in this,' said the doctor.

Something deeply bothered Max.

The thing is, he thought, *how can I remember getting a D for the essay if I'm still in hospital? That happened weeks later because my wrist was still wrapped in the bandage when I handed it in. Mrs. McCabe told me the bandage needed replacing because it had gone a horrible beige colour which was unsanitary, and she said she had first aid training and could clean and replace it herself, but I said no because I hated her.*

'I don't remember a car crash,' said Max.

Max also couldn't remember why he hated Mrs. McCabe. She was one of the few teachers who liked him. She hadn't even reported him when she found him torturing the pigeon. Maybe he resented her because of the time he'd called her "Mum" in class once by mistake, and everyone had laughed mercilessly about it for days. He remembered seeing Mrs. McCabe's eyes filling with tears, and how she tried to disguise it.

Max thought at the time that she was crying with laughter, but he later found out she'd had a recent miscarriage and was now unable to have children.

When Max asked his mum what a miscarriage was, she said, 'It's what happens when you lose a baby.' Max asked her how it was possible for Mrs. McCabe to lose a baby, and his mum said, unhelpfully, 'Because she left it too late.'

Max didn't understand, but left it at that.

'What's the last thing you remember?' asked Doctor Brooke.

'Lying on the pavement,' said Max. 'I thought I was dying, and was angry with my clumsiness. Pain rising. Getting cold. The moon had a halo of mist around it. I worried my dinner would go to waste and my goldfish needed feeding, and my bike was broken and my parents would be cross with me.'

The doctor furrowed his brow.

'Anything else?'

'No,' said Max. 'Are my parents angry with me? Is that why they're not here?'

The door was opened by a policewoman wearing a stab-proof vest and a full complement of harmful-looking equipment around her waist. She owned the hard face with the beady eye.

She let in two plain-clothed police detectives, one older than the other, then she went back into the corridor and shut the door.

The older detective took the doctor aside and they began a quick low-voiced discussion which Max couldn't hear.

The younger detective folded his arms and stood looking at Max with a strange smile on his lips. They were the two men from before. The older man was the senior in rank. He was paunchy, grey in pallor, and in his late fifties. His colleague, in his thirties, looked like he had once been in the army, or maybe a boxer. Max could smell his bad breath from across the room.

After their short discussion, the older detective sat in a chair by the bed and got out a pen and a writing pad.

'When can I go home?' asked Max.

'He's suffering memory loss,' said the doctor.

'Yeah, right,' said the younger detective, rolling his eyes.

'He suffered bleeding on the brain from the head trauma,' said the doctor.

'You said he's recovered remarkably well,' said the older detective.

'Physically, yes, but I'm not sure about his mental state. I have some concerns,' said the doctor.

The older detective began to cough. It sounded like a phlegmy death rattle. His face went puce.

Max tried to recoil in disgust, but couldn't move far because of the still-too-tight sheets.

The older detective put a handkerchief to his lips and barked a huge glob of spit into it.

'Want some water?' asked the younger detective.

The older detective shook his head and produced an inhaler which he sucked on deeply. The cough subsided, but he wheezed breathlessly for a while longer.

'Hospitals always do this to me,' he gasped. 'It's the air.'

'I need to check his pulse,' said the doctor.

Max thought he meant the older detective's pulse, but the older detective indicated him towards Max.

'Go ahead.'

Doctor Brooke came around the side of the bed, pulled out the sheets, then lifted them off Max's left arm.

Max offered his wrist to the doctor. Clank – a handcuff attached his wrist to the bed rail.

Max could see bruises at different stages patterning his arm, like late-summer roses whose petals were turning. The arm didn't look like his at all. He viewed it with curiosity.

The doctor moved the handcuff to access Max's pulse, then he pressed down on the vein. Max felt unpleasant little throbs of blood pounding beneath the doctor's fingers. The pulse raced. Each one throbbed in his ears. It made him light-headed.

'What are the handcuffs for?' asked Max.

'You are, are you not, Maximillian Hope?' said the younger detective.

'Max. Just Max,' said Max, testily. 'Only my mum calls me Maximillian when I've done something bad.'

Doctor Brooke finished taking Max's pulse, then he tucked the sheets back in.

'You do not have to say anything, but it may harm your defence if you do not mention now anything you later rely on in court. Anything you do say will be given in evidence,' said the younger detective.

'Shouldn't he have a lawyer present?' asked the doctor.

'Are you having a laugh?' replied the younger detective.

'You sound like you're arresting me?' said Max.

'You have been arrested and charged with four counts of murder,' said the older detective.

'But I'm only eleven!' protested Max.

The younger detective took a mobile phone out of his pocket and held it in front of Max's face. He took a photo, then showed the screen to Max.

Max looked at the photo. A man in early middle age with black rings around his eyes and slightly jaundiced skin looked back at him. The man had fading dyed black hair and grey beard stubble.

'Who's that?' asked Max.

'It's you, Max,' said the younger detective, with relish. 'It's you.'

4

Max crouched by the edge of the pond in the back garden of the Hope family home. The garden was unusually large for suburbia, and it had an overgrown area at the far end where Max disappeared for many an hour of his childhood, alone.

Flies bobbed and weaved like embers in the dappled haze. The pond's surface sparkled and shimmered with intricate distorted patterns. Tiny concentric circles rippled outwards. Max saw his fifteen-year-old face reflected in the water, lit by a shaft of sunlight which ruptured through cumulus clouds on the horizon.

Ancient oak trees towered overhead, survivors from a rural time before the semi-detached urban sprawl. Autumn leaves of yellow and orange and red fell in silent acquiescence onto a carpet of mossy lawn.

Max slid his hand into the water and gently lifted out a tadpole. It wriggled in the cup of his palm, opening and closing its mouth as if singing a silent requiem. Max carried it over to a rose bush, then knelt down and impaled the tadpole onto a thorn.

Slime oozed out of the piercing. The tadpole struggled for a moment, then it shivered ever so slightly and died. Max observed, fascinated.

Almost every thorn had an insect similarly spiked on it; his randomly chosen previous victims.

As always, Max felt a pang of remorse.

'Max, stop doing that!' shouted his dad, from inside the house.

Deep crimson flooded Max's vision. He stood up and shielded his ears from a great unending scream penetrating nature – then found himself in the park next to his high school.

Claire walked by, aged fifteen, framed in the gold of a summer evening.

Her beautiful shy eyes transfixed him.

'Are you stalking me, Max?' she asked playfully, without stopping.

'You never knew what I truly thought about you,' said Max. 'I regret not asking you out. I was afraid you'd say no.'

Claire glanced back at him and smiled.

'You had fifty percent chance of a yes,' she said. 'Pretty good odds.'

Max watched, the same way he'd longingly watched her walk home through the park a thousand times.

'Would you have said yes?' he asked, catching up with her. 'I know you liked me.'

'Don't you think it's time you moved on?' asked Claire.

'No,' said Max. 'A day hasn't gone by where I haven't thought about you. In fact, as the years pass, my feelings for you increase.'

'That's sweet,' said Claire. 'But too late.'

'We always had an unspoken bond between us since junior school,' said Max. 'We were meant for each other.'

'You're using me as a tokenistic symbol of idealistic femininity,' said Claire. 'There's no way I was as perfect as you remember me. It's impossible.'

'Believe me, you were special. I remember,' said Max.

'Memories are unreliable,' said Claire. 'They rewrite themselves to fit a narrative.'

Mist surrounded them now. Snowflakes fell in drifts. Naked trees stood like sentinels amongst the milky whiteout.

'With you, I wouldn't have needed to hide in life,' said Max, 'I'd have been normal. I didn't have the courage to reveal my feelings at the time. You're the love of my life, and I hardly knew you.'

Claire stopped walking. She listened for something.

'They're coming, Max. You should run,' she said.

Max could hear voices in the mist. His name was being spoken.

'I don't want to run anymore,' said Max. 'I want to be with you. I don't want to lose you again.'

Claire continued walking. Max stood rooted to the spot. He watched her disappear into the blanket of vapour.

'So, what's the plan, Peter Pan?' he heard her say.

***

Max opened his eyes.

Room 9. Daytime. Doctor Brooke was at the foot of the bed having strong words with the younger detective.

'He's faking,' said the detective. 'He's notorious for faking.'

'He's not ready for interrogation,' said Doctor Brooke. 'He can barely sustain consciousness. Look at him.'

Doctor Brooke and the detective looked at Max. Both were surprised to see him looking back.

Max shut his eyes and squeezed them tight.

'Go away. Leave me alone,' he whispered. 'I want to be with Claire.'

He felt a hot tear run down his cheek.

***

When he opened his eyes again it was night-time. Someone sat in a chair by the door, looking at a glowing iPad.

Max moved slightly. The person looked up at him. Blackout.

***

Max opened his eyes. Again. Daytime now. Outside, an airliner cut a vapour trail across a clear cerulean sky. He couldn't see the plane itself because it was too high up. He watched the straight chalky line thread across the deep blue. His heavy lids closed.

***

An old recurring dream: a darker shade of blue. Underwater, in a vast unbroken sea, Max is sinking down. Splinters of sunlight penetrate the surface into the absolute darkness below.

Deeper and deeper. He reaches up to the light. It glints tantalisingly through his outstretched fingers. He tries to scream. Silver bubbles of discordant sound fill his vision. Lungs fill with salty water. A tsunami of panic pumps through his capillary system.

A monstrous great white shark weaves with sickening intent through the gloom. It cruises towards Max. Black doll's eyes. Serrated teeth bared in an angry red lipstick of gums.

***

Max jolted awake, gasping for breath. It was still daytime in Room 9.

Doctor Brooke was standing at the foot of Max's bed, holding a red clipboard. The doctor smiled. It didn't suit him. Chipped wonky front teeth.

'Welcome back,' he said.

'What the hell is happening to me?' asked Max.

'There have been some complications. We put you under heavy sedation to deal with a new blood clot on your brain. You were having seizures. Don't worry, you're out of the worst of it.'

Max's eyes turned towards the window to see if there were any more planes leaving pretty vapour trails, but the sky was shrouded in grey.

'How old am I?' asked Max.

'Forty-one,' said the doctor.

'Impossible,' said Max.

He furrowed his brow. A bandage was wrapped around his head.

'We had to shave your hair,' said the doctor, who resumed studying a chart on the clipboard.

'What exactly am I supposed to have done?' asked Max.

'I'm not at liberty to say.'

'Tell me,' said Max. 'Please,'

Doctor Brooke's face flushed. He glanced around at the door, but no one was there.

'You really can't remember?'

'I thought that had been established,' said Max.

'It will come back to you.'

'That detective said four counts of murder, didn't he?' asked Max.

'I advise you to rest for the time being,' said Doctor Brooke.

'I didn't murder anyone,' said Max.

'I'm afraid I can't discuss this with you, it's a police matter,' said the doctor, as he hastily went to the door.

'Don't go,' pleaded Max.

'Sorry, I have other patients to see.'

Doctor Brooke left.

Max lay on his own in that stupid bed with the stupid handcuffs on in that stupid room in that stupid hospital with the stupid grey sky above and all those stupid people doing all their stupid things in this stupid world in this stupid galaxy in this stupid stupid universe.

'I haven't murdered anyone,' Max said aloud.

He kept repeating it to anyone who came within earshot.

Nurses regularly came in and gave him superficial checks.

'I haven't murdered anyone,' Max said to whichever nurse happened to be on duty. They all ignored him.

A Caribbean porter came in that evening to clear away the food and detritus on Max's bedside table.

'I haven't murdered anyone,' Max said.

The porter sucked his teeth and said, 'Sure, sure,' then left.

Over the following days, Max's strength improved. He rattled the handcuffs on the bedrail with inert frustration.

A police officer was now stationed in the room.

'You can't keep me here. I haven't murdered anyone,' said Max to the police officer.

'On the contrary,' replied the officer.

Max faced daily humiliations with as much dignity as he could muster. He dreaded bed baths, along with the unwanted erection each one inspired. He considered it part of a sinister programme to try and break his spirit. Only after persistent arguing about the violation of his self-respect was he finally allowed, under supervision, to attend to his own ablutions.

The first time he stood up, the effort exhausted him to such an extent that he collapsed back onto the bed.

Max's limbs soon strengthened enough for him to stand unaided. By sheer force of will he began making unsteady forays to the toilet using a Zimmer frame, accompanied by an impassive heavily armed police officer, like he was some sort of dangerous monster.

The exertion of these first shuffled attempts along the eerie deserted hospital corridor covered Max in an oily sweat.

When he saw himself in the bathroom mirror, his heart sank. His head was still bandaged. Grey stubble covered his gaunt face. Bruises on his arms, legs and ribs were turning angry shades of purple, remnants of injections, drips and the mysterious "car crash".

He wore carpet slippers and a thin one-piece disposable hospital gown made of a strange papery material, no doubt good for absorbing stray bodily fluids, if nothing else. Such utility-wear only served to magnify his vulnerability.

'Is that really me?' said Max to the police officer.

'It isn't anyone else,' replied the police officer.

Max discovered a new hurdle to his lack of privacy – the indignity of taking a shit while being listened to. It removed all enjoyment from it. He tried to be as quiet as possible in the cubicle, but was unable to avoid the inevitable stool splash. The sound, followed by cold water licking the underside of his scrotum, made Max wince.

'Can you wait outside, please?' he said each day to the police officer on duty. 'I'm not going to escape down the u-bend.'

Next, Max was escorted to a disabled shower room. He manoeuvred his naked Gollum-like body into it, then sat and let lukewarm water rain down on him. It took on the quality of a literal and psychological cleansing; sloughing off the ugly broken current Max Hope.

The me I never knew, he thought.

He willed himself to cultivate a better version of the person he could no longer remember being.

One day Max burst into tears in the shower. Great heaving sobs of emotion poured out. It took him by surprise. He wasn't sure what he was crying about, and it felt alien to him.

I don't deserve this, he thought, *Why is this happening to me? I'm a good person.*

He was glad it happened in the shower so no one witnessed it. After, he rubbed his skin raw with a towel, making himself bleed. The pain felt satisfying.

Max was returned to Room 9 and handcuffed to the bed.

'Do you really think I'm going to run away?' he said to the departing police officer. 'I can barely stand up.'

The days and nights merged into one another, like a montage. Max tracked the waxing and waning of the moon.

The hospital food tasted awful, like budget airline stuff. The plastic packaging had more nutritional value. Max didn't realise he could demand takeaways, but the police didn't tell him and he didn't know to ask. He had yet to be assigned a lawyer.

Doctor Brooke said he could have a TV in the room for an hour a day, but Max declined the offer. Max got the impression it was a ruse, like they were trying to soften him up. He couldn't even remember what programmes he liked anyway.

An array of bland people visited. One was a legal supervisor. One was a liaison officer. One was a representative of some organisation.

There were others, one at a time, morning and afternoon. Max didn't listen to any of them. He usually pretended to fall asleep while they droned on at length in patronising tones about legality and procedural things that sounded serious and oh-so important.

'It's in your best interests,' said one.

'You need to consider your options,' said another.

'We would appreciate your cooperation,' said the next.

Each time, the person became annoyed at Max's lack of engagement.

'Retard,' muttered one.

'I'll leave the forms here for you to fill out,' said another.

'I know you can hear me,' said the next.

Max found it quite amusing. Fucking petit bureaucrats. These wanker pen-pushers had dedicated the best years of their lives studying all of this garbage.

Max did contemplate the prudence of being courteous and cooperative, but then rejected the idea because of the negative vibes he was getting from their body language.

They had already made up their minds about him: guilty.

5

Detective Superintendent Kate Lamb held up a photo and asked Max, who was sitting in bed in Room 9, to look at it.

Lamb had been assigned to Max's case after the sudden and untimely death the previous week of the older detective (Max never learned his name). A severe asthma attack, apparently.

Also present was Detective Inspector Hicks (he of the rancid breath), and a watery-eyed insignificant-looking man with a scruffy beard, scruffy hair, scruffy jacket, woollen tie, creased shirt and trousers, and scuffed shoes (one of them orthopaedic). He introduced himself as Ched Hazzard, a name which didn't suit him at all. He was a legal aid barrister, appointed to represent Max as his defence lawyer. This filled Max with initial disappointment, but when Ched Hazzard asked him if he was being treated okay and did he have any complaints, Max began to warm to him, slightly.

'We'll have one of those handcuffs off for a start,' said Ched Hazzard. A police officer reluctantly removed the one from Max's left wrist.

'Do you recognise the people in this photo?' Lamb asked Max.

'You're not obliged to say anything, Max,' said Ched Hazzard, pulling at a loose thread on his shirt button and feigning boredom.

Max gave the photo a cursory glance.

It was a photo of a very overweight attractive woman in her thirties, sitting in a garden with two teenage girls and a slightly older boy. They were smiling, but only out of instinct.

'No,' said Max. 'I don't recognise those people.'

'Sure?' asked Lamb.

'Yep.'

'Look again. Think.'

'This is not standard police protocol,' sighed Ched Hazzard.

'Due to the unusual nature of this case,' said Hicks, 'what with your client's health circumstances and the continual delay in procedure that has been incurred, not to mention my colleague's unfortunate demise, we have been unable to follow prescribed protocol.'

'Doctor Brooke should be present,' said Ched Hazzard.

'Doctor Brooke is unavailable at the moment,' said Lamb.

'Then you should have waited.'

'I have talked to the doctor separately and he has given me all the information I need,' said Lamb.

'Then he will have told you my client is suffering from a form of amnesia. Your questioning is pointless at the current time. I must say, it strikes me as quite amateurish.'

'Hey,' said Hicks to Ched Hazzard, in a reproachful manner.

'I'm hoping the photo will jog Max's memory,' said Lamb.

'Are you a trained neuropsychologist?' asked Ched Hazzard, with a hint of sarcasm.

'Please,' said Lamb to Max, 'have another look.'

Max looked at the photo again.

'Sorry,' he said. 'Not a Scooby.'

'There. My client has given you an answer.'

Lamb sat completely still for a moment.

'Okay,' she said, putting the photo into a folder. 'Thank you.'

Lamb and Hicks left.

'Hot, huh?' said Ched Hazzard to Max when they were alone.

'What is?'

'Detective Lamb.'

'Is she?' said Max.

Ched Hazzard had a leery grin on his face.

'Absolutely,' he said, holding up his hands. 'In my opinion.'

Max shrugged. Lamb had nice eyes, but her skin was puckered with old acne scars and her hair was cut too short and badly bleached. It made her head look too small for her body.

'Was she wearing a wedding ring?' asked Ched Hazzard.

'I didn't notice,' said Max.

Ched Hazzard put his hands on his hips; except he didn't put them on his hips, but almost under his armpits. It made his body sag, and his stomach inflate like a balloon. He adopted the pose frequently.

'Beauty is in the eye of the beholder,' said Ched Hazzard. 'I'm no oil painting myself, but my grandmother used to say that in a certain light I resembled Robert Donat.'

'Who?' asked Max.

'Robert Donat. The film star.'

'Never heard of him,' said Max.

'Ever seen the Hitchcock version of *The 39 Steps*? Robert Donat was the star of that film.'

'Not sure,' said Max.

'What about *Goodbye Mr. Chips*? Seen that?' asked Ched Hazzard.

'I can't remember,' said Max, yawning.

'Robert Donat won the best actor Oscar that year, beating Clark Gable in *Gone with the Wind*,' said Ched Hazzard. 'No one remembers old Robert Donat anymore. Pity. Great actor. English, too.'

'Much as I'm enjoying this fascinating conversation about obscure movie stars, who were the people in that photo?' asked Max.

'What photo?'

'The photo detective Lamb showed me. Were they the people they're claiming I killed?'

Ched Hazzard removed his hands from his armpits. His stomach deflated, and he sat on the edge of the bed.

'To put it succinctly, yes,' he said.

'I didn't do it,' said Max.

Ched Hazzard's face clouded over.

'Unfortunately, Max, you did.'

Silence.

'Not the response I was expecting,' said Max. 'Aren't you supposed to be defending me?'

'We need to be truthful with each other if we're to have any hope in this situation, Max. There are a lot of barriers in our way.'

'I'm not sure what the fuck this situation is,' said Max. 'I haven't been told anything.'

'You have, Max, you just haven't listened. Also, I have been somewhat hamstrung by legal restraints. I would normally have established all the preliminary background stuff with you by now, but the police investigation has been incompetent, to say the least. Most of all, I need to know your side of the story so I can prep you for the trial.'

'I presume it was the car crash, right?' said Max. 'If I killed those four people, was I drunk driving?'

'A car crash?' said Ched Hazzard.

'Well?' asked Max, impatiently.

Ched Hazzard sucked in air through the gaps in his front teeth, which made a hissing sound. Deposits of white spittle were in the corners of his mouth.

'You really can't remember, can you?' he said.

'No,' growled Max.

'We can work with that,' said Ched Hazzard. 'You see, to all intents and purposes this is a cut and dried case – there are no other suspects, and so much actual and circumstantial evidence against you, frankly it's laughable, but maybe we can go with diminished responsibility.'

'I don't understand,' said Max.

'I'm also considering a plea of insanity,' said Ched Hazzard.

'For you, or for me?' asked Max.

'I'll only use it as a last resort,' said Ched Hazzard, almost to himself, with a wry chuckle that annoyed Max.

'I'm not insane. I'm the sanest person around here.' said Max.

'Quite,' chuckled Ched Hazzard. 'Quite.'

'So, what's to be done?' asked Max.

'Normally, a solicitor and me would interview you to establish your side of the facts so a statement could be submitted for the trial. That isn't possible, because you have no recall of the events in question.'

'How did they die?' asked Max.

The chuckle seemed to get stuck in Ched Hazzard's throat. Max felt an overwhelming urge to rip out the man's larynx.

'It was... somewhat gruesome, actually,' said Ched Hazzard, avoiding eye contact.

'Tell me,' said Max.

'I'm unable to give you that information in case it falsely influences your recall.'

'What?' asked Max.

'You've been recommended for psychological treatment, you see, and the psychologist has requested that the full details of your case be kept from you for the time being.'

'That doesn't make sense,' said Max.

'It is most unusual,' said Ched Hazzard, 'but we must abide by it. I tried to have the procedure rescinded, but they refused.'

'So, I'm not allowed to know the exact reason for my arrest?'

'You have been arrested and charged with four counts of murder. I thought that had been made clear?'

'I've never seen those four people before!' shouted Max.

'Mm. Mm,' said Ched Hazzard. 'Mm. That's the problem, you see – no one's going to believe you.'

'That's not fair!' shouted Max.

'The psychological evaluation, whatever it will involve, may prove to be beneficial,' said Ched Hazzard. 'Or detrimental, depending on its findings, the validity of which I expect to be negligible at best. You will no doubt be required to do tests of varying degrees in order to delve into the deepest recesses of your subconscious and jog your memory, as it were. It all sounds like a load of old hooey to me, but them's the given circumstances.'

'What evidence is there to link me to the murders?' asked Max.

'Oh, lots. Lots. You did it, Max. No question.'

'I don't believe you,' said Max. 'I don't believe any of you. I think you're all in on this. It's some kind of conspiracy.'

Max's body language made Ched Hazzard get up and retreat to the window.

'Now, now, there's no need for that kind of talk. I assure you there is no foul play at work here, Max.'

'You would say that.'

'I deal in truth, and nothing but the truth.'

'You're a lawyer. You're a professional liar.'

'I'm here to help you.'

Max rattled the handcuff on his wrist.

'So, get me out of here. I'm innocent.'

'I can't do that,' said Ched Hazzard.

'Then what good are you to me, you moron?'

Ched Hazzard smiled unhappily. His watery eyes blinked with saline, and he wiped them with a stained beige handkerchief.

'You don't seem to understand the severity of your situation. I'm the only person who can help you.'

'But even you are convinced I'm guilty.' said Max.

'Whether I believe you are guilty or not is beside the point. My main objective isn't to get you out of here, or to prove your innocence, as that is a foregone conclusion. My job is to try and reduce the punishment you will receive, and represent you to make sure you get as fair a trial as possible.'

'This is bullshit,' said Max. 'I hope I'm still in a coma, and you're a figment of my imagination.'

'I'm afraid not, Max. He-he,' said Ched Hazzard with another high-pitched nervous giggle. 'He-he. Nope.'

Max pinched himself.

'I must have died in that car crash,' said Max. 'This is a level of purgatory. There can be no other rational explanation. None of this shit adds up. It's totally implausible.'

'Sometimes fact is stranger than fiction,' said Ched Hazzard.

'Maybe, but this is taking the piss,' replied Max.

The door opened and Doctor Brooke entered. He had a patch over one eye.

'What happened to you?' asked Ched Hazzard.

'I was attacked by a hawk,' said the doctor.

Max looked at Ched Hazzard and raised a wry eyebrow.

'Okay, that is implausible, I'll grant you that,' said the lawyer.

'You're to begin sessions of physiotherapy tomorrow,' said Doctor Brooke, offering no further information on his hawk attack.

'About time too,' said Ched Hazzard. 'My client's physicality has atrophied. He could sue for gross negligence.'

'We had difficulty finding anyone willing to work with your client,' said Doctor Brooke. 'His reputation somewhat precedes him.'

'My client is not a danger to anyone.'

'I demand to know who the four people who died were,' said Max.

There was a momentary silence.

Ched Hazzard sucked in more air through the gaps in his teeth.

'Has he not been told yet?' asked the doctor.

'No,' said Ched Hazzard.

'Why not?' asked the doctor.

'Some nonsense has arisen about not telling my client the details until the psychologist checks him out. As far as I'm concerned, withholding of this vital information is anathema, and therefore my client has every right to know the answer to his question.' said Ched Hazzard, raising his hands again. 'In my opinion.'

Doctor Brooke nodded and looked confused.

'Yes. Well. I'm not a psychologist myself,' he said.

'Here's the thing,' said Ched Hazzard, turning to Max. 'The people in that photo were your family.'

Max narrowed his eyes at Ched Hazzard.

'Your wife and three children,' clarified the doctor. 'You murdered them.'

'My family, huh?' said Max.

Doctor Brooke glanced at Ched Hazzard. 'Are you sure we're allowed to give him this information?'

'Too late now,' said Ched Hazzard.

'Do you think I'm an idiot?' said Max. 'I've never been married, and I don't have any kids.'

'How do you know?' asked the doctor.

'I'd remember,' said Max.

'It's my understanding that you remember nothing of your adult life,' replied the doctor.

'True. Very true. My client remembers nothing,' said Ched Hazzard excitedly.

And it was true. Max could remember nothing.

6

The following days were a relentless blur of questioning by more dull people asking Max questions which seemed to have little relevance to anything. Max mostly answered, 'I don't know,' and Ched Hazzard would reply with, 'My client doesn't remember.'

Lamb and Hicks were usually present. Max noticed Ched Hazzard was often blunt and abrupt with Lamb. He guessed it was a strange flirtation technique. Or maybe misogyny.

One slow afternoon, Doctor Brooke showed Max a series of cards with pictures on. A duck. A ball. A tree, etc. He asked Max to say what they were, and to describe them. Max found it childish. Then the doctor said a few sentences and asked Max to remember and repeat various details, which Max easily did.

The doctor diagnosed him with selective retrograde amnesia, to which Detective Hicks rolled his eyes and replied, 'How convenient.'

Max remembered numbers, words, phrases and useless trivia, but an impenetrable wall cut off his entire adult life.

Doctor Brooke assured him the situation was temporary.

Max could now wear pyjamas and order takeaways. All Ched Hazzard had to do was mention breaches of Max's human rights, and the police caved in to his demands. The term "human rights" scared them.

Max was handcuffed to a wheelchair after breakfast and taken to a fitness centre connected to the hospital by a walkway. Someone kept shouting 'Murderer!' in his direction, so several officers walked in front and behind him for protection. They also threw a sheet over his head, which made him feel like a circus freak.

The fitness centre stank of sweat, narcissistic onanism, desperation and general inadequacy. Although glad to be out of the confines of Room 9 for a while, Max's skin crawled at being in such a temple of vanity. He viewed it with nothing but contempt.

This harsh assessment stemmed from his school PE visits to a local leisure centre. Those occasions were always fraught with intimidation and embarrassment; the removal of clothing in damp fungal-infested changing rooms where paedophiles prowled around looking for pretty boys like himself.

The PE teacher regularly shouted at Max for not putting enough effort in by calling him 'a useless bag of skin'. That teacher died of a heart attack while playing squash during Max's final term, and Max laughed about it for days afterwards. 'Who's the useless bag of skin now, fuck-face?' he muttered at the school memorial assembly.

Max's physical rehabilitation was the responsibility of a big muscle-bound personal trainer and physiotherapist called Rutger, a blond blue-eyed walking cliché with an indistinguishable European accent.

Max guessed at Denmark.

Rutger put Max through a light regime of weights. The repetitiveness became boringly satisfying.

Rutger never smiled. He never said much either, and had no personality. Max wasn't sure whether to befriend him or not, but decided against it, simply because the guy chose to wear lycra all day.

Rutger didn't seem to hate or judge Max. Max was getting used to the hatred and judgement of strangers. Most people nervously glanced in his direction, and hardly anyone spoke to him unless it was about legal or official police business.

All Rutger would say of Max's fitness regime was, 'It's all about the tic tacs.' Max eventually realised he meant "tactics".

Each day the heaviness of the weights went up incrementally, and Max made good progress.

The rooms in the fitness centre were cleared of the public before Max entered, as if the sight of him would turn people to stone. He found it absurdly strange at first, but soon grew to like it. He didn't want anyone watching him in his condition.

Rutger would then do some exercises with him in the swimming pool. Max enjoyed this most of all. It involved relaxing and floating. There was far too much chlorine in the water, but Max didn't complain. At least he wasn't handcuffed to the bed.

Max recognised a certain cruel irony to his current leisurely existence. Here he was with a personal trainer, a fitness centre seemingly for his use alone, bodyguards, 24-hour security, doctors and nurses nurturing him, and free food and drink. And why? So he could be locked away in prison for the rest of his life. An innocent man reduced to the status of an evil pariah.

The severity of his apparent crime, which of course was a travesty of justice, as he hadn't even committed it, meant he would be very old by the time of release. If he was ever released. He was never going to be released.

Life suddenly felt very claustrophobic.

As he floated with the attentive Rutger by his side and a police officer watching from a row of benches, Max contemplated likely methods of suicide. They all seemed difficult, plus he was under too much scrutiny for any of them to be possible. He guessed his captors had already pre-empted this and put him under suicide observation from the start.

But wouldn't suicide be an admission of guilt?

He tried to imagine how he would cope with decades of incarceration stretching before him. What a waste. What a humane and enlightened liberal waste of a life.

And then one day I'll be exonerated, he thought. *They had the wrong person all along. It was a set-up. They needed to make an example of someone, and I happened to be the unlucky stool pigeon. Poor bastard.*

Never saw it coming. I'll receive some paltry compensation, but it will be too little too late.

The previous day, Max asked Ched Hazzard if his parents had been in touch yet. No, he said, although they had issued a press release saying they wanted nothing to do with him. Same with his sister.

Max wrote them insulting letters, but didn't send them.

Everyone was convinced he had perpetrated the crimes. The evidence seemed conclusive. Max determined to look into this matter further.

The warm water made him feel drowsy.

He wondered what Claire would be doing right now. What was her reaction when the news about Max broke? Was she shocked? Upset?

And what about Mrs. McCabe?

***

Ten minutes later, Max stood towelling himself off in the empty locker room. The ubiquitous police officer watched him.

'Pervert,' said Max. 'Do you get a thrill out of watching a man dry his undercarriage?'

The police officer averted his gaze.

Max looked down at his unflattering nakedness. His nipples looked like two beady bloodshot eyes; his bellybutton resembled a pursed mouth set in a dumpy paunch. His flaccid mushroom penis was lost within a hirsute immersion of wiry grey and black pubes. (He asked to shave it all off, but they only allowed him to shave under close supervision.) Accompanying his penis in its repulsive aesthetic, a baggy turkey-neck scrotum hung beneath. His whole body looked like the result of an awkward design compromise.

Max put on his pants. Soon he'd be handcuffed to that bed again, and he'd lay there dreaming of walking through flower meadows at sunset with Claire.

It was important to Max that he didn't look like a criminal. They allowed him special dispensation to wear a shirt and jeans with slip-on shoes (the result of Ched Hazzard throwing the words "human rights" about again).

'Their deaths were probably an accident, you know?' said Max, as he put on socks. 'I didn't kill anyone. I'm innocent. When this debacle is over, I'm going to sue every fucking one of you.'

'Do you want a kick in the balls?' said the police officer.

Max wondered if he could overpower the police officer. Maybe grab the pepper spray, or the Taser gun on his belt, then stun him and make a run for it.

No, there were more heavily-armed officers outside the door. He couldn't take them all on in his fragile condition. Anyway, where would he run to? How would he survive? The world was his enemy.

He shuddered at the thought of Claire being an enemy too. No, not Claire. Not mysterious, beautiful, sublime Claire.

The defining quality of beauty is manmade. Beauty is an intellectual and cultural concept, made up and defined by humans. The sublime is different – it's created by God or Nature. A garden is beautiful, but a mountain is sublime.

I bet Claire married some undeserving prick, thought Max.

He remembered one dull maths lesson when he and Claire amused each other by doing silly comedy double-takes, like in old movies.

I was smitten, he thought.

But Max married someone else, they said. The woman in the photo, of whom he had no recollection. What a strange thing a life is. Who was his wife? Did he love her? And those teenagers were his kids, apparently. He couldn't imagine himself being paternal.

More police officers arrived. They sat Max in the wheelchair, then handcuffed him to it and threw a sheet over him.

***

As Max was pushed back to Room 9 surrounded by his police escort, he ruminated about the facts so far presented.

Four people were dead. A woman and her three teenage children died in a gruesome, as yet unspecified, way. The woman was Max's wife. The children were Max's children. Max had been charged with their murders. There was no doubt in anyone's mind that Max did it. Max had so far been given no motivation for the murders. There had been a car crash which erased his memory of the events from his adult life from an unspecified time, possibly his late teens onwards. It was still unclear whether he had been driving the car they died in, or if he had driven into their car.

Well, thought Max, *I'm in a bit of a pickle.*

'Murderer!' a voice shouted.

An egg splattered against Max's head. Through the sheet, he could see runny yolk. A slight commotion occurred, but within seconds Max was in a lift.

'Lucky me, they could have used hard-boiled,' said Max.

The lift moved upwards with a hydraulic hum.

An idea still nagged away at Max. All he had to go on were the details he'd been told. What if they were all lying? What if this was a bizarre experiment? An elaborate hoax of some kind? Why him? And to what purpose?

He was at the mercy of strangers. None of it seemed to add up. How could he be sure if anything they said was true? What evidence did he have that the murders even happened? The people in the photo could be anyone. He'd taken it all on trust.

'I want to see my lawyer,' Max said under the sheet. He then worried the lift might have a pause button between floors. The police could beat him up just for the hell of it. But he concluded those buttons only existed in movie lifts for contrived plot convenience.

They removed the sheet when they entered Room 9. The two officers stood in front of him, as per procedure. One of them threw the sheet into a laundry trolley. Max was transferred from the wheelchair and handcuffed to the bed rail, then – careful not to make any sudden movements – he slid onto the bed. Every time, he noted the two officers looked visibly relieved to get this manoeuvre over with. They were scared of him.

Good boy, Max. Obedient slave. A microcosm of the power dynamic in society as a whole. The erosion of civil liberties. Don't make a fuss. Don't question. Don't get involved. Be submissive. Docile.

'I want to see my lawyer,' he repeated.

One police officer exited. The second officer sat in the corner and stared at a mobile phone. Max found it difficult to distinguish between any of his guards. They were like clones. He'd tried making friendly small talk with some of them, but none wanted to engage. They were losing their fear-value to him.

Max kicked off his shoes and lay down.

'Maybe someone tried to kill me,' said Max. 'Did anyone check the brakes on the car to see if they were sabotaged?'

'Forget about the car crash,' said the police officer.

'That's the problem,' said Max. 'I have forgotten.'

Max looked up at the ceiling. He noticed a spider in the corner of the room, one of those ones with long spindly legs and a tiny abdomen. Daddy-long-leg spiders. Probably not their entomological name. It was suspended in a wispy web with a sheath of empty exoskeleton dangling from it, the relic of its earlier self. He would monitor the situation. If the fucker moved too far from the web, Max would have it destroyed. If it kept its distance, he would respect its right to live, in spite of an image of the spider landing on his sleeping face during the night and laying eggs under his eyelids.

'Maybe an enemy framed me?' said Max.

'Shut your mouth,' said the police officer.

'Charming,' said Max, getting cocky. 'I thought you and I might become best friends after this miscarriage of justice is resolved. Let's backpack around South America together.'

Max tried to remember if he had a best friend. He couldn't recall any friends at all, apart from the school ones, and he was certain he'd lost contact with them long ago.

'Believe me,' said the police officer, 'you're not going to be travelling anywhere for the foreseeable future, apart from in a van taking you to prison.'

'I'm confident of being acquitted of all charges,' said Max.

'I wouldn't put money on it,' said the police officer.

'I enjoy our cerebral banter,' said Max.

'You think you're clever, don't you?' said the police officer, slightly rattled.

'Compared to you, yes,' replied Max.

Max couldn't help himself. He knew it was counterproductive, and it would come back to bite him when in a tight spot.

The police officer looked up from his phone.

'When I'm on holiday in Florida in a few weeks' time, I'll be lying on a sun lounger drinking a cold beer, and I'll think of you in your prison cell. Who'll be the clever one then?'

'Touché,' said Max.

I am clever, he thought. *Intellectual, even. I know a lot of stuff. Books. Philosophy. Culture. Damn, if only I could remember any of it. If only I could remember who I used to be.*

7

Ched Hazzard appeared a few hours later, as Max requested. He took great pains to assure Max that everything was real, and yes, an actual murder trial was pending; and no, this wasn't an elaborate hoax, or an experimental new TV show. No conspiracies or foul play by a third party were suspected, either. Max still wasn't entirely convinced.

'What took you so long to get here?' he asked.

'I was on a date,' said Ched Hazzard. 'Someone I found online. They claimed to be a sexy female dancer, but it turned out to be a muscly man with a beard. Nice bloke, actually. I could have got angry about his subterfuge and the waste of my time, but the food was too good. Then he offered to give me a Rusty Trombone, which turns out to be an unusual sexual practice. Needless to say, I made my excuses and left him to pay the bill.'

'Go away quickly,' groaned Max, pulling the sheets over his head.

***

The next morning in the gym, Max tried the rowing machine, then the cycling machine. Both bored him.

Afterwards, Max floated in the pool. He began to suspect people were deliberately pissing in it. A sulphurous odour hung around that wasn't there before, and the water stung his eyes.

Even Rutger stopped getting in. He stood at the side of the pool saying, 'Tic tacs. Tic tacs.'

The police officer on pool duty had a smirk on his face. He looked like the one Max insulted the day before.

Max imagined the staff and police officers lining up and taking long steaming pisses in the pool shortly before his arrival, laughing as they did so. What larks. How long would it be before he felt the dreaded unwelcome nudge of a massive floating turd?

Max played along with their game for now. He wore water wings and a swimming cap with pink flowery design. His trunks were a size too small and chafed terribly, but Max said nothing. He knew his fitness privileges would end the moment he recovered his health. He needed to be careful not to make too much progress, and reckoned he could squeeze two more weeks of this before being transferred to... where?

Some grim institution? An insane asylum?

A curious incident happened in the changing room ten minutes later.

Max took off his swimming trunks and walked around the corner to the shower cubicles. The smirking police officer waited, as usual, with a towel near the lockers, just out of sight, a duty all the police officers found demeaning.

'I feel like a bloody servant,' he heard one officer say. 'I did not sign up for this.'

Max switched on the shower and stood under the soft flow of water.

There was a maintenance door opposite this particular cubicle. Max had noted it was always locked.

But today it was ever so slightly ajar.

Max, covered in lather, stepped out of the shower and, almost without thinking, pushed open the maintenance door. Beyond it, a service stairwell went down to a small vestibule where cleaning products and mops and buckets were kept. At the bottom, an open doorway led out to a sunlit corridor.

Max looked to his right to see if the police officer was in view. He wasn't.

With an insouciance he could barely believe, Max stepped into the stairwell, pulling the door shut behind him. The temperature dropped several degrees compared to the shower room. Being wet and naked made all the hairs on his body prickle.

He cautiously squelched down the steps to the vestibule.

This is obviously a trap of some kind. It's too easy. They're testing me, thought Max.

He expected to walk through the doorway to be confronted by several police officers, who would indulge in an orgy of Taser-related justice before sending him straight to solitary confinement in the worst prison known to mankind, for trying to escape.

He turned to go back, then paused.

'I have nothing to lose,' he said, turning back to the vestibule entrance.

As a precaution, Max armed himself with a bottle of citrus bleach with lime scale deterrent. He acknowledged the futility of this gesture, but instinct had kicked in. Only with the benefit of hindsight did he realise the mop might have made a better weapon.

Max steeled himself for a couple of seconds, then he walked into the bright corridor.

He was alone. Stark naked and wet, but alone.

A glass wall faced him which ran the length of a ground floor corridor. It looked out onto a nondescript grassy area at the back of the fitness centre with garages and a service alleyway full of overflowing rubbish bins to one side. To his right was an emergency exit. To his left, the corridor led off into other parts of the building.

Max stood there, frozen with indecision. It only took a few short steps and a push on the bar of the door and he would be in the outside world.

He calculated that the service alleyway must lead into the residential street glimpsed just past a row of conifers. He wouldn't need to climb any fences, or negotiate a security gate. His nakedness presented a problem, but he would deal with that somehow.

He imagined a charity clothes bank being just around the corner, and saw himself ripping open bin bags bulging with unwanted clothes and inside one he'd find an expensive linen suit with a wallet full of cash carelessly left in a pocket. In the next bag he'd find a shirt and pair of shiny brogues, along with a snazzy fedora hat he'd wear at a jaunty angle. He would be totally inconspicuous.

Max suddenly realised he had an erection. It was extremely erect. So erect, it actually hurt. It seemed like unfortunate timing. Being thought of as a murderer was bad enough, but also being considered a naturist pervert made for an inconvenient bout of unwanted self-consciousness.

Just as he was about to make his move, a cleaner walked down the corridor towards him pushing a trolley.

Max turned to face her. She saw him, then stopped.

Time stood still for just under an eternity.

Max felt cool air circulating around his body. It made the tiny bubbles of remaining lather pop on his skin.

The cleaner's eyes fell upon Max's pulsating gland. She regarded it, then raised her eyes to meet his.

'I highly recommend this product,' Max said, referring to the citrus bleach in his hand. 'Is it all right if I leave it here?'

The cleaner nodded slowly.

Max bent down and put the bleach on the floor.

He casually walked back into the vestibule, then ran up the flight of stairs and back into the shower room. He shut the maintenance door behind him carefully and hopped into the steaming shower, just as the police officer appeared around the corner holding Max's large fluffy towel.

'Time's up, princess,' said the officer.

Max jumped in fright.

The police officer saw Max's erection. He threw the towel on the floor and walked away.

'I wasn't masturbating,' said Max.

His heart raced wildly. He could hardly catch his breath because of the exertion and the sudden steamy change in temperature.

Max felt lightheaded. A wave of nausea overcame him.

I'm having a heart attack, he thought.

He collapsed, hitting his head on the floor. He lay half in and half out of the shower. His penis, with an alarming speed, retreated flaccidly amongst the forest of pubes.

How humiliating, thought Max. *Even in death there's no dignity. Next I'll shit myself. That's what happens.*

Max tried to call to the police officer, but no sound came out.

Maybe it's better this way, he thought, going numb. *For me, anyway. What a piece of work is a man. The paragon of animals. I should have gone through that emergency exit when I had the chance. I would be free now. Fuck.*

A blinding white flash of light ripped through his brain, along with a terrifying roar of electrical energy.

***

The light and sound stopped.

Max was somewhere else: the living room of a large detached house in leafy suburbia. A purplish-grey sky bathed everything in twilight. All appeared uneasily calm.

Max recognised the room, but he didn't know why. Chinese rugs. Shiny polished floors. Expensive furniture, tastefully arranged.

Opera played loudly – Maria Callas sang "Mon coeur s'ouvre a ta voix" from Saint-Saens' *Samson and Delilah*.

Max looked in a mirror. His reflection stared darkly back, covered in warm congealed blood. The face grinned.

Blackout. Silence.

***

Max woke up, choking. He tried to raise his right hand to his face, but he was once again handcuffed to the bed in Room 9. He opened his eyes, which streamed with tears.

No tubes or wires were attached to him. No bleeps from heart monitors could be heard. Early afternoon sunlight shone through the blind.

Doctor Brooke stood nearby, reading the clipboard chart. The police officer sat in a chair by the door, flicking angrily through a newspaper. Neither seemed particularly interested in helping Max, who convulsed into paroxysms of coughing.

'Water,' croaked Max.

Doctor Brooke pointed towards a beaker of water on the table to Max's right.

Max reached across and awkwardly grabbed the beaker with his left hand, then gulped down the water, spilling most of it onto his pyjama top.

The liquid balm made him splutter until he finally lay there, exhausted and breathing heavily.

'What happened to me?' he eventually rasped.

'Nothing serious,' said Doctor Brooke.

'Nothing serious?' said Max, 'I thought I died.'

'Wanking in the shower,' said the police officer. 'I caught you doing it.'

'I wasn't wanking,' said Max. 'I was having a heart attack.'

'It wasn't a heart attack,' said the doctor. 'There's nothing wrong with your heart. More likely a result of your little escapade.'

'I got a right bollocking because of you,' said the police officer to Max.

'What do you mean?' asked Max.

'You caused quite a stir,' said the doctor. 'The police who were alerted to the scene of your collapse found the maintenance door next to you unlocked, and your wet footprints leading down into a service corridor below.'

'I got a right bollocking for it,' repeated the police officer. 'It wasn't even my fault. I just stand there with a towel, like a mug. Do you have any idea how much paperwork I'll need to fill out?'

'You almost got away,' said the doctor. 'What made you come back?'

'I missed you all,' said Max.

'Everyone's seen the CCTV footage,' said the police officer. 'What the fuck were you doing with that citrus bleach?'

'The cleaning lady has been fired for gross negligence,' said Doctor Brooke, to Max. 'She left the door unlocked by mistake. She was also found to be working in the UK illegally and is now due to be deported. I hope you feel happy with yourself.'

Max didn't feel happy with himself. He didn't feel anything, except a vague sense of despondency. (Everyone had seen his penis.)

'All actions have consequences,' said the police officer, with genuine earnestness.

'Very true. Very true,' said the doctor, who then pointed at Max's forehead. 'You hit your head. Small bruise. You'll live.'

'Yay,' said Max.

'You were due to have your first appointment with a neuropsychologist today, but it's been postponed until tomorrow,' said the doctor.

'Fat lot of good that will do,' said Max.

'I wouldn't be so sure,' replied the doctor.

'Am I still allowed to use the health facilities?' asked Max.

'I don't see why not,' said the doctor. 'The security detail will have to be improved, though.'

'It wasn't my fault,' said the police officer. 'I got a right bollocking for it as well.'

'Yes, so you've said several times,' said the doctor.

'I nearly got sacked. I've got a wife and two kids to provide for, and I nearly got sacked because of that piece of shit,' said the police officer, pointing at Max. 'I have to protect that child-murderer. That wife-killer. He killed his wife and his children in

cold blood, and he lies there with a smug grin on his fucking face.'
(Max didn't have a smug grin on his fucking face.)

'Now, now,' said the doctor.

'He really pisses me off,' continued the officer. 'My wife wishes they'd bring back capital punishment for people like him, and I have to protect him. Mug!'

'This is not the time or place,' said the doctor. 'If you have a problem, take it up with your superiors.'

'Oh, I will do,' said the police officer, his face reddening. 'I'm not the only one who feels this way.'

The police officer glared at Max, then returned to his newspaper.

'Don't you have something more important to do, like direct traffic?' said Max.

'That's enough,' said Doctor Brooke.

Something moved in Max's peripheral vision. He looked up into the corner of the room. The spider had caught a fly. It twanged silently in the web as the spider's spindly legs eagerly wrapped around it. Within seconds it succumbed to the greedy thirst of the arachnid's devouring fangs.

There's subtext for you, thought Max.

8

The next morning, Max was on the running machine in the gym. He built up to a decent walking pace, then broke into a jog, but Rutger slowed the machine down and told him to take it easy. Tic tacs.

Max felt mentally exhausted. He'd woken up in the night screaming and soaked in cold sweat. It happened regularly now. He could never remember exactly what had disturbed him, though the faintest imprint of various shadowy phantasms plagued his daylight hours. He thought he saw things – people – in the periphery of his vision, but when he looked, no one was there.

After the gym work, Max swam a few lengths of the smelly pool. This also seemed a bit creepy now – being alone in such a large (dark) body of water. It made his leg twinge, but he didn't know why.

He showered (they'd padlocked the maintenance door), dressed, then his two guards wheeled him under a sheet towards another area of the hospital. An egg missile hit him again.

'Murdering bastard!' shouted the usual unseen assailant.

Today, Max was meeting the neuropsychologist. His mind conjured up images of a Joseph Mengele-type in full surgical outfit ready to shove lobotomy probes into the darkest recesses of his unconscious. Doctor Brooke assured Max it would be conversation-based.

The way Doctor Brooke said "conversation-based" made it sound like he meant "bullshit".

Max removed the sheet. He was being wheeled down a gloomy silent corridor. There were offices on either side, all with closed doors and seeming to be devoid of life. At the end of the corridor they stopped at a door with "Doctor Digby Shah" written on it, followed by lots of medical qualification letters.

A wave of anxiety rushed through Max. He felt like a dog going to the vets to be neutered.

'What do you reckon? Electrodes to the head, or to the balls?' he said to the two police officers.

'Both, hopefully,' replied the first officer.

The second officer knocked on the door.

Footsteps approached from the other side.

Max suddenly needed to shit, but he puckered his sphincter and affected a casual look.

The door was opened by a woman of around fifty years of age. She had attractive dirty-blonde hair and wore a black trouser suit.

'Come in, Max,' she said.

They wheeled Max into a comfortable consultation room. A leather swivel chair was one side of a coffee table. A couch was against the far wall. Large potted plants were in the corners. Rothko prints jostled for space on the walls between impressive-looking framed medical certificates. Double-glazed windows looked out onto mature trees in an empty park.

The woman sat down in the swivel chair. She had nothing else with her, except a small tablet computer.

'Remove his handcuff, please, then close the door on your way out,' she said.

The police officers looked confused.

'He's a dangerous criminal,' said one.

'One of us has to remain in the room,' said the other.

'That won't be necessary,' said the woman, softly. 'It will hardly be confidential if someone is listening to our conversation.

I insist on the removal of the handcuff, and to be alone with Max, please.'

Fifteen minutes elapsed while the police officers consulted superior officers on their walkie-talkies. Confused overlapping dialogue and contradictory instructions finally led to an agreement.

The police officers searched the room, looking for sharp objects or an escape route, then they checked the windows were locked and secure before nodding with satisfaction to each other.

'Crazy,' muttered one of them as they slowly unhooked the handcuff.

'You're eating into our allotted time,' said the woman.

'If we hear anything in here,' said one officer to Max, 'we're coming in fully armed. We mean business.'

'And don't lock the door,' said the other officer to the woman.

'I haven't got the key,' she replied, unfazed.

The police officers waited for a moment, then went into the corridor and shut the door.

Max regarded the woman.

She was scrolling down a page of writing on her tablet.

Max's eyes scanned the room for cameras, or maybe a two-way mirror, but nothing untoward could be seen.

'You can sit on the couch,' said the woman, without looking up.

Max hesitated, then stood.

'Are you not intimidated by me?' he asked.

'Should I be?' she replied.

'It's the general vibe I get from people,' said Max.

A hint of a smile played on the woman's lips.

'Interesting,' she said. 'Do you like to intimidate people?'

'No. I don't think so. I haven't really got the build for it, but I suppose my reputation precedes me. Apparently, I'm a notorious murderer.'

'How does that make you feel?' asked the woman.

'Innocent,' said Max.

Max went to the couch and sat down. It felt strange. Too casual. He tried to think of the last time he'd sat on a couch, but couldn't remember. He was hunched up at one end.

'You like Rothko?' asked Max, to fill the silence.

'Rothko?'

Max nodded towards the nearest print.

The woman looked at it.

'No, not really.'

'Why do you have them on your wall?'

'It's not my wall,' she said.

'So, you're not Digby Shah?'

'No, I'm not Digby Shah. I believe he's a male consultant.'

'Why are we in his room?' asked Max.

'I was allocated it. I've never been here before.'

'Where's Digby Shah?' asked Max.

The woman turned and looked at Max.

'I have no idea,' she said, with a smile.

Max picked up a cushion and placed it on his lap as a comforter, then he immediately put it back in case it looked as if he was trying to hide an erection, which he wasn't. He blushed.

'It's upside down,' he said.

'What is?'

'The Rothko. An easy mistake.'

'Oh?' said the woman, glancing once again at the print. 'How can you tell?'

'I studied his work for an art project at middle school. I picked him because his stuff looked easy. But it's deceptive.'

'Yes, I suppose so. You like his work?'

'No,' said Max.

'What sort of art do you like?' asked the woman.

Probe, probe, probe, thought Max.

'Is this part of the session?'

'No. Just a preamble.'

Max tried to think what art he liked. The only pictures he could think of were the *Mona Lisa*, and Van Gogh's *Sunflowers*. He didn't want to say either of them. Too obvious. Too philistine.

'The one with the dogs playing poker,' he said as a joke. 'I don't know. Art isn't a high priority to me right now. Everything is still jumbled up in my head.'

'I'll bring a book on art for you to look at,' said the woman.

'Why?' asked Max.

'As an exercise. Art can be a useful tool for the mind.'

'Cool,' said Max, with a hint of sarcasm.

The woman looked at him. Her eyes seemed to penetrate his skull.

Max couldn't help but find her attractive, although her face was bony, but flawless. Intelligent, but like a mask. Twenty years ago, she must have been stunning.

Max averted his eyes to the window.

'My name is Lee,' she said.

'I prefer the name Digby Shah,' said Max.

'Just call me Lee.'

Max nodded vaguely and brushed non-existent lint off his trousers.

'So, you're a psychologist?' he asked.

'I straddle the line between psychology and neuropsychology,' said Lee. 'I don't see why the two need to be mutually exclusive, although some of my colleagues differ in that opinion. Psychology is a diverse field.'

'I'm sure it is,' replied Max.

'The human brain is the most complex thing in the known universe. We still don't fully realise its capabilities, or its vulnerabilities,' said Lee.

'I've been getting a pretty good idea of that lately,' said Max.

'No doubt,' said Lee.

A momentary lull ensued. Max realised he was tightly gripping the arm of the couch. He released it.

'Are you going to record what I say, or make notes?'

'I keep it all in here,' said Lee, tapping her head.

Max's sphincter squeezed out a silent, painful fart. He was concerned it might lead to a follow-through, so he clenched his buttocks tight. He would suffer stomach cramps for it later. Right now, he felt the need to attain a certain decorum in front of Lee. Dignity at all times.

He wondered how many people had sat on this couch while they were given a terminal diagnosis by Digby Shah.

How many cried? How many stared in disbelief? How many were now dead?

'I didn't kill anyone,' said Max.

Lee said nothing. The countenance on her face didn't change. A poker face. Or was it Botox?

'No one believes me,' he continued. 'I don't expect you do, either.'

'There's rather compelling and conclusive evidence that proves you committed those murders,' said Lee.

'So I've been told. But I have no memory of it. For all I know I could have been set up.'

'Not possible,' said Lee.

'Oh? Why can it be dismissed so easily?'

'The time for conspiracy theories has passed,' said Lee. 'You have to move on from such denial and accept responsibility.'

'Why should I trust anything you say?' asked Max.

'I promise not to lie to you. You simply must have faith,' said Lee.

'I have no faith in anything or anyone,' snapped Max.

He realised his hand was gripping the arm of the couch again. He saw Lee's eyes flicker to it. Max released his grip.

Fuck, she saw. Mustn't let my guard down, he thought.

'Are you intimidated by me?' asked Lee.

'No.'

'Are you intimidated by strong intelligent women?'

'I'll let you know when I meet one,' Max shot back.

He blushed with regret at the misogyny of the comment, then blurted out a few half-completed sentences of apology, even using the words "inappropriate overt patriarchal stereotyping".

Lee leaned forward slightly.

'Don't apologise,' she said. 'Say what you mean.'

'I don't know what I mean. If you know what I mean,' said Max. 'I'm not a misogynist. It was a flippant remark.'

'Doctor Brooke tells me you have selective retrograde amnesia,' said Lee, leaning back in her chair, eyes unblinking.

'Apparently so,' said Max.

'There are medical and legal reasons for these sessions,' said Lee. 'I have to establish if your dissociative disorder is factitious or not. The CAT scans have proved inconclusive. We also have to determine the length of your amnesiac state, and whether the temporal trauma or an emotional trauma is causing the block.'

'They say I was married with children,' said Max. 'They showed me photos of them. I had no idea who they were. People are judging me, criticising me for showing no remorse, but how can I have remorse if I don't recall the existence of my so-called family? To me, they're just strangers in photos. It might sound cold-hearted, but if they're dead, that's unfortunate. It has nothing to do with me.'

'Interesting,' said Lee. 'You're so certain.'

'I mean,' said Max, 'maybe I fell asleep at the wheel? Has no one considered that the car crash may have been an accident?'

'The car crash?'

'Yeah. From what I can gather, I was driving my supposed wife and kids in a car, and it crashed. Right?'

Lee's forehead wrinkled for half a second. There was definitely Botox in there somewhere.

Max continued, 'Just because I was the only survivor, doesn't mean I'm a murderer. I want to see police reports. Vital evidence is being withheld from me. My lawyer's a fucking idiot who's more concerned with shagging the detective working on my case. I'm surrounded by morons. Maybe I'm the victim here? I've woken up in a Kafkaesque nightmare. I don't know who the hell I am. I don't know who I used to be. No one is talking to me. I don't deserve this treatment. No one even seems willing to give me the benefit of any doubt. Is that fair? Everyone has automatically come to the conclusion that I'm guilty. Since when has that been the law in this country? I'm innocent unless proven guilty, right?'

Lee busily scrolled through her tablet.

'I'm afraid I'm to blame,' said Lee, without looking up. 'I want certain aspects of your case to be withheld from you for the time being until we establish the extent of your memory loss. I thought such rudiments had been relayed to you. Surely you have been visited and questioned by legal and medical representatives? It's a basic prerequisite.'

'Various people visited me in the days after I woke up, but I wasn't in the right frame of mind to listen to them, what with me being half-dead and dosed up on enough medication to knock out an entire herd of fucking elephants,' said Max.

'Yes. Of course,' said Lee, turning off the tablet. She looked up at Max and smiled thinly. 'Thank you for coming today.'

'Is that it?' asked Max.

'For now,' said Lee.

A few minutes later, Max was handcuffed to the wheelchair and heading back to Room 9. In the lift, he looked at the two police officers.

'It was a car crash, wasn't it? They died in a car crash?'

'Shut up,' replied one officer, as he threw the egg-encrusted sheet over Max.

9

Dawn. Max restlessly slept. A nightmare played somewhere inside the labyrinth of his mind. He waded through lakes of treacly blood and entrails while being chased by unseen phantasms. Hands reached out of the morass and tried to grab him.

After returning to Room 9 from his first session with Lee the previous afternoon, Max had become increasingly agitated and angry. He made demands to see his parents and sister, but when told to calm down, he started shouting and threw a tray of food at a wall. For his own safety, Doctor Brooke heavily sedated him.

***

Max's childhood contained a poetic strangeness. There were few relatives. No network of aunts or uncles or cousins.

Both sets of grandparents were dead. He remembered, just, his elderly grandfather, a man with liver-spotted hands and a kindly smile. At his unemotional funeral, Max nearly retched at the smell emanating from the coffin. He found the service funny for no particular reason and kept giggling, so Dad told Margot to take him outside.

When smoke came out of the municipal crematorium roof, it dotted his coat with ash. Max asked Margot what it was.

'Granddad snow,' said Margot, absently.

Max never wanted for anything growing up. He had toys. A warm bed. Food. An education. In many ways, privilege, which he rarely found an appreciation for. His life was suburban and uneventful, and nothing much was expected of him.

Max couldn't wait to leave the creepiness of childhood behind. The early bedtimes. The empty playgrounds at dusk. The swings in the park that creaked. (The two older boys in junior school who tried to lure Max into the dark toilets at the end of the long corridor. Max wet himself rather than go in.) The corruption of innocence.

Sometimes, he missed childhood. Marvelling at hoar frost in winter. The thrill of kicking through autumn leaves. Sparklers. Presents. Long summers. Intense fleeting friendships. The promise of future potential. The lack of responsibility and pressure.

**

Max woke up screaming and drenched in a cold sweat. It was morning. He sat up in bed. The police officer on duty in Room 9 looked at him.

'You've soiled yourself,' said the officer.

**

For the first time since his recovery began, Max refused to go to the gym. Rutger and his tic tacs would have to wait.

Max was scared at the prospect of more spectral encounters. The very thought of getting into the swimming pool and being dragged under to his doom by supernatural entities filled him with dread, even if it did run counter to his notions of rationality.

He had a shower, but kept his back to the wall and his eyes wide open.

All he could think about was getting back to Digby Shah's office and talking to this Lee person.

First, he had a session of cerebellar tests with Doctor Brooke. They were an extension of basic cognitive assessments he had undergone shortly after waking from his coma, where Doctor Brooke moved his finger back and forth in front of Max's eyes and Max had to follow it.

Max now had to stand on one leg and close his eyes while counting to ten, then repeat it with the other leg. Simple. He also had to look at a monitor and follow a moving X on its screen. Various coloured dots appeared and disappeared around it, like a rubbish computer game, and Max had to say 'Yes' whenever he saw them.

'Does this really help?' he asked the doctor.

'We're not doing it to amuse ourselves,' came the reply.

Afterwards, police escorted him to have an EEG scan. The noise the scanner made unnerved him. He expected a gentle humming sound, but this one must have been ancient, because it made a loud clatter, like someone hitting a sheet of metal with a hammer. Max thought it was going to explode. He panicked and shouted to the nurse to be let out.

***

An hour later Max was in the hospital lift, heading to his appointment with Lee. He sat handcuffed to the wheelchair. The two police guards stood either side. They cuffed his left wrist now, because his right one was covered in friction burns.

'I'm not an invalid. Why am I wheeled everywhere?' he asked from under a freshly-laundered sheet.

'Health and safety,' came the curt reply from Officer One.

'Why do I have to have this sheet over me?'

'So your photo doesn't end up in the press,' said Officer Two.

'And health and safety,' said Officer One. 'We can't have you injured by food-based missiles, can we?'

'But we're in a lift,' said Max.

'We don't want to look at you,' said Officer Two.

Max pulled the sheet off himself out of defiance.

'Happy now, you moany bugger?' said Officer One, to Max.

'Ecstatic,' replied Max, smarmily. 'I'm giddy with delight.'

They wheeled Max down the corridor. He readied himself to demand answers from Lee, but as soon as he arrived in Digby Shah's room he became strangely obedient and quiet, much to his own surprise.

Lee was already sitting in the swivel chair, looking calm and composed.

A smile displayed her expensive dentistry.

As before, the police searched the room, then unlocked the handcuff.

'He's been causing trouble,' said Officer One. 'Are you sure you want us to leave?'

'Yes, thank you,' said Lee.

'He's a slippery customer,' said Officer Two. 'Don't be fooled by him, he can turn nasty.'

'Oh, don't worry,' said Lee. 'I'm trained to a high standard in several martial arts. I could take all of you out before you knew what hit you.'

The officers stood silent.

'Good to know,' was the only riposte one of them could muster.

They left the room and shut the door.

Lee stared at her tablet computer. Without looking up, she gestured for Max to sit on the couch.

Max did as he was gestured, although he sat in the middle of the couch to avoid gripping the arm.

'You're waking up each morning screaming and soiling yourself. Can you recall any details of your nightmares?' asked Lee.

Max thought.

'There's often snow. And lots of blood. I'm usually wading through it, or sinking in it, unable to escape from something chasing me. There's dark water, too. A sense of dread. Inevitability.'

'Do you recognise anyone or anywhere in the dreams?'

'No.'

Lee looked up at Max with an unblinking lizard stare. A slight lopsided closed smile played on her lips.

She stood up and approached Max.

'Here,' she said, offering Max her tablet computer, 'I have photos for you to look at.'

Max took the tablet from her. Lee then went over to the window and stared out at the park.

Max looked at the screen of the tablet. On it was a photo of himself as a baby.

'Where did you get this photo from?'

'Your mother,' said Lee.

'You've spoken to her?'

'Briefly.'

'You spoke to my dad, and my sister?'

'Again, briefly.'

'And yet they won't speak to me?'

'No.'

'Are my parents still together?'

'Yes.'

'Are they well?'

'Your father recently had a severe stroke. The stress of losing all three of his grandchildren affected him very badly.'

A well of emotion stirred within Max, but quickly subsided.

'And my mother?'

'She's coping.'

'So, my sister has no children of her own?'

'No.'

Max looked at the tablet screen again.

'What do I do with this thing?'

'Put your finger on the screen, and swipe it to the left,' said Lee.

Max did so. Another photo slid onto the screen: Max, aged seven, in a chimney sweep costume.

'That was a primary school play. I liked dressing up and pretending to be other people.'

'There are remarkably few photos of you,' said Lee.

'I hated having my picture taken,' said Max.

He swiped the screen: a middle school portrait photo of himself aged ten, smiling awkwardly.

'I never understood why the school insisted on taking our photo every year whether we wanted to or not,' he said. 'They charged for it, too. I think this is the only one my parents ever bought.'

He swiped again: Max, aged twelve, in a stiffly posed photo with his mum, dad and Margot on a windswept shingle beach.

'Cornwall. The weather was miserable, and so were we. It was the only proper family holiday we went on, other than day trips. We spent most of the time sitting in dreary cafes near Land's End waiting for the rain to stop. It didn't, so we went for bracing walks along a beach and I got pneumonia. My parents were very annoyed with me.'

'You make them sound like monsters,' said Lee.

'They were never the most affectionate of people,' said Max. 'But no, not monsters. They're frighteningly normal.'

'It sounds like a lonely childhood,' said Lee.

'I didn't know any different. My parents never encouraged me to bring friends home. It didn't seem odd at the time.'

Max swiped to the next photo: Max, aged fourteen, looking dapper in a white shirt and a thin black leather tie, laughing with Paul Finch at one of the only parties Max went to. He and Paul Finch were chummy for a while, but they fought each other later that night when Max kissed Paul's sister, Daisy, with tongues during a game of spin the bottle, and they never spoke again.

'You didn't have many friends,' said Lee. 'I spoke to contemporaries of yours from school, but no one seemed to remember much about you, or they confused you with other people.'

'Really?' said Max, with surprise. 'I thought I was quite popular. Did you speak to Edgar Parr? Or Mike Barrow? Or Steve Glock? Or Paul Finch? They were all friends of mine.'

Max wanted to ask if she had talked to Claire, but something held him back from mentioning her. He guessed that Claire had forgotten him. She probably married some idiot, and now had five kids. Maybe it's better not to know.

'The people I spoke to,' said Lee, 'remembered an incident at a school reunion about five years ago, when you became violent and assaulted someone.'

'I have no recollection of that,' said Max, as he swiped through some teenage photos of himself with greasy hair and acne. 'Did you speak to Mrs McCabe? She was my form teacher in middle school.'

'She died two years ago. Cancer,' said Lee.

'Shit,' said Max.

'I read your childhood and teenage journals,' said Lee. 'They're full of clever, witty ideas, poetry and vivid imagination. Why did you stop writing them?'

'Don't know. What is the point of this little trip down memory lane?' asked Max, more tetchily than he intended. 'I have good recall of that period of my life. Can we move on?'

'Okay,' said Lee.

'I hope the rest of my life is more interesting,' said Max. 'I'm going to be so disappointed if I didn't become an international spy and playboy among the rich and famous.'

His eyes became fixated on a square of sunlight lying across the wall and ceiling opposite him. It glinted off the polished potted rubber tree leaves. Max imagined the square sliding down the wall, warping in shape as the day progressed, unobserved by human eyes. He thought of all the squares of sunlight in all the empty rooms along the corridor and throughout the world. Empty rooms. Empty life. Emptiness.

'Max?' said Lee.

Lee was now back in her swivel chair.

'Sorry?' said Max.

'I said, you left school with few qualifications and little interest in academia, yet you managed to scrape into a college to study English Literature. Do you recall that?'

'Yes. I used college as a delay tactic to prevent myself from becoming a fully-fledged adult. I didn't feel ready. I wasn't academically gifted, but I was an intelligent auto-didact. I willingly read Descartes, and Montaigne, Virginia Woolf, Waugh, Hermann Hesse, Camus, Sartre, Dostoyevsky, Flaubert, Rimbaud, Plath, Byron, Milton, James Joyce, Baudelaire and Shakespeare.'

'Do you remember being thrown off the college course?' asked Lee.

'No,' said Max.

'You physically attacked your tutor. You pinned him to a wall by his throat and tried to strangle him,' said Lee.

'Nonsense,' said Max. 'I was a geek. I remember my time at college, and I was quiet and studious.'

'Swipe to the next photo,' said Lee.

Max did so: a police mugshot of Max aged nineteen.

'Whoa!' said Max.

'The charge of assault was eventually dropped, but you were kicked out of college.'

'I… I don't remember,' said Max.

Lee leaned forward.

'We're not yet clear on why you murdered your family. Only you can tell us what motivated you. I want to help you recover your memories up to the time of the murders.'

'How?' asked Max.

'Hypnosis,' said Lee.

An alarm sounded throughout the building. The two police officers burst through the door with Tasers raised.

'Don't fucking move!' they shouted at Max.

'Relax,' said Lee, calmly. 'It's just a fire alarm.'

'We need to evacuate the building immediately,' said Officer One.

They pushed Max into the wheelchair and handcuffed him. As he was wheeled out, he looked at Lee.

'What happened next?' he asked. 'What happened next?'

10

What happened next: the police rushed Max down to a room on the ground floor with more police officers guarding him.

They stayed there for two hours until the fire alarm was found to have been set off by a patient in the terminal ward who'd attempted suicide by setting themself on fire with the candles on their birthday cake.

This inconvenience annoyed Max greatly. His appointment with Lee had elapsed and he'd have to wait until tomorrow for the next instalment of his life.

Selfish suicidal fucker, thought Max. *I hope they survived.*

***

Arriving back in Room 9, Max found Ched Hazzard waiting for him, dressed in an oversized white cable-knit sweater, with a lumberjack shirt underneath and brown corduroys with socks and sandals.

'Hey, Max, how's everything going with the shrink?' he asked.

'Not sure. We haven't got very far,' said Max.

'What kind of stuff is she asking you?'

'Oh, you know, what my favourite ballet is, and she's eager to know my views on macramé.'

'Really?' said Ched Hazzard.

'No,' said Max. 'I don't know what to make of her.'

'She has a reputation for being a little unconventional.'

'She wants to hypnotise me,' said Max.

'Ghurhur,' chortled Ched Hazzard.

'I'm serious,' said Max.

'Oh. Hypnosis? Jesus. That's old-school.'

'My sentiments exactly,' said Max.

'Well, it's a novelty,' said Ched Hazzard.

'This whole thing seems pretty wacky if you ask me.' said Max. 'And talking of wacky, what in the name of Christ are you wearing?'

Ched Hazzard looked down at the clothes. He put his hands on his hips, making his midriff sag as before.

'I'm going on a date,' he said. 'Why, is this apparel not conducive to such propriety?'

'You're going a date dressed like that?' asked Max. 'Are you taking her on a deep-sea fishing trip to the 1970s?'

'I think I look debonair,' said Ched Hazzard, slightly hurt. 'This is my smart-casual look.'

'I presume it will be the first and last date?' scoffed Max.

'Ask me who I'm dating.'

'I couldn't give a shit,' said Max.

'It's Detective Superintendent Kate Lamb.'

'Fuck off,' said Max with disbelief. 'Did you hypnotise her?'

'Ghurhur. No, I used a bit of the old Ched Hazzard charm. It works every time.'

'I thought *I* had more chance of going on a date with her than you.'

'What can I say?' said Ched Hazzard, with a wink. 'When you've got it, you never lose it.'

If I had a pencil, I'd stab your fucking eyes out, thought Max.

'It's only a pub lunch,' continued Ched Hazzard. 'Best to keep the dates informal and cheap to begin with.'

'Informal and cheap. You romantic devil,' said Max. 'Remember to use protection.'

'Oh, I always carry pepper spray,' said Ched Hazzard.

'I mean condoms.'

'Sex condoms? For sex?'

'No, condoms for grouting tiles with; yes – sex condoms. For sex.'

'I hadn't considered that eventuality,' said Ched Hazzard. 'Now I'm scared.'

'What are you doing about my case?' asked Max, irritably.

'I'm doing everything I can, Max,' said Ched Hazzard. 'I'm exploring every avenue. All legal procedures are being followed, but they take time. It's a really complex business. A minefield of red tape. Half the time I don't understand what's going on.'

'That fills me with confidence,' said Max. 'Do you have an assistant, or a legal team helping you?'

'Well, my mother does my typing, if that's what you mean.'

Max ground his teeth.

'Haven't you found anyone who is willing to vouch for me? Anyone to give me a positive character reference, or an alibi?'

Ched Hazzard busily rummaged for loose change in his pockets.

'Um, not really,' he said, pulling out a fifty pence coin. 'Is that enough for a packet of three?'

'I'm fucked,' muttered Max.

***

Max was taken down for a swim in the pool. The water now stank like a sewer. He complained to Rutger that there was more piss in it than actual water, but Rutger said it was probably "only baby piss", as the mother and toddler group used it first thing. Max said he didn't care whose piss it was, it was unsanitary, then he started ranting about his human rights. Rutger didn't understand.

***

Once again, an egg hit Max's head with remarkable accuracy as he sat under the sheet, being wheeled through the hospital foyer.

'Murderer!' someone shouted.

'Bring back hanging!' shouted another.

'Why don't you stop them doing that?' Max asked the police officer pushing him.

'They're entitled to their opinion,' said the officer.

'Doesn't missile throwing constitute as assault?' asked Max, with egg seeping through the cotton and polyester mix.

'Not when it comes to you, no,' came the reply.

'I'm innocent,' said Max.

**

Max lay on the bed in Room 9. He had an hour until his next session with Lee. It felt like a Friday, but could have been a Tuesday.

He looked up at the spindly spider. It hadn't moved for days. It just waited patiently for an opportunity to present itself, for an innocent creature to blunder into its web. The inevitability of misfortune. A blood sacrifice repeated over billions of years. A moment of sudden violence would occur, followed by a small horrific unlamented death.

Such infinite varieties of bloodlust were happening every second in trillions of tiny places. Kill. Eat. Discard. Next. No compassion. No guilt. No mercy. Pure instinct. Survival at any cost. The lust for life. The random chaos of existence. Godless.

A rustling sound came from near the door. Max lifted up his head and saw a morbidly obese police officer sitting in the chair. Max watched him surreptitiously take a pork pie out of his pocket. The man drooled as he tore the wrapping off, and was just about to ravish the comestible when he noticed Max looking at him.

'I'm bloody starving, me,' said the officer. 'Do you mind if I…?'

'Be my guest,' said Max.

The police officer greedily devoured the pork pie in two messy gulps, then licked each one of his greasy fingers with a satiated groan of satisfaction.

'That was something,' said the officer.

'You're telling me,' said Max, laying his head back on the pillow.

'I'm not supposed to eat on duty for some reason, you see, but needs must.' burped the officer.

Max turned over on his side and closed his eyes.

'What are your views on hypnosis?' he asked.

'I'm sorry, but I'm not allowed to engage in verbal conversation with you,' said the officer.

'Feel free to use interpretative dance,' said Max.

'Actually,' said the police officer, 'I did go to a magic show a while back, and a hypnotist made the whole audience cluck like chickens, me included. I felt such a fool. It was very funny.'

'Sounds a hoot,' said Max.

From somewhere on the floor above, noisy hammering, drilling and sawing began. Max put the pillow over his head, but the thudding reverberated through it.

'Is this some kind of psychological torture?' he said, sitting up.

'It's from the terminal ward,' said the obese police officer. 'They're fixing the fire damage from yesterday. The person died.'

'Suicide by birthday cake. How absurd,' said Max.

'Death by birthday cake would be my method of suicide, as it goes,' mused the police officer.

'Yes, but you'd cram the cake into your gob and choke on it, rather than burn to death,' said Max.

'Hey,' said the police officer, offended. 'That's discrimination, that is. You're judging me because of my appearance.'

'Arrest me,' said Max, lying down again.

'I can't help my genes. I attract food,' said the officer.

Max heard a crisp packet rustling.

'You'll get diabetes,' said Max.

'Already got it, but only type two so far, touch wood.'

The hammering, drilling and sawing became louder. Max dived under the pillow again. He heard the police officer say something.

'What?' asked Max, lifting the pillow.

'I said, you're pretty handy with a saw, aren't you?' said the officer.

'What do you mean?' asked Max.

'You know,' said the officer, emptying the contents of the crisp packet into his mouth.

'No, I don't know,' said Max, sitting up.

'Yes you do,' said the police officer. He had a silly grin on his face. He winked at Max.

'I really don't know what you're talking about,' said Max. 'You're talking in riddles.'

The police officer stopped himself mid-chew and put his hand to his mouth.

'Bollocks, I've said too much, haven't I?'

'Was I a carpenter, or something?' said Max.

The police officer mimed zipping his mouth.

'Oh, come on,' said Max, 'Don't leave me hanging.'

The police officer shook his head.

Max could glean no more information from him. The police officer pretended to ignore Max from then on, and even hummed quietly to himself.

Max lay back on the bed and looked at his hands. They didn't look like the hands of a manual labourer.

Max enjoyed woodwork at school, but he never considered it to be a potential vocation.

'Jesus Christ was a carpenter,' mused Max, aloud. 'It's an honest trade. I wonder if Jesus was good at joinery? I don't think the Bible goes into detail on His qualifications or employment history. No, I couldn't be a carpenter. Or a manual labourer. I'm an intellectual of some kind.'

Max sat up in a sudden panic.

Who am I? he thought. *What did I do with my life? Why am I wasting time?*

The police officer produced a saveloy and offered it to him. Max shook his head. He observed the officer swallow it in one gulp. 'Good God, man.' said Max.

A pretty nurse entered carrying a tray with Max's pills and a paper cup of water.

'Your pills, please,' she said in a flat Polish accent.

Max looked at the pills: one pink, one white, one yellow.

'Know what they're for?' asked Max, as he did every day to each new nurse.

'I not know,' said the nurse.

'You not know?' asked Max, playfully. He looked at the rotund police officer. 'She not know.'

'There's no need to patronise her,' said the police officer, dabbing the crumbs off his stab-proof vest.

'They stop me from exploding. Boom!' said Max to the nurse, then he started to laugh.

The nurse didn't react.

'I not understand,' she said.

'No, me neither, Dorota,' said Max, reading her name badge. 'Me neither. Oh well, bottoms up.'

Max picked up one pill at a time, leaned his head back and dropped them into his mouth with a gulp of water. He swished them around theatrically before swallowing them, followed by a satisfied burp, as if he'd enjoyed them.

'Yum-yum pigs bum,' he said. 'Delicious. My compliments to the chef.'

Max smiled at Dorota. Dorota didn't smile back.

'That is all,' she said, then she left the room.

'Nice girl. Great personality,' said Max.

'She's Polish,' said the police officer.

The hammering, drilling and sawing became more intense.

'Can't a guy get some peace around here?' shouted Max.

He swung his legs off the bed. As he did so, a ray of sunlight fell upon him. His image reflected back in the window, like a mirror. In the harsh unkindness of the light, his appearance resembled a concentration camp inmate.

'My looks have gone, along with my youth,' he said. 'I can't remember the last time I got laid. Or the first time. I can't remember anything at all, except being a carpenter, right?'

He looked at the police officer for clarification, but the police officer merely gave a nervous grin.

Max sighed, then closed his eyes and bathed in the warm sunlight.

Why am I not interested in things? he thought. *I'm existing in this odd tiny vacuum of nothingness. I don't know what's going on in the world. I'm not particularly bothered, either. I'm devoid of interest in politics, and music and films and TV and general culture. I have no great desire for anything. But I'm not depressed. Why am I not bored? I'm suitably absorbed by myself, by this blank that is me. Who am I? Who was I? What are my wants and needs? I simply don't know. I don't appear to be in any rush to find out, either. It's like I've just accepted this as my reality now. What is reality anyway?*

Max suddenly opened his eyes.

'I wrote a novel,' he said.

11

'Was my novel published?' asked Max.

Lee sat opposite him in Digby Shah's consultation room.

'Self-published,' replied Lee.

Max looked disappointed.

'Have you read it?'

'Yes,' said Lee.

'Is it any good?'

'I'm not a literary critic,' said Lee.

'That's an evasive answer,' said Max.

'It's an interesting novel. Difficult. Somewhat abstract. Esoteric.'

'I want to read it.'

'In good time,' said Lee.

'No, now,' said Max, raising his voice.

Lee remained still.

'In good time,' she repeated.

Max realised he was gripping the arm of the sofa again. He slowly released it. Lee was inscrutably calm and collected. Max desired to see her naked.

'My dad tried to write a novel,' he said.

'I didn't know that,' said Lee.

'I just remembered it. He spent many hours in his room tapping away at a big boxy computer, but eventually he gave up on it, I think. Yes, I remember one autumnal evening, I was about sixteen, I watched from my bedroom window as he took the only manuscript copy of it down to the end of the garden and lit the barbeque, then he fed each page one by one into the flames. My mum told him to stop, but he didn't. Then he took a USB stick with the novel on, clamped it with tongs and held it over the fire until it melted into liquid.'

'And how did you feel about that?' asked Lee.

Max shrugged.

'Soon afterwards, I wrote a novella. I wanted to impress my dad. When I finished it I let him read it. "You pretentious little prick," was his only informed critique. Nice, huh?'

'What happened to that novella?' asked Lee.

'I deleted it. It was a thinly-veiled self-pitying cri de coeur about my life at the time; an attack on my parents and my school. Looking back now I see the hallmarks of a nervous breakdown. I knew I wouldn't pass my exams. I'd made vague unrealistic plans to be an actor, or a writer. No doubt my parents were concerned about my prospects. Then my sister attempted to commit suicide.'

Max stopped short, surprised by his own revelation.

'Go on,' said Lee, leaning forward.

'I… I was about seventeen. My parents had gone away for a few days. I arrived home one night with… with someone… a girl…'

Max stared into the middle distance, lost in thought.

'What girl?' prompted Lee.

'Her name was… Zoe,' said Max.

Lee nodded slowly. 'Good. Go on.'

'Oh fuck, I didn't marry her, did I?'

'Keep going, Max,' said Lee. 'Think. Concentrate.'

Max shifted uncomfortably on the sofa. His face flushed. His irises dilated and he looked as if in a trance.

'I joined an amateur dramatic society. In a galling example of naivety, I convinced myself I had natural thespian talent, and movie producers in the audience were bound to spot my brilliance and beg me to star in their award-winning films. I met Zoe at a rehearsal for Goethe's *Faust*. Zoe played a nymph. I'd been given a tiny one-line role as a courtier. I hardly noticed her at first. I was attracted to another girl in the cast who typically wasn't interested in me at all. Zoe flirted with me during the dress rehearsal and we started hanging out, as friends. I didn't find her attractive, but she was sweet-natured. After the final performance there was a party and we both got a bit drunk, then I took her back to my house. But when we got there, the front door was ajar and all the lights were on. Some overwrought ballad by Whitney Houston played loudly on a loop in the living room. Margot had trashed the place and lay semi-comatose on the floor among empty vodka bottles and pills. She'd made a half-hearted attempt to cut her wrists because her latest boyfriend had dumped her. I called an ambulance, even though Margot begged me not to. Paramedics came and took her to hospital.'

'Then what happened?' asked Lee.

'I didn't go to the hospital with Margot. Instead, me and Zoe lost our virginity that night. She pulled me down amid the suicide detritus and we had sex. I remember blood being on the carpet. Margot's blood, and Zoe's hymenal blood. It scared me because I thought I'd hurt her. I tried to clean it up, but I made the stain even worse. My parents came back from holiday early. I told them it was a wine stain, but they knew it wasn't. They brought Margot home the next day. She didn't speak to me. She moved out soon after.'

'Why didn't she speak to you?' asked Lee.

'Embarrassed, maybe,' said Max. 'Or ashamed. She wanted to be dead. I don't know what happened next. Remind me.'

'I want you to tell me,' replied Lee.

'I can't remember!' shouted Max, coming out of the trance. 'What is the relevance of this?'

Max immediately looked contrite.

'Deep breaths, Max,' said Lee. 'I know it's frustrating.'

'My memories are there,' said Max. 'I can feel them.'

'That's good, Max. It gives us something to work with. I want you to receive your memories progressively and in chronological order. We must try and avoid the possibility of implanting false memories in your subconscious. With practice, you'll start to unlock the truth.'

The door opened. One of the police officers looked in.

'I heard a raised voice. Everything okay in here?'

Lee nodded, waving her hand dismissively.

The police officer eyed Max with suspicion, then retreated.

'They want to move you to a high-security psychiatric hospital,' said Lee. 'I'm the only reason you're still here.'

Max looked down at the soil in a large rubber tree plant pot next to the couch. It was bone dry, which annoyed him. The leaves had a polished leathery sheen, but were beginning to brown at the edges. He wanted to touch them, but stopped himself. How strange, he thought – these plants had grown freely for millennia before humans appeared, and now here they were, cultivated prisoners reliant on their neglectful captors, held in an alien environment to add visual nuance to bland offices.

'You appeared in *Arsenic and Old Lace*,' said Lee.

She showed Max the screen of her tablet. On it was a photo of an amateur dramatic society cast, lined up on stage in front of a cheap set in unconvincing 1940s costumes. Among them was teenage Max in an ill-fitting American police uniform. Next to him stood Zoe, as a maid.

Max sat for a while pondering.

'I have no recollection of that at all.'

'Let's try something else to help push things along,' said Lee.

Out of her bag, she produced a plastic black box the size and shape of a Polaroid Instamatic camera and placed it on the table in front of Max. It had two lenses, similar to camera flashes. She switched it on.

'This is a prototype invention of mine,' she said. 'It will help you focus.'

The lenses flashed on and off in sequence, slowly at first, one purple, one yellow, although sometimes the colours changed. A metronomic click accompanied each flash. Max squinted at them, mesmerised, then he looked away.

'Just keep looking at the colours,' said Lee.

Max's eyes were drawn back to the flashing lights. The speed at which they changed began to vary. Sometimes they appeared both together. It became strangely soothing. After an unspecified time, Lee said, 'You've now entered an altered state. Don't fight against it. There is nothing to worry about.'

'How long have I been under?' asked Max.

'Not long,' said Lee.

Max looked at the room.

'Everything is the same,' said Max.

'Not quite,' said Lee. 'Open the door.'

'Open the door?' asked Max.

'Tell me what you see,' said Lee.

Max smiled. He stood up and walked to the door, feeling woozy as he put his hand on the doorknob. He cracked the door open, flinching at the expectation of attack by the two police officers.

Max peered through the crack. The corridor had gone. In its place was the theatre dressing room from his local amateur dramatics theatre.

Max shut the door.

'What the fuck is going on?' he asked.

'Go through the door.'

'What have you done to me?'

'It's a memory regression technique. I had amobarbital sodium put in your coffee earlier. It's not a widely-recognised method anymore, but I find it gets results when used in conjunction with the light box.'

'You've drugged me?' said Max. 'Is it LSD?'

'No,' said Lee. 'Trust me, it's perfectly safe. I want to get to the heart of who you are. Your memory needs a kick-start. Maybe it will work, maybe it won't. You won't actually leave this room. At an appropriate time I'll stop the light box and you'll come out of the altered state. Go through the door and explain in detail everything that happens.'

Max hesitated, then cracked open the door. The theatre dressing room was still there.

'Curiouser and curiouser,' said Max.

He went through the doorway.

***

Max stood at a mirror, tugging at the much-too-tight collar on his police costume. Opening night. Nervous anxiety. He looked as miscast as he felt; too young for the role, but they didn't have anyone else. (He had white make-up painted onto his temples).

Clothes and belongings of the cast were in heaps on chairs and tables. Some had rushed straight from work. On a crackly Tannoy, the actors on stage could be heard saying dialogue amidst a cacophony of boiled sweet wrappers and competitive audience coughing.

'I'd better begin at the beginning,' one actor said in an American accent veering wildly between continents. *'It opens in my mother's dressing room, where I was born – only I ain't born yet...'*

Max smoothed down his heavily lacquered hair and put his peak cap on as Zoe entered from the stage corridor, pulling off her maid wig.

'I'm sure this thing's got fleas,' she said, scratching her scalp.

Her long frizzy hair fell down near to her waist. Max hated her long frizzy hair. He kept finding them attached to his clothes, and it made him reflexively gag.

'You should cut your hair shoulder length, and straighten it,' he said.

'But I like my hair,' said Zoe, looking hurt.

Max was about to exit into the corridor, but Zoe grabbed him.

'Kiss me,' she said, puckering her lips.

Max pecked her on the cheek.

Zoe loved public displays of affection. She insisted on holding hands (she had clammy hands) when walking, and liked kissing in front of people (her lips were overly moist – Max always wiped his mouth, when she wasn't looking). He did things to appease her, then he felt emasculated for not taking the initiative. He found Zoe's theatricality initially endearing (she was a terrible actress, hence the minor roles), but it quickly began to grate on his nerves.

Max was infatuated with a beautiful actress (again) in the cast, but she didn't pay him any attention at all (as usual); she only had eyes for the oily prick playing Teddy Brewster.

'It's our five-week anniversary,' Zoe whispered in Max's ear. 'Come back to mine tonight. We can try anal if you want.'

She smiled coquettishly, then blushed.

Zoe's face was wan and pretty, but Max had become alarmed by the noticeable amount of downy hair sprouting on her top lip. He didn't know how to broach the subject of depilation with her.

Max headed straight down the corridor towards the stage.

Cliques had inevitably formed amongst the cast. Max didn't belong to any of them. He found it difficult to bond. Friendships were awkward for him. He was always polite and friendly, but something about him made people reluctant to engage further. They could never put their finger on why.

He stood in the wing, next to an elderly prompt who followed the script via torchlight. The guy playing Police Officer Klein to Max's Police Officer Brophy (both minor roles) was already there, looking petrified.

They nodded to each other.

Max didn't understand the plot of the play. He only paid attention to his own scenes at the rehearsals. The actors had laughed indulgently at each other and made it sound funnier than it actually was. To Max it seemed like a creaky old pile of shit.

Their cue line came: *'I pulls my guns – braces myself against the wall – and I says – "Come in."'*

Max and the other guy stepped onto the stage. Max opened his mouth to say the line 'What the hell is going on here?', but he only got as far as *'What the—'*, when he tripped and fell flat onto the stage. His police cap rolled into the front row and his lacquered hair wildly plastered itself over his face.

The audience laughed.

Two actors helped Max to stand up.

'Biggest fucking laugh we've had so far,' said one of them as a private aside to the other.

'What the hell is going on here?' said Max, unheard above the laughter.

The laughter began to subside.

'What the hell is going on here?' said the prompt, loudly in the wing.

The audience went silent.

Max didn't want to say the line again, but the actors on stage looked at him, expectantly.

'What-the-hell-is-going-on-here?' said Max with staccato venom, and not in his character's accent.

'He forgot his line,' said an old lady to her neighbour in the front row.

'No I didn't,' said Max, flattening his hair back down as sweat poured off him, stinging his eyes.

An audience member threw the cap back to Max.

The scene continued in a tense, haphazard way. All eyes were on Max, who delivered his lines with contained anger.

'The Lieutenant's on the warpath. He says the Colonel's got to be put away some place,' said Max, crossing the stage and lifting the receiver of a heavy wall-mounted Bakelite telephone, as per his directions. He dialled too aggressively. The phone fell off the wall and smashed a vase full of water, which was not supposed to happen.

90

Max tried to reattach the phone to a hook on the chipboard wall, but the set collapsed backwards.

'Fucking cunt!' shouted Max.

There was a collective intake of breath from the audience, followed by whistled readjustments of hearing aids.

'You stupid arsehole,' growled one of the actors, who swung a punch at Max, but missed completely and went crashing into the wing.

Chaos ensued; people backstage tried to push the set back up, others tried to help the actor in the wing who noisily crashed into the prop table. Max froze. Several audience members began to boo and heckle him. A stage manager ran on with a mop and a broom to clear away the broken vase and water.

The prompt, unaware of what was happening, repeated the next line louder and louder. 'Say, do you know what time it is? It's after eight o'clock in the morning.'

Through stinging tears, Max saw his mum and dad getting up from the third row and leaving. He'd specifically told them not to come. Then the stage lights went out and people screamed in panic. At that very moment, Max decided the stage and the world of thespianism was not for him.

Brushing past Zoe in the dressing room (she didn't make eye contact), Max grabbed his belongings and rushed out into the night. He trudged aimlessly in the rain for a while in his police costume, through moonlit woods, only stopping now and then to vomit and dry-retch from shock. He made a pitiful attempt to drown himself in a stream, but it wasn't deep enough.

He prayed he would catch pneumonia and die the next day, or perhaps catch a life-ending disease from all the sewage in the water. Oblivion seemed a preferable alternative to the rawness of humiliation. But there was no escape from his fate. His punishment was to live and be snared in the relentless trap of existence.

When he got home, his dad sat in the living room watching TV.

Max tried to sneak up the stairs. Halfway up, he heard his dad begin to sarcastically slow-clap.

'Proud of you, son. Hollywood is only a phone call away,' he said.

'It wasn't my fault,' said Max, barely above a whisper.

He passed his mum on the upstairs landing. She opened her mouth to say something, then thought better of it.

'Oh, Maximillian,' she said, shaking her head.

Max went to his bedroom, defeated and ashamed. He cried all night.

***

Lee switched the light box off. The clicking stopped.

Max perched on the couch opposite her, his heart beating rapidly.

'This is progress,' said Lee.

'In what way?' asked Max.

'Your memories seem to be intact. You didn't remember that episode before, but now you do, vividly.'

Max was quiet for a moment.

'I'm hardly cock-a-hoop,' he said. 'I'd rather that debacle remained forgotten.'

'Would you like to talk about it?' asked Lee. 'Tell me about how you are feeling.'

'What am I supposed to say?' said Max. 'It was a horrible experience. It doesn't prove I'm a murderer. It's irrelevant.'

Lee took a sip of water.

'Okay, let's push onwards,' she said. 'What do you remember of your time studying English Literature at college?'

'Like I said, I was a nerd.'

He stood up and walked over to the door. Lee remained in her chair and made no effort to stop him. Max opened the door – the corridor and the two police officers were outside. They both stood up and put their hands on their Tasers.

'It's all right, Officers,' said Lee. 'This is part of the session.'

Max closed the door and sat back down on the couch.

'Tell me about the murders,' he asked.

'You're not ready to know what happened yet.'

'This whole thing is illogical.'

'I know it isn't easy, Max.'

'Just give me a straight answer, or I swear I'm going to—'

Lee started the light box again. Click-click-click-click…

Max was under her power.

'We haven't much time before the amobarbital sodium wears off,' said Lee. 'Please open the door again and go through.'

Max found himself mechanically doing as he was told.

The hospital corridor and the police officers were gone again, this time replaced by the classroom at the local college he attended, aged nineteen.

This is insane, thought Max.

***

'You're late,' said Reynold (the tutor), as Max entered the classroom.

'No, the rest of the world is early,' said Max in riposte.

Reynold was a square-headed little man in tweed. Max hated him. The feeling was mutual.

'Oh, very droll, very droll,' said Reynold.

Max sat down in his usual seat. Three long tables placed end to end created one long u-shape. Around it sat several greasy no-hopers who somehow washed up onto the shore of this bland provincial tertiary college of modern education to study Eng. Lit. Most of them seemed unable to read or write.

Max considered himself too good for the place. Reynold disagreed.

He'd had it in for Max from the first day, when he overheard Max larking around in the toilets telling another student that Reynold was a notorious paedophile. Max didn't realise Reynold was taking a dump in one of the cubicles. The false paedophile rumour quickly spread, so Reynold used every opportunity to make sure Max and his work suffered.

'Thank you for gracing us with your presence, Mr Hopeless,' said Reynold with mock courtesy. It was the sort of snide thing Max's dad might say.

Max kept arriving late to class because of an unusual fetish he had discovered: stripping naked in a local overgrown cemetery and wandering around amongst the gothic mausoleums. He couldn't understand why he did it, but it gave him a strange pleasure, like a risky compulsion. There didn't seem to be a sexual motive, just the fear/thrill of being naked and vulnerable in a public place, as well as an element of sacrilege. Max rationalised it to himself with the notion, *we all do weird irrational stuff from time to time.* His legs prickled satisfactorily with nettle and bramble welts.

It was a short-lived fetish. He only did it once more, later in the year. On that occasion he thought someone was following him, so he dived naked into a copse and tore his scrotum open on a thorn. He almost fainted at the amount of blood. He would always have a tiny scar as a reminder.

'Perdition,' Reynold said, looking at Max. He held Max's short story assignment aloft with the tips of his fingers, like it was used toilet paper. 'I want you to explain to us what the word perdition means.'

Max felt hot.

'Don't you know?' asked Max, trying to buy time to think.

'You use the word twice in your short story, Maximillian.'

'Just Max,' said Max through gritted teeth.

'I find it very odd, just Max, how you can use words that you don't know the meaning of. It's not the only example in your work either. I can appreciate if someone has idiosyncrasies in their style, or if they are exploring post-structuralism, but you take liberties. I asked for a 2000-word story based on the notions of dialectical myth and allegory within the rhetorical and temporal thematic shifts of *Beowulf.*'

'Aren't you supposed to be encouraging us to write?' snorted Max.

'If someone has talent, yes. But you, just Max, haven't.'

'You can't have much talent yourself if you're working here, you square-headed twat,' muttered Max.

A shockwave of giggles rippled through the room.

'Get out of my class, you guttersnipe,' barked Reynold. 'And don't bother coming back.'

Max's mouth suddenly went dry. He wondered how he was going to explain this latest humiliating failure to his parents. What would he do now? Where would he go? He stood up and walked towards the classroom door, planning lies and incorrigible excuses.

'You'll be hearing from my lawyer,' said Max.

'Out!' shouted Reynold, his face turning purple.

'This isn't fair,' said Max. 'I listen to you praise everyone else when they read their barely-literate stories aloud, yet you always criticise mine, which are far superior.'

'What we have here,' said Reynold to the class, 'is a typical entitled smart-arse with an over-inflated sense of ego. Not only is he talentless, but he does not listen to the instructions of the exercises. I did not ask for a pornographic stream-of-conscience abomination on the aesthetics of the female pudenda, which this filth is.'

'I was trying to be different. I write with passion,' said Max.

'Get out and take your filth with you,' said Reynold, scrunching up Max's assignment and throwing it at him.

It hit Max's eye. Before Max knew what he was doing, he'd pinned Reynold against a wall and started choking him.

Several classmates lifted their camera phones and pressed record.

***

Lee switched off the light box.

Max gripped the arm of the couch with a white knuckle. His muscles were tight.

'And relax,' said Lee.

Max's body immediately went limp.

'The fucker deserved it,' gasped Max. 'What was I supposed to do, meekly walk out of the room so he could continue taking the piss out of me?'

'You nearly put him in hospital,' said Lee.

'Why are you making me relive such shit stuff?' said Max. 'This is not a true reflection of who I am.'

'Who are you, Max?' asked Lee.

'I'm... I'm... I...' Max trailed off, then sank further into the couch. 'I am not a murderer.'

'I believe,' said Lee, 'that the bicycle accident you had when you were eleven had a major impact on you, much more than you or anyone else realised. When you hit your head on the pavement it changed your personality. Before the accident, you were a well-liked boy with top marks in exams. After the accident, you became withdrawn with sudden mood swings. Your grades dropped, and your journal entries turned dark and disturbing before they stopped abruptly.'

'Can a head trauma change someone that much?' asked Max.

'I've known cases where people have hit their head and can suddenly speak fluently in different languages, or they can play piano concertos without ever having taken a lesson,' said Lee.

'But what talent was I given?' asked Max. 'I'm a broken man. Will that count for anything at my trial?'

'I'm not a legal expert,' said Lee. 'And the world doesn't always have easy answers.'

'You're saying I'm mentally ill,' said Max. 'It makes sense. I've never felt normal. I never fitted in.'

'You're making good progress,' said Lee. 'These exercises are proving you have access to your memories. Your brain is rewiring itself and strengthening the neural pathways. It's like a computer rebooting itself after a major system failure.'

'But if my life is going to be revealed as a compendium of humiliation, why should I participate any further?'

'Because something is missing here,' said Lee. 'There's more to this, and it's at the root of your condition. You must try and think.'

Max took a deep breath, then frowned with concentration.

'I remember being put in a cell at a police station after attacking that teacher,' he said. 'I remember the fear. All charges were dropped and my dad picked me up that evening. I can see the look on his face.'

'You see? You remember more than you realise,' said Lee.

'I was taking driving lessons at the time,' said Max, surprised. 'But I can't remember how to drive.'

'You passed your driving test first time,' said Lee.

'Wow,' said Max. 'Success at last.'

'During your first lesson, you drove the car into a lake, but I'll spare you the details on this occasion,' said Lee.

'Probably for the best,' said Max.

'Do you remember your first car?' asked Lee, carefully.

A fuzzy picture emerged in Max's mind.

'I think it was blue... A Fiat?' he said.

'Good. Correct,' said Lee, with something resembling a benevolent smile. 'Keep flexing those memory muscles.'

'Who was my wife? How did we meet?' asked Max. 'Please tell me her name.'

The shutters on Lee's face came down.

'Next time,' she said.

'What did I do with myself during my twenties and thirties?'

'Next time.'

'Why not now?' asked Max.

'Time's up.'

Max looked at the clouds outside the window.

'I always considered myself artistic and creative by nature. How did I end up as a manual worker?'

Lee's forehead furrowed.

'What do you mean?' she asked.

'One of the police officers who guards my room said I was handy with a saw,' said Max, turning to look at Lee.

Lee's eyes seemed to flash with fire.

'Which officer said that?'

'The morbidly obese one,' said Max.

'Did he say anything else?' asked Lee.

'No.'

'And from his comment you presume you were a manual worker?'

'I'm not sure,' said Max, showing his palms to Lee. 'But these are not the hands of a manual worker.'

Max expected a reaction from Lee. Her face went blank.

'Next time, Max.'

As if on cue, the two police officers entered.

Max allowed them to take him back to Room 9 without a fuss.

***

On entering Room 9, a small Indonesian woman was cleaning. She quickly began to gather up her equipment.

Max winked playfully at her.

As he lay on the bed to be handcuffed, he glanced up at the corner of the room. The spider and its web were gone.

Max sat up.

'Hey, what happened to the spider?' he said to the cleaner.

The cleaner nervously picked up a can of insect spray and made a hissing sound.

'Murderer,' said Max.

12

Max was doing sit-ups on his bed when Ched Hazzard arrived at Room 9 carrying a satchel.

A low sunset reflected off the hospital's south wing windows. Hostile clouds of deep purple were creeping ominously overhead. Lights began to be switched on for the evening.

The police officer by the door gave the satchel a cursory check, then nodded for Ched Hazzard to enter.

'How did the date go, stud?' asked Max.

'Oh, it went,' said Ched Hazzard.

'Give me the sordid details,' said Max. 'Did you make beautiful music together? Did the angels weep?'

'Not quite, no. Rather disappointing, actually.'

'Oh? Explain?'

'She—' Ched Hazzard looked at the police officer. 'I need to talk to my client about important confidential business.'

The police officer went outside. Ched Hazzard continued, 'She threw up. Twice. Something she ate.'

'Are you sure it wasn't a reaction to your clothes?' said Max.

'No. The waiter warned us the scampi was potentially dangerous, but she took a reckless gamble. Silly, really.'

'How sick are we talking?' asked Max.

'Projectile. It was terrifying. She only has herself to blame.'

'Are you seeing her again?'

'I don't know. Maybe. She's threatening to sue me.'

Max stopped doing sit-ups.

'Thus, ever did true love run smoothly,' he said, amused.

'They got rid of the rotund fellow,' said Ched Hazzard as he rooted around in the satchel.

'Who?' asked Max.

'The police officer.'

'Why?'

'Loose lips sink ships,' said Ched Hazzard, pulling a couple of large glossy coffee table books out of the satchel. 'These are for you.'

He handed the books to Max. They were about the history of art.

'Who are these from?' asked Max.

'A secret admirer,' said Ched Hazzard.

'Really?'

'No. They're from Lee, your psychologist. She said she promised to give you them.'

'You got any porn in that satchel? I'm desperate.'

'No. But I have something else.'

Ched Hazzard took out a bundle of letters and gave them to Max.

'What are these?' asked Max.

'They really are from your secret admirers. Love letters and marriage proposals. You get about thirty each day. That's just a selection.'

'Really?' asked Max.

'Yeah.' said Ched Hazzard. 'There's a lot of sick and lonely people in this world.'

'No offence taken,' said Max.

Max's nostrils were suddenly attacked by various comingled cheap perfumes permeating off the paper. They were from many women, badly spelled, and on pastel-coloured notepaper. On one, written on Hello Kitty paper in capital letters and green biro: 'I AM A LADY OF MATURE AGE AND I WOULD LIKE TO

MARRY YOU. I LIVE IN A HOSE (sic) IN BATH WITH MY DACHSUND, MINNIE. WE READ ABOUT YOU EVERY DAY IN THE PAPER AND THINK THAT YOU LOOK LIKE A DECENT CHAP, THE QUADRUPLE MURDERS NOTWITHSTANDING, AND—'

Max handed the letters back to Ched Hazzard.

'You keep them. Might give you a thrill on cold winter nights.'

'Thanks,' said Ched Hazzard, with genuine appreciation. 'Oh, there's a big international football match on TV tonight. I can get a TV put in here. We can watch it together.'

'No, I don't think so,' said Max.

'You don't want a TV in here?'

'No, I don't want a TV in here.'

'Don't you get bored?'

'Only with boring people,' said Max. 'I prefer my own company. It's the only intelligent conversation I get. Besides, I've got these books to entertain me now.'

'Whatever floats your boat,' said Ched Hazzard.

Max opened the first book at a random page and looked at a photo of Edvard Munch's *The Scream*.

'Appropriate,' he said.

'I'm sorry they killed your spider,' said Ched Hazzard. 'I heard you were quite upset.'

'He was my only friend in this world,' said Max. 'A brave and noble companion, and a fine poker player to boot.'

'I'm your friend,' said Ched Hazzard.

'No you're not,' said Max. 'You're paid to be here. In any other walk of life I wouldn't even acknowledge your existence.'

'Bit harsh,' said Ched Hazzard.

***

A few hours later, Max had eaten beef stew with mashed potatoes and soggy vegetables (using flimsy plastic cutlery). He now sat up in bed dressed in cotton pyjamas looking at pictures in one of the glossy art books, lit by an overhead lamp. He quickly skipped through the crude early cave paintings of animals being hunted, paused briefly at ancient Egyptian hieroglyphs, moved through European religious ephemera, only stopping to inspect a detail of Satan devouring the damned in hell, from Fra Angelico's *The Last Judgement*. He spent time examining the demonic hybrid creatures of Bosch and Breughel, then shuttled past many portraits of obscure aristocrats and monarchs, and landscape paintings containing anatomically incorrect animals (the bodies were always too big and the heads too small).

He reached the Enlightenment, infused with Hogarth and Gillray's cynical satires, pricking timeless bubbles of human hypocrisy.

Max then reacquainted himself with gothic. How often death and love were interlinked. Consumptive poets in moonlit churchyards.

The romance of young life snuffed out.

He lingered over several examples of Fuseli's phantasmagoria, such as *The Nightmare*, and a William Blake picture of a ghostly figure sitting with head bowed in a cave. A caption read: "The forms of virtue are erect, the forms of pleasure undulate".

'Lucky them,' sniggered Max.

The police officer by the door looked up from a paperback book. 'What?'

'Nothing,' said Max. 'What are you reading?'

The police officer lifted the book. It was a true-life crime account about the Kray twins.

'*Tess of the D'Urbervilles?*' joked Max. 'You surprise me. I won't give away the ending, but she gets executed.'

The door opened and the corridor officer poked his head in. From another room, a TV could be heard broadcasting the football match.

'It's going to penalties.'

'But what about him?'

'He's not going anywhere.'

The police officer stood up.

'I hope both teams lose,' said Max, as the two officers exited the room.

Max turned the page and stared at a picture by Goya, of a wild-eyed man biting the head off a human torso. It was titled: *Saturn Devouring His Son.*

The door of Room 9 opened and a shifty-looking man darted in wearing a doctor's white coat. He had a stethoscope around his neck, which made Max immediately suspicious.

'This is nice, isn't it?' said the man, sarcastically.

'You're not a doctor,' said Max. 'The stethoscope gives you away. It shows you're trying too hard.'

The man reached into his coat. Max presumed he was about to become the victim of an assassination. He didn't think to press the emergency button. He didn't think to do anything.

The man pulled out a camera. Max breathed a sigh of relief.

'Look at you sitting there,' said the man. 'What kind of justice is this?'

He took a photo of *Saturn Devouring His Son.*

'What do you want?' asked Max.

'This is like a bloody luxury hotel,' said the man. 'The NHS is shutting down wards, yet you're taking up valuable resources in a private room at taxpayers' expense. You should be in prison. It's outrageous.'

The man took pictures of Max. Max raised his hand to shield himself from the flashes.

'Leave me alone,' pleaded Max.

'Why did you kill your family, eh?' said the man, as he moved around the bed trying to get a better angle.

'I didn't kill anyone,' said Max.

'Yes you did, you lying sack of piss. Why'd you do it?' said the man, getting up close and teasing Max to grab the camera off him.

Max lurched forward and almost grabbed it, but overbalanced and fell onto the floor with one wrist still handcuffed to the bed. The man continued taking photos. Max hid behind the sheets.

At that moment, the two police officers returned. A melee ensued, although Max was unable to see it. After a struggle, they got the man under control and bundled him out of the room.

'It's too late,' the man shouted. 'I've already uploaded the pictures to my agency.'

Max peered out from behind the sheets. Nurses were looking through the doorway at him.

'Is he dead?' asked one.

'Unfortunately, no,' said another.

***

Following an incident-free sleep, Max woke up with the dawn, feeling curiously cheerful.

The morning progressed. Rutger. Run. Swim. Shit. Shower.

The sun shone brightly. Max returned to Room 9. He was surprised to find Detective Superintendent Kate Lamb (still looking ill from food poisoning), and several senior police officers waiting for him. None of them wanted to be there.

'Max,' began Lamb, 'on behalf of all my colleagues, I would like to personally apologise to you regarding last night's unacceptable breach of security.'

Max, convinced she was going to vomit in his face, took a cautious step back. She really shouldn't have been at work.

Lamb planned to say more, but couldn't continue. She shook her head and beckoned to someone. Detective Hicks carried in a ridiculously large, yet cheap-looking decorative fruit basket with a powder blue bow around it. The fruit was slightly bruised because Hicks had been kicking it around in the corridor. He didn't try to conceal his seething disgust as he plonked the basket onto a table.

'As a tokenistic gift,' said Hicks through gritted teeth, 'please accept this fruit basket as a gesture of goodwill.'

'You shouldn't have,' said Max with a shit-eating grin. 'Really, you shouldn't have. I'm touched.'

'Is there anything you would like us to do, Max?' asked an anonymous senior officer.

'Yes. Set me free,' said Max.

Max and several of the officers chuckled falsely.

An awkward silence followed.

The police began to shuffle out of the room.

Hicks muttered an audible 'Motherfucker,' as he passed Max.

Ched Hazzard was waiting to come in. He and Detective Lamb glanced at each other in passing, but said nothing.

When the room cleared, a police officer handcuffed Max to the bed.

Ched Hazzard entered.

'Help yourself to some fruit,' said Max.

'No thanks. Trying to give up.'

Max opened one of the art books and flicked through random pages: an empty room with open doors, by Hammershoi; *An Experiment on a Bird in the Air Pump*, by Joseph Wright; *The Death of Marat*, by David.

Ched Hazzard perched himself on the end of the bed and idly picked at a loose cotton thread.

'Any news for me?' asked Max.

'Nope.'

'So, what's this visit in aid of?'

'I was passing,' said Ched Hazzard.

'What exactly are you doing for me?'

'There's a lot of red tape, Max. Progress is slow. It's complex.'

'So you keep saying,' sniped Max.

He turned another page. *Standing Nude, Facing Front (self-portrait)*, by Egon Schiele stared back at him. It reminded Max of himself.

'I do have some news, actually,' said Ched Hazzard. 'The prosecution lawyer has issued a statement to the press calling you a ruthless, cold-hearted manipulative liar, a violently abusive psychopath, and also a malicious and calculated murderer.'

'Everyone's a critic,' said Max.

'Don't worry, I issued a counter-statement saying, "No he isn't".'

'Wow,' said Max. 'If that doesn't convince them, nothing will.'

Doctor Brooke (still wearing an eye patch) entered the room holding a tray with a steaming cup of coffee on it.

'How are the neuropsychology sessions going?' he asked Max.

'That hypnosis shit works,' said Max.

'Really?' said Doctor Brooke. 'You surprise me.'

'Me too, Doc, me too, but I'm buzzing. I've got new memories coming out of my arse, if you'll pardon my French.'

Max flicked a few pages ahead and stopped at an expressionist triptych of mutilated twisted lumps of agonised meat with screaming mouths – *Figures at the Base of a Crucifixion,* by Francis Bacon.

Max shivered.

'Well, you'd better drink that coffee. You have another appointment with her shortly,' said Doctor Brooke.

Max picked up the cup and smelled it theatrically.

'Mmm. Just like mother used to make. Coffee laced with amobarbital – the warm beverage of champions.'

He drank the whole cup in one gulp.

'Deeelicious!' he said.

13

Thirty minutes later in Digby Shah's consulting room, words were spilling out of Max's mouth. He paced up and down excitedly while Lee listened in her chair.

'It was a blue Fiat with a dent over the front left wheel arch and a little patch of rust over the petrol cap, and third gear would never properly engage so I had to hold the gearstick in third to stop it popping back to neutral, and I bought the car myself for £300 with money I saved, and my mum and dad paid the tax and insurance, and that car was a piece of shit but I loved it more than anything in the world and the first opportunity I got I drove it all the way down to Newquay for no reason at all, and I slept in that little blue Fiat overnight, then drove back home the next day and even when the engine overheated and I had to be towed back the last fifty miles, I still forgave it, and when I got home I found a gormless spoddy university student had moved into my bedroom even though I'd been gone less than a day, and my parents said they were renting out my room because I didn't have any prospects and I wasn't pulling my weight and I needed to get a job and I had a big row with them and I stormed out. And do you know what? They hadn't rented my sister's room, even though she had left home by then!'

'And that's all just come back to you?' asked Lee.

'Yes!'

'Good. Then what happened?'

Max became still. He frowned.

'I can't remember,' he said, disappointed.

Lee switched on the metronomic light box.

'Sit down. Concentrate.'

'Don't I need to go through the door?' asked Max.

'No need,' said Lee. 'Just watch the lights.'

Max sat on the sofa. Within seconds his eyes became fixated on the sequence of lights and the metronomic clicks.

'Where are you now?' asked Lee.

***

Max sat in the driver's seat of the blue Fiat. Midday. A Friday. He was twenty-one. In his haste to leave after the argument with his parents, he'd forgotten to take any possessions with him. He was effectively homeless and friendless, with only half a tank of petrol, no food, and a grand total of nine pounds in his pocket.

He'd driven in a random direction and parked in an unfamiliar side street in London because the engine threatened to overheat again. While waiting for it to cool down, he got out and wandered over to a public park. It was an unseasonably chilly day. The park was empty. Max saw some swings swaying in the light breeze. He went and sat on one.

'Life must be leading me somewhere,' he said to himself. 'This can't be all there is. There has to be a purpose to what I'm experiencing.'

He began to think of all the people he'd known at school. Where were they? What were they doing now? Probably at university, or beginning their careers in middle management. Starting families too.

And what about Claire? Where did she go? Max felt like crying, but didn't know why.

At that exact moment, he noticed a lone figure – a female –

walking in the distance along a path on the edge of the park. He squinted his eyes at her.

It was Claire. Or was it? Surely not. Too coincidental.

The closer she got, the more Claire-like she became. Without seeing him, she turned off and walked to an exit gate.

Max prepared to call out to her, but then thought better of it. What would he say?

'Why would Claire be here?' he said aloud.

He stood up and jogged towards the exit she had taken. He'd follow her and… and what? Stalk her? What if she caught him?

She was out of sight by the time he reached the gate. He stood on the pavement and looked both ways. The street was deserted. For the next hour he searched the surrounding area for her, but to no effect.

'It probably wasn't even her,' he repeated to himself many times, unconvincingly.

By two o'clock he'd given up the search. He walked along a parade of scruffy shops in an obscure side road: a laundrette, a closed Chinese takeaway, a charity shop with cracked windows. The few other shops stood forlorn and empty.

A sudden cloudburst made Max take shelter in the doorway of the last shop along. He stood there watching the rain come down when he noticed a small sign in the window. It read: *Staff wanted – apply within. No experience necessary, only a curious mind.*

Max turned and peered through the dirty window. The first thing he saw was a complete neck vertebra and skull of a giraffe, surrounded by a collection of dusty tat: Venetian masks, moth-eaten taxidermal animals, and tables full of crystals, fossils, minerals and accumulated antiquity. The shop, called "The Emporium", had nothing in common with its surroundings apart from its dereliction.

Max opened the door.

Some sort of sickly-sweet incense was burning, creating a hazy effect in the foetid air. A Chopin nocturne played on a gramophone.

Max walked inside the crammed space and picked up a few objects: a pack of tarot cards, some glass plate portrait photographs of unhappy Victorians, a voodoo doll with a grotesque face.

He stopped and looked at a table full of unusual specimen plants and vicious-looking cacti. A Venus fly trap busied itself breaking down the enzymes of an unfortunate bluebottle whose legs were twitching in its maws.

'Plants,' said a man's refined voice in a shadowy back area of the shop, 'are merely the horticultural whores of human whimsy. They prostitute themselves with aesthetic abandon. I refuse to water them. Fuckers!'

Max wheeled around in surprise. He couldn't see anyone.

'Excuse me?' he asked.

Something stirred in the darkness of the back room. The owner of the voice made a languid step forward into a sliver of light. He was thin, pale and interesting, perhaps in his thirties, with long flowing black dyed hair. He wore a velvet frock coat with a waistcoat and cravat, incongruously teamed with Y-fronts and fluffy bunny slippers.

'They'll have the last laugh, of course,' said the man, resting his head against a pillar and looking bereft of vitality. 'Long after humans are extinct, the plants will thrive while our bones decalcify. They will be our captives for now, but listen closely and you can hear them deriding our hubris. My God, life is miserable, and it isn't long enough. I could easily endure another decade of this torture. Alas, I am fated to die.'

The man pulled out a cigarillo from a silver case and lit it with a match. His fingernails were painted black. His hands shook.

'I've come about the job,' said Max.

'What job?' said the man, framed in a wraith-like veil of smoke. He watched the flame burn out on the match.

'There's a sign in the window,' said Max.

'Not buying, then?'

'No.'

'Pity. Oh well, you'll do. Welcome aboard.'

'What is the job?' asked Max.

'Don't know. Whatever you like, as long as you're quiet. I can't pay much. Is £200 per day sufficient?'

'£200 per day?' asked Max, surprised.

'All right, £400 per day, cash. You drive a hard bargain, you bastard.'

The man pulled out a thick wad of £50 notes, then peeled off eight and threw them towards Max.

'How long does the job last?' asked Max, picking up the notes.

'Until fate decides otherwise.'

'When do I start?'

'You already have,' said the man, retreating back into the gloom.

'My name's Max, by the way.'

'Rex.'

'No, Max.'

'My name is Rex, you whoreson!' barked Rex.

Max cautiously followed Rex into the backroom, which was divided from the shop by a beaded curtain.

Rex sat cross-legged on a stained futon, freebasing heroin, surrounded by the detritus of various drugs and drug-taking paraphernalia.

'Do you partake of narcotics?' asked Rex with a sweet smile. His teeth were brown.

'Um, no,' said Max.

'What hard drugs do you imbibe?'

'None.'

'None? How do you fill up the days?' asked Rex.

'I smoked marijuana once,' said Max.

'Marijuana is not a drug. Marijuana is what you take while waiting for the drugs to arrive,' said Rex with a cackle.

The sensible side of Max advised him to take the £400 and run, as this job, whatever it entailed, was obviously doomed to fail. But he didn't.

He found himself intrigued. Besides, he had nowhere else to go and nothing else to do. There was potential here for a spot of exploitation.

'Do you get much passing trade?' asked Max.

'Passing trade?' scoffed Rex. 'It's stopping trade we need. All anyone does is pass, and I don't blame them. Who wants to buy any of that old garbage? It's ridiculously overpriced. Like life itself, it is a pointless endeavour. I pray only for my death to be mercifully swift.'

'How do you stay open?'

'Because of Mummy!' screamed Rex.

Rex calmed down with a deep inhalation of heroin.

'I don't understand,' said Max, somewhat alarmed.

'Then allow me to explain, my dear Max,' said Rex, drowsily reposing and possibly now in a different dimension. 'I am from an ancient and obscenely rich family. Inherited wealth, of course. We are interbred to the nth degree. I have uncles with cleft palates the size of frisbees and Adam's apples the size of cricket balls. Such wealth brought us great privilege along with inevitable catalogues of misery and tragedy over the centuries, and now we find ourselves washed up on the plastic bottle and used disposable nappied shore of the 21st century, totally moribund. My mother appropriated this vanity establishment to give me a purpose. I am merely the decorative frontispiece, banished from the family home due to my huge intake of drugs and predilection for necrophilia. I care not a shit for this business, or anything else for that matter, and since I receive an allowance of several thousand pounds per week, I have no ambition or motivation, other than to die dramatically.'

'So, you have no customers at all?' asked Max.

'I wouldn't know a customer if I saw one. People occasionally come in to steal merchandise. I let them get on with it, I'm not one for confrontation. We are, however, open from 9-5, 365 days a year. One must maintain discipline.'

'Why do you need staff?' asked Max.

112

'Isn't it obvious?' growled Rex. 'I can't run a business. I can barely wipe my own arsehole.'

Rex immediately fell asleep and began snoring.

Max liked his new employer very much.

He went straight home and informed his parents he had started a high-powered and important job as curator at a gallery of objets d'art. They were initially sceptical, but gave him the benefit of the doubt when he produced his first day's wages to them as rent. Max went upstairs to his bedroom and threw all of the university student interloper's possessions out of the window. The student returned later that evening and collected up his stuff (scattered across the lawn) without any trace of ill will, and they never saw him again.

Max went back to The Emporium the next morning.

'Max, I thought I'd imagined you!' said Rex, shoving several £50 notes into Max's hand. It was always £50 notes. Rex seemed unaware of there being any other monetary denominations. 'Get me a coffee, will you, I am simply gagging for a frothy latte. And keep the change.'

Max drove off to Knightsbridge and did some shopping for himself, then went to the Savoy for lunch.

When Max returned, he found Rex blissfully puffing on an opium pipe.

'I couldn't find any coffee,' said Max.

'What coffee?' asked Rex. 'I hate coffee. Never touch the stuff. Do you know what that shit does to you?'

'I'm uncomfortable around drug use,' said Max, hoping to be fired with a large severance pay-off.

'Me too. Me too,' said Rex. 'I wish I could buy ethically traded drugs. Drugs are horrible and destructive and dangerous and socially evil, and they help fund gangs and cartels and scumbags, and buying it creates a demand and supply in time-honoured capitalist style which exacerbates my various guilt complexes. Drugs perpetrate nothing but negativity, and they leave a trail of destruction and death in their wake. There is nothing glamorous or clever in drug addiction, and I will never defend drug-taking. But, fuck me, I enjoy them.'

Over the following days, it transpired that Max's job involved running pointless menial errands for Rex, and keeping him company. (On the third day, Rex tasked Max with finding a golden fleece. Max sat in the pub for two hours, before returning empty-handed.)

Max earned £2000 per week basic, plus commission on any sales he made. Rex had a terrible memory, so Max worked out he could tell Rex he hadn't been paid that day, even if he had, and Rex would pay him double.

By the third week Max bought himself a second-hand Porsche. When he showed the car to his dad, he took Max aside and asked him if he was prostituting himself sexually.

By the fifth week, Max started looking at property in Kensington.

One sunny afternoon, he decided to take his three-hour lunch break in the park. He sat on the same swing ruminating about his recent good fortune when a figure in the near distance caught his eye – the woman from before. Claire.

This time Max didn't let her out of his sight. He got up and followed her out of the park and down a few streets until – she stopped outside The Emporium.

Max hid behind a tree and watched her.

Claire waited outside, seemingly in two minds whether to enter or not. After a minute of anxious hesitation, she walked away. Max didn't follow her any further. He couldn't. He was rooted to the spot. His heart fluttered.

Claire was looking for *him*.

***

Lee stopped the light box. Max sat on the couch, drenched in sweat from the effort of remembering.

'Holy shit,' he said.

14

Lee handed a glass of water to Max. He took a few sips, then after a pause, said, 'It all seems so absurd, but it happened. It's so vivid. I began to doubt the veracity of my memories, but they're real.'

'Who was Claire?' asked Lee.

'A girl I knew from school,' said Max, clamming up.

Lee returned to her chair. On her tablet computer, she surreptitiously wrote down the word 'Claire.'

'You're a very unusual case, Max. Your memories unfold to you and reveal themselves without premeditation. Do you remember them only as they happen?'

'Yes.'

'But you can't see beyond each moment?'

'Correct.'

'You really don't know what happens next, do you?'

'No.'

'Then we need to continue in a linear order,' said Lee, with her hand poised over the metronomic light box.

'These strange detours must be relevant,' said Max. 'I see patterns forming. I see myself forming.'

'It's for your own benefit as well as ours,' said Lee. 'Before long, we won't need the light box anymore. Take a deep breath, and continue.'

She switched on the light box. The colours clicked on and off again. Max stared at them.

***

Max spent a whole week painstakingly rearranging The Emporium's window display, but only so he could keep looking out for a sight of Claire. So far – nothing. The window display looked no different from before, but Rex sobbed and called it a triumph.

Rex went into the back room and snorted large quantities of cocaine to celebrate. Unfortunately, cocaine made him pontificate.

'The problem, dear Max, is modern atomised society. Depression and dissatisfaction are at record levels. Life has no purpose or meaning beyond its own experience. There's a strange autistic detachment to existence. Even love has diminished to the point of irrelevance. We may just as well not exist at all. We failed collectively as a species by default, but no one is willing to—'

There was a dull thud. Max recognised the familiar sound of Rex's head hitting the floor. Rex collapsed unconscious on a regular basis. Max went over to the gramophone. Rex's falls made the needle skip. He nudged it; a crackly old recording of Elgar's *Sospiri* continued.

Max listened to it for a while, then he went into the back room, where Rex flailed helplessly on the floor in a pool of vomit.

'You need help,' said Max.

'I am a silly billy,' said Rex, with blood gushing out of his septum.

Max lifted Rex into a chair.

'I thought I was fucked up. You make me look normal,' said Max.

'It's you and me versus the world, Max,' said Rex. 'We're better than all those fuckers out there put together. We know the score. The game is lost before it's begun. Let us drink copious amounts of Dionysian death juice. Beg Bacchus for the balm that kills regret and numbs the stinging nettles in the blood.'

Rex opened a bottle of Napoleon brandy. Max, not much of a drinker, sniffed it with distaste.

'I can't work in this sort of environment,' he said.

'Is it the money? I'll double it,' said Rex, stuffing a wad of crumpled £50 notes into Max's hand. 'Only, drink with me. Please. You're my only friend in this god-awful world.'

Max sighed.

'Fine. Pour.'

'It will take the edge off,' said Rex.

'Take the edge off what?'

'The open wound of the human condition. It will make you forget.'

'Forget what?' asked Max.

'I can't remember!' laughed Rex as he poured Max a crystal goblet of golden liquid. 'Bottoms up!'

Max watched Rex drink the rest of the bottle in one long gulp. It was pathetic. Max regarded him with the pity he deserved.

When he'd drained the bottle, Rex slid down onto the stained futon.

Before blacking out again, he whispered:

"With eyes fixed on the stars, I often fall,
And can't distinguish fact from lie, it seems;
Guard your precious fantasies,
The wise can only envy madmen's dreams."

Max drank the glass of brandy. He found he liked it. Over the next few days he helped himself to Rex's vast drinks cabinet, and even began to dabble in the cocaine scattered over most of the surfaces of the office.

Copious vomiting became a nuisance.

'Get the poison out,' encouraged Rex. 'Then you can get more in.'

Max started to find lots of dents and scratches on his Porsche, so he bought a 1960 Bentley Continental in British racing green using a cheque he "borrowed" from Rex. Max claimed it as a company car.

When Max got home that night, he nearly ran over his dad who was mowing the front lawn.

'What the bloody hell are you doing, Max?' shouted his dad.

Max unsteadily got out of the Bentley. He'd driven through the privet hedge and the rockery. He pulled out some £50 notes.

'All right, don't get excited,' said Max. 'Here, take this cash.'

'I don't want your money,' said his dad, grabbing the bank notes and counting them, before stuffing them into his own pocket.

Max proffered a half-empty bottle of brandy.

'Drink this. It will take the edge off.'

'I don't like the path you're taking, Max.'

'You're just jealous of me because I'm richer and more successful than you,' drawled Max.

'You're not successful. You're a ponce,' said his dad.

'Well you're a cunt!' said Max.

'Don't come back here.'

'You'll never see me again!' said Max, getting into the Bentley. He reversed through the garden hedge, then gave his dad a parting shot of an extended middle finger, before speeding off.

A minute later, Max returned. He entered the house and went up to his bedroom to get the one possession he wanted – his goldfish, Trumpet.

He came down the stairs with the goldfish bowl, green water spilling everywhere.

'Maximillian!' said his mum, rushing from the living room.

'I'm moving out,' said Max. 'You're cramping my style.'

'Who do you think you are?' asked his mum.

'I don't know,' he replied. 'I really don't know.'

He jumped into the Bentley and sped away.

Rex gave Max the key to his flat in Chelsea. The huge mansion flat was furnished like an Edwardian gentlemen's club. Dust covered everything. Rex never used the place. He preferred living in the genteel squalor of the shop.

Max placed Trumpet on the dining room windowsill overlooking a park. Whether Trumpet appreciated his new surroundings, Max couldn't be sure.

Max felt grown up suddenly, although his total lack of knowledge regarding important real-world affairs like finances and tax (Annuities? Investments? Mortgages? Pensions?) baffled him and gave him pause in moments of sobriety. Scary adult stuff. He chose to ignore it.

Max stepped up his earning power by pocketing small items; a trilobite fossil here, a shark tooth or a crystal there, then he'd tell Rex customers had been in and bought them.

'Those trilobites are flying out the door,' said Max.

'Max, you're my guardian angel,' Rex replied, giving him more cash as commission. 'What would I do without you? You are a true friend indeed.'

Max sold the items privately to other dealers, usually at a loss. He felt guilty for exploiting Rex's vulnerability, but it didn't stop him.

Max's job description developed into "Paid Drinking Buddy". Entire days drifted by in a haze of strong alcohol and drug abuse.

'I hate the taste of alcohol so much, I have to get drunk to drink it,' Rex said one afternoon, slumped on the futon in the back room of the shop.

'I have no friends,' said Max, gloomily. (It was the gin).

'You've got me, old duck,' said Rex. 'What more do you need?'

'I have no talents or skills,' said Max. 'I have no qualifications. I can't speak any languages or play any musical instruments.'

'At least you don't have to wear nappies,' said Rex. 'Be thankful for small mercies. I'm a martyr to incontinence.'

'I have a horrible feeling my life will end in abject failure,' said Max, as he busied himself dusting some tribal shrunken heads.

'Dare to fail,' said Rex. 'I dared to fail. Then I failed. It didn't do me any harm. Just remember – success is failure in disguise. Of course, it helps that my family are rich beyond the dreams of avarice, but my point is heartfelt and just as valid.'

'But there are so many things I want to achieve,' said Max.

'Like what?' sniffed Rex.

'I don't know,' said Max. 'Write a novel. Have a girlfriend. Travel. Be successful.'

'Oh, how boring,' said Rex. 'Don't be so bloody generic.'

'I'm an alpha male,' said Max, staring at the pink feather duster in his hand. 'I'm ambitious.'

'My dear deluded friend,' said Rex, 'you're falling for the same bullshit trick that has confounded and frustrated generation after generation. We are nothing more than genetically predetermined animals. Rebel against it. Rage at its futility. Ambition is so bourgeois. I have rejected all the conventions of life, and look at me.'

Rex's clothes were flecked with vomit. His eyes were bloodshot and his face was puffy with a green complexion.

'Okay, bad example,' he concluded.

Every morning, Max got into the routine of taking a long bath, then he sniffed a few toots of cocaine, followed by a chaser of champagne, before driving to The Emporium. If Rex was comatose, Max turned around and went home to listen to classical music at full volume. The neighbours kept knocking on the door to complain about "The Ride of the Valkyries" playing on a loop all day.

One afternoon while at a loose end, Max determined to find Claire. He bought an enormous bouquet of flowers and drove to a house he vaguely remembered her living at. For courage, he drank half a bottle of cognac with some Xanax. When he arrived, he could barely stand up.

The door was answered by a man he'd never seen before.

'Claire?' drooled Max, offering the bouquet.

The man slammed the door in his face. Max considered this rude. He banged on the door and shouted insults, then urinated on the doorstep.

'Now I think of it, Claire never lived in that area,' said Max, later, to Rex in the back room of The Emporium.

'Fuck this,' said Rex, rousing himself from the futon. 'Let's escape this suffocating ennui. I feel like doing some culture.'

They drove over to an art gallery in Hoxton where pretentious hipsters milled around looking at an exhibition of new work.

Rex bought a wall-sized silk screen print of King Ludwig II of Bavaria in the style of Andy Warhol. Max pointed to a random landscape painting nearby.

'How much is that piece of shit?' he asked a woman standing by it.

'I'm the artist,' she said. 'It's £500, but for an ignorant drunken bore like you, £5000.'

Max lifted the painting off the wall, then punched his fist through it and hung it back.

The artist slapped Max around the face.

'Violence is the ultimate artistic expression,' said Rex, handing the cash to the artist. 'Plus, he's improved your work no end.'

Over the following weeks, Max and Rex spent all their time together in nightclubs and seedy 24-hour bars, surrounded by good-looking people of dubious means. Max enjoyed the novelty of bohemian debauchery for a while, but it soon made him cynical and nauseous.

'We are the architects of our own downfall. The seeds of destruction are sown in youth,' said Rex to him one night while being fellated at a bar by a woman in a gorilla costume. 'I fell hopelessly in love, once. Alas, she died. Well, they cremated her, so I can only presume.'

Unsexy sex was everywhere. Max observed the degradation with his brandy-glazed eyes, half-amused, half-sickened at the feral activity all around him. He didn't know any of these people, or why they had chosen this reckless lifestyle. Did they really derive pleasure from it?

Was it really worth all the disease and abuse?

'Want to go to a private room with me?' a naked young woman asked Max one afternoon in an expensive brothel near

Piccadilly Circus. Her face was caked in make-up to disguise her acne scars.

'No, not really,' replied Max, reading *The Picture of Dorian Gray*.

'Are you shy?' she asked, unzipping his fly.

'No, just bored.'

'Aren't you having fun?' she asked.

'I'd like to line you up in a row and manually punch bullets into your degenerate skulls,' said Max to the people around him.

They laughed, thinking it was dry humour. But Max meant it.

He caught sight of himself in a mirror. Apart from the dark rings under his eyes and the pallid skin, he looked quite raffish with his thick dark hair and goatee beard, and the faux fin de siècle Victorian clothes he now adopted, borrowed from Rex. Or maybe the dimmed lighting and alcohol played tricks on him. He attempted a suave smile, but only a leery drunken grin appeared on his face.

'How sad it is,' murmured Max, with his eyes fixed upon his own reflection. 'I shall grow old, and horrible and dreadful. A meat puppet at the mercy of fate's caprice. I'm dead inside. I'm only twenty-two, and I'm already dead.'

***

Lee stopped the metronomic light box.

Max sat on the couch, drained.

'Jesus,' he said. 'What an arsehole.'

The two police officers entered the room. Max, with the gentleness of a child, allowed them to put him in the wheelchair and handcuff him.

'You're making great progress,' said Lee.

'I don't recognise myself,' said Max.

'That's what they all say,' said Lee.

'Do I find Claire?' asked Max.

'That's for you to tell me,' said Lee.

The police put a sheet over Max and wheeled him out.

15

'Max, this is Ophelia,' said Ched Hazzard, introducing a woman in her twenties, wearing preppy clothes, bright green lipstick, a beanie hat and numerous tattoos.

'I'm Ophelia,' said Ophelia to Max, as if he was deaf.

Max sat on the bed in Room 9 eating a curry (bhuna), which Ched Hazzard and Ophelia were rudely interrupting.

'Ophelia is a brand manager to a public relations company. I had an idea that maybe we could rebrand you,' said Ched Hazzard, turning to Ophelia. 'Is rebranding the right phrase?'

'Absolutely,' said Ophelia. 'Max tested very low in our focus groups. He has a negative image in the general public's perception, but we've come up with some exciting ideas on how to upgrade his profile with approval-rating positive media content.'

'Is this a joke?' asked Max.

'Show him, Ophelia,' said Ched Hazzard.

Ophelia produced a glossy A4-sized catalogue and showed it to Max. It contained photos of male models dressed in everything from casual clothes to evening wear. She pointed to a picture of a man in a shiny suit with the arms rolled up, a vest underneath and loafers.

'It's about appealing to people's irrational desires,' said Ophelia.

'It's definitely a look, Max,' said Ched Hazzard. 'What do you think of the loafers?'

'I think you're crazy,' said Max.

'The 80s look will soon be back in vogue,' said Ophelia. 'Imagine the impact it will have if you turn up to your court hearing dressed in the *Miami Vice* look? With some fake tan, designer stubble and hair gel you could be an influencer, or the fashion icon of murderers. We can also open Twitter and Instagram accounts highlighting your softer, more playful side, and—'

'Fuck off,' interrupted Max.

Ophelia looked stunned.

'Excuse me?' she said.

'Take that, and pummel it up your arse,' said Max, throwing the catalogue towards the door.

Ophelia gathered up her belongings and picked up the catalogue.

'I told you there was nothing I could do with him,' she said to Ched Hazzard. 'I mean, look at him.'

'Ophelia, please…' pleaded Ched Hazzard.

'I hope they lock you up and throw away the key,' said Ophelia over her shoulder as she left the room. 'You rude, vile pig.'

'Bollocks,' said Max in reply.

'Well, that was uncalled for,' said Ched Hazzard after Ophelia had gone. 'You can be a rude vile pig, do you know that?'

'She was talking about media content and approval ratings, for fuck's sake,' said Max, tucking back into his curry.

'Max, you have to think about your future media responsibilities. I'm taking meetings now regarding book deals and image rights and film options before leeches cash in and exploit this tragedy.'

The irony wasn't lost on Max. He rolled his eyes with derision, then stuffed a chunk of naan bread into his mouth.

***

The midnight moon appeared high and full. Wispy ethereal clouds scudded across its face, creating a beautiful spectral corolla.

Max looked up at it from his bed in Room 9. He imagined himself in the open somewhere; in a flower meadow, or walking along a stream maybe, or down an empty country lane with only a hush of breeze rustling through the trees for company. The hoot of an owl. A wisp of sparkly gossamer.

But Max was here, in the urban sterile contained environment of the hospital. He would soon be in a prison cell. Then a coffin.

Sleep came intermittently. Night sweats plagued him. Something deep in his subconscious held him in a vice-like grip of anxiety and he couldn't shake it off.

I am insignificant. The moon is insignificant. Earth is insignificant. The human race is insignificant. The Milky Way is insignificant. Nothing matters, nothing does. Why? Because, because.

'If the universe is expanding, where is it expanding into?' he said, then peered over the bed sheets in the hope of engaging the police officer in a conversation. The officer stood in the corridor, chatting to the door guard.

Max rested his head back on the pillow.

What a strange life I've led, he thought. *A stupid life. A wasted life.*

He tried to think of memories involving Rex at a later period, but only repeats came back to him, as if in a feverish dream. Things he found amusing then, now seemed disturbing.

He tried to think of Claire as an adult, but only fragments of school memories presented themselves. Her eyes. Her smile.

There was that time he asked Claire if he could walk her home from school, and she said yes, and they didn't say a word all the way. He used to think it had been a romantic experience, but now he saw it as awkward and strange. Max expected to be invited into her house, but she didn't offer. He hadn't understood at the time that it was a sign of rejection. He'd failed to impress her.

He scrunched up his eyes and tried to force his memories forward, but he couldn't move beyond the point of the acne-faced girl in the brothel giving him a hand job.

Frustratingly, he still needed amobarbital and the light box.

The next morning, Max sat on the couch in Digby Shah's room. Lee sat opposite in the swivel chair. The session began.

'How do you feel?' asked Lee.

'I've stopped pissing blood. It's a small triumph, but I'll take it.'

'Have the nightmares stopped?'

'I'm going to kill four people,' he said. 'I still don't know why. So, no, the nightmares continue.'

'You accept that you killed them?' asked Lee.

'No. Yes. Maybe. No. I don't know. It's a paradox,' said Max.

'How do you feel about that?'

'Innocent,' said Max.

'Are you ready to continue?' asked Lee.

'Sure. I have a window in my schedule,' said Max.

Lee put her finger on the metronomic light box "on" button.

'Wait,' said Max. 'I need a moment to steel myself for the carnival of horror I'm sure you're about to reacquaint me with.'

He took a few deep breaths, then nodded to Lee.

Lee pressed the "on" button. Max stared at the colours once again.

***

Word got around that Max was a successful businessman. So much so that his old college, which had expelled him for violent anti-social behaviour, invited him to give a speech to the business students on "How to Be a Success".

Max stood behind the curtain of the college lecture theatre, drinking a bottle of brandy to steady his nerves. Rex had come along to give his protégée encouragement. He thrust some pills into Max's hand.

Max guzzled them all down in one gulp with the brandy.

'What were those pills?' asked Max.

'Suppositories. You're supposed to insert them in your anus.'

'Why are you giving me suppositories, you berk?' asked Max.

The senior lecturer poked his head through the curtain.

'Ready?' he asked Max.

'I was born ready,' slurred Max, as a wave of nausea coursed through his entire system.

The lecturer sniffed the air, then grimaced.

'What's that smell?'

'I think my business associate has shat himself,' said Max.

'Occupational hazard,' said Rex, with a shrug.

'Get rid of him,' hissed the lecturer, retreating through the curtain.

'Yes, will do,' said Max, as pockmarks of sweat suddenly dotted his dark suit.

'A kiss for luck, my dear Piers Gaveston,' said Rex, lunging to kiss Max on the lips.

'No,' said Max, pushing him away. 'I refuse to be your catamite.'

Max looked at the speech cards he'd prepared, but they contained nothing but meaningless drunken scribble. He'd have to freestyle.

The lecturer began his introduction.

'It's a pleasure for me to introduce an alumnus who has graciously given up his busy day to offer us the secrets to his business acumen…'

Rex took his trousers down and inspected the gusset damage.

'It's diarrhoea, Max. It's runny diarrhoea!' he said.

Max tried to usher Rex off the stage.

'… so please welcome, Maximillian Hope.'

The curtain lifted, revealing Max on his knees, desperately trying to pull Rex's trousers back up.

Max shoved Rex into the stage wing, then, slipping in diarrhoea, approached the podium mic.

Laughter rippled through the audience.

'It's Max. Just Max. Only my mum calls me diarrhoea when I've done something bad,' he said into the mic.

Twenty seconds of Max's nervous amplified breathing followed.

Max looked at the audience – a sea of apathy looked back.

'Good evening,' he said eventually, even though it was midday. Sweat stung his eyes.

'In conclusion,' he said after another long pause, 'don't listen to your tutors. They couldn't make it in the real world, that's why they teach.'

Another ripple of laughter. Max, encouraged, continued.

'Why do we do what we do? Is it complacency? Denial? What are you doing here today? Youth doesn't last long. The sun is shining outside. Do you want to be stuck in offices doing menial work for the rest of your lives? Do you really have so little ambition and imagination? Thirty years from now, you'll realise you lost your life to the traps and snares you're setting for yourselves now. You'll realise too late that you made a mistake. You will regret your decisions. You made them because you were afraid. You're going to be interns, or take shitty minimum wage jobs just to pay off your student debts. You have no guarantee of anything when you leave here. Does that seem sensible to you? We're taught from birth to be hostages to outdated models of career-fascism. We gullibly enslave ourselves in the great bourgeois capitalist lie of society. Next time you're in a cemetery, remember that all those dead people were like you, once. One day you'll be like them.'

There was a rumbling of discontent around the lecture theatre.

'Who is this prick?' shouted one of the tutors to the head lecturer.

'This is not what we asked for!' shouted another.

'You want to know my secret to being a successful businessman?' asked Max. He turned and pointed at Rex, who wandered out of the wing naked from the waist down, openly urinating. 'Chance upon a buffoon who's as rich as Croesus, then bleed the fucker for every penny he's got.'

Rex gave Max the thumbs up.

'Take it all, dear Max. Take it all.'

The curtain was brought down. The head lecturer tried to stop Max from continuing, but Max brushed him aside and shouted into the mic, 'We are nothing more than individual survival machines. Life is short. Kill your friends. Let chaos hold dominion over all! Nothing matters! Everything is nothing!'

Rioting began. Students started throwing chairs and setting fire to their books. A fire alarm sounded. Sprinklers came on. One student stripped naked and started running around. Other students attacked each other.

Rex appeared through the curtain and patted Max on the back.

'Our work here is done,' he said.

'My dad was right,' said Max sadly. 'I am a ponce.'

Max touched the microphone. He shuddered as a huge electric shock passed through him. His life was saved by the head lecturer, who punched him in the face.

Max fell down and lay supine on the stage. He was capable, just, of admiring the pretty spectrums of colour refracting through the lights as cascades of water came down from the ceiling. Rex dragged him outside and bundled him into a waiting taxi.

'That was fucking brilliant!' laughed Rex, still half-naked and soaking wet. As they drove away, he trilled:

'How thoughtless, and how thankless we must seem,

to those for whom cold death is not a dream,

devoured by an endless black nightmare.'

'This is so fucked up,' said Max. 'I am so fucked up.'

'Nonsense,' said Rex. 'Look out of the window.'

Max looked out of the window. The taxi drove down a busy street full of office workers on lunch breaks.

'Those people are fucked up, dear Max. We are not like those worker drones; their whole lives are a compromise. They serve a purpose, but nothing more. We are the tribe of the moon, you and I. We dance in the twilight. We dine with the ancients. We are delicate chrysanthemums in an unweeded garden that grows to seed; things rank and gross in nature possess it merely.'

'But look at us!' cried Max. 'We're a couple of useless drunk wankers. You're covered in your own shit and piss and you have no trousers or pants on. I'm drugged out of my fucking mind, I just started a riot and I nearly died. It's irresponsible. It is not normal.'

'Exactly! Isn't it fun!' said Rex.

'Not really, no,' said Max.

Rex moved away from him.

'Don't go all normal on me, Max. I can forgive most failings in people, but not normality. Normality, and its evil twin ordinariness, are the most beastly crimes imaginable.'

When the taxi pulled up outside The Emporium, Max paid the driver with a soggy £50 note, then followed Rex.

Rex halted just inside the shop doorway and looked towards the back room with an uneasy gaze.

'Ladies, darlings, I think not creatures,' he said.

Someone was sitting in the back room. A woman.

'Who's that?' asked Max.

'My sister.'

Rex's sister stood up and stepped forward into the light.

'Hello,' she said.

It was Claire.

16

Lee switched off the light box. Max continued to stare at it for a while.

'Why have we stopped?' he asked, eventually.

'You need a break,' said Lee.

Max stood up and paced around the room.

'It couldn't be Claire,' he said.

'Why not?' asked Lee.

'I feel like I'm being manipulated,' said Max, suddenly angry. 'You told me to trust you, but I don't. I'm not sure I trust myself anymore.'

'Nothing untoward is happening,' said Lee.

'Claire was an only child,' said Max. 'Something isn't right.'

Lee pursed her lips. She gestured for Max to return to the couch.

'Please,' she said.

Max sat back down and took a deep breath.

'This isn't easy,' he said.

'I never said it would be,' said Lee.

'I apologise,' said Max. 'I'm not questioning the integrity of these sessions. I know everything I'm seeing happened. I remember them when I see them. I want to go back in straight away. I'm ready right now.'

'Okay,' said Lee. 'Just relax and breathe normally.'

Lee switched on the metronomic light box. Click, click, click, went the lights. Max's pupils dilated once again.

***

'Who's that?' asked Max.

'My sister,' said Rex.

Rex's sister stood up and stepped forward.

'Hello,' she said.

'What are you doing here?' sneered Rex.

'Rex, I can see your cock and balls,' said Rex's sister, averting her eyes.

'Don't be so bourgeois, Juno,' said Rex.

'Juno?' said Max, staring at Juno.

'Yes, my sister Juno,' said Rex. 'Are you okay, old duck? You look like you've seen a ghost?'

'I'm... fine,' said Max.

'You've probably met each other before,' said Rex.

'How?' asked Max.

'She's the most promiscuous slut in the south east.'

'Shut up, Rexy,' said Juno, blushing.

'A joke, dear heart,' said Rex. He turned to Max, and whispered, 'No, really, she is a complete whore.'

Rex kissed Juno on the lips, then disappeared into the back room. Juno held her nose as he passed.

'Oh Rexy,' she said. 'You stink of dung.'

'It's all Max's fault,' said Rex. 'He's a bad influence on me.'

Juno looked Max up and down.

Max wanted to say something clever, but couldn't think of anything.

Juno lost interest and turned away from him.

'We're all terribly worried, you know,' she said.

'So you're here to spy on me?' said Rex. 'Plus ça change. What will you report to Mummy and Daddy this time? That

I'm having far too much fun and I must be sent to a monastery again?'

'I'm not going to stop you doing anything,' said Juno. 'I just don't want to watch you kill yourself.'

'But there's something tragically heroic about the waste of youthful promise snuffed out,' said Rex. 'I'd hate to be too old to die young. I hate old people. Old people should be killed at birth.'

'Let's not argue,' said Juno.

'I'm not arguing, Rosencrantz. Or is it Guildenstern? I'm thirty-five. Horrifyingly ancient. My youth is gone. All that is left is a decaying husk. The grave yawns open before me like a big yawny thing.'

'Mummy and Daddy are going to cut off your allowance,' said Juno.

Rex reappeared, wearing a skirt.

'Those fuckers wouldn't dare!' he declaimed.

'It's the truth.'

'Then I shall self-immolate forthwith,' said Rex, holding a teaspoon to his neck, threateningly.

'Rexy, that skirt is hideous,' said Juno.

'Now is not the time for sartorial criticism,' said Rex. 'Besides, all of my pants and trousers need to be scraped clean.'

'Ick,' said Juno.

'Anyway, so what if I die? Bring it on, say I. You'll inherit the lot.'

'I don't want the money.'

'Neither do I. Money disgusts me,' said Rex.

Max made the smallest of throat clearances. Rex and Juno looked in his direction.

'Max, why are you lurking?' said Rex. 'If you stand there much longer I'll put a price tag on you.'

'And for goodness sake, turn some lights on,' said Juno.

'Don't! It will attract customers,' hissed Rex.

Max couldn't take his eyes off Juno. She was the absolute double of Claire, albeit in her early twenties.

'Does he always stare at people like this?' asked Juno.

'No,' said Rex. 'I think he likes you.'

'How unfortunate,' said Juno. 'I'm here to fire him.'

'What?' asked Rex. 'You can't fire Max. He's a close personal friend and business partner of mine. He's also my top salesman.'

'It's been noted by the family accountants that your spending has been haemorrhaging since the arrival of Mr–?' Juno looked at Max.

'Hope. Max Hope,' said Max.

'Hope Max Hope? Unusual name,' said Juno. 'Only last week Rexy, you spent over £48,000. What on earth are you spending it on?'

'Overheads and sundries,' said Rex.

'You're wasting it on drugs, and no doubt Mr Hope Max Hope is helping himself to the rest.'

'How dare you slander his good name,' said Rex.

'My name is just Max Hope,' said Max.

'See?' said Juno. 'He even lied about his name.'

'If Max goes, I go,' said Rex.

'Please spare me such empty gestures of fraternal solidarity,' said Juno.

'I'm standing my ground on this issue,' said Rex.

'Okay, he can stay.' sighed Juno.

'Oh, thank God,' said Rex, deflating like a balloon. 'I thought you were going to call my bluff.'

'You didn't let me finish my sentence,' said Juno. 'He can stay on one condition: you must make at least one transaction within the next five minutes. Go.'

'Juno, that's beastly of you,' said Rex. 'Business is slow. We haven't made one transaction in five months.'

'The clock is ticking,' said Juno.

Rex panicked and ran into the street.

'Buy something from us, you bastards,' he shouted towards a nearby council tower block. A volley of abuse came back at him.

A car approached. Rex tried to flag it down. The driver had no intention of stopping, so Rex jumped onto its bonnet and he and the car continued down the street and out of sight.

Max and Juno looked at each other.

'Well?' she said.

Max went over to a drawer and took out a small crystal magnifying glass attached to a silver necklace.

He showed it to Juno.

'I think this would look perfect on you. It's mid-Victorian,' he said.

Max went to put it around her neck. 'Would you mind?'

Juno shook her head slightly, intrigued.

Max placed the necklace on her.

She held up the magnifying glass and looked at Max through it.

'You're soaking wet. You look like a drowned rat,' she said.

'I scrub up quite well,' said Max.

Juno smiled, then noticed the price tag of the magnifying glass.

'£9000? That's outrageous.'

'Luckily, I have a staff discount,' said Max, taking out several £50 notes and putting them in the till. 'This counts as a transaction, does it not?'

'Yes, I suppose it does.'

'So, I have a stay of execution?'

Juno nodded.

'Is this necklace a gift for me, then?' she asked.

'Do you like it?'

'I love it. I shall wear it always.'

'Good,' said Max.

'I hope you don't think this automatically allows you access all areas in my knickers,' said Juno. 'Contrary to my brother's warped view of me, I'm not promiscuous at all. In fact, I'm rather chaste by modern standards. Does that bother you?'

'Not at all,' said Max.

'Fine. Then you have permission to woo me,' said Juno.

Max laughed.

'You and your brother speak like characters from Evelyn Waugh novels.'

'Careful now. Don't ruin it,' said Juno.

A moment later, Rex returned in a more distressed state than before. He held a broken car wing mirror in his hand.

'It's no good, Max. The game's up, old duck. I couldn't persuade any of the philistines out there to invest in objet d'art. I'll arrange a bloody good redundancy package for you, and—

Rex was confronted by the sight of Max and Juno sucking each other's faces off in the back room.

'Bugger me,' he said, smiling.

***

'Murderer!' shouted a voice.

The metronomic clicks and flashing lights abruptly stopped.

Someone had rushed into Digby Shah's room, but they were already being dragged away by the police officers.

Commotion could be heard out in the corridor.

Lee shut the door. Max blinked. His vision blurred back into focus.

'What's going on?' he asked Lee.

'Another security breach, it seems,' said Lee, flustered.

Max noticed the light box was lying broken on the floor.

Lee sat down in her chair. A bead of blood began to run down her forehead.

'You're bleeding,' said Max.

Lee lifted her hand to her face and touched the blood.

'I stopped someone from attacking you,' she said. 'I think we'll end today's session here.'

'The light box is broken,' said Max.

'You don't need it anymore,' said Lee. 'It was only a device to help you concentrate.'

Max took out a handkerchief and approached Lee.

'May I?' he asked.

Lee stiffened slightly, but nodded.

Max dabbed the blood and cleaned the small cut.

'It's just a scratch,' he said. 'You won't need a stitch, or even a plaster.'

Lee nodded again.

'Have you read that book on the history of art I sent you?' she asked.

'Nearly. Why?'

'When you get back to your room, look at the last few pages of modern art. There's one painting in particular that might interest you,' said Lee.

***

When Max returned to Room 9, a woman was waiting. Detective Hicks stood with arms folded.

'Always a pleasure to see you, Hicks,' said Max. 'Are you here to offer me another fruit basket?'

'In a way,' said Hicks through gritted teeth. 'This lady here is from a liberal religious charitable organisation. We are legally obliged, for some reason, to allow her to talk to you.'

'Oh hell,' said Max.

The police officers handcuffed Max to the bed.

The woman turned to Max with a rehearsed sincere smile.

'I'm Sally,' she said. 'My organisation believes it is inhumane for anyone to be detained or incarcerated for any crime.'

Hicks could be heard grinding his teeth.

'As human beings,' continued Sally, 'we're all fallible. We all stray from the path of righteousness and are swayed by the lure of evil. I just want you to know that I am praying for you. I know in my heart that one day you will seek to embrace the bosom of our Lord.'

'Jesus Christ,' sighed Max.

'That's right,' said Sally. 'He will forgive you, and cleanse you in His love. For there must be no borders. We are all as one in the eyes of God. We were created equal. My church believes in freedom for all people, because all people are love.'

'Even the murderers?' asked Max.

'Yes, even the murderers,' said Sally.

'What about Hitler? What about child rapists?'

Sally's smile faltered for a second.

'We forgive everyone. We don't believe in punishment. We believe everyone should be free. Freedom is love. Freedom is equality. Freedom is empowerment and—'

'What you're saying is well-meant,' interrupted Max, 'but it doesn't take away from the fact it's bullshit. Bullshit is bullshit, Sally. I'm not saying it to be rude, I'm saying it because it's the truth. What you're saying is childish wishful thinking. Please free me by leaving now.'

Hicks tried to prevent himself from laughing.

'That is your freedom of choice, and it is beautiful,' said Sally.

Sally didn't move. She beamed a smile.

'This has been so enlightening,' said Max. 'But the door is over there.'

'I'll leave these pamphlets here for you to peruse.'

'Please don't,' said Max. 'I've just remembered I embraced Satanism this morning, but I appreciate your sentiments.'

Sally continued smiling as Hicks escorted her out of the room.

'I will pray for your freedom,' she said.

'Thank you,' said Max. 'Safe journey back to your planet.'

Max picked up the art book Lee had given him. He flicked through the last few pages, which dealt with modern art. Most of it was crap, but one picture took his eye – a painting of a pair of woman's breasts with the word "Tits" underneath. The caption of the picture read,

Tits, by Juno Hope.

17

The picture in the book nudged open a volcanic fissure in Max's brain. It projected montages of lost moments from his life into the darkness, like the aurora borealis. He viewed the waves of light and sound with curiosity, observing his younger self somewhere in time. Nothing at all remained of that person. He was there, a figure in a landscape, an entity in the midst of a relentless forward motion of existence. He remembered being there, but at a remove.

The strange internal logic of human motivation. Wants. Needs. The way we just are. Were. Will be. We accept it without explanation or reason.

Max lay on the bed in Room 9, present, but absent.

Juno Hope. Juno Hope. Juno Hope.

***

Juno invited Max over to her house. She lived with her parents in a huge mansion in Hampstead. She had the whole top floor to herself, with a glass-ceilinged artist studio in the roof.

Max looked at a row of almost-finished paintings. Juno was some kind of rising pop art star. Her latest work was a self-portrait of her posterior with the words *My Bum* painted underneath it.

'That's my bum. Do you like it?' she asked Max.

'It's a very nice bum,' said Max.

'I might exhibit my other stuff soon.'

'What's this one?' asked Max, tilting his head in front of one painting which looked like an open knife wound.

'It's called *My clitoris, No. 11*. I've dedicated it to Georgia O'Keeffe,' said Juno. 'And this one is called *Back of my knee*.'

'I see a pattern forming in your work,' said Max.

'It's post-conceptual. Post-structuralist. Post-everything,' said Juno.

Max thought the paintings were naive and too similar to the work of Pauline Boty, but maybe they were Juno's knowing homages.

'And this one?' asked Max.

'That's a favourite of mine. It's called *My colon*.'

'Self-explanatory.'

'Self-exploratory too,' said Juno. 'I inserted an endoscope inside me for authenticity.'

'Ace.'

'Come downstairs and meet Mud and Fud,' said Juno.

'Who?'

'Mummy and Daddy.'

'Gulp,' said Max.

They went downstairs to a dining room where Mud was sitting alone at a long dining table. Juno introduced Max as "The Boy". Mud was a once-attractive woman in her late fifties with an expensive coiffure, a Nehru-collared suit, and large impenetrable sunglasses which she never removed. A snappy little dog sat in her lap, growling constantly at Max.

'Well, he's better than the last one,' said Mud. 'The Rastafarian.'

'Mud is a terrible racist,' giggled Juno to Max.

Juno sat down. Max joined her.

'I don't know what it is with my children,' said Mud, 'but they often make me wish I had ripped out my uterus and drop-kicked it off a cliff when I was a young girl.'

'Isn't she a gas?' laughed Juno.

'Tight,' said Max.

A very old man was wheeled into the room by a sexy uniformed nurse. Juno jumped up and ran to the old man. She smothered him with kisses.

'Juno, you know I abhor public shows of affection,' said the old man, loving the attention.

Max initially took him be Juno's grandfather, but it was her dad.

'Oh Fud, don't be a horrendous grouch,' said Juno in a baby-talk voice.

The nurse pushed Fud to the head of the table.

'Who the bloody hell is that?' said Fud, pointing at Max.

'Max, Fud, Fud, Max,' said Juno, as an introduction.

'He's the new Boy,' said Mud.

'What do you do?' asked Fud, leaning forward with intent.

'He's Rex's business associate,' said Juno.

Mud and Fud gave brief audible groans of contempt.

'Actually, I'm a writer,' said Max.

'Oh?' said Fud. 'Might we be familiar with any titles in your canon?'

'I'm writing my debut novel,' lied Max. 'I expect it to be successful.'

'Really? What are the odds?' said Fud.

Juno returned to Max's side and rested her hand on his groin.

Two servants appeared with bowls of soup which they placed in front of the four people at the table. Max hadn't asked for anything and wasn't hungry.

He felt Mud's eyes glaring at him behind her sunglasses. She hardly ever moved, and reminded Max of a shop mannequin. A servant put a cigarette (in a cigarette holder) in her mouth and lit it. Her snappy little dog lapped up the soup. Juno tucked a napkin into Max's shirt collar. The nurse ladled soup into Fud's mouth.

'What are your intentions for our daughter?' Fud asked, through slurps.

***

Max didn't find out what answer he gave. Next, he and Juno were in a nightclub, dancing. They were surrounded by beautiful rich young men and women he didn't recognise.

'Eugenics in action,' Max shouted to Juno.

***

Then Max was in the back of a taxi with a drunk Juno curled into his lap. They were driving through dark early-morning London streets that glistened with a wet patent leather sheen.

'I want us to be symbiotic,' whispered Juno sleepily.

Max looked down at her. She looked just like Claire. But she wasn't Claire. Claire was somewhere else. Claire was with someone else.

And that was a problem.

'I'll never love you,' said Max, stroking Juno's hair.

Juno mumbled something, but she was already asleep.

***

Next, Juno and Max were walking hand in hand around Lord Leyton's house museum in Holland Park on a hot summer afternoon.

'I want to meet your Mud and Fud,' said Juno.

'My family are dysfunctional,' said Max.

'Darling, all families are dysfunctional.'

'Another time, perhaps. Where to next?'

'Sir John Soane's house in Lincoln's Inn, then Thomas Carlisle's in Chelsea,' said Juno. 'Then I want to go home for a bonk.'

***

Evening. Max and Juno lay in bed, post-coital.

'Do you think your parents heard us?' asked Max.

'Hope so,' giggled Juno.

'If we're not careful, you'll get pregnant.'

'Would that be such an awful thing?'

Max said nothing.

***

Max was driving his Bentley fast down a country lane. Juno sat in the passenger seat, cowering. They were going to some old friend of hers' wedding in Gloucestershire, but they were lost.

'Fucking fucking fuck!' shouted Max, as he swerved dangerously past slow-moving cars.

'Calm down or you're going to kill us,' said Juno.

'Good!' said Max. 'I didn't want to go to this wedding anyway! I don't know these fucking people! Stuck-up toffee-nosed pricks!'

He sped around a corner, narrowly avoiding a moving tractor.

'CUNT!' Max screamed at the farmer.

Max bounced up and down with rage in his seat and almost ripped the steering wheel off its column.

'Max, you're scaring me,' said Juno.

Max was scaring himself. He didn't know what had triggered this anger. He knew it was unnecessary, but he couldn't help himself. His blood boiled. He'd woken up in a bad mood, and it culminated in this embarrassing display. There was no excuse for it.

They arrived on time at the wedding, but Max didn't speak to anyone for the whole day. He sat at the church and the reception fuming, and he hated himself for it.

Juno hadn't seen this side to him before.

***

Max and Juno floated down the Cam in a punt one weekend in early autumn.

Max watched the light sparkle on the water and idly thought about Rupert Brooke. He'd recently memorised his poetry in preparation for this little weekend trip, but he couldn't remember a word of it now. Poor, handsome, long-dead Rupert Brooke. Anyway, Max always confused Brooke with Wilfred Owen and Siegfried Sassoon.

God, did any of it matter?

'When will your novel be ready?' asked Juno, trailing her hand in the water.

'What novel?' asked Max.

'You said ages ago that you were writing a novel.'

'Oh. Yes. I am.'

'What's it about?' asked Juno.

'It's bad luck to discuss a book before it's finished.'

'I can't wait to read it,' she said.

'Mm,' said Max.

Just as they were going under the Bridge of Sighs, Juno cuddled up to him and whispered in his ear.

'I'm pregnant.'

She looked at Max, excitedly. The look on his face didn't change. He simply nodded a couple of times, then returned to staring at the water.

***

Next, Max was in an expensive hotel bedroom, staring at himself in a mirror, nursing the worst-ever hangover.

Morning light slanted through a window, which highlighted several silver hairs on the side of his head that had appeared almost overnight.

He regarded them with horror.

'Happy birthday,' said Juno, flatly, as she walked in from the bathroom, with a visible baby bump. 'I see you're enjoying my present.'

Max looked around. All the alcohol in the mini-bar had been drunk. Miniature bottles were scattered across the floor.

'Where are we?' asked Max.

'Look out the window,' sighed Juno.

Max carefully pulled the curtain aside to be confronted with the skyline of Manhattan.

'Whoa. I don't remember getting here,' he said.

'I'm not surprised,' said Juno. 'You drink so much. You've been permanently zonked out of your head for weeks.'

Juno began to sob quietly.

'Why are you crying?' asked Max.

'I thought I could make you happy. But you're never happy.'

'I am happy,' said Max. 'Look.' He made a huge effort to smile, but it looked like an agonised grimace. It made Juno laugh.

***

Juno showed Max around New York. She'd been there lots of times.

Outside the Dakota building, Max lay down on the pavement and pretended to be a dying John Lennon. Juno told him to stop, as it was an insensitive thing to do.

Then they walked down Broadway, through Times Square, and went up to the Empire State Building observation deck. A cab to Wall Street. A sober visit to the 9/11 memorial. A boat over to the Statue of Liberty. A cab to the Chelsea Hotel (eerily semi-derelict at the time; Max was convinced a splat of vomit on the floor was Dylan Thomas' ectoplasm).

At dusk, they ate ice creams in a horse-drawn carriage clopping through Central Park.

'Now I'm with puppy, Mud and Fud insist we get married,' said Juno.

'Okay,' shrugged Max.

'Is that all you have to say?' asked Juno, irritated.

'Sure,' shrugged Max again.

In frustration, Juno stuck her ice cream on top of his head. The cone looked like a small pointy clown hat.

For comic effect, Max made no attempt to remove it. He let melting ice cream run down his face.

Juno smirked and shook her head at him.

'You are such a cock.'

They saw *Phantom of the Opera*, then went for a meal at Sardi's, but didn't see any celebrities.

Later, Max sat at the window of their hotel room looking down at the incessant crowds in Times Square, while Juno undressed for bed.

'What do all those people down there think they're doing?' asked Max.

'They're having experiences,' said Juno.

'Is that all there is – experiences?' asked Max.

'I think you're depressed,' said Juno. 'You should see someone when we get home.'

Max didn't respond. He wanted to open the window and jump out.

They took an early morning flight back to London. Max sat in a First Class window seat drinking brandy, and listened to Khachaturian's *Adagio to Spartacus and Phrygia* through headphones as the sun rose over the Atlantic. It bloomed like a slow nuclear explosion through the clouds on the horizon. Max had never witnessed anything so sublime. He almost screamed with delight, then recalled how Immanuel Kant had connected the sublime with terror. As the orchestra reached its rousing crescendo, so did the magnificence of the firmament fretted with golden fire. Tears flooded Max's eyes. He glanced around to see if anyone else was sharing the moment, but everyone was asleep and all the blinds were down.

Juno snored gently beside him.

She's carrying my child, he thought to himself. *I hope we crash.*

A few days later, Max stood outside a house in Fulham. He'd picked the name of a psychiatrist randomly from the phone book and made an appointment to see a Dr L. Baum.

Max pressed the doorbell.

Through pebbly glass in the front door, a figure approached. Max felt the old instinct to run away. Hide. Don't engage. Too late.

The door was opened by Lee.

'Hello,' she said. 'You must be Max? Come in.'

18

'Max?'

'He's not responding.'

'Max? Can you hear me?'

Max blinked a few times and found himself back in Room 9. In front of him stood Doctor Brooke and two police officers.

'What?' asked Max.

'You were in a trance of some kind,' said Doctor Brooke.

'You shouldn't have disturbed me,' said Max.

'Your sister is here. She wants to see you.'

The police officers handcuffed Max to the wheelchair and wheeled him down the corridor to a deserted refectory. At the far end behind a table, sat Margot and a woman he didn't know.

Max was brought to a halt at a slight distance. Margot's eyes were raw from crying. She looked haggard. Max hardly recognised her.

'Dad's dead,' said Margot, without looking at him.

A long awkward silence.

'Oh,' said Max emptily.

'He died from the stress you put him under,' said Margot. 'You killed him. Are you pleased with yourself? That's what you wanted, wasn't it? Death is all you're good at.'

'Margot, I can't remember what I've done,' said Max.

Margot turned to the woman next to her.

'See? No emotion. He couldn't give a shit.'

'I'm sorry, Margot. I'm truly sorry,' said Max.

'Sorry?' said Margot. 'You're sorry?' she repeated, louder.

The woman held Margot's hand to calm her down, then put an arm comfortingly around her shoulder.

'I don't know what else to say,' said Max.

Margot looked at him.

'This is the last time we'll see each other, Max. I want nothing more to do with you. Neither does Mum. Don't bother trying to contact us, we are not interested. You're not invited to the funeral. As far as I'm concerned, I have no brother. You are the devil.'

Max nodded slightly, then was still.

He turned to one of the police officers next to him.

'I think we're done here.'

As they wheeled Max out of the refectory, Margot shouted at him, 'You evil bastard! Burn in hell! Murderer!'

Max then realised it was Margot who threw the eggs and shouted at him, and who had tried to attack him the day before.

***

A short while later back in Room 9, two novels Max requested arrived. *The Catcher in the Rye* and *Steppenwolf* were cherished favourites of his teenage years. He settled down and read them both in one sitting, but found them disappointing.

Holden Caulfield no longer resonated with him in the same way. And what the hell was *Steppenwolf* about?

He put the books aside and picked at itchy scabs on his wrists, making them bleed.

A nurse came in to check on him.

'Tsk,' she said, at seeing the bleeding scabs. Then she left.

Max lay down and slept a deep dreamless sleep.

***

The next morning, after a workout with Rutger, Max promptly found himself back on the couch in Digby Shah's room, supping a coffee laced with sodium amobarbital.

He updated his new memories to Lee.

'And then?' she asked.

'You opened the front door and let me in,' said Max. 'That's as far as I got before being interrupted with the news about my dad.'

'How do you feel about your father's death?'

'I don't know. We never got on. That's bad, isn't it?'

'It's honest,' said Lee.

We're all carrion, thought Max. *We get devoured by trillions of microbes every second of our temporary lives. One day, the inevitable catastrophic collapse of civilisation will begin with one sneeze. Then the end game will occur; the die-back of our myopic hubristic species, followed by the next great extinction. Nature will welcome our fall. She'll reclaim and heal the vast damage of the parasitic human scar. As it was in the beginning, so shall it be in the end.*

'Honesty is the best policy,' said Max.

Lee gave one of her crooked little smiles. It disturbed Max.

'You were a client of mine once,' said Lee. 'That's why I wanted to help you again. So now you know.'

'You're a sly one. You've known me all along,' said Max.

'Shall we continue?' asked Lee.

'Okay. You were right. I no longer need the light box.'

Max stared at the wall for a while. His eyes dilated.

***

Max was sitting in Lee's consultation room in her house in Fulham. Lee sat opposite him. Both were twenty years younger. The shelves were full of psychology and philosophy books. A ceramic phrenology head sat on her desk. Framed certificates hung on the wall. Children could be heard playing and screaming in a distant junior school playground. Why do children scream in playgrounds?

150

'How can I help you?' asked Lee.

'I was hoping you'd tell me,' said Max.

Lee smiled. Yes, she'd had some facial work done since then. Filler.

'You're here for a reason,' said Lee.

They sat in silence for nearly a minute.

'I'm sorry. I think I'm wasting your time,' said Max.

'By taking the effort to come here, you've already made an important step in acknowledging you have a problem you wish to address.'

The school bell rang in the distance. Playtime was over. The learning of mannered obedience resumed.

'There's something missing in me that others seem to have,' said Max.

'In what way?' asked Lee.

'I'm disconnected. I feel dead inside, like a ghost wandering aimlessly through a maze of dead-ends. I don't belong. I'm generally hopeless.'

'Have people told you that?'

'They don't need to. My ineptitude is staggering.'

'So this is purely a subjective view of yourself?' asked Lee. 'It's quite common. It's called warped perception.'

'I feel vulnerable,' said Max. 'Afraid. Angry, yet timid. Intelligent, yet obtuse. Contradictory. Displaced. I don't enjoy life, I endure it. I find life a grind. I feel guilty for feeling this way, because my despair feels indulgent.'

'Are you on any medication?' asked Lee.

'No.'

'I can refer you to a doctor, if you like?'

'No.'

'Do you have financial worries?'

'No.'

'Any sexual problems?'

'Not really.'

151

'Does your family have a history of depression?'

'I don't think so. We don't talk. We're estranged. We don't see eye to eye. I drink too much. I snort lots of cocaine too.'

'Are you under the influence of stimulants right now?' asked Lee.

'I had a snifter on the way here, to take the edge off,' said Max.

'To take the edge off what?'

'The fear. The horror.'

'How long have you felt like this?'

'Always. I disguise it, just. It's my default position.'

They conversed for a few minutes about his childhood; whether he'd been physically or mentally abused, etc. Max adamantly rebuffed the questions and said they were irrelevant.

'What do you do for work?' asked Lee, changing tack.

'Nothing, really. But I get paid well for doing it.'

'What do you mean?'

Max explained about The Emporium, and Rex.

'You need to curtail your intake of drink and drugs,' said Lee. 'They will only perpetuate and magnify your problems. You're using them as a crutch, and also as an excuse.'

'But sobriety fills me with beige,' said Max.

'I insist upon it,' said Lee.

It was quiet outside now. The children had returned to their desks and were being taught to be civilised animals, with all the social rules and complex rituals that necessitates. Please and thank you. A is for Apple. $Z \times 4 + Qw9 = 7V$. Á la recherche du temps perdu. Je ne mange pas ca pour les raisons philosophiques.

A flurry of red and gold leaves tapped past the window in the breeze.

'I feel nothing half the time,' said Max. 'The rest of the time I feel too much. It's exhausting. I don't even love my girlfriend.'

'Have you talked to your girlfriend about it?' asked Lee.

'No. That's another thing – she's pregnant, and her parents are forcing us into a shotgun wedding.'

'No one can force you to do something like that,' said Lee.

'It's going to happen anyway. Resistance is futile. I will get married. I will be a terrible husband and father. Stuff will happen. Events. We'll visit people and places half-heartedly. We'll smile. Hellos. Goodbyes. More kids. Rush around. Bumble unhappily along in a vague forward and sideways motion. We'll argue over trivial nonsense, resent each other, and we'll spend interminable hours being bored and miserable at restaurants and hotels and friends' houses where I'll pretend to be normal and people will say behind our backs, "I like her, but not him" and won't invite us again. Then one day, quite suddenly, it'll be over.'

'That's a very cynical and reductionist view,' said Lee.

'No, it's a realistic view,' said Max. 'Can you prescribe medication for me? The powerful stuff? Lots of it?'

'It would be exchanging one set of chemical dependency for another. First, reduce the drugs and alcohol. Then I recommend you reconnect with your family. We all need connections. It appears you have cut yourself off, and it's affecting you detrimentally. You're in denial of that. I also suggest you consider getting a job that fulfils you in some way. Do you have any hobbies?'

'No.'

'What do you like doing most of all?'

'Sleeping.'

'Anything else?'

'I've always wanted to write a novel,' said Max.

'Good. That's a start.'

Max noticed an engagement ring on Lee's finger.

How old is she? thought Max. *Thirty-two? Thirty-three? There are no photos on display. Maybe she deliberately gives nothing away about herself. All the doors are shut. Is she here alone? Does she feel safe being alone with a stranger? What makes her laugh? What turns her on? Does she ever masturbate in this room? Does she have children? Had they been screaming in the nearby playground? No tell-tale signs. No scrapes on the walls, or dirt on the carpet. No small scuffed shoes discarded haphazardly by the front door. How many clients does she have? How many people had sat here droning on to her?*

Max vaguely desired to use her toilet.

'Why don't you love your girlfriend?' asked Lee.

'She's a proxy,' said Max.

'In what way?'

'She looks exactly like a girl at school I once knew. The great unfulfilled cliché of my life.'

'Would you like to talk about her?' asked Lee.

'No,' said Max.

Max's mind drifted off to thinking about mayflies he used to see in the pond in the back garden of his parents' house when he was young. The mayflies waited patiently for years as mundane larvae, only to briefly blossom into glorious flying insects for the final few hours of their lives, fulfilling their genetic obligation in a danse macabre.

With giddy rapture, they'd take to the air in a desperate speed-date with death, mating in the last moments before their dying fall, if they were lucky. Most never got that far. Nature's cruel indifference. But are we any different? We pretend we're above it all, but we're not. We're weaved within the same fabric of mystery.

Lee watched Max, but said nothing.

She's judging me, thought Max. *What will she write in her notes? That I deserve nothing but contempt? That I'm a narcissistic, self-pitying and conceited waste of humanity?*

Max looked at her and gave a shy smile.

'You drifted off,' said Lee. 'What were you thinking about?'

'Mayflies.'

'Mayflies?'

'And death,' said Max.

'Any particular reason?' asked Lee.

'No reason.'

'Do you think about death a lot?'

'Doesn't everyone?'

'Do you ever have suicidal thoughts?'

Careful, Max. Careful.

'No more than most,' he replied.

'Have you ever harboured dark thoughts about harming yourself, or harming other people?' asked Lee.

Yes, thought Max. *If I had a gun, I'd go on a rampage and murder lots of people.*

'No,' lied Max.

Lee nodded, then scribbled something down in a pad.

This will be over shortly, thought Max. *Time goes so fast. Why was I so afraid? Is life just a relentless series of tasks to overcome, one after the other? I'll leave here and probably never return. It helped pass time. But it would have passed anyway. This moment next week I'll be wasting time somewhere else. I'll think, "I was at that psychiatrist's house about now. Hasn't the week gone fast?" What a boring thought. Pacing time incrementally on the march towards oblivion. Sex. Eat. Sleep. Try not to die. In a few minutes, I'll be driving in my car. Off to the next meaningless thing. Where? Pub? Park? Flat? The Emporium? See Juno in her studio? What a small inconsequential life. I must try to keep occupied and curious. Smile. Be nice and polite. Kindness is a virtue. Empathy. Courage. Integrity. Why don't I just drive and keep going? Start a random new life. New name. New place. New people. Same old problem: me.*

Max paid Lee in cash and booked another session for the following week. He went back to his (Rex's) flat. The front door was broken open. The flat had been vandalised. Graffiti covered the walls, and furniture was missing. Someone had taken a dump on the living room carpet. Piss filled the fish tank. Trumpet floated on the surface.

As twilight fell, Max took Trumpet's corpse down to the pond in the park, placed him on a toy boat, and set it alight. The boat floated across the pond like a small Viking funeral pyre.

Max opened a bottle of brandy and started drinking.

***

At the rising of a blood red sun, Max awoke on a deserted beach with sand as soft as talcum powder. His head throbbed. He waited awhile, trying to remember where he was. Blank.

Eventually, he approached a friendly amused fisherman who told him this was Papua New Guinea.

'How did I get here?' asked Max.

'Maybe osmosis?' laughed the fisherman.

'How will I get home?'

'Fly, like a bird.'

'I'm never drinking again.' said Max.

He walked along the shore in a state of low-level panic. It was a very beautiful place. Why not stay? Become a beach bum.

No. Want to go home. Right now.

He patted himself down and found his passport and credit card, then wandered through a mangrove forest until he came to a road. Hailing a passing car, he asked the driver to take him to the airport as fast as possible. The driver said, 'Okay,' and drove at breakneck speed along dangerous potholed roads, paying no heed to personal safety.

On the flight home, the plane flew into an electrical storm and shook violently. Max remembered Trumpet had died. He sobbed, and a flight attendant told him to stop as he was upsetting other passengers.

At Gatwick Airport, Max discovered his Bentley had been impounded for being parked illegally. He paid his last £300 to release it.

Max went straight to The Emporium and made Rex give him a couple of thousand pounds in cash, then he drove over to see Juno.

Juno was having a bath in a large free-standing ceramic tub. The water steamed. Juno's cheeks were red from the heat.

'Get in,' she said.

156

Max took his clothes off and climbed in. They sat looking at each other.

'This water is too hot. We'll prune,' said Max.

'I tried to call you. Where have you been?'

'Papua New Guinea.'

'Why?'

'I got drunk. Trumpet was murdered.'

'You have my sincere condolences. How did he die?'

'Someone pissed in his tank.'

'How beastly.'

***

Juno and Max went to San Lorenzo's for dinner. Juno got talking to a male pop star at the next table who was celebrating getting to number one in the charts. Max marvelled at how charming Juno could be, but her flirtatiousness irritated him.

At one point, the pop star briefly took her away to a secret VIP area, but Max wasn't invited.

'Don't worry,' Juno whispered to Max. 'He's gay.'

***

Later that night, Juno and Max lay in bed. Max read Sartre's *Nausea* by torchlight.

He underlined several sentences.

My memories are like the coins in the devil's purse: when it was opened, nothing was found in it but dead leaves.

And –

We find it so difficult to imagine nothingness. Now I knew. Things are entirely what they appear to be and behind them... there is nothing.

And –

I do not think therefore I am a moustache.

Christ. Existentialism. It's enough to make anyone depressed. All that dizzying angst overloading life with the arbitrary nothingness we so desperately try to avoid.

'I want you to meet my parents,' said Max.

'About time,' said Juno.

***

Negotiations began. Phone calls with awkward silences and stilted pleasantries happened. A time and date was arranged.

***

A week later, Max and Juno were driving over to his mum and dad's house.

'Are you going to buy a present for them?' said Juno, checking her make-up in the vanity mirror.

'Why?' asked Max.

'It's the usual protocol in these situations.'

'It's only my parents.'

'Seems a bit mean. Not even flowers?' asked Juno.

'Don't be so bourgeois,' said Max.

***

Max rang the doorbell. Margot answered, wearing dungarees and a faded Sex Pistols T-shirt.

'Hello stranger,' she said.

'What are you doing here?' asked Max.

'I live here, you tool. Come in.'

'Juno, my sister Margot. Margot, Juno.'

Juno and Margot air-kissed each other's cheeks.

Coats were removed in the hallway.

'I thought you owned a flat somewhere?' Max asked Margot.

'It got repossessed,' laughed Margot.

'What happened to your start-up business? The one that made the stuff for things?'

'The economy is in meltdown,' said Margot. 'Have you not noticed?'

'You should have asked me for financial help,' said Max.

'Yeah, right,' snorted Margot.

'What do you do now, Margot?' asked Juno.

'I work part-time at a laser hair removal salon. Well, I volunteer there, and I love it,' said Margot, her face clouding over.

Mum and Dad appeared. Nods and smiles were exchanged.

'Empty-handed I see?' said Dad.

'Told you,' said Juno, nudging Max.

Max took out a wad of £50 notes and peeled off several. He offered them to his mum.

'Holy shit,' said Margot.

'We don't want or need cash handouts, Max. It's vulgar,' said Dad.

'I'll leave it here, just in case.'

'Put your money away, Max,' said Dad.

'It's no problem. You can—'

'Put the money away, Maximillian,' interrupted Mum.

'Come through,' said Dad, to Juno. 'We're having beef.'

'I'm vegetarian,' said Juno. 'Didn't Max tell you?'

'Max never tells us anything,' said Dad.

'I think there's a lasagne in the freezer,' said Mum.

'Does the lasagne have meat in it?' asked Juno.

'I can scrape the meat out,' said Mum.

'Doesn't that sound appetising?' said Margot, arching an eyebrow.

'Come through,' repeated Dad.

They went and sat in the dining room. Max used to think it was big, but it was only half the size of the one in his (Rex's) apartment, and a quarter the size of the one in Mud and Fud's house.

'I'd offer you alcohol, Max, but you're driving,' said Dad.

'I've stopped drinking,' said Max.

'Really? It was the only thing you were good at,' said Dad.

'His psychiatrist advised him to stop,' said Juno.

'You see a psychiatrist?' asked Mum.

'She's not a psychiatrist. More of a psychologist,' blushed Max.

'What's the difference?' asked Margot.

'It's spelled differently,' said Max.

'Money down the drain,' scoffed Dad.

Max noticed his dad was knocking back large glasses of wine. His eyes were already glazed, which was a bad sign.

'I was sorry to hear about Trumpet,' said Margot.

'I gave him a good send-off. He's now in piscine Valhalla.'

'Never mind dead fish, let's talk about the bump,' said Dad.

'Huh?' said Max.

'The baby, you prat. The baby,' said Dad.

'Yes, congratulations,' said Mum.

'Thanks,' said Juno. 'It was totally unplanned.'

'Do you know what it is yet?' asked Mum.

'We're not fussed,' said Juno.

'Well I'd like to know,' said Dad, abruptly.

'As long as it's healthy, its gender doesn't matter,' said Juno.

Dad huffed with barely disguised disapproval, and poured himself another glass of wine.

'Sexual categorisations don't matter anymore,' said Margot.

'Yes they do,' said Dad. 'Of course they do. Unless it's going to be a hermaphrodite freak, or something.'

'Insensitive, Dad,' muttered Margot.

'I'm sick of all this gender-neutral bullshit,' said Dad. 'It's a con. A fad. Everyone wants to be gay or bisexual or transgender, like it's a fashionable lifestyle option, rather than a genetic abnormality. People are turning gay and bi and trans simply because it's permissible. It's indulgent and selfish, and it's time someone said so.'

'This isn't the time or place for bigoted opinion, Dad,' said Margot.

'Have you set a date for the wedding?' asked Mum.

'It'll be in December,' said Juno.

'I presume we're invited?' asked Dad.

'Of course,' said Max. 'We're sending the invites out next week.'

'Who's paying for it?' asked Dad.

'My parents,' said Juno.

'Whew,' said Dad.

'We're renting a country house for the weekend,' said Juno.

'Where's the ring?' asked Dad.

'Max hasn't got me one yet. He hasn't actually proposed.'

'What a weird set up,' said Dad.

'Am I going to be a bridesmaid?' asked Margot.

'Um… okay,' said Juno.

'At least one of my kids has spawned. Surprised it was him,' said Dad.

'David,' said Mum to Dad, with a censorious tone.

'Margot's had herself sterilised,' said Dad.

Silence. Margot scowled.

'Why?' asked Max.

'So she can screw with impunity,' said Dad.

'Shut up, Dad!' said Margot.

'No, you shut up!' barked Dad. 'This is my house!'

'You're drunk,' said Margot.

'I've earned it,' said Dad.

'I don't want to bring a child into this world, okay?' said Margot.

'What sort of logic is behind that thinking?' asked Dad.

'There's going to be nine billion people soon. It's unsustainable,' said Margot.

'Oh, so one more is going to make a lot of difference!' scoffed Dad.

'There are millions of orphans I can adopt,' said Margot.

'Sure, it's as easy as that,' said Dad.

'Stop being such a prick about it. It's your generation that caused all the problems,' said Margot.

'If you had done any research into this,' said Dad, 'you would have seen that the birth rate for indigenous Europeans has fallen through the floor. That's why all these migrants are being allowed in. It's a deliberate and cynical social engineering exercise. It will fail horribly, of course. The whole thing is a total disaster. It's all about algorithms affecting global social trends, and binary digits. The warning signs are all around us. It's all there in the history books. There's a certain irony in the fact that education, and feminism, and liberalism, and atheism and permissiveness and prosperity will lead to our downfall. You can sit there and sneer and judge me all you like, but I know what's going on. I speak the uncomfortable truth, because no one else has the balls to. I don't expect any of you to understand.'

'So your solution is to get drunk and insult everyone?' said Margot.

'It's infinitely better than your extreme solution,' replied Dad.

'I knew you wouldn't like or agree with my decision, but you can at least show some respect for it,' said Margot.

'You have to earn respect, Margot. You have to earn it,' said Dad.

'You always have to have the last word, don't you?' said Margot.

Dad opened his mouth, then hesitated.

'Oh, what's the point?' he said. 'I won't waste my breath on you lot.'

'I think we should leave,' said Juno to Max.

'You only just arrived,' said Mum. 'We haven't even eaten. I made a tiramisu.'

'I've lost my appetite,' said Max.

Dad brought his fist down hard onto the table, sending glasses and cutlery bouncing into the air.

Everyone looked in his direction. He raised his arm, which began to bleed. Somehow, he had cut himself.

'Now look what you've made me do,' he said.

There was a loud dull thud.

***

Max's eyes refocused. He sat on the couch in Digby Shah's room, back in the present moment.

He saw Lee looking towards the window.

Max followed her gaze. On the window was a ghostly white imprint of a pair of spread-out wings. Between them, a thin vertical line of red ran down the pane. Both were highlighted by a sudden shaft of sunlight.

Lee stood up and went over to the window. She looked down.

'Oh!' she said.

Max got up and joined Lee at the window. He looked down at a narrow ledge underneath it.

'Poor thing,' he said.

Two police officers entered the room.

'We heard a noise,' one of them said.

'Do these windows unlock?' asked Lee.

'No. Why?'

'Look,' said Max.

One police officer went to the window and looked down at the ledge.

On it was a white bird. Its neck was broken and blood poured from its beak. It twitched with finality.

'Can it be saved?' asked Lee.

'No,' said Max.

'It's only a pigeon,' said the officer.

'It's a dove,' said Max.

'A dove?' said the officer.

'Like in the Bible,' said Max.

19

Lee ushered the police officers out of Digby Shah's room, then sat back in her chair. Max returned to the couch. The dove remained on the window ledge, twitching.

'I don't have the capacity to murder anyone,' said Max. 'Least of all my wife and children. The very notion is abhorrent to me. I can now see I'm a flawed individual, but I'm not a murderer.'

'I'm afraid that's not good enough, Max,' said Lee.

'Then why don't we cut to the chase and push forward to just before the murders took place?' said Max. 'That would be logical wouldn't it? We could prove my innocence.'

'I shouldn't have to remind you that the point of these sessions is not to determine *if* you committed the murders, but *why* you committed them. The exposition is what we are chiefly interested in exploring. It is important that you reboot your memory in linear sequence, and we are running out of time by questioning the process. Everyone has the capacity to be a murderer. You are no different.'

Max looked flustered for a while, then he stared with concentration at a blank space on the wall again.

'Okay. I can see a boat on a lake, and a Regency-style country house in a dawn mist. I think it's the morning of my wedding.'

'Good. Go on,' said Lee.

***

Max and Rex were sitting in a rowing boat on a lake, both wrapped in shawls to protect them from the biting December cold. Their breath came out in plumes. A purple ball of fire on the horizon was burning through early morning mist that clung to the parkland and woods.

'I can no longer feel my extremities,' said Max. 'I want to go back to bed.'

'Bathe in the aesthetics, old duck,' said Rex. 'This is your last dawn of freedom. Feast your eyes upon the supreme orb of Ra. Embrace your sentient ability to appreciate such magnificence. We must remember moments like this. Bliss was it in that dawn to be alive. Mother Nature hath opened her legs wide for our ocular pleasure.'

'That's very eloquent, however I'd rather not have fucking pneumonia when I get married in a few hours,' said Max.

'It's all practicalities with you, isn't it?' said Rex. 'Bollocks to the wedding, this is more important.'

Rex pulled a bottle of champagne out of the water and poured two flutes.

'You feel guilty about not giving me a stag party, don't you?' said Max.

'I feel like a beastly cad, Maxie. I had mega plans for a trip to Morocco, but Mummy took me to The Priory to have me *drained.*'

He and Max clinked glasses.

'I don't want to get married, or have children,' said Max.

'Never mind,' said Rex. 'Remember, nothing intrinsically matters. One day, everyone will be dead and everything will be forgotten.'

'Yes,' said Max. 'That's a comfort.'

They rowed back to a jetty, then walked up to the hired country house, scrunching through frost on the lawn as they did so.

'I'm a very lucky bugger,' said Rex. 'Unfortunately, I've wasted most of my life treating my privileges like a burden. I've taken it for granted instead of appreciating my rarefied position. I forget that most people live God-awful lives in abject poverty and adversity. I've had it easy. I don't wish to sound patronising. I'm genuinely fascinated by the lives people lead. Nothing we do in life makes any sense, which is lovely. Conceptually myopic, but horribly lovely. So macabre and twisted. We spend our little lives in a constant state of anticipation, never knowing what might happen next, running blindly through the fields of wheat until we're scythed down by the unknown. What a way to exist! The will to live is so powerful. To enjoy life and rage against the dying of the light is the aim. To love and laugh and dance while knowing the abyss of eternal oblivion could occur at any second with no warning, is beautiful. So frighteningly beautiful. So wretched and despicable and exhausting, yet so fucking beautiful!'

'Bloody hell, Rex,' grinned Max. 'Are you sober?'

'How dare you,' said Rex. 'I'm a very sick individual. I may expire before breakfast. If this is close to sobriety, then hell is empty and all the devils are here.'

They went upstairs and changed into black tailcoats, grey spongebag trousers, waistcoats, stiff-collared dress shirts with dark cravat ties, and black Oxfords. Green carnation buttonholes were Rex's idea.

They sat in Rex's room and smoked some opium. It didn't have much effect on Max, except to make him feel a little more despondent.

'I apologise for not loving your sister,' he said.

'Don't worry about it, dear brother,' said Rex.

'I don't love anyone, you see,' said Max. 'Not even my parents. I'm incapable of love.'

'What about that girl you told me about? Claire.'

'Oh, yes. Claire. I loved Claire. Still do.'

'Maybe you'll marry her one day.'

'I doubt it,' said Max.

They went downstairs where guests were mingling. Max pretended to be a good host by making bland small talk with people he didn't know. He smiled and said thank you a lot. All the guests were from Juno's side. Max's mum, dad and Margot had arrived late the evening before, but kept to themselves. They quickly realised they had almost nothing in common with Mud, Fud and their ilk.

Dad had grown a bushy beard, which Mum hated. A noticeable friction still stood between them and Margot. Margot looked desperately sad. She decided not to be a bridesmaid.

Fud took Max aside and said he was going to get him a proper job in finance at a City firm. Max told him he didn't have any qualifications, and Fud laughed.

The guests made their way into the adjoining chapel. Max lingered alone outside in a cloister. An open archway nearby led into a sunny topiary garden. Max had a great urge to run far away.

I have no ambition to be anything in life, he thought. *I'd be content to be a tramp.*

Max walked over to the archway. He took a deep breath and dared himself to keep going. He imagined himself chancing upon a road, flagging down a car and getting a lift to... somewhere. Anywhere. If the driver asked him why he was dressed as a groom, he'd breezily say he'd been to a fancy-dress party.

'Maximillian,' said his mum. 'Come inside.'

Max nodded.

***

Max and Rex stood at the altar with a vicar. The *Wedding March* by Mendelssohn struck up on an organ. No backing out now. Max would have to make vows to a God he didn't believe existed.

He turned around and watched the bride and Fud (pushed by his sexy nurse) approach down the aisle. There were gasps from the congregation at the sight of Juno in a deep crimson wedding dress and veil. Her face was caked in white pancake make-up, with kohl-rimmed panda eyes and black lipstick.

'Christ,' said Rex, under his breath.

Max's mum and dad wore disapproving looks on their faces. Margot glanced at Max and mouthed, 'What the fuck?'

'She's always had a flair for the recherché,' said Rex, leaning towards Max's ear.

A long tedious ceremony took place.

'You may now kiss the bride,' said the vicar, eventually.

Max lifted Juno's veil. She smiled, cracking the white make-up. A tear rolled down her cheek, making the kohl run.

Max regarded her with a neutral mask concealing inner horror.

They kissed.

***

The ballroom filled with wedding freeloaders.

Fud gave a boring speech about himself and his great achievements in the financial sector. It was very self-indulgent and grandiose, and he got Max's name wrong twice.

Rex attempted to give a Best Man's speech, but slurred his words and giggled like a buffoon. His own family heckled him, and eventually he gave up amid a chorus of boos.

Max simply said, 'Thanks for coming,' as a speech, then sat down.

He thought it wise to be succinct, but could tell it hadn't gone well from the murmurs that followed.

He quickly drank an entire bottle of wine.

A string quartet struck up. People danced.

Max wandered into the garden alone at sunset and overheard his new mother-in-law bad-mouthing him to another guest on a terrace.

'I have no idea what Juno saw in him,' she said. 'He's a complete blank. A nonentity. And his parents are ghastly oiks.'

Shortly, Margot joined Max. They strolled in a rose garden for a while, talking about nothing in particular.

'You look like a condemned man going to the gallows,' she said.

'I do get myself into situations, don't I?' said Max.

'I like Juno and Rex, but the rest are snobs,' said Margot.

'Yes, they're horrible people,' said Max.

'Still, you've hit the jackpot, haven't you? You're loaded with cash now. You've become part of the despised plutocracy.'

'Believe me, no one could despise me more than I do,' said Max.

'I'll never despise you,' said Margot.

'Cheers,' said Max, absently.

'Great speech, by the way,' said Margot, dryly.

'Yeah. I improvised most of it.'

Max stared into the distance. Margot looked at him.

'Whenever I talk to you, you seem like you're somewhere else. Where are you right now?'

'Sorry. I'm here,' said Max.

They continued walking. Silvery spectral mist crept across the rapidly darkening landscape.

'I'm a lesbian,' said Margot, apropos of nothing. 'Are you shocked?'

'Not really. This is the 21st century,' said Max.

'I know, right?' said Margot. 'But I can't face telling Mum and Dad. They're still reeling from the whole sterilisation episode.'

'How long have you been gay?' asked Max.

'Always, I think,' said Margot. 'I used to bang boys hoping it would make me straight. But I never enjoyed it. I fantasised about girls. I need to be true with myself. It's like my whole life has been a lie. It's time I liberated myself. I'm moving in with a girlfriend soon. The atmosphere at home is toxic.'

'Yoo-hoo! Maxie!' called Rex through the twilight.

Rex and Juno approached, arm in arm. Both held lanterns.

'Can Max come out to play?' Juno asked Margot.

'Yes, but try to bring him back in one piece,' said Margot.

'We promise,' said Juno.

Rex and Juno grabbed Max's arms and led him away.

'Where are we going?' asked Max.

They went down to the lake, swathed in a low-lying mist. At the jetty was the rowing boat, now covered in petals and flower garlands. Rugs and warm blankets were inside it.

All three got in.

Rex ignited a flaming torch placed at its bow, then he rowed them out to the middle of the lake. Juno and Max snuggled up. She placed his hand on her distended stomach and he could feel the baby kicking.

Juno turned on her iPod and played Beethoven's *5th Piano Concerto in E Flat Major, opus 73*.

Rex stood up, and began reciting Rimbaud's *Ophelia*.

On the calm black water where the stars are sleeping, Ophelia floats like a great white lily; floats very slowly, lying in her long veils – In the far-off woods you can hear them sound the mort.

For more than a thousand years sad Ophelia has passed, a white ghost, down the long black river. For more than a thousand years her sweet madness has murmured its ballad in the evening breeze.

'That's a beastly poem,' said Juno. 'It's all about death. Haven't you got anything more appropriate?'

'You interrupted my flow!' shouted Rex. 'I hadn't got to the bit about how the fucking *ruffled water lilies are sighing about her* and *A mysterious anthem falls from the golden stars,* but you've ruined it.'

Juno hooted with laughter.

'You really are such a banana head,' she said.

'I've never been so insulted in my life,' said Rex, giggling. 'All right, what about a bit of Omar Khayyam:

The moonbeam splinters night's skirt with light –
Drink wine, there is no better time than this:
Be glad, but remember how long for moonbeams
There'll only be your grave and mine to shine on.

'It's about death again,' sighed Juno. 'Either do a light-hearted one or keep your trap shut.'

'Tough room,' said Rex. 'Okay: *The owl and the pussycat went to sea in a beautiful pea-green boat. They took—*'

Rex's hair touched the naked flame of the torch. The highly flammable hair product he used engulfed him in a huge fireball. He stood silently flapping his hands at his head to no effect.

Juno screamed.

Max rushed to assist Rex, but Rex pushed him away.

'Jump in the water, you stupid fucker!' shouted Max.

Rex collapsed overboard.

The water sizzled. Smoke smelling of fried skin and hair lingered in the freezing night.

Max and Juno peered into the inky black water.

'Where is he?' whimpered Juno.

'Hold the lamp over the side,' said Max.

Max jumped in. The cold stung his skin and took his breath away. He almost lost consciousness and his clothes were like lead weights. The light from Juno's lamp above was just enough to pick out Rex's sinking form. Adrenaline made Max swim down further.

Whistles of pressure screeched in Max's ears. Coloured dots flashed before his eyes. With great difficulty and bursting lungs, he grabbed Rex, and hauled him up to the surface.

***

Max sat in front of a roaring fire in the library, swaddled in bath towels.

'Is he going to live?' he asked through chattering teeth.

'Touch and go,' said a concerned-looking paramedic.

***

There was a knock at the door. The two police officers entered, breaking Max's concentration. He shivered on the couch in Digby Shah's room.

'Poor Rex,' he said. 'Did he die?'

'Tomorrow will be our last session, I'm afraid,' said Lee.

'But we're no nearer to a conclusion.'

'They're transferring you somewhere else.'

'Where?'

'A high-security prison facility.'

'Oh fudge,' said Max.

20

Afternoon. Room 9. Max lay handcuffed to the bed, thinking about a moment from his childhood when he first became aware of mortality.

He was eight years old and sitting in the living room watching TV with his parents. A disturbing documentary came on about the work of coroners. An announcement at the beginning stated the programme contained upsetting images. His mum told him it was time for bed, but Max lied and said he had indigestion.

There was a section of the documentary where a husband and wife had to identify the body of their young son who drowned in an accident.

The cameras followed them into a morgue where the boy lay under a sheet.

'Exploiting other people's private grief,' said Mum, riveted.

The sheet was lifted and the husband and wife both nodded, then they held each other and dissolved into sobs.

'I hope we never have to do that for you, Max,' said Dad.

For weeks afterwards, Max didn't sleep with sheets on his bed.

***

Evening. Room 9. Max pretended to be asleep while Ched Hazzard quietly argued with Detective Lamb, Doctor Brooke and two official-looking people with laminated lanyards.

They were talking about him. Negotiating. Something about getting the procedure right. Logistics. Documents needed to be signed. Legalities to be considered. Ched Hazzard mentioned human rights.

'How many more times are you going to use the human rights card?' said Lamb, with disdain.

'We shouldn't be having this conversation in front of...' said the first official, glancing at Max, 'in front of the subject.'

'Can we reconvene this in the corridor?' said the second official.

'Why has no one mentioned post-traumatic stress disorder yet?' said Ched Hazzard. 'Wasn't it the initial diagnosis? My client is sick, and you are disregarding this fundamental issue.'

'That's true,' said Doctor Brooke. 'It's been brushed under the carpet somewhat. I believe it could be a major contributory factor to his general behaviour.'

'Are you advocating that he stays here longer?' said the second official to Doctor Brooke.

'That simply isn't possible,' said the first official. 'Is he medically and psychologically fit to be moved? That's all we need to agree.'

'My client's PTSD is being egregiously ignored. We are talking about someone suffering from a severe mental trauma here.'

'This is another one of your delay tactics, Hazzard,' said Lamb.

'Oh, I'm sorry, are you medically trained, Miss Lamb?'

'Are you?' said Lamb. 'And it's Detective Superintendent Lamb, you rat.'

'Now, now,' said the first official.

'I'm not denying that PTSD wasn't a contributory factor,' said Lamb, 'but many other people are diagnosed with it, and none of them murder anyone as a result. That's why we disregarded it.'

'It's a very flawed judgement,' said Ched Hazzard. 'If you applied that argument to almost any other situation it would collapse under scrutiny. All medical cases must be taken on an individual basis. You cannot expect everyone in a given situation to react in identical ways. My client did not receive counselling after the bus incident, and it has never been taken into consideration.'

'We've had this conversation many times already,' said Lamb.

'My notes say he was offered counselling, but he refused,' said the first official.

'That's not the same argument,' said Ched Hazzard. 'Moving my client right now will be detrimental to his physical and psychological recovery and general wellbeing.'

'We are given to understand he has no recollection of the… event,' said the first official, 'which seems to preclude the likelihood of PTSD in his current condition, therefore it seems to me we have reasonable grounds for moving him.'

'Is he physically fit?' asked the second official.

'In my opinion, yes,' said Doctor Brooke.

'Then it's agreed,' said the first official.

'I can hear you, you know?' said Max. 'I'm right here.'

Max opened his eyes. High up in the sky another unseen airliner drew a clean white vapour trail across the blue stratosphere.

Ched Hazzard, Detective Lamb and the two officials left the room, still arguing.

Max picked up a copy of *Madame Bovary* on his bedside table and began reading: *And she was ravishing to behold, with the teardrop trembling in her eye, like the moisture a passing storm might leave in the cup of a blue flower.'*

***

Max looked at Juno. She was looking up at him, and yes, a teardrop trembled in her eye, like the moisture a passing storm might leave in the cup of a blue flower.

Max tucked stray strands of Juno's hair behind her ears.

If only she were Claire, he thought.

'He's going to die, isn't he?' said Juno. 'His immune system is shot to pieces. It can't cope with pneumonia. He's so vulnerable.'

They stood by Rex's bed in a private hospital room. Rex lay unconscious, hooked up to a drip, a ventilator and a heart monitor. His head and hands were wrapped in bandages.

'He might pull through,' said Max, wearing a borrowed tracksuit.

Rex opened his eyes with a sudden jolt.

'Old duck,' he whispered, on seeing Max.

Rex tried to move, and seemed in a state of agitation. Juno soothed him until he calmed down.

'I have seen heaven,' said Rex, with a beatific smile. 'God held out His hand to me and caressed my cheek. He told me not to worry, and showed me all the wonder to behold.'

'Just rest, darling,' said Juno.

'A choir of archangels sang a requiem for me,' continued Rex. 'There is no such thing as death. There is only life eternal.'

Rex closed his eyes.

'He's delirious,' said Max.

'No,' said Rex. 'It's all real. Paradise... paradise.'

'I'll get Mud and Fud,' said Juno.

Juno left the room.

Rex's heart monitor suddenly started pinging with an alarm. He opened his eyes and stared wildly at Max.

'The prophets in the temple told of the Beast,' said Rex, grabbing Max by the arm and squeezing tightly. 'It's you! It's you!'

There was commotion in the corridor. Max tried to pull away from Rex, but his grip tightened like a vice.

Max prised Rex's scab-encrusted fingers off one by one, then he ran into the corridor to find Juno being wheeled away by nurses. A puddle lay on the floor.

'Her waters have broken. It's early,' a nurse said.

***

Max and Fud sat in a maternity corridor. Behind closed doors, Juno was screaming.

'Are you not going in?' asked Fud.

'No,' said Max. 'I find childbirth revolting.'

'Same here,' said Fud. 'It's a miracle, but it's a revolting miracle. All the blood and exposed flesh can put you off your tea.'

'It's going to be a boy,' said Max.

'Do you have a name for him?'

'Aldous.'

'Aldous?'

'After Huxley.'

'Yes, I get the literary reference.'

Max looked at his watch.

'This time yesterday, the wedding was starting,' he said.

'Seems like years,' said Fud.

'The honeymoon will have to be postponed,' said Max.

'The honeymoon is over, Max. The honeymoon is over,' said Fud.

***

Max left Fud and went to check on Rex, but when he got to his room it was filled with nurses and doctors. Rex was in the throes of a cardiac arrest. A doctor applied a defibrillator which made Rex's body jerk and stiffen in a distressing way.

'I told him,' said Mud, sitting alone by a water cooler in the corridor, her eyes hidden, as usual, behind huge sunglasses. 'I knew the drink and drugs would get him eventually. I must take some of the blame. I gave him his first gram of coke when he was nine.'

Her yappy little dog sat on her knee. It growled and yapped at Max.

Mud made no attempt to silence it.

Max looked through the door of Rex's room again. Black and yellow liquid was spurting out of Rex's contorted mouth. His heart monitor began to make a single flatline note, then panic ensued.

Max wandered off down the corridor in a daze and found himself at a nurse's station. A doctor in a white coat stood there looking at some paperwork.

'I want to be a doctor,' said Max.

The doctor peered over his glasses and looked Max up and down.

'Oh, do you now?' said the doctor, sceptically.

'Yes. How do I train?'

'What kind of doctor do you want to be?'

'I want to save people,' said Max.

'Very noble, but that's not what I asked.'

'Just a general doctor.'

'Just a general doctor?' said the doctor, frowning. 'Do you know it can take more than ten years to become a qualified doctor?'

'Really? That's a big commitment,' said Max.

'Sorry to burst your bubble,' said the doctor. 'I recommend you apply to take a clinical aptitude test to begin with, if you're serious.'

'I am serious. What does it involve?'

'It tests your aptitude. For instance, are you skilled at verbal reasoning?'

'Not particularly.'

'What about decision making?'

'Er... yes. No. Not sure,' said Max.

'How good are you at quantitative reasoning, or abstract reasoning, or situational judgement?' asked the doctor.

'I believe my aptitude in those subjects to be somewhat limited,' said Max.

'Then you're wasting my and your time,' said the doctor. 'Piss off.'

'Thank you,' said Max.

Max walked back to Rex's room. The room was now empty. The bed had been removed.

Mud still sat by the water cooler, like before. Her yappy dog growled at Max again.

'Where's Rex?' he asked.

'The morgue,' said Mud.

***

Max returned to the maternity wing, with Mud in tow.

'It's arrived,' said Fud.

'Is it alive?' asked Max.

'Of course it's alive. Why wouldn't it be?'

Max looked through the door and saw Juno holding a wriggly purplish little thing in her arms. She smiled at Max and gave him an exhausted thumbs-up.

'Our beautiful boy is dead,' Mud said to Fud.

Fud let out a long crestfallen sigh.

'Why couldn't it have been him?' he said, pointing at Max.

Max mouthed 'Rex is dead' to Juno, but she didn't understand. She mouthed back 'Can't hear you', then gestured for him to come in and hold the baby. Max didn't want to. He shook his head.

***

Max took a taxi back to his (Rex's) mansion flat in Chelsea. He'd had it expensively redecorated since being vandalised.

He sat in a Chesterfield armchair and smoked a cigar. He didn't like the flat anymore. It reminded him of Trumpet. Fud said he would buy Max and Juno a big family home.

Max then drove over to The Emporium and sat in the back room. He watched night fall while listening to the gramophone play a scratchy old recording of *Pagliacci – Vesti la Giubba*.

Images of Rex lying in the refrigerated morgue made him sombre. Then a great cloak of fear overwhelmed him. Life and death and nothing but decay and coldness and unknowing and the dark and the dark and the dark.

He heard something move in the shop, but when he looked, no one was there.

'Rex? Is that you?' he asked.

Max felt a chill. He walked out of the shop and went into a nearby warm public library. In the medical section he browsed through books on how to become a doctor.

Ten years of training, at least, they all said. A medical degree, then foundation training, then a foundation year, then core medical training, then speciality training, then general practice training, followed by exams in maths, science, biology, chemistry, physics and more.

Max already knew he would drop out in the foundation year.

What did he want to specialise in? Neurology? Dermatology? Surgery? Psychiatry? Pathology? Immunology? Anaesthesiology? Ophthalmology? Internal medicine? Radiology? Paediatrics? Pharmacology? Osteopathy?

'Fuck all that,' said Max, attracting looks from other library users.

The future weighed heavy on him. How would he fill up the days? He had adult responsibilities now. If he sat in The Emporium all day doing nothing he'd end up like Rex. He needed a purpose in life. But what? It needed to be something requiring minimal social interaction; something quiet and intellectually stimulating, like writing a novel.

A novel. Of course. He would write the novel he'd been lying about writing. He went to a pub to celebrate the good idea. He also toasted his new son, and his newly-dead best friend.

It was almost Christmas – the season of forced jollity and temporary goodwill. Another great idea struck him: he should go on honeymoon by himself. The tickets to Venice were still valid, so why not? He'd set the novel in Venice. The trip was justifiable as research.

The next morning, when he landed at Marco Polo airport, he rang Juno to ask if it was okay for him to go solo to Venice.

'No,' she said. 'Come to the hospital and see your son.'

'I have important business to attend to,' said Max. 'I'll buy you and the boy something nice.'

Max took a speedboat across to San Marco.

***

A hospital porter noisily pushed a food trolley into Room 9, breaking Max's concentration.

'I'm a terrible human being,' said Max.

'Yep. Total scum,' replied the porter. 'Beef or chicken?'

21

Max sprinted at full speed on the running machine.

'Careful,' said Rutger.

'Yeah, tic tacs,' said Max, with beads of sweat on his brow.

His heart pounded, but he pushed himself.

I'm innocent, he thought. *Need to keep my strength up.*

He swam ten lengths of the pool with resolve, before getting out and shaking Rutger's hand goodbye.

'Remember the tic tacs,' said Rutger.

'You do know the word is tactics, don't you?' asked Max.

'Sure,' said Rutger.

***

Two police officers wheeled Max along the corridor to his last session with Lee. The door to Digby Shah's room was open. An Indian man holding a box of personal possessions stood talking to Lee inside.

'I trained for ten years,' said the man. 'Then they make me redundant so they can knock this building down to replace it with a multi-storey car park. Parking is more lucrative than saving lives, they tell me. The priorities are all wrong.'

'I sympathise with you,' said Lee.

'It's a sad day.' said the man, shaking his head as he left.

'Was he the mysterious Digby Shah?' Max asked Lee.

'Yes,' said Lee.

The room had been stripped of everything except two chairs and the rubber tree plants. Ghostly square outlines where the Rothko's once hung seemed stencilled to the walls.

'I believe I was severely long-term depressed,' said Max, when they were alone. 'I should have been on medication. From what I have learned of my former self, I was in a continuous mentally vulnerable state. I even got diagnosed with PTSD. I heard Lamb and Hazzard arguing about it.'

'You're getting ahead of yourself,' said Lee. 'Have you recalled any more memories?'

Max updated her.

'Tell me about your trip to Venice,' said Lee.

'Is it important? We're almost out of time,' said Max.

'Try to remember,' said Lee. 'Everything is important.'

Max sighed. He struggled to think. Then he relaxed. His eyes dilated.

***

Max sipped a bitter liqueur at a table outside Florian's Café. San Marco was almost deserted, except for pigeons. The sun glowed like the disc of a full moon behind the cold grey winter clouds.

Max got up and strolled across to the basilica. Inside, a service of some kind was happening. Incense burned. Voices of a choral mass echoed high up into the dome. The obscure ancient mysteries of religion and its architectural aesthetic of gory iconography seemed bizarre to Max. It contained a beguilingly poetic power, focusing on guilt and pain and retribution and sorrow, yet its opulent masquerade of greedy hypocrisy made him nauseous. When people were starving in the streets, gold leaf and marble were being lavished on rooms no one would see.

'Religion, after charity, is the biggest con trick ever invented,'

Max said to himself. 'A brilliant, fraudulent money-making exercise. Why would anyone want to believe in this?'

'Light a candle for those who are deceased,' said a blind priest sitting next to a stand of tapers, for two euros each.

'It would be a tokenistic gesture,' said Max. 'The dead are dead.'

He went next door to the Doge's Palace, where politics and law were once performed like plays. He crossed the Bridge of Sighs and wandered alone around the prison with only echoes for company.

On a gondola ride, he asked the gondolier not to speak or sing. They glided silently along empty canals.

Darkness fell. Max became lost in a maze of misty cobbled streets. He stopped a few times and looked behind him, feeling followed, then chanced upon a piazza with a trattoria. Max was the only patron.

Eating cannelloni and drinking a bottle of red wine, he attempted small talk in stilted Italian with the owners, but they didn't reciprocate.

I should have lit a taper for Rex earlier, he thought, gloomily. *Isn't all religious faith about the suspension of disbelief? My philistine atheism dismisses the spiritual symbolic power beyond intellectual understanding. I'm ashamed of my lazy rationalism.*

Max headed back to his hotel and almost fell into a canal on the way.

The next day he went to Harry's Bar. An attractive American woman sidled up to him at the bar to buy a drink. Max recognised her as a film actress, but couldn't remember her name or anything she'd been in.

'I'm a big fan,' lied Max. 'Please have that drink on me.'

She thanked him and they exchanged a few pleasantries.

'What are you in Venice for?' asked the actress.

'Writing a novel,' said Max. 'You?'

'Shooting some scenes on that island where they make the glass.'

'Murano,' said Max.

Max wanted her to invite him back to her hotel room, but only so he could reject her with 'Sorry, I'm newly married.' But she didn't. She just smiled and said, 'Good luck with the book.'

Max returned alone to his hotel room and sat for hours thinking about what his novel might be about. He scribbled a sort of manifesto onto a sheet of hotel paper:

It will address contentious issues, and not be some fucking airport novel that gets forgotten about after ten minutes. It will have to change the way people think. It will challenge people's perceptions.

It will be serious. No childish jokes. It will deal with a spectrum of idealistic subjects informing the human condition, but it won't be preachy. It will be accessible, but intelligent. It will feature zombies in a post-Apocalyptic Venice. It will address contemporary reactions to poverty, religion, victimhood and injustice.

Excited that he had made a breakthrough with the novel, Max went out and got paralytic drunk in an Irish bar.

The next morning at the airport, he bought some hideously over-priced festival masks as panic gifts.

Back in London, Max sat by Juno's hospital bed, showing them to her.

'That one's for Aldous,' he said, pointing at a brightly painted one with sequins and feathers on it.

'What the fuck is he supposed to do with that?' asked Juno. 'Are you lining him up to perform at Gay Pride in about twenty years?'

'He can play with it,' said Max.

'It's not a toy, Max. Aldous could choke on the sequins.'

'I didn't think. I was upset about Rex.'

'So you ran away?' said Juno. 'Does that seem sensible to you? Is that what you do in times of trouble, you run away?'

'I made a breakthrough with the novel. I wrote a manifesto. Do you want to hear it?'

'No, I fucking don't!' shouted Juno.

Max put the masks back in the bag to fill an awkward silence.

'Did you know that there's no explanation for the conception and evolutional development of eyes?' he said.

'What?' scowled Juno.

'Physics, biology, anthropology and Darwinian principles have never properly explained the evolutionary conception and development of eyes,' said Max. 'There are assumptions and theories surrounding it, but no satisfying explanations about how eyes came about. *The Origin of Species* offers only the vaguest conflicted theories about it.'

'Are you high?' said Juno.

'It's like speech,' babbled Max. 'Where did language come from? No one knows. For over one hundred and fifty years the consensus said linguistics was an evolutionary tool, but if that was the case, why are humans the only creatures with the ability to speak? No one is even sure how language works.'

'Stop speaking, or I'll punch you in the dick,' said Juno.

'Also,' blithely continued Max, 'the Big Bang Theory is only a theory, not fact. Hence the word "theory". It's the best one we have regarding the origins of the universe, but no one knows for sure what the origin of the universe actually is, so they made clever assumptions which have become understood as scientific facts. Evolutionary theory itself doesn't quite make sense, but we blindly assume that it does. If you look into any principle closely enough you find we know far less than we like to think. All theories fall apart under scrutiny.'

'Fuck off, Max,' said Juno. 'Just fuck right off. I'm not in the mood.'

***

The day of Rex's funeral arrived. Juno wore her wedding dress, dyed black. Black horses with black plumes pulled a glass carriage with the glossy black coffin (purple velvet interior) in front of a fleet of black limousines. The large number of mourners surprised everyone. Max's mum, dad and Margot also "showed their faces".

186

The cortege snaked through the cemetery to a church in Highgate.

A short ceremony followed. Verdi's *Requiem* was played. Juno cried uncontrollably. A priest gave a Bible reading which had nothing in connection with Rex. *Abide With Me* played on an organ.

Max and Juno visited the funeral home the night before to look at Rex, which Max found ghoulish. The mortician had done a lot of work on Rex's face. He reminded Max of the creepy wax-faced figures of Jesus and various saints he'd seen in the churches of Venice.

Max was asked to give a eulogy, but declined.

At the end of the funeral service, Max helped to carry the heavy lead-lined coffin outside, to the strains of Sid Vicious's *My Way*.

Snow fell as the mourners trudged along a muddy path towards the family mausoleum – a large decaying gothic construction with stone gargoyles dissolved by acid rain.

Its rusty door was opened up. They placed Rex's coffin inside, next to older coffins covered in pigeon and bat droppings. The roof leaked. A foul odour hung in the damp gloomy air.

'That space is reserved for us,' said Juno, pointing to an empty shelf.

Max gladly went back outside. Some mourners hung around offering words of consolation. They asked if there was a free bar at the wake, and when told 'Yes', rushed off.

Max noticed a grave digger preparing a new plot nearby. Max picked his way amongst broken marble angels and gravestones choked with undergrowth. He looked down into the oblong hole of wet clay. The bottom was full of brown water. The grave digger, cheerfully laying AstroTurf at the edges, smiled at him.

'Bleak, isn't it?' said Max.

'Depends,' shrugged the grave digger.

'Depends on what?' asked Max.

'Which way you look at it.'

'I can't see any positives,' said Max.

'Well, that's debatable,' said the grave digger. 'We've all got to die, and we've got to be disposed of somehow. I wouldn't like to be put down here myself, but that's just an opinion. I'm being cremated.'

'Was there a body already down there?' asked Max.

'At one time. But the bones decalcify after so long. You only find fragments of coffin. And the rusty handles.'

'Do you enjoy your work?'

'I do,' said the grave digger. 'It's satisfying. I like to do a decent job. I often find jewellery, but I always put it back, out of respect.'

'Good to know,' said Max.

'The bodies rot so quickly in this wet clay, you see,' said the grave digger. 'No drainage. After a few weeks, all the flesh has gone. I've exhumed a few in my time. It is what it is. Best accept it. You sleep better at night.'

***

The post-funeral gathering took place at Mud and Fud's house, with finger food. Max's mum, dad and Margot went straight home.

'He didn't leave you anything,' Juno told Max, behind a black veil.

'I didn't want anything,' lied Max.

'He didn't own anything,' said Juno. 'All he had was weekly pocket money from Mud and Fud, which he spent. And he didn't have a trust fund because of his profligacy, although his pocket money was horrifcally generous and indulgent. Mud and Fud feel so guilty now.'

Max was broke. He expected some kind of windfall from Mud and Fud now he was family, but received nothing. He'd grown accustomed to a certain standard of high living, but had no way of sustaining it.

Max and Juno moved into Rex's old flat until the new house was ready.

(Rex didn't even own the flat. Max regretted wasting so much money redecorating the place.)

'What are you going to do for money now?' asked Juno.

'I'm writing my novel.'

'That won't make you any money, darling. Fud said he can get you a position in his old city firm.'

'I'd rather eat my own neck,' said Max. 'Anyway, I still work at The Emporium. I expect a wage.'

'The Emporium is a moribund establishment. You were never a proper employee there. Now Rex has gone, we have no need of it.'

'My novel is important!' shouted Max. 'I cannot be distracted.'

'All right, all right,' said Juno. 'If it means that much to you, perhaps I can persuade Mud to keep The Emporium going until something better comes along. I can give you per diem to tide you over.'

'Like pocket money?' sniffed Max.

'No, as a sort of artistic patronage, or an advance,' said Juno. 'I want you to be happy. But I can't have you mooching around at home all day. You'll drive me and Aldous bonkers. Write at The Emporium.'

'I'll need money for a computer,' said Max.

Juno gave him £2000 in cash.

Max bought a laptop. It gave him lots of trouble and he took it back to the store twice, ranting about how nothing ever works properly and no one knows what they're doing. Eventually they fixed it. (It had a virus downloaded from a hardcore porn website he visited).

Max sat in the back room of The Emporium for hours every day staring at the blank glowing screen of the laptop, his hands poised over the keyboard in anticipation for the tsunami of words which the literary muse was bound to bestow on him.

He typed the word *The*, then deleted it.

'Man, this is more difficult than I thought,' he said to himself.

***

By the following April, nature was pregnant with spring, and Juno was pregnant with twin girls, Perdita and Willow (Juno's choice).

Fud bought the newlyweds a large detached modern family home in a cul-de-sac of a quiet affluent suburb. Juno had an art studio in the attic, and Max had an (unused) writer's shed in the back garden.

Max took an instant dislike to the house and the area, which he found characterless and petit bourgeois. The house lacked architectural merit in his opinion. And there were pampas bushes in every front garden.

Max dug his out and burned it on the first day.

Juno filled the house with her mildest artwork, with only the odd labia or gonad on display. The one concession was a large painting of Max's anus with the cheeks pulled apart, called *Starfish*, which hung in the downstairs toilet.

Juno made an effort to ingratiate herself to the neighbours. Max didn't.

He spent more and more time at The Emporium, trying to write his novel and avoiding the burgeoning chummy little social microcosm of nosey neighbours Juno busily accumulated.

Sometimes he'd get home to find Gaz and Nat from next door in his living room. Gaz was a flash prick who ran a luxury car showroom. Nat sold beauty products online. Max instantly despised both of them, but Juno said they were nice.

Gaz kept trying to sell Max a new car because the Bentley was so old and dented. Nat was constantly hard-selling moisturisers and creams to Juno.

'They don't come over here for social reasons, they come over for commercial reasons, and you're too gullible to see it,' said Max.

'You hate me having friends, don't you?' replied Juno.

Juno organised a barbeque one weekend and invited all the neighbours, much to Max's annoyance. Two of the six houses made lame excuses for non-attendance, which annoyed Max even more.

'Who do they think they are, snubbing us?' he said.

Max opened the door for each guest with a smile that almost convinced in its sincerity. He made drinks and dull small talk, but left the cooking to Juno (and Gaz, who claimed to be an expert at everything).

Max kept disappearing for long intervals with the excuse of checking on Aldous. Max used Aldous as an excuse for absenting himself from most situations. Otherwise, interactions with his son were minimal. He point-blank refused to change nappies or bathe him, and he never got up in the night to stop him crying.

'Bring Aldous down. We'd love to see him,' said Nat.

'Maybe later,' said Max.

Max went upstairs to escape Gaz's constant sales patter. In Aldous's room, he peeked down at the people in his garden and mimed shooting each of them. Then he sat by Aldous's cot and read aloud Edgar Allen Poe's *The Cask of Amontillado* to him.

'So this is where you're hiding!' said Gaz, barging into the room and making coo-chi-coo noises to Aldous. 'I've got the perfect Lexus for your daddy,' he continued, without a hint of shame.

As the day progressed, Max grew tired of pretending to listen to what people were saying to him. He nodded as if interested, and he smiled when they smiled, and laughed when they laughed, and said, 'Wow,' and 'Really?', but he wanted them all to fuck off.

At one point, when Gaz didn't realise he was in hearing range, Max overheard him say to a neighbour, 'It's pretty obvious Juno's the one with the money. Fuck knows what Max does. Bugger all, by the look of it. I'm going to flog that mug a Lexus, if it kills me.'

I'll sort you out, you cunt, thought Max.

At dusk, when they were finally alone, Max casually said to Juno, 'Margot's texted me. She wants me to pop over and help her move some furniture.'

This was a lie. He hadn't been in contact with Margot for weeks. He went into the garage, grabbed a large can of petrol, put it in the boot of the Bentley, then drove a couple of miles away. He parked in a side street, and walked off with the can of petrol in a carrier bag.

A few minutes later, he stood opposite Gaz's car showroom. It was a Sunday evening – no one around. Max noted two CCTV cameras. He put a baseball cap on, then went over to the far corner of the forecourt and hid.

He poured a large puddle of petrol out of the can, then walked away, trailing a line of it behind him. At a safe distance, he lit a match and ignited the trail of petrol.

The whoosh of flames was more powerful than he expected. Within seconds two cars were alight. Then a third (the Lexus), then a fourth.

Max crossed the road, tugging the baseball cap lower, and walked back to the Bentley.

As he reached the street corner, an explosion lit up the night sky. A chain reaction of bangs followed. The entire forecourt was ablaze.

'You're the mug, Gaz,' said Max, to himself.

He drove home and pulled quietly (with lights off) into his garage.

'That was quick,' said Juno, when Max entered the living room.

'I was halfway there when Margot texted to say she didn't need me after all,' said Max.

He went upstairs and watched the glow in the distant sky. Fire engine sirens could be heard. Then Max went into the bathroom and threw up.

Shortly, he joined Juno on the living room sofa and pretended to read a newspaper, but he couldn't because his hands were shaking with fear and adrenaline. He put the paper down because he didn't want Juno to notice.

The police were bound to knock on the door at any moment.

Surely he'd been filmed by an unseen camera. The baseball cap was a pathetic disguise. He'd been so sloppy. Someone must have seen him. What was he thinking? He hadn't thought it through properly. It was a spur of the moment thing; personal retribution on a world full of cunts like Gaz. He wanted to confess his criminality to Juno. He wanted to go to a police station and hand himself in.

Gaz ran out of his house next door, then jumped into a loud Maserati and sped off in the direction of his showroom.

What if someone has been killed? thought Max.

Max couldn't sleep that night. There was a lot of coming and going next door. Curtains twitched throughout the cul-de-sac. A police car arrived. Officers talked to Nat in the street and she started crying.

Juno went out to see what was happening. She brought Nat inside and made her a cup of tea.

Max went down and pretended to be sympathetic. He surreptitiously kept sniffing his fingers to detect if there was any petrol residue still on them, and he continually glanced at himself in the mirror to see if he looked guilty.

Gaz returned in the early hours, shell-shocked.

'I've lost the lot. The whole showroom's gone,' he said.

The next day, Max heard Gaz shouting at someone on the telephone, 'What do you mean, there's a discrepancy? I filled out the relevant forms. Are you insinuating I'm an arsonist?'

Nat interjected with a nervous,

'What's wrong, Gaz? What's wrong?'

Gaz said,

'They're not going to pay out the insurance, because they think I set fire to the showroom as an insurance scam.'

Nat started crying again.

Gaz came around and sat at Max and Juno's kitchen table that night.

'What happens now?' asked Juno.

'I'm totally fucked, pardon my French,' said Gaz. 'It took my whole adult life to build that business up, then wham, it's gone in a puff of smoke.'

'Literally,' said Max. His heart raced.

'We'll have to sell up,' said Gaz. 'Move in with Nat's parents. I had everything invested in the business. Why would someone do this to me? It doesn't make sense.'

'Do the police have any leads yet?' asked Max.

'No. Nothing.'

'And no one was injured?' asked Max.

'Thankfully, no.'

Max breathed a silent sigh of relief.

Aldous started crying, so Juno went upstairs.

'I have something to tell you,' said Gaz, fixing Max with a hard stare.

Max nearly shit himself.

'What?' asked Max.

'I have previous with this,' said Gaz. 'Twelve years ago, I set my first showroom on fire when things were going bad. But I swear to God, I had nothing to do with this. Do you believe me?'

'I believe you,' said Max.

'Thank you,' said Gaz. 'You're a friend.'

Poor bastard, thought Max. *You're thanking the motherfucker who's ruined your life. Not as clever as you think you are, are you Gaz? All you pricks out there, you underestimate me, yet you're not worth the steam off my piss. This is my world, and all you pieces of shit are just living in it. I can't explain the things I do. I can't justify them, either. Shit just happens.*

***

Max jolted back into Digby Shah's room.

'Blimey,' he said. 'I was a nasty piece of work. Did you know about any of this?'

'Yes,' said Lee. 'You came back to see me in Fulham shortly after and confessed to me. I must admit, I didn't believe you at the time. I thought you were grandstanding; maybe something of a fantasist.'

'It's all true,' said Max.

He stared again at the wall and let his memories resume.

***

Within a few days of the showroom fire, Max's paranoia subsided. (He stopped thinking every passing car and helicopter was monitoring him). He still woke to every sound in the night though, and he assumed the phones were tapped.

Gaz and Nat moved out. Juno was sad to see them go. Max waved as they drove away. Gaz gave him a forwarding address so they could stay in contact, but Max scrunched it up and threw it in the bin.

Gaz and Nat were soon replaced by Deepak and Shilpa. Max liked Deepak, apart from the permanent grin he wore on his face, but he saw Shilpa as a potential problem. Deepak was a quiet-spoken doctor who worked punishingly long hours at the local hospital. Shilpa was an over-friendly little social dynamo, who wore too much make-up and thought too much of herself. She set about redesigning everything about her new house and garden, so workmen hammered and sawed and drilled there every day for months, which drove Max crazy.

He regretted getting rid of Gaz and Nat, especially when Deepak and Shilpa's two young children ran around the garden screaming all the time.

'Those noisy little fuckers,' Max said to Juno. 'I can't use my writing shed, even if I wanted to.'

'I can't hear them,' Juno replied.

Max told Shilpa he needed peace to write his novel, but she didn't take the hint. Instead, she always asked him the same questions.

Shilpa: 'How's your memoir coming along?'

Max: 'It's a novel.'

Shilpa: 'How many pages did you write today?'

Max: (under his breath) 'None of your fucking business.' (aloud) 'Five.'

(actually, only five words).

Shilpa: 'What's it about?'

Max: 'It's about a seemingly-normal suburban psychopath who murders his annoying neighbour and her noisy kids.'

Shilpa: (giggling) 'Ooh, that sounds creepy.'

Max put in a daily 9-5 shift at The Emporium. No customers ever came in, despite a twenty-percent-off sales drive. He vacuumed all of Rex's remaining cocaine off every surface using his nostrils, hoping it would give him the energy and impetus to write. But it didn't.

He sold off items of stock to make extra cash so he wouldn't need to rely on Juno's (quite miserly) allowance. In restaurants, he still insisted on paying. There were also astronomical household bills to pay. Juno said she would cover them, but Max said he was capable.

'Okay Mr Patriarchy, I won't emasculate you with my feeble feminist 21st century principles,' she would say, fluttering her eyelids.

***

Max took long strolls in the park while waiting for inspiration. One day he sat on a bench and a woman pushing a baby in a pram asked if he wanted a free hand-job. Max shrugged, then nodded. They went into a nearby toilet and she masturbated him, but he was unable to climax so she gave up and left. Max never saw her again and he didn't think to ask her why she did it or what she got out of it.

***

Max's hair was getting greyer by the day, so he began dying it. When Juno saw his new unnaturally black hair for the first time, she smiled but said nothing. Max tried to make a joke by saying,
'I'm a marvel of modern science. I'm rejuvenating. It's a miracle.'
Juno started singing *You're So Vain* to him.

***

At nine months, Juno's stomach had ballooned to comic proportions.
Max's mum and dad visited the house for the first time.
They had a photo of themselves taken with Aldous.
'He doesn't look like either of you,' said Dad. 'Although he's got his father's farts.'
Dad also kept making snide remarks about Juno's artwork. He walked around her attic studio pointing at each painting and saying,
'How much is this one?'
'Ten thousand pounds,' said Juno.
'People actually buy this kind of stuff?'
'Sometimes.'
At the dining table, Dad said to Max,
'How's that play going?'
'It's a novel,' said Max.
'Which millennium will your magnum opus be finished by?'
'Says the man who burnt his own novel,' said Max.
'I realised I had no talent,' said Dad. 'I didn't waste time indulging in a frivolous pastime for longer than necessary. It's important to know your limitations.'
'And yet you've persisted in being an accountant,' sniped Max.

197

'I've always made money,' said Dad. 'You and Margot never wanted for anything.'

'Except affection,' said Max.

'Maximillian, that's not fair,' said Mum.

'Show me some respect in my own home,' said Max, fixing his dad with a death stare.

'This isn't your home, it's your wife's home,' said Dad. 'Like that junk shop isn't yours, either.'

'It's an antique and objets d'art showroom,' growled Max.

'Don't make me laugh,' said Dad.

'If you can't think of anything positive to say, either say nothing at all, or fuck off,' said Juno to Max's dad.

Silence.

'I apologise,' said Dad, contritely. 'I'm out of order. It's the drink. It makes me say things I don't mean. Please forgive me.'

'Let's eat,' said Max.

***

The police officers entered Digby Shah's room to take Max away. It broke his concentration. He rubbed his eyes.

'I'll try to see you in the next location,' said Lee.

'I keep getting side-tracked by trivial details,' said Max.

'Nothing is trivial. It all helps,' said Lee. 'Keep remembering.'

'I must figure this out,' said Max. 'Someone murdered my family.'

'I'm intrigued by Claire,' said Lee. 'I'd like to talk to her. I should've done so before. I feel she's important.'

'If you find her, give her my love,' said Max as he was handcuffed to the wheelchair and pushed out of the room.

22

Evening drew a shroud over the hospital. Max sat on the bed in Room 9 watching rain falling in silvery sheets. Lightning illuminated distant thundery cloudscapes.

His few belongings were packed into a sports bag: a few clothes, some books, a flannel, a toothbrush and toothpaste. Even they weren't really his. Ched Hazzard said all his belongings had been incinerated.

Rex was dead. Dad too. And Juno. And Aldous. Even as-yet unborn Perdita and Willow. All dead, potentially because of him.

Now I am become death, the destroyer of worlds, he thought.

He closed his eyes.

***

Max sat in the back room of The Emporium. He typed:

Boz said: "What lingers is a fragile melancholy. A haunting melody of glacial silence. An unbreakable kiss of dialectic fracture. Embrace nihilism's shadow. Survive the transition of loathing. Immerse in the texture of interior hate."

Not bad, thought Max. *I don't know what any of it means. But not bad.*

The phone rang. Max answered, expecting to hear automated sales bullshit.

'The Emporium, Max Hope, head of sales and acquisitions speaking, how may I help?' he said.

'It's me, you dickhead,' said Juno, hyperventilating. 'The babies are coming. Shilpa's taking me to the hospital.'

'I'm on my way,' said Max.

He hung up and felt resentful at his concentration being interrupted.

Max stayed seated. He returned his eyes to the laptop screen. The first fifty pages of his novel were written. Flaubert agonised for years over every syllable of *Madame Bovary*. Bram Stoker took seven years to write *Dracula*. Max read somewhere that Schiller needed the scent of rotting apples in his desk in order to write, so he put a Granny Smith in his, but it didn't help at all.

Max's novel was developing into a dystopian stream of consciousness narrative about a man called Boz, a novelist, sex addict, philosopher, ex-exorcist, ex-SAS, ex-test pilot, ex-cult leader, ex-heroin addict and keen amateur gynaecologist.

Max toyed with the title, *A Hegemony of Twats*.

***

Max arrived at the maternity ward.

'No flowers?' asked Shilpa.

'What's the point?' said Max.

'It's a nice gesture,' said Shilpa.

'They're expensive, and they get thrown away the next day,' said Max. 'I can appreciate the aesthetic protocol of fresh flowers, but ultimately they are nothing more than a wasted expenditure.'

'Oh, well…' said Shilpa, staring blankly at him.

'Does Deepak work here?' asked Max.

'On the sixth floor.'

'I need to talk to him. Now.'

'What about Juno?' asked Shilpa.

'She's not going anywhere.'

***

Max found Deepak in a sixth-floor corridor attempting to resuscitate a woman by thrusting an adrenaline needle through her breastplate and into her heart.

'Sorry to bother you Deepak,' said Max, 'Can I shadow you for a day?'

'What?' said a distracted Deepak.

'As research for my novel,' clarified Max. 'I think my main character yearns to be a doctor, and I, or rather he, needs to learn about—'

'I'm quite busy right now, Max,' interrupted Deepak, mid-thrust.

'Tomorrow, perhaps?' asked Max.

'Tomorrow will be better, yes.'

***

Perdita and Willow Hope were born that evening. Shilpa told Max to film their births, but he declined.

'You should eat the placenta,' suggested Shilpa.

'Yuck,' squirmed Max.

***

Max arrived at the hospital early the next morning. He briefly visited Juno and the babies, then rushed up to see Deepak.

'I just want to observe,' said Max. 'Can I wear a white coat, please?'

'Why?' asked Deepak.

'To blend in. I don't want anyone to think I'm a voyeur.'

Deepak unlocked a cupboard containing lab coats and green scrubs.

Max put on a white coat. Deepak handed him a visitor ID lanyard.

'This is unorthodox,' said Deepak. 'I'm doing this as a favour. And grab a coffee. It will have the effect of making you look purposeful, but casually so.'

Max picked an empty coffee cup out of a bin.

Deepak showed him around an unused operating theatre, then an unused ward and unused consultation rooms and offices. They also passed an Accident and Emergency reception area crammed with ill and injured people.

'Why aren't those patients being dealt with?' asked Max.

'Cutbacks,' said Deepak.

'Glad I'm not ill,' said Max.

'Me too,' said Deepak.

Max felt good playing at being a doctor. He went into a toilet and took photos of himself in "doctorly" poses.

'Now,' said Deepak (the benign smile never leaving his face), 'I have to do rounds on this ward, and afterwards I want you to tell me if you can sense anything unusual about the patients.'

Deepak led Max into a normal-looking ward. There was a mixture of men and women of all ages in pyjamas and gowns reading books and newspapers, chatting to visiting relatives, or sleeping.

Nurses attended to their duties.

Max tried not to make eye contact with anyone. He stayed close behind Deepak, who studied charts at the end of a selection of beds and asked patients vague questions and received vague answers.

'Max?' said a surprised female voice.

It was Zoe. She sat in the next bed, knitting a woolly shawl. She put it down and gawped at Max. Her hair was in a gamine bob which made her look prettier than Max remembered.

'Zoe?' said Max.

'You're a doctor?'

'Yes,' lied Max.

'Wow,' said Zoe.

'I know, right?'

'The thespian calling didn't work out?'

'My talents lay elsewhere.'

Both smiled awkwardly and nodded for no reason.

'I tried to call you after the *Arsenic and Old Lace* debacle,' said Zoe.

'I needed to reassess my life options,' said Max.

'Becoming a doctor was a good choice.'

'I'm also a novelist and dealer in antiques and objets d'art.'

'An unusual combination,' said Zoe.

'I like to keep busy. I'm married with three kids now.'

'Max Hope, you are full of surprises.'

'Some have greatness thrust upon them,' shrugged Max, conceitedly.

'They certainly do,' smiled Zoe.

'You married? Any kids?' asked Max.

'No. One day, hopefully, when I get healthy again,' said Zoe.

'What's wrong with you?'

'It's my lungs. I was jogging each morning, but found I got more and more out of breath. Then I collapsed. I mainly breathe through a ventilator now. It's lung cancer. I know it is, but my family don't want to tell me.'

Max pressed his fingertips to Zoe's neck, then felt along her clavicles with a look of concentration on his face.

'You'll be fine. Trust me,' he said.

'Do you think so?' asked Zoe, suddenly wheezing.

'Absolutely,' smiled Max.

'I want to get out of here,' said Zoe. 'This is no place for someone my age. I have big ambitions. I spent three years doing a useless degree at university and I have nothing but debt to show for it.'

'Life is pain,' said Max.

'I can't believe you achieved so much,' said Zoe. 'You're successful and talented and settled down. I'm so happy for you. Life throws some weird tangents, doesn't it?'

'Yes,' said Max. 'My best friend, who also happened to be my best man and brother-in-law, burned to death at my wedding.'

'Yikes,' said Zoe, her lips turning blue.

Some other doctors entered the ward to do rounds. They glanced at Max curiously.

'Max?' said Deepak, indicating a hasty exit.

'Good luck with the scarf,' said Max to Zoe. 'See you.'

Zoe put a ventilator mask on, and waved breathlessly to Max.

Deepak ushered him out of the ward.

'Well? Did you notice anything unusual in there?' asked Deepak, when they were at a safe distance.

'No,' said Max.

'Good. You weren't meant to. That's a terminal ward. Two weeks from now, all those patients will have passed away and others will be in their place.'

'Even the girl I was speaking to?' asked Max.

'Yes. Inoperable final stage lung cancer.'

'But she didn't look terminal?'

'The end, when it comes, is often benevolently sudden.'

Max stopped and turned to go back. Deepak stopped him. For the one and only time, the smile on his face dropped.

'Max, one important lesson to take away from this is that you must never become emotionally involved with the patients. It's difficult, and it sounds clinical, but it's the only way to get through it without your heart being broken on a daily basis. We have to be rational and philosophical. Why do you think so many doctors burn out, or take to drink? I've helplessly watched dozens of beautiful children die. I can remember all of their faces. I remember their smiles. Some nights, I get home to Shilpa and the kids, and I feel like bursting into tears. But I can't. I hold it together for their sakes. Do you understand?'

Deepak gripped Max's arm.

'Yes, I think I do,' said Max.

Max immediately went down to see Juno with the intention of

giving her a hug, but when he got to her room, Mud and Fud were there.

'Look what the cat dragged in,' said Mud, with contempt.

***

Boz stood marvelling at the Byzantine architecture of the basilica. As he did so, he couldn't help but realise how irrelevant its ancient narrative was becoming. The world's social cognitive chronicle is rapidly changing, he thought, and a time will come when the organised religions will be superseded by data technology and the worship of a singularity of algorithms. This new religion will not offer false hope in non-existent future utopias, but will allow us to feel safe and content in the biological meaninglessness of the here and now, unchained by the burden of any conceptual illusions such as free will, or soul. Such determinism won't necessarily be an improvement, it will simply be a new narrative which will eventually be replaced itself by something as yet unseen. Religious buildings are already viewed as relics of a bygone age; one day, unfortunately they will all be pulled down and wiped away.

Boz felt a chill at these thoughts, but also smugness because he had foreseen the inevitability of the future.

He lit a candle for himself to gain the affection of a non-existent God, then walked out of the basilica, into the warm sun in the piazza. His linen suit became drenched in sweat, and his haemorrhoids burned with anger.

Max reclined in his chair in the back room of The Emporium and put his hands behind his head. A feeling of satisfaction stole over him.

'This is going to be a literary game changer,' he said aloud.

He wasn't sure about the haemorrhoids detail, though.

***

That evening, Max was home alone. He lay naked, except for the white doctor's coat (which he accidentally-deliberately forgot to return), on the sofa in the living room with all the lights off.

A car's headlamps illuminated the walls in refracted oblongs. It was Deepak's car pulling into the next door drive. Max imagined Deepak putting on his rational smile, then greeting his wife and kids, before going up to the bathroom and bursting into frustrated tears.

Poor bastard, thought Max.

Poor Zoe, too. He resolved to take her some flowers the next day.

***

A huge clap of thunder rattled the windows. Max was back in Room 9.

Doctor Brooke, Ched Hazzard, Detective Lamb and four armoured police officers were looking at him.

Angry deep purple storm clouds loured over the hospital.

'He's faking,' said Lamb.

'He's back,' said Doctor Brooke.

'Where were you, Max?' asked Ched Hazzard.

'The living room at home,' said Max, realising for the first time that it was the same living room he'd seen in the nightmare which had disturbed him weeks earlier.

'Is he fit to be moved?' Lamb asked Brooke.

'I don't see why not,' said Brooke.

'Let's roll,' said Lamb to the police officers.

'I'm being moved now?' asked Max.

'Sorry, Max. Nothing I could do,' said Ched Hazzard.

Max felt sad about leaving the familiar cocoon of Room 9.

Taser guns were raised as Max was uncuffed, then transferred and recuffed into the wheelchair.

'For God's sake, he's not Hannibal Lecter,' said Ched Hazzard.

'I have more sympathy for Hannibal Lecter,' said Lamb.

'Bit harsh,' said Max.

23

Garbled voices. Shouting. Flashes of light. Max was at the epicentre of the storm. The press were here for him. Jostling. Ravenous. They'd probably kill him if they got to him. Max represented the toxic underbelly of the human animal.

He felt a degree of safety under the sheet, and held it tight to himself so no one would see his unshaved face and grey hair.

An egg splattered against his head. He shut his eyes.

***

Max bought a bouquet of flowers. They were quite expensive, and the flower seller blatantly coerced him into buying dearer ones than he intended.

'Who are they for?' asked the flower seller.

'An ex-girlfriend. We took each other's virginity. She's dying of lung cancer,' said Max, immediately regretting over-sharing.

'Then you need these ones,' said the flower seller.

Max now stood at the nurse's station outside the terminal ward.

'Could you give these to Zoe in bed twelve, please?' said Max.

The nurse looked at a list of names on a computer screen. She glanced at Max, then back at the screen.

'Are you a relative?' she asked.

'An ex-boyfriend,' said Max.

'I'm afraid Zoe passed away early this morning.'

'But I was talking to her yesterday.'

'She became poorly in the night, and went downhill very quickly. We couldn't save her. I'm very sorry,' said the nurse.

Max pictured Zoe waving goodbye to him the day before. Now she was dead. She didn't even finish knitting her shawl.

***

'Get him in the back of the van. 1-2-3.'

The police lifted Max up in his wheelchair and pushed him into a dark metal container. Doors slammed shut behind him.

The van began moving. Hands banged on the sides. The van picked up speed. Max pulled the sheet off his head. He was in a cage.

***

'I bought you these,' said Max.

'Wow. Flowers. Unlike you,' said Juno.

Perdita and Willow were in her arms. Max smiled. Tears filled his eyes.

***

After a series of twisty back streets, the van drove along either a dual carriageway or a motorway. Max had been given no information on his destination. He wondered if he was being taken to be executed. His heart beat a little faster at the thought. He reasoned his death wouldn't make any difference.

'This is claustrophobic,' he shouted to an unseen driver in the cab, but received no answer.

***

'My wife and newborn daughters come home tomorrow,' said Max.

'How do you feel about that?' asked Lee.

Children were screaming again in the distant playground.

'I don't know. Mild dread. Anticipation. Distraction.'

'Is it not important to you to be a good husband and father?'

'It's important,' said Max. 'I just don't think I'm cut out for it. I don't have any paternal feelings for my son. He looks at me with suspicion. It annoys me. But I'd never hurt him. Now there'll be two more. And what worries me most of all, I think I'm turning into my father.'

***

The van slowed down and pulled onto a ramp. Max kept twisting his head to see if he could recognise anything through the toughened glass windows at the top edge of the van. Gates opened and the van entered into a high-walled compound.

***

Juno sat on the sofa in the living room with Aldous in her arms. Perdita and Willow were in the next room making gurgling noises. Their hired nanny made goo-goo noises back.

Helium balloons jostled on the ceiling. Congratulatory cards were on the coffee table, along with a half-eaten cake with pink icing that Shilpa made.

'Are you going to that girl's funeral?' asked Juno.

'No,' said Max. 'It's one of those odd humanist ceremonies. She's being buried in a wicker basket.'

'You can go if you want,' said Juno.

'I don't want to,' said Max.

***

The van stopped. The rear doors opened. Max was lifted out into an underground car park.

'Is this where I get a bullet in the back of my head?' he asked one of the police officers.

***

Juno showed Max the newest paintings in her studio.

'That's Leda and that's the Swan, after Rubens,' she said. 'I'm going through a classical Greek mythology allusion phase.'

'I don't remember the bit in that story where Leda wears a strap-on dildo and rapes the swan?' said Max.

'I've taken artistic licence with it. It's a post-feminist diatribe about toxic masculinity and rape, in this case, Zeus.'

They moved on to the next painting.

'Why are Abelard and Heloise cross-dressed?' asked Max.

'It's a comment advocating transvestite and transgender rights. My work is becoming more politicised.'

The next painting.

'Freud and Jung impaled on a double-ended vibrator?' asked Max.

'Self-explanatory,' said Juno. 'It's provocative. My agent says there's a lot of buzz in New York for my stuff right now. There's a bidding war going on for *Tits*. Did I tell you I'm off to Manhattan next week? I have an exhibition at the Lincoln Center.'

'Are you taking the kids with you?' asked Max.

'Don't be ridiculous,' said Juno.

***

Police officers wheeled Max along a corridor with strip lighting. They passed a reception area where Ched Hazzard was remonstrating with some prison officers.

210

'Do the words habeas corpus mean anything to you people?' he was saying.

'Get this clown out of my face,' said a warden.

They wheeled Max into a room. An armed guard stood by the door.

A flustered-looking Ched Hazzard came in.

'Is this a remand prison?' asked Max.

'Yep,' said Ched Hazzard.

'Will I be offered bail?'

'Nope.'

A prison officer holding a clipboard entered, followed by two police officers.

They shut the door.

'Maximillian Hope?' asked the prison officer.

'Just Max,' said Max. 'Only my mum calls me Maximillian when I've done something bad.'

'You have done something bad,' said the prison officer. 'Max Hope, you are being detained at this facility until further notice, pending trial. I'm Officer Walker. I've been assigned as your personal officer.'

'Woop-woop,' said Max, flatly.

'Our medical records show you as having no alcohol or drugs in your system, and the course of medication you were on has ceased. A member of prison staff will sort out with you what clothes to wear. You will have to wear prison clothes on these premises. A member of staff will make a list of everything you brought with you. You may be able to keep some things. Everything else will be kept in a safe place.'

'All I want is my books,' said Max.

Walker made a note.

'You will now be searched. Are you capable of standing up?'

'Yes.'

'Why is he in a wheelchair?' Walker asked Ched Hazzard.

'Health and Safety.'

'Lose the wheelchair,' said Walker to a police officer.

Max's handcuffs were removed. The wheelchair was taken away. An officer patted Max down.

'Clean,' said the officer.

'If you wish,' said Walker, 'you may see a doctor, a prison chaplain, or a representative of another religious denomination on request.'

'No,' said Max.

'You're allowed one phone call to your family—' Walker stopped short, then cleared his throat. 'Or the Samaritans.'

'No,' said Max.

'You can have a bath or shower if you want one.'

'Is my room ensuite?' asked Max.

'Do you realise why you're here?' asked Walker.

'I presume that's a rhetorical question?' said Max.

'Don't answer any further questions, Max,' said Ched Hazzard.

'Is this joker really your lawyer?' Walker asked Max.

Max nodded.

'Christ,' muttered one of the police officers.

'Do you realise why you're here?' repeated Walker.

'I'm still gathering evidence,' said Max.

**

'Doctor?' said a voice.

Max was standing alone in a hospital corridor, looking at notices on an activity board. He wore the white coat. A stethoscope hung around his neck, along with a lanyard which had the word "visitor" blotted out, and replaced with "doctor" in biro.

He'd spent the morning roaming around wards checking the clipboards at the end of beds. No one stopped or questioned him.

'Doctor?' repeated the voice.

Max looked in the voice's direction. A nurse stood in a doorway.

'Yes?' Max heard himself say.

212

'Can you come here, please?'

Max's heart fluttered nervously as he walked into a room where the nurse and a young trainee doctor were looking at a man in obvious pain, lying on a bed.

'This patient can't speak any English,' said the trainee doctor. 'We've worked out he has an abdominal problem, but we'd like your opinion.'

'Of course,' said Max.

A sudden large bead of sweat appeared on Max's forehead.

Run, Max, run.

Max looked at the man on the bed.

'Where on the abdomen precisely?' he asked.

The trainee doctor frowned. He pointed to the patient's abdominal area.

Max nodded thoughtfully, before prodding his finger into the man's abdomen. The patient screamed in agony.

'Jesus, what are you doing?' asked the trainee doctor.

'Making sure the abdomen was the problem,' said Max.

'I already told you.'

The patient cursed in distress in a language they didn't recognise.

'This isn't really my area of speciality,' said Max, edging towards the door. 'I'll get one of my colleagues.'

'I haven't seen you before,' said the nurse. 'What's your name?'

'Honeydew. Doctor Honeydew,' blurted Max.

'It says Doctor Hope on your lanyard,' said the nurse.

'That's my maiden name,' said Max, panicking.

'Come back here,' said the trainee doctor. 'Who are you?'

'Call security,' said the nurse.

Max hurried out of the room and down a corridor. He ducked into a stairwell and ran down several flights, throwing off the white coat as he did so.

The ground floor door opened out into an A & E reception area full of people with minor wounds and ailments.

Max covered his face with his hand to hide from any CCTV cameras. He jogged towards the automatic entrance doors, expecting the clamp of a security guard's hand on his shoulder.

None came. He kept going.

His Bentley was parked in a nearby side street to avoid paying the exorbitant hospital car park fee.

On the drive home, he pulled over and threw up.

***

'Do you have any special dietary requirements?' Walker asked Max.

'I don't like tapioca,' said Max.

***

Max paced up and down behind the curtained window of the living room. He kept peering through them, fearful of approaching police cars.

'I'm such a prick,' he said, slapping his face. 'Why do I keep putting myself into dangerous situations? Why can't I be normal?'

He heard a sound and realised the nanny was watching him from the next room, bottle feeding Perdita and Willow.

***

'This is your cell,' said Walker, opening a heavy door.

He flicked a switch. A fluorescent light came on. Max looked inside the small room – a single bed, a sink, a toilet, and a TV high up on a shelf. The walls and floor were bare. A lantern window in the ceiling provided the only source of natural light.

Max gingerly entered.

'Where are my books?' asked Max.

'If you need assistance, ring the bell,' said Walker.

'Where are my fucking books?'

Walker slammed the door shut, then locked it outside.

Max felt claustrophobic again. He took a few deep breaths and sat on the bed. At least he was in a single cell, he reasoned. And he was no longer required to wear handcuffs.

He lifted up the thin bed cover. The bedspread and pillow looked new and clean. The room smelled of disinfectant.

He wore blue prison garb. It stripped him of identity.

They had taken his photograph and his fingerprints, and given him a prison number.

Prisoner 320042, Hope, M. lay down and, much to his own surprise, promptly fell asleep.

24

Aldous toddled around the living room.

'Aren't you a clever little boy?' said Max's mum.

'I could do that at his age,' said Max.

'No, you were a late starter,' said Mum. 'Very late.'

'When does Juno get back?' asked Dad.

'Don't know,' said Max. 'She turns up for a day or two to see the kids, then goes off somewhere else in the world to mix with celebrities and the glitterati. She's in LA at the moment.'

'I don't approve of such gallivanting,' said Mum.

'Juno is a good mother,' said Max.

'Then she should be here,' said Mum.

'I can't say I like her paintings,' said Dad, 'but they do sell for crazy money. What's the one with the tits called?'

'*Tits*,' said Max.

'Yeah. You see that painting everywhere now. It's iconic.'

'Doesn't she invite you to her social engagements?' asked Mum.

'She knows I'm not interested in all that nonsense,' lied Max.

'You need to be careful, or you'll lose her,' said Dad. 'She might be banging someone successful right now. Did you sign a pre-nup?'

'Juno would never cheat on me,' said Max.

'Don't be so sure,' said Dad. 'Alpha women need alpha men.

She's hanging around good-looking rich guys. What do you think she sees when she comes back here and you're mooching around like a village idiot with dyed hair?'

'That's uncalled for,' said Mum.

As much as Max felt like ramming a pen into his dad's carotid artery, he knew he was making a valid point.

'I'm making a valid point,' said Dad. 'You're letting yourself be made a fool of by your own wife.'

'That's enough,' said Max firmly, to his dad.

The nanny was in the room. Max found her attractive and didn't want to lose face in front of her.

***

Max lay on the bed in his cell watching a star twinkling through the lantern skylight. He wondered how far away it was. One million miles? One hundred million miles? He felt overwhelmed with insignificance.

***

'Can I come out to LA?' asked Max.

'Why?' asked Juno, on the phone from LA.

'To see you.'

'You'd find it incredibly boring out here.'

'I've never been to LA. I could fly out tomorrow.'

'I have meetings all week.'

'What, twenty-four hours a day?'

'People work long hours out here. It's so competitive.'

'What are the meetings about?' asked Max.

'They want me to host a TV show about American art and culture. They like my acerbic English wit and natural eccentricity. They're offering a fuck-load of money and it'll be good for my career. I'm gonna be here for, like, longer than I planned.'

It grated Max that Juno already spoke with a slight American twang in her voice, although it did sound sexy on the phone.

'So you don't want me to come out?'

There was a long pause.

'How are the babies?' asked Juno.

'They're fine.'

'Put Aldous on the phone. I have some friends here who would like to hear him.'

'Friends? What friends?'

'Just friends,' sighed Juno.

'The kids are asleep. It's late here,' said Max.

'Oh yeah. I forgot about the time difference.'

Max could hear laughter in the background. Juno put her hand over the receiver and said something to someone.

'Juno? Juno?' asked Max.

'Darling, I have to go,' said Juno.

'I'm coming out there tomorrow.'

'There's nothing for you to do out here.'

'It's LA for fuck's sake,' said Max. 'I'll go to fucking Disneyland if you're too busy to spend five minutes with me.'

Juno sighed again.

'All right. I'll get my assistant to arrange a flight for you. Happy now?'

'I'm giddy with anticipation,' said Max.

***

He was angry to find Juno had only bought him a Premium Economy ticket. When he boarded the flight, they refused to upgrade him to First Class, so he got drunk and abusive.

'Do you know who I am?' he shouted at a steward.

When he landed at LAX, police escorted him off the plane and interrogated him for three hours.

Humid rain fell as Max finally pulled up in a taxi outside

Juno's rented Spanish-style villa in a fashionable Beverley Hills canyon.

A pall of orange smog hung over the city.

Max rang the bell four times. Juno finally answered the door holding a martini in her hand. She was slightly high on Xanax and dressed like a 1960s flower child.

'Not the best start, eh?' she said, raising one eyebrow contemptuously at Max's exhausted crumpled appearance.

Although she was alone, the house smelled of people.

That night, Juno tried to instigate sex, but Max pretended to have a bad back brought on by the cramped conditions of Premium Economy. She gave him a blow job instead. Max noticed she was more accomplished at it than before. She even sucked on his balls, but he didn't enjoy that. In fact, he found it disconcerting. He got the impression she'd been practicing this new technique on someone else.

The next morning dawned sunny and warm. Max sat by the villas pool, drinking a beer.

Juno spent most of the time on the phone to her manager, or organising her schedule with a personal assistant, Mia, a woman attractive enough to be a catwalk model.

A very camp clothes designer and his assistant arrived with a rail of dresses for Juno to try on. They also brought a tux for Max, because there was a gala awards ceremony Juno reluctantly agreed to take Max to later.

The designer and his assistant looked disapprovingly at Max with his beer and his pot belly.

'Is he with you?' the designer asked Juno.

***

Juno's limousine joined hundreds of identical limousines in a long winding queue which crawled towards an exhibition centre. Max wore the tux; Juno wore a horrible off-the-shoulder emerald satin dress. A hairdresser had made her hair into something resembling a 1970s afro. Juno said she loved it, but Max could tell she didn't.

'What's this ceremony for, anyway?' Max asked Juno.

'Not sure. I've been to so many of these things lately. What is this one?' Juno asked Mia, who sat opposite in a little black dress and resembled the women in Robert Palmer's *Addicted To Love* video.

Max felt intimidated by her.

'The Independent American Cultural Arts and Sciences Television Choice Pilot Season Spirit Gold Awards,' said Mia.

'Are you nominated for anything?' Max asked Juno.

'No. I'll just be walking down a red carpet,' said Juno. 'People will take my photo and I'll be asked simple questions by reporters. Stand near me and smile. And only speak if you're spoken to.'

'Don't worry, they won't speak to him,' said Mia.

'I'm an accessory,' muttered Max. 'Arm candy.'

'It's important Juno is seen at events like this,' said Mia to Max. 'It shows that she's somebody.'

'Isn't everybody somebody?' asked Max.

'Not necessarily,' said Mia, as she pinned a 24-carat diamond "END POVERTY NOW" badge to Juno's dress.

'Compassion porn,' laughed Juno at the badge. 'Virtue Viagra.'

'Remember not to smile,' said Mia. 'Smiling is so out right now. And don't say anything important. Keep answers short and trivial.'

The limousine stopped in front of the exhibition centre. The door opened and Juno stepped onto a red carpet. Max was about to follow, but Mia blocked his way with her arm and said 'Wait' while Juno was showered in a blitzkrieg of flashbulbs. He watched as Juno put one hand on her hip and manoeuvred herself into unsmiling poses.

'Okay, go,' said Mia to Max, once the flashes stopped.

He followed close behind Juno. They were shepherded like cattle into a roped lane. The B-list lane, Max noted. The recognisable people in the A-list lane received fawning praise from an over-eager cacophony of press and fans. The B-list lane was quieter. Max glanced at the C-list lane, where less good-looking people were being ignored.

'Smile for God's sake,' said Juno, smiling.

'Mia said not to smile,' said Max.

'No one smiles when posing. But we're on the red carpet now. Smile.'

'I wasn't aware of the complex smiling protocol,' said Max, smiling.

'Don't grin, you look insane,' said Juno.

Max attempted a better smile, which looked worse. He started sweating profusely and the collar on his shirt chafed.

'This feels ridiculous,' he said. 'Who dresses up at two o'clock in the afternoon?'

'People who are going places,' said Juno.

'So why does everyone look desperate?' asked Max.

'They're not desperate, they're ambitious,' said Juno.

'It looks glamorous on TV, but it's a meat market,' said Max.

'I told you you wouldn't like it here,' seethed Juno.

They were shunted along in front of a row of underwhelmed reporters who asked Juno inane questions. She responded with rehearsed bland answers about feminism and lack of diversity in the arts.

***

Max sat alone at a separate table in the prison refectory eating a meal of school dinner quality. Other inmates sat at a distance, glaring at him.

'Why are some allowed to wear civilian clothes?' he asked a warden.

'They haven't been convicted of anything yet,' said the warden.

***

'Do you think Nature marvels at human endeavour?' Boz addressed the crowd. 'No, it sees us as nothing more than a fungal infection.'

There was a murmur of discontent from those gathered, but Boz didn't care. He continued, 'What's more, one day Nature is going to find a cure for our resilience. As a species, we have forgotten that we are just guests on this planet, but we act like we're at home. Our collective egotism will lead to our downfall.'

Max stopped typing and sat back in the chair. Having recently returned from LA, he had ensconced himself in his writing shed in the garden.

Juno had introduced him to lots of "industry" people, but they were all shallow and awkward encounters. Max made no impression.

Juno rang home from LA most days. They talked briefly on the phone, but it was the nanny she wanted to speak to. The trip to LA had been a failure.

***

Max stood in the cold concrete exercise area under a slate grey sky. A few other prisoners milled around in small groups. He kept away from them. He'd been led to believe prisons were quite luxurious now, but this one was almost Dickensian in its austerity.

He began thinking about Juno, Aldous, Perdita and Willow. Dad, too.

Funerals took place where mourners refused to mention Max's name.

Max the unmentionable. Max the despised.

A well of sadness overcame him. But he didn't cry.

***

There was a large boggy patch in the back garden that never drained. It bothered Max. He kept staring at it.

An expensive gardener came once a week to upkeep the landscaped lawn and shrubbery, but attempts to improve the boggy area always made the problem worse.

Max put on a pair of Wellington boots, grabbed a shovel and started frenziedly digging out the bog.

'What are you doing?' asked the nanny, who brought Aldous out to watch.

'Digging a pond,' said Max.

'Is a pond wise with young children around?' asked the nanny.

Max stopped digging, annoyed at being interrupted.

'I'm doing it for them,' he said. 'They can learn about nature from it. It's no good wrapping children in cotton wool. Neither I or my sister ever drowned in the pond at home.'

The hole started filling up with muddy brown water. It reminded Max of the grave at Rex's funeral.

'You're sinking,' said the nanny.

***

'Have they set a date for the trial yet?' asked Max.

'No. Soon,' said Ched Hazzard, with a troubled look on his face.

'What's wrong?' asked Max.

'It's your sister. She's taken her own life.'

***

Juno was on a brief visit home to see the kids.

'What on earth is that monstrosity?' she said, looking out at the back garden.

'It's a pond. For the kids,' said Max.

'It's a muddy ditch,' said Juno.

'Give it time.'

'Christ, it looks like the Somme battlefield out there,' said Juno.

'Eventually, it will become a nature reserve just for them,' said Max.

'Mumumumum,' said Aldous, clinging to Juno's leg. 'Mummy,' Juno and the nanny looked delightedly at Aldous.

'That's his first word! He called me Mummy!'

'He called me Daddy yesterday,' lied Max.

'No he didn't,' said the nanny.

'Mumumumum,' repeated Aldous.

'It could mean anything,' said Max.

'Mum. Mum. Mum. Mummy,' said Aldous.

25

Max lay on the prison cell bed. The TV up on the wall mutely showed a cookery programme. Max had complained about the TV having no sound. When an inmate – an electrical expert – examined it, he said, 'There's a dry turd crammed into the speaker,'

Walker promised to replace the TV, but nothing had happened.

***

Max stood in a bunker on the sixth fairway of his local golf club. He was there because Deepak invited him for a round. Max bought golf shoes and a Pringle jumper especially. He'd never played golf before, and hacked at the ball in frustration, throwing up clouds of sand. The ball rolled back down every time with Sisyphean defiance.

Deepak marked off every shot Max took in a little book.

'You're hitting it all wrong,' Deepak kept saying, bemused by Max's ineptitude.

Shortly, when they were on the putting green, Deepak, lining up a putt, said casually,

'A strange incident happened at the hospital recently. Some imposter dressed as a doctor tried to treat a seriously ill patient.'

'Oh?' said Max, with flushing cheeks.

'Yes. It's a criminal offence, you know,' said Deepak.

'No doubt,' said Max.

'Dangerous, too. What sort of sad idiot does that?' said Deepak.

'The mind boggles,' said Max.

'They have extra security now, so it can't happen again,' said Deepak, as he found the perfect line into the hole.

You know it was me, thought Max. *That's why you invited me to play golf. To warn me.*

Max took ages lining up his own putt, but it ended further away from the hole.

'Max, can I be honest with you?' asked Deepak.

'Sure,' said Max, cautiously.

'You suck at golf,' said Deepak.

***

An episode of *Murder She Wrote* silently played on the TV now. That silly old cow Jessica Fletcher was sticking her nose into someone else's business, as usual. Why didn't the murderers kill her first?

***

Max sat in a pub with Margot, who'd split up acrimoniously with her latest girlfriend and suddenly needed Max as a shoulder to cry on. She drank gin, which only made her more maudlin.

'Max, life is a giant fucking nightmare, you know?' she said. 'It's a complete shit-storm. We're all trapped in a nightmare, and we're all trying to wake up. How can we enjoy ourselves with the knowledge we have of the Holocaust, the wars, the terrorism, the genocides and senseless destruction we cause? We're sick.'

'I'm listening the shit out of this,' said Max.

Eye shadow tears streaked Margot's cheeks.

'We should be ashamed, Max. Who the hell do we think we are as a species? I feel such guilt. We all feel it, but we don't acknowledge it. It's fundamental collective guilt for the crimes we've perpetuated

226

throughout history. The crimes are still happening right now, faster and more intensely all over the world. It will get worse in the future. The relentless conflict. The collateral damage incurred in making this great human project, this ugly arse crack of human endeavour. We all have blood on our hands. Literal and symbolic blood. Blood of nations. Blood of whole races. Blood of entire species. That's the underlying trauma inside us, the uncomfortable truth, the root of our problems. That's where despair and depression come from. It's guilt.

I lie awake at night and the guilt overwhelms me. Is it any wonder so many choose to die? Is it any wonder we try to forget? We collude in a mass denial, while aware of the horror of how we reached this point, yet it doesn't stop us. It doesn't make the horror go away. It's always there. Time doesn't diminish it. We can try to ignore and dismiss the carnage and pass responsibility by saying it isn't done in our name, but it is, and we have the full glaring burden of self-awareness to constantly remind us. We're snared by the crimes we've committed, Max. Snared in the same cognitive delusion, yeah? There's no escape from it. We're all condemned. Our conscience won't let us get away with it. We are all guilty. We are all culpable. We are all evil. All of us selfishly continue the damage. All of us, without exception.'

Margot began sobbing and laughing at the same time.

'You must have really liked that girl,' said Max.

'The sex was fantastic,' blubbed Margot.

***

There was now a programme on the silent TV about people buying junk at car boot sales, then selling it at an auction, which seemed like a lesson in futility to Max.

***

'Me lub Mummy,' Aldous said repeatedly.

'You lub Daddy, too,' Juno said to Aldous.

227

Aldous shook his head.

'Me lub Mummy.'

'Isn't he adorable?' said Max, in a flat tone.

They were in the dining room at Max's mum and dad's house. Juno, Max, Aldous, Mum, Dad and Margot were all wearing party hats to celebrate Mum and Dad's wedding anniversary. Perdita and Willow crawled around on the floor.

Mum and Dad were impossible to buy presents for. Margot gave them book tokens. Max wanted to impress them.

'I bought you this,' he said, sliding a sheet of formal paper across the table to Dad.

Dad studied the writing on the paper.

'Are you fucking kidding?' he asked.

'What is it?' asked Mum.

'A double burial plot,' said Dad.

'Very expensive, too. And it's all yours,' said Max.

Margot stifled a laugh.

'Jesus, Maximillian,' said Mum.

'It's important to plan for the future,' said Max.

'I did tell him it was a rather macabre present, but he didn't listen, as usual,' said Juno.

'Me lub Mummy,' said Aldous.

***

Another cookery programme. This time, Z-list celebrities were doing the cooking rather than anonymous members of the public, although Max didn't recognise any of them.

***

Max's writing shed was full of spiders. The more he sprayed it with insecticide the more spiders appeared, as if they thrived on the stuff.

He started having a recurring nightmare where spider legs grew

228

out of his face instead of hairs. The long black hairy spider legs moved and twitched, and every time Max shaved them off, more instantly sprouted.

'Look out!' Max heard the nanny shout while he sprayed a corner of the shed with a particularly hardy arachnid infestation.

Max poked his head out of the door and saw Aldous standing at the edge of the pond, about to fall in. The nanny grabbed him.

'That pond is dangerous!' she scolded, more to Max than Aldous.

Aldous cried for his mummy, but she was in Morocco filming a new segment of her TV show about art.

The spiders seemed to be mocking Max. They were representative of all his frustrations in life.

He went into the garage, grabbed a hammer, then set about smashing the shed into thousands of pieces. It took hours. When he finished, the shed was nothing more than a large pile of matchsticks. He collapsed, exhausted.

Aldous stood nearby watching.

'You a stupid,' he said, pointing at his father.

***

Another programme about people buying junk at car boot sales, then selling it at auction. This time, Z-list celebrities were doing the buying, rather than anonymous members of the public, although Max didn't recognise any of them.

***

Max sat at his dining table, pushing spaghetti Bolognese around his plate which the nanny had cooked. She sat opposite him.

'Do you not like it?' she asked.

'It's fine,' said Max.

He felt under constant scrutiny from the nanny. She probably reported everything back to Juno. He always pretended to be busy around her.

'How's your novel going?' she asked.

Max wanted to tell her the truth; he sat in The Emporium jerking off to weird internet videos most of the day. The novel was stuck on page 122. The character of Boz was becoming stale and repetitive and Max feared another great juggernaut of disappointment and failure heading his way.

'Good,' he lied. 'All good.'

The nanny's name was Livia. She lived in a room above the garage. She was twenty, and Swedish, but spoke perfect English with only a trace of accent. Max noticed she dressed more formally when Juno was home, but usually walked around the house in only a T-shirt and shorts when Juno was away. Max liked to think Livia was sending out a signal to him. Although tempted, he didn't take the initiative in case he was wrong. Anyway, her boyfriend picked her up on a motorbike every so often. Sometimes, Max heard them screwing in her room. She made Max feel middle-aged, even though the age difference was just five years. He knew one day soon, she'd leave and he'd never see her again. He knew he would think about her a lot over the years, but she wouldn't think about him at all.

'You're very lucky,' said Livia.

'In what way?' asked Max.

'You have an easy life.'

'Oh?' said Max, slightly riled. 'You think this is easy?'

'Yes. Compared to most people. But you always look sad. Why?'

'It's none of your business,' said Max.

'It is my business. I care about your children,' said Livia.

'But you don't care about me,' said Max.

He immediately regretted the curious comment. He didn't know why he said it. It sounded like he blamed her for his sadness, which wasn't the case. It also came across as forced and self-pitying.

An uncomfortable silence followed.

Max started to inwardly panic, unsure whether to make a joke of it, or to try and back-track. The silence continued too long for either option to be viable.

'I'm not attracted to you,' said Livia, eventually.

'No, me neither,' said Max, absurdly.

Livia left the room to do some washing, and the subject wasn't brought up again.

***

There was a fabric softener advert on the silent TV in Max's cell. It featured a beautiful woman wandering through a flower meadow at sunset. For the briefest of moments, Max imagined himself in that meadow, with Claire walking towards him in silhouette, and she was smiling.

***

'Did anything happen between you and Livia while I was away?' Juno asked Max one night in bed.

'No. Why?' said Max, reading *Paradise Lost*.

'The two of you seem to be avoiding each other.'

'I hadn't noticed,' lied Max.

Juno turned onto her side and faced Max.

'I want to read your novel.'

'It's not ready.'

'I want to read what you've got so far.'

'Why? To check up on me?'

'I might be able to help you with it, or give you useful feedback.'

'Thank you, but I don't need feedback,' said Max.

'Well, how much longer will it take? Mud and Fud keep questioning me about it. They don't think you're writing anything at all.'

'I couldn't give a fuck what they think,' snapped Max.

'Well you should!' said Juno, turning away from him. 'You should utilise your plentiful free time more usefully. Get qualifications, or volunteer for a charity, or something.'

'Fuck this,' said Max.

He got out of bed, threw some clothes on and left the house.

He drove aimlessly for a while, until chancing upon a dogging hotspot in a country lane car park, where he watched ugly couples having sex in Volvo's. The suspicious eyes of masturbating perverts clocked him nervously in the dark, their faces half-lit by headlamps. When a woman asked Max if he wanted a 'spunky tit wank', he made his excuses and left.

Max's phone beeped with a message from Juno.

'Sorry, darling. Please come home,' it read.

Max drove home, but when he went up to the bedroom, Juno was fast asleep and snoring.

***

Max switched off the TV. He sat up. There was a foul stench coming from the toilet next to the bed. Several times a day an effluvium of extreme potency emanated from it, filling the small cell with a funk like rotten eggs. Max kept complaining to Walker about it, but to no effect, and he suspected they were trying to break his spirit.

Max's nose began to bleed. It happened the day before, too. He secretly hoped a fatal brain haemorrhage would carry him off quickly and fairly painlessly. But after a short while it stopped.

His books were piled up in a corner, un-looked at since his arrival. He noticed one he didn't recognise, so picked it up. It was nicely bound and the cover had a shadowy cracked-glass design.

Slush Pile, by Max Hope.

Max's hands slightly trembled. He opened the cover. A post-it note stuck inside had *'I promised to give you this – Lee'* written on it.

Printed on the flyleaf page, a dedication read: *For Juno, Aldous, Perdita and Willow, nymphs in my orisons.*

He flicked to a random end-of-chapter page.

Boz stood on the mountaintop with a feeling of triumph. He had made it to the summit, or so he thought. But when he looked into the distance all he saw was bigger and higher mountains stretching to the horizon.

Tears began to roll down his cheeks, but crystallised as they reached his beard.

'All for nothing,' he cried. 'All for nothing.'

Drops of blood blotted onto the page.

Max blacked out.

26

Max was rushed to the prison infirmary. He spent the night lapsing in and out of consciousness while haemorrhaging copious amounts of blood. The doctor said he should go to hospital as his condition could turn critical, but resources were stretched due to a terrorist incident, so the doctor monitored him there.

Some sort of quantum leap happened in Max's brain that night. The landscape of the next few years of his life, into his thirties, unfolded before him like in a hall of mirrors. Most of it ached with dullness and predictability; he saw himself enduring interminable evenings with so-called friends and associates of Juno. Max had no friends of his own. His life diminished in small increments of social awkwardness. He became "Juno's husband"; a nondescript kind of entity. The flame which burned inside him struggled to stay alight.

A recurring theme at social engagements involved inquisitive people being initially intrigued by meeting a novelist. But Max's guarded facade of mystery rapidly crumbled under interrogation. His vague answers caused suspicion. Juno always stepped in to try and rescue him by saying how talented a writer he was, and how he was on the verge of major success, but it only served to make Max look and feel like a fraud.

He began to withdraw from life in general. Everyone else seemed so busy and successful with proper careers and full lives. Max couldn't reconcile his "otherness". He hated small talk, and he disagreed with Juno's friends' political opinions, but he resolved to give nothing of himself away. This in turn made people think him aloof, or shy (or plain rude), and he usually spent evenings silently staring out of his host's windows, which Juno found embarrassing.

'Don't come in future,' she said to him in a taxi home one night.

They stopped having sex by unsaid mutual agreement. Juno bought him a moorland green 1963 Bentley Continental as compensation, not that he had anywhere to go in it.

Juno's series on art was shown on TV. The American producers made her exaggerate her English accent and her eccentric fashion sense so she came across as a rude upper-class snob, a fashionable conceit for US/British relations at the time. The show got recommissioned. Juno was in the ascendant. Max floundered. He kept reminding himself to be grateful for his good fortune. To moan about such a privileged life seemed churlish.

'I opened two beautiful gifts this morning – my eyes,' he often said.

But it wasn't good enough. There was something missing in him that others seemed to have.

One day, Max saved Aldous from drowning in the garden pond. Aldous was six at the time. He found him floating face down, but managed to get him breathing again. Max had never been so scared. As soon as the boy spluttered water out of his lungs, Max reflexively smacked him.

Aldous screamed and ran next door to Shilpa.

The nanny was out with Perdita and Willow. Juno was in LA.

Moments later, Shilpa brought a cowering Aldous back.

'He's soaking wet. He said you hit him,' she said.

'I saved him from drowning. I hit him to get all the water out.'

'Daddy hates me!' cried Aldous. 'I want Mummy!'

Aldous rang his mother. Juno gave Max a trans-Atlantic bollocking.

'Would you rather he drowned?' Max responded.

235

'Fill in that fucking pond!' replied Juno.

Max tried to bond with his son. He sat with him the next day watching episodes of Aldous' favourite cartoon, about a pig that enjoyed eating ham, or something, but Max found it mind-numbingly tedious.

'This is utter crap, Aldous,' said Max. 'It's childish crap.'

'I'm six,' replied Aldous, indignantly. 'This is a programme for 4-8 year olds, so I fit its age demographic perfectly.'

'Where did you learn the word "demographic"?' asked Max.

'I'm intelligent,' said Aldous. 'Like Mummy.'

Another time, he caught Aldous impaling insects onto a rose bush.

'Don't do that. It's cruel,' said Max.

'Suck my bum hole,' said Aldous.

Max kneeled down next to Aldous and calmly said,

'Let me tell you something, little man – if you talk to me like that one more time, I'm going to impale your hamster on this bush. That would not be nice, would it?'

'No,' said Aldous, his lip quivering and his eyes filling with tears.

'So, apologise to me,' said Max.

Aldous thought for a long moment.

'Sorry,' he mumbled.

'Sorry, what?'

'Sorry, Daddy.'

'That's better.'

Max and Juno had a big argument later that day. Accusations they both later regretted flew backwards and forwards. Juno said Max was a cold and unemotional father, and that Aldous was scared of him. Max said that if they weren't careful, Aldous would grow up to be a snivelling entitled little prick.

'That's your son you're talking about!' shouted Juno. 'He told me you threatened to kill his hamster.'

'The boy was rude to me. He needs discipline,' said Max.

'You sound like your father,' replied Juno.

Max tried to book another session with Lee, but she had moved away and changed her number.

The writing of the novel slowed to a snail's pace. Max's sedentary lifestyle and increased alcohol and junk food intake made his pot belly swell, which made him more self-conscious. His confidence shattered.

After thirty, he started cutting his own hair to avoid the chit-chat of barbers. His hairline began to recede, so he took expensive dietary supplements which promised rapid hair follicle regrowth, but a news report said they caused cancer and were no better than placebos.

Max attempted to nurture a love of literature in his children. On their birthdays, instead of toys, he bought them works by writers such as Nabokov, and Meyrink. It became an odd family ritual which they learned to put up with. Aldous defaced most of his books with erect penis drawings, or he would deliberately lose them.

Max read Huysmans' *Against Nature*, and Proust's *Á la recherche du temps perdu* to Perdita and Willow as bedtime stories. The girls pretended to fall sleep, hoping he'd go away. Max realised this, but persisted with it out of bloody-mindedness.

'Try *Wind in the Willows*, or *Alice in Wonderland* like normal people,' advised Juno.

Livia, the nanny, announced out of the blue one morning that she was leaving to travel around India on a motorbike with a new guy she'd hooked up with. She loved the children, she said, but she had to follow her heart. So she left. The children were upset. Max was, too. He still harboured vague fantasies of having an affair with her, despite her lack of interest in him. He dressed in preppy smart/casual clothes, thinking it might make him more attractive to her, but when he saw a photo of her boyfriend, (grungy with a bushy lumberjack beard and long tangled scruffy hair), Max realised he'd been wasting his time.

Juno, from America, organised a new nanny. A large matronly woman of late middle age, called Miss Cronk, arrived in a formal grey uniform.

She took a very dim view of Max immediately.

'You've never cooked or cleaned for them?' asked Miss Cronk.

'I'm quite a hands-off father,' said Max.

'Sounds like an evasion of responsibility,' said Miss Cronk.

'Hey, I get them excellent take-out food from local restaurants.' said Max 'And I've learnt how to use the washing machine. Well, Aldous taught me how to use the washing machine.'

The children were growing up fast, (and were very independent for their ages) so Miss Cronk spent time instilling discipline in Max. He became more domesticated. He vacuumed. He made sure bills were paid. He found he enjoyed going to the supermarket to buy groceries.

He mowed the lawn once a week, because he wasn't happy with the way the gardener did it in horizontal strips.

Max started taking Perdita and Willow to junior school. It gave him a new sense of worth. Then he'd drop Aldous off at middle school and return to an eerily empty house.

Safety in the sanctuary of his own company resulted in a short-lived contentedness. His life felt wrong. It was boring. Emasculating. Undemanding. He could feel life passing him by.

Max teetered on the edge of dangerous loneliness. He wandered the house in just a vest and boxer shorts, and didn't bother to shave or bathe for days at a time. He watched TV news all day, a continuum of repetitive depressing carnage. War relentlessly raged somewhere. UN personnel had been killed in a bombing raid. Terrorists had murdered dozens of holiday-makers somewhere. Phone footage of blood-smeared people running down a street. Politicians made impassioned speeches condemning the atrocities. Vows of solidarity. The usual rhetoric.

Max sat on Perdita's bed one afternoon when he was home alone. Like Willow, the pictures of Disney characters on her walls had been replaced with pictures of guinea pigs and horses. Before long, they would be replaced with pictures of pretty boys from pop groups, then douchebag actors and rappers, until they too would be deemed embarrassingly out of date and finally replaced with blank space.

It only seemed like a few months since the kids were in nursery school. Aldous played a sheep in one ultra-liberal non-denominational nativity. He was wrapped in cotton wool and his face was painted black, which one parent complained was racist. When all the children were handed lit candles, Juno became very agitated – flashbacks of Rex turning into a fireball. She almost jumped onto the stage, but Max stopped her.

Afterwards, a teacher assured them the cotton wool had been sprayed with flame retardant, but Aldous said the teacher was lying.

Max felt a chill of panic at the relentless speed of life. Summer always went so quickly, yet winter went on and on. Was it nearly Christmas again already? The kids were busily developing personalities and networks of noisy friends. They rushed off to endless birthday parties and outings to one place or another in monitored social whirls. The two girls were chatty social butterflies like their mother, while Aldous was brooding and serious and interested in grime music, fast cars and ultraviolent computer games.

Both sets of grandparents showered the kids with presents in an almost competitive fashion, which annoyed Max. The attic was a time-line of their childhood represented in discarded toys.

A vast range of hamsters, rabbits and goldfish lived and died in a blur of short blameless enslavement, all for his children's folly.

Similarly, Margot managed to get through an array of girlfriends. She introduced Max to the first few, who were always 'The One', but next he would hear they had split up and Margot blamed herself every time because she wasn't sure if she was a lesbian, or bisexual, or maybe even asexual. It was a recurring problem with her.

Max got the impression Margot regretted getting sterilised. She made lots of broody enquiries about adopting a child from Cambodia.

Margot was a good aunt. She'd show up (unannounced) with gifts for the kids every now and then, and they liked her. She took them to the zoo once, but a monkey threw shit through the bars of its cage at them, making Willow cry hysterically. The episode knocked Margot's confidence. She never took them on trips again.

Max wished he could see Margot more often, but she lived her own life. She went through a phase of risky casual sex with people she met online. When Max tried to intervene, Margot put up a wall of silence and a long period of disconnection happened between them.

Time passed. Neighbours came and went. Everyone kept to themselves.

There were no more barbeques, or invitations to other people's houses. The idea seemed a quaint bygone relic. Avoidance became the norm. No one bothered to know each other's names any more. Impersonal nods of recognition when putting the dustbins out were the only form of social nicety that remained. People were more guarded. Distrustful. Private. It was a microcosm of the fractured new landscape of social cohesion.

It's like a collective autism of society, Max thought to himself.

Around that time, Shilpa got run over at a zebra crossing and had her right leg amputated. She became a recluse. Deepak tried to get her to walk with a prosthetic leg, but she didn't take to it.

Max noticed Shilpa and Deepak aged quickly from then on.

Claire still occasionally fluttered through his mind. He kept expecting to bump into her at the school gates, or see her out shopping, and he rehearsed various witty off-the-cuff things he'd say to her. But it never happened. Some days she didn't cross his mind at all.

Juno's TV show was cancelled after two series, and her contract wasn't renewed. She tried to put a brave face on it by saying she was glad she didn't have to do all that awful travelling anymore and she preferred to make art rather than talk about art. But Max found her in her studio one afternoon crying in front of a blank canvas.

After a few months of being a devoted wife and mother, Juno became restless and yearned to escape back to the world of celebrity. However, when she emailed her showbiz friends in LA, none replied.

Mud and Fud pressurised Juno into sending Aldous away to a vastly expensive private school where it was hoped his education and attitude would improve. Aldous vehemently opposed the idea at first, but soon thrived. He started as a day pupil, then only came home at weekends, then only every second weekend, by choice.

Perdita and Willow soon followed him.

Max missed them sometimes, but when they came back, the house would fill with discord and he was glad when they went away again.

Max and Juno received outraged criticism from people they considered friends about how appalling it was to board their kids at private school, and how they could never do the same to their kids as it was a barbaric and elitist system, tantamount to child abuse.

Max told them all to get a fucking grip.

His novel progressed in increments. He went through periods of hating it, like a millstone around his neck, but he persevered and reminded himself of the future masterpiece it would become. He'd show all those bastards who mocked and doubted him. The book needed to be written.

The world needed it.

He sent the first three chapters to ten literary agents, along with a carefully written synopsis and introductory letter. Eight never replied. Two sent standard rejections months later.

***

Max opened his eyes. He lay in a bed in the prison infirmary. It took several minutes until he moved his stiff body.

A doctor approached.

'Oh. You're alive,' said the doctor.

'I want a second opinion,' said Max, groggily.

27

Max was doing yoga stretches on the prison infirmary floor.

'You need to rest,' said the doctor.

'Rest?' said Max. 'I've been unconscious for three days.'

'Aren't you mentally exhausted?' said the doctor. 'A lot of restless brain activity took place.'

'I'm not tired at all,' yawned Max.

'You had a visitor,' said the doctor.

Please be Claire. Please be Claire. Please be Claire.

'Who?' asked Max.

'A weird little guy. Said he was your lawyer.'

'Oh, him,' said Max, disappointed.

'A woman visited you too.'

Please be Claire. Please be Claire. Please be Claire.

'Who?' asked Max.

'She said she was your psychiatrist.'

'Oh, her,' said Max, disappointed again.

'You should be in hospital, you know?'

'No, I like it here,' said Max. 'I'm buzzing. My memory is returning.'

'We'll keep an eye on you,' said the doctor.

'If you insist,' said Max.

The doctor didn't move.

'Why did you do it?' he asked.

'Excuse me?' asked Max.

'Why did you kill your family? You killed them in cold blood. I was a fan of your wife's TV show. Were you jealous of her? Why did you have to kill the kids too? It doesn't make sense. I have a young family myself. How could you do such a thing?'

'You can go now,' said Max.

The doctor hesitated, then left, locking the door behind him.

Max sat and stared at dappled light on the wall.

***

He found himself sitting under a parasol on a beach staring out at the sparkling Mediterranean sea. He hated beaches. The heat and the sand made him feel unclean.

The kids loved the beach. Juno did too. She lay in the sun in a damp one-piece bikini with wet sand in her hair, texting. The kids were in the surf, splashing around.

'Why don't you have a swim with Aldous?' suggested Juno.

'There are probably sharks in there,' said Max.

Juno looked at Max. He was fully clothed, with Camus' *The Outsider* in his hand.

'Please,' she said.

Max sighed, then mechanically took off his shirt.

'It's obvious who wears the trousers around here,' he said, taking off his trousers.

'Get some vitamin D on that body,' smiled Juno.

'I'll burn.'

'Put some lotion on.'

'No. I'll sizzle,' said Max.

'Please yourself.'

Max stepped out from under the parasol. His skin shrivelled at the heat. He grimaced. The sand was almost molten. He tiptoed towards the sea, self-conscious of his tight trunks and pale untoned body.

'Fucking hell,' he muttered several times.

'Everyone's looking at you!' teased Juno.

Max looked back at her and did a bodybuilder pose, which made her laugh.

'Daddy!' said Perdita and Willow, playfully splashing him with water.

Max pretended to enjoy it, but he didn't. He wished he was in a bar on his own drinking a cold beer.

'Hey, Aldous, I'll give you 20 euros if you can beat me to that buoy,' said Max, pointing to a buoy about one hundred metres out.

'There are sharks,' said Aldous, sitting on a lilo.

'No there aren't,' said Max, nervously scanning the water.

'We'll do it!' squealed the two girls.

'The offer is only open to Aldous,' said Max.

'That's not fair,' said Perdita.

'It's sexist,' said Willow.

'50 euros,' said Max to Aldous.

'All right. When?' asked Aldous.

'Now,' said Max, diving into the surf.

He swam at full throttle, determined to beat Aldous. It took about two minutes for him to reach the buoy. He clung to it, out of breath, then looked back to see how far behind Aldous was.

Aldous still sat on the lilo, splashing around with his sisters. He hadn't even bothered.

'For fuck's sake,' said Max.

Max wanted to get back to shore. Something about the ocean creeped him out. A primal fear. A feeling of unease. You were vulnerable in the sea. It was a deceivingly dangerous and alien place.

The inviting swimming pool blue went about fifty metres out, then it deepened into an ink blue. Max hadn't noticed this from the beach, which now looked quite far away. Doubts began to form whether he could make it back. He'd have to swim against the current, and he already felt tired.

He pushed away from the buoy and began to head back. He

swam twenty metres, then something bumped against his leg. Max froze.

He felt simultaneously hot and cold and dizzy with terror. What the fuck was it? A bump, or a bite? Was the leg already gone? He tried to call out, but his throat constricted. His arms flailed numbly and he began to lose buoyancy. Salt water stung his eyes and filled his mouth.

His heart raced. A shark! A shark!

Christ, the sky was such a beautiful and vivid cerulean. People were relaxing on the golden sandy beach. His children and his wife were so close, but taking no notice of him.

Max suddenly regretted not being a better husband, father and son. He had failed his family, and failed himself. Death by shark was his forfeit.

In those frantic seconds he made a vow: if he lived he would embrace his family with love, and promised to be a kinder person generally. He didn't want to be eaten. Or drown. Or drown while being eaten. Punch the fucker. Gouge out its black doll's eyes. Kick the cunt's gills.

Max pushed on forward, expecting to be dragged under and to feel serrated teeth slicing through his flesh; water turning red, a painful dull crunching of bones, and then nothing for eternity.

An image flickered through his mind of his mum answering the phone at home and reacting to the news of his violent death.

The surf came into sight, but a strange calm came over him. Let go. Surrender. Nothing to fear. Escape into the warm welcoming arms of death. Max accepted the invitation. He stopped struggling.

Another bather, seeing Max's distress, dragged him onto the beach.

A crowd gathered. Max glanced at his legs – no damage. He vomited. Perdita and Willow stood nearby, crying. Aldous watched, concerned.

Juno fell to her knees next to Max.

'What happened?' she asked in a panic.

'A shark bumped against my leg,' gasped Max.

'There are no sharks in these waters,' someone said. 'It was a jellyfish, or a piece of junk. Maybe a refugee corpse. Lots get washed up here.'

Max sat on the hot sand, shivering and feeling foolish.

That night at a restaurant, Max and Aldous watched Juno dancing with Perdita and Willow.

'I think it was a shark, Dad,' said Aldous.

'Thank you,' said Max.

Aldous was becoming a handsome young man.

Juno indicated for Max and Aldous to join them on the dance floor, but both shook their heads.

'Boring,' shouted Juno, who continued dancing with the girls.

'Do you ever get bullied at school?' Max asked Aldous.

'No.'

'You'd tell me if you did, wouldn't you? You never tell me anything about school.'

'You never ask,' said Aldous.

'Do you want to go to a rugby match when we get home?'

'I don't like rugby. I prefer football.'

'Okay, a football match, then,' said Max.

'Sure,' said Aldous.

A recurring nightmare about drowning in dark water plagued Max for the rest of the holiday. He didn't even go into the hotel swimming pool from then on.

When they got home, a fragile vulnerability hung around him, but he didn't like to acknowledge it.

Max took Aldous to a football match. Before it began, announcements were made advocating respect and equality and tolerance, but as soon as the game started the opposing sets of supporters shouted venomous abuse towards each other, and sang insulting songs with a thuggish tribal gloating.

Max joined in the volleys of hate by loudly calling the referee a cunt several times, but only to fit in. He couldn't really see the point of caring deeply about something so arbitrary. In fact, he struggled to see much point in anything. What compulsion drove people to such illogical fanaticism?

Aldous didn't enjoy the game either. And their team lost 4-0.

Juno flew to Australia to be a contestant in a TV reality show where celebrities had to survive in a jungle for three weeks.

'What's the concept?' Max asked Juno before she left.

'We're given basic rations and have to avoid cannibalism,' said Juno.

'For entertainment purposes?' asked Max.

'My manager says it will boost my profile.'

When Juno got there, they told her she was only a stand-by, in case another celebrity pulled out, which they didn't, so she spent all her time in a hotel room binge-eating and she returned home four stone heavier. The irony was lost on no one.

Unfortunately, she kept on pigging out and put on more weight. Max privately felt ashamed of Juno's new appearance, but he said nothing. She was obviously unhappy. Since the huge success of *Tits,* her art had failed to maintain popular momentum.

Max's pot belly grew larger too, which he hated, although Juno said it suited him. She painted it, with the title *Spare Tyre.* It didn't sell.

Max felt guilty for everything. He'd held Juno back with his social awkwardness. He wanted to spill out his angst to Lee, but couldn't, so he kept it bottled up inside.

On a whim, Max hired a private detective to look for Claire. He met the shifty-looking guy in a café.

'Why do you want to track her down?' asked the private dick.

'Is it important?' asked Max.

'I need to make sure you're not a deranged stalker.'

'Just find her,' said Max. 'Take some photos. I want to know if she's married, or has kids, okay? That's all.'

A week later he met the detective again.

'I couldn't find anything,' he said. 'She's not on any electoral register. I drew a blank.'

'You didn't try hard enough,' said Max.

'She's the first person I've ever failed to find,' said the dick. 'I feel like I've been on a wild goose chase.'

Max paid the guy, then dismissed him.

Shortly afterwards, Max began to suffer intense migraines. One was so bad he temporarily lost his sight. Certain it was a brain tumour, he put off having a scan. He wanted to die.

Max went through periods of fear, anger, denial, sadness, regret, but struggled with acceptance.

Anticipating death, he wrote long friendly letters to Aldous, Perdita and Willow at their school, ending them with, 'Love, dad.'

Juno noticed a mellowness in him, and observed that TV charity adverts made his eyes well with tears every time they came on.

When she asked if he was okay, he'd wipe his eyes and say,

'Those poor people.'

Eventually, he plucked up the courage to have a brain scan.

The result revealed it wasn't a tumour, but a lesion from his childhood bike accident. The doctor told him to take it easy, and do nothing extreme like bungee jumping or deep-sea diving, otherwise it could rupture and cause a haemorrhage.

Max felt relieved. His self-imposed death sentence had been revoked, albeit temporarily.

***

Click, click, click.

'Max?' asked Ched Hazzard, clicking his fingers in Max's face.

Max blinked back into the prison infirmary.

'Oh, it's you,' said Max.

'The prisoner is to be taken back to his cell,' said a guard.

'He doesn't look well to me,' said Ched Hazzard.

'The doctor signed him off,' said the guard.

'I'm remembering so much,' said Max.

'Good. That's good,' said Ched Hazzard.

'I couldn't have killed them, though,' said Max. 'I loved my family. They've got the wrong person.'

'They've set a date for the trial. It begins in two weeks,' said Ched Hazzard.

'Well, that's something,' said Max.

Max showered, dressed, and returned to his cell. It seemed smaller than before. Colder. Lonelier. The light rapidly faded outside. His books were still stacked in a corner, *Slush Pile* on top.

Max stared at the book, but didn't pick it up. What horrors of literary banality lay within its pages? Thousands of unread words. Hundreds of hours spent birthing its unloved and unwanted text.

What a waste of a life. A fool's errand. Mrs McCabe predicted it. His dad predicted it. Everyone predicted it.

What pleasure am I to derive from life now? he thought. *I'll never be free. I'm to be surrounded by inhospitable sterile cold walls, with people who wish to do me harm. I wish a shark had killed me that day. My family would still be alive.*

He pondered for a moment over the veracity of his memories. How accurate were they? Memories are generally unreliable. Didn't Lee tell him that? Or did Claire? How much could he trust? How much could he trust himself?

28

Max woke up at 2am. His circadian rhythm was out of sync. He lay still for a while, watching blobs of colour appear and disappear in the darkness of his cell.

Stomach cramps alerted him to an imminent faecal impaction. He drew an intake of breath, then manoeuvred his bare buttocks onto the cold stainless-steel toilet by his bed. He waited.

Nothing happened. His stomach was distended with methane. Max pushed and strained, but a pain shot through his heart, so he stopped.

Evelyn Waugh and Elvis died on the toilet, thought Max. *I'd be in distinguished company.*

Shit. Piss. Vomit. Stomach acid. Bile. Mucus. Phlegm. Blood. Semen.

We are such stuff as dreams are made on.

He switched the TV on with a remote, but the signal had been lost. An angry interference flickered across the screen; the supposed electrical microwaves created by the Big Bang. Or something.

The toilet seat grew warm. Max remained on it, staring emptily at the monochromatic fuzzy glow.

***

Shortly after his thirty-fifth birthday, in the grip of an early middle-aged crisis, Max searched online for discreet female companionship.

He surfed dubious dating websites full of people asking for very odd and quite dangerous perversions to be done to them. Max considered some tempting, but fear prevented him enquiring.

He looked at escort classifieds and was surprised by how many "sex-workers" there were in the local area. Every photo featured women in come-hither poses, wearing tight Basques and assorted cliché fetish clothing. (A disturbing number were dressed as schoolgirls.)

They all accepted "contributions" or "tributes" for "appointments", but the terminology couldn't disguise the often-desperate nature of their business. Max didn't like to judge.

He deliberated whether he wanted to contribute to such an exploitative industry. He had morals.

So fucking what? Life is short.

But it's like cheating.

So? Juno cheated on me, probably.

But it's ethically wrong.

Fuck you, you spineless liberal hypocrite.

Max was attracted to the no-commitment, no-consequences empty nature such interactions afforded. The fake names. The secrecy. The potential danger. Everyone did it to some extent. Prostitution was a continuous background hum.

Max found a website of "natural girl-next-door" types who offered a "girlfriend experience" option, which involved kissing and cuddling, followed by a mutual shower, then a massage with a "happy ending". Max loved the creative euphemisms.

He smiled at their faux-innocence. It turned him on and appalled him in equal measure. He tried to justify his new compulsion as potential research for the novel. Boz could develop a predilection for such odd behaviour.

A huge furtive twilit subculture happened 24/7 in plain sight amidst the respectable façade of society. It ignited an impulse of risk inside Max.

It had been a while since he'd had sex. He'd never considered himself particularly good at it, or even enjoyed it very much. Most of the time he didn't miss sex, but he felt it important to prove to himself that he was still capably virile.

Max chose three potentials. One was called Crystal. The second was called Jasmine. All the prostitutes used pseudonyms like Crystal or Jasmine. None of them were called Susan or Doreen.

He texted them both (he didn't want to have an awkward chat on their mobile phones), but their replies were brisk, tarty, and full of terrible grammar, plus they wanted a deposit via credit card, which Max considered suspicious.

Number three, called Harper, looked pretty in her photo, with bright blue eyes. She politely replied to say she was available the next day at noon for the price Max wanted. She lived at a discreet address in Earls Court. Max booked an appointment under the name "James".

He then tried to put it out of his mind, as experience taught him that over-thinking created anticipation which always ended in disappointment. Reality never lived up to fantasy.

The next morning, Max showered, trimmed his pubic hair (a modish gesture of courtesy), then drove to Harper's address in a surprisingly smart leafy road.

He parked the Bentley at a short distance and waited until the allotted time. It was an unseasonably warm sunny day. Lots of people were out and about doing nothing in particular. Max wore a baseball cap as a disguise, and pretended to be conversing on his phone when anyone passed by.

(Anxiety. The thought of being unable to achieve an erection).

He switched on the radio. The news said sixty percent of all animal species would be extinct within twenty years due to increased human activity. The numbers were dropping alarmingly.

'What a lovely species we are,' Max muttered to himself. 'The paragon of animals, indeed.'

(He wasn't even in the mood for sex. He wanted to go home and avoid the potential humiliation of impotence.)

He removed his wedding ring and put it in his pocket.

(Was Harper even real? Was he being lured to his death by a murderer? Was a violent pimp waiting inside to rob him?)

Max started the engine. Then switched it off.

'Stop catastrophising,' he muttered. 'Whatever happens, happens. If I wasn't here, I'd be bored. I yearn to live in the moment.'

Moments later, Max approached Harper's apartment block. It was set back from the road behind well-maintained gardens and security gates, but they were open. He walked through to its entrance portico.

He texted Harper: *It's James. I'm outside. What number?*'

She immediately texted back: *'7.'*

Max pressed 7 on the front door intercom. The door buzzed and he went inside, then up two flights of stairs. Feelings of dread filled him, but a rush of adrenaline mixed with curiosity compelled him forward.

He couldn't believe a call girl worked in such a genteel, eerily quiet, building.

The door to apartment 7 was ajar. Before Max could knock, Harper opened it. She was pretty, in her twenties, with bright blue eyes, like in her photo. She smiled and indicated for him to be silent, then she ushered him inside and closed the door.

'Hi,' whispered Max.

'I have to be careful of my nosy neighbours,' whispered Harper.

She wore a negligee-type dress, which displayed a slim, slight figure.

A corridor led off into a large gloomy apartment, but Harper pointed to the first room on the left. The curtains were drawn. A futon draped in colourful silk sheets and cushions was on the floor. Harper went inside.

Max followed her.

'It's a hundred for one hour,' she said.

Max handed her the cash.

Harper put the money into a locked drawer, then she opened a laptop computer. A business-like spreadsheet appeared on its screen, which Harper updated with the added £100.

'Take your jacket and shoes off, please,' she said.

Max sat on a stool in the corner and obediently did so.

Harper switched on some strange Arabic music, then lit an incense stick (Max hated incense, but said nothing) and sat on the futon.

She looked at Max. He felt like a gauche teenager.

'So, James, what can I do for you?' said Harper, in an unusually old-fashioned cut-glass English received pronunciation sexy purr, which occasionally betrayed a European inflection.

'Um… not sure,' said Max, with a nervous laugh.

'I don't do full intercourse, or anal, although I don't mind fucking you with a strap-on,' said Harper. 'What do you like doing?'

'I'm kind of new to this,' said Max, inwardly cringing.

'You're a virgin?' asked Harper.

'No. Not at all,' said Max, his throat suddenly bone dry.

'Sit here with me,' said Harper, patting the futon.

Max moved and sat awkwardly on the edge of the futon. Even though he considered Harper very attractive, his penis shrivelled. He became self-conscious about his breath smelling, and he'd forgotten to bring mints. He desperately wanted to fart.

'Unusually warm weather for the time of year,' said Max, initiating pitiful small talk.

'You're very tense, aren't you?' said Harper. 'There's no need. I'm not going to bite. Unless you like biting?'

They both smiled, then Harper massaged Max's shoulders.

'You're good at that,' said Max. 'Did you train?'

'Take off your shirt, please,' said Harper.

Max did as he was told. She continued massaging him, then said, 'Would you like me to kiss you?'

255

'Sure,' said Max.

They kissed. It had been a long time since he'd passionately kissed a woman. He enjoyed it. His penis stirred.

Harper told him to lie down, then she undid his trousers, slowly pulled down his (fresh) boxer shorts, and initiated oral sex.

'Are you enjoying this?' she slurped.

'Very much indeed, thank you,' said Max.

'It's my best talent, according to my boyfriend.'

'Your boyfriend?' said Max, sitting up.

'Relax, he's away on business,' said Harper, switching to hand relief.

'Does he know you do this?'

'Yes. He likes me earning my own money. I do too. It's empowering. Besides, I have overheads. I need to earn so much a week just to pay my mother's mortgage back home.'

'Where is back home?' asked Max.

'France.'

'How come you speak the way you do?'

'Promise you won't laugh,' said Harper.

'Try me.'

'There's an old British movie called Brief Encounter, and it starred an actress called Celia Johnson. It's always been my favourite film.'

'I've seen it. Trevor Howard's in it too,' said Max.

'Yes!' squealed Harper. 'They fall in love and have a chaste affair. It's so romantic. We live in such unromantic times.'

'I agree,' said Max, noticing his penis becoming flaccid in her hand.

'It was the only film in English I watched growing up,' said Harper. 'I presumed everyone in England still spoke like that, so before moving here I took elocution lessons to speak like Celia Johnson, and now I can't get rid of it. Isn't it frightfully silly?'

'I think you have a lovely accent,' said Max.

Harper looked at Max's penis.

256

'Oh dear. You appear to have lost momentum,' she said.

Harper continued working on Max for another five minutes, but his penis didn't improve. He needed to fart really badly now.

'I think I heard my phone beep,' said Max, pulling up his trousers.

'I didn't hear anything,' said Harper.

Max got up and looked at his switched-off phone.

'Yep, thought so,' he said. 'Sorry. Work. I have to go.'

'But you didn't come,' said Harper. 'And you booked for an hour.'

'I'm on emergency call,' lied Max.

'Are you a doctor?'

'Yes.' Max nodded. 'I'm a doctor.'

'Well, it was awfully nice to meet you. Do come again,' said Harper.

She gave him a hug, then Max exited.

At the bottom of the stairwell, he let out a very long and loud wet fart. It echoed throughout the building.

Days passed. Max couldn't stop thinking about Harper. He booked another appointment and returned to her apartment fully intending to fulfil his sexual desires.

She answered the ajar door of apartment 7 in an approximation of a nurse's uniform, although Max hadn't requested her to do so.

'I thought you'd like me like this,' she whispered, with a giggle.

They went into the same room. Max gave her £100, then took off his coat and shoes and felt just as awkward as before.

'What sort of things do you do with your clients?' he asked.

'All different.' she said. 'One likes me to tread on his balls with my stilettos. Another likes me to take a shit on his stomach. One likes to fuck my armpit.'

'Wow,' said Max. 'How recherché.'

'I enjoy the variety,' said Harper.

'And what do you like to do?' asked Max.

'I like to shower with my clients. I like the sensation of skin on skin, but also because most of them have poor hygiene. I like massage too. And mutual masturbation. And kissing and cuddling. And dirty talk.'

'But no actual sex?' asked Max.

'Sex I can take or leave,' shrugged Harper. 'Actually, I'm repulsed by the male organ.'

'That makes two of us,' said Max. 'Is your boyfriend still away?'

'Yes. He never wants sex with me. He prefers to pay for whores.'

Max noticed a well-thumbed book about Seneca next to the futon.

'Seneca?' he enquired.

'I'm studying for a PhD,' said Harper. 'You never know when a dead language will come in handy. Would you like me to teach you some third-conjugation verbs?'

'Another time, perhaps,' said Max.

'In that case, let's get naked and have a shower,' said Harper.

'Okay,' said Max.

'You're not going to rush off on an emergency call today, are you?'

'No, not today,' said Max.

They soon stood with their lips locked under the warm water in the shower. Then he and Harper towelled each other dry and lay naked on the futon, caressing and kissing. It was a sexual re-awakening for Max. Harper even said she loved his pot belly. Maybe she said it to all her clients.

His relationship with Juno had become almost like that of housemates, but he wouldn't consider leaving her. The possibility of Juno finding out about Harper filled him with horror. After each appointment, he scrubbed his body clean of her scent.

One time, he forgot to put his wedding ring back on and Juno noticed. Max made an excuse that it had become bent out of shape and was at the jewellers being mended.

'You're fucking someone, aren't you?' she said.

Max froze. He glanced at Juno. She started chuckling.

'I'm joking. Who'd want you?' she said, returning her attention to the TV and stuffing her chubby face with crisps.

29

Morning light crept in through the ceiling window. The door to Max's cell clanked open. Walker looked in.

'That's got to be the longest shit in history,' he said to Max, who still sat perched on the toilet, staring at the flickering TV.

Max didn't respond at first.

'I was remembering,' he said.

'Get dressed,' said Walker.

Max showered, then, as usual, had breakfast separately from the other inmates. Some whistled and cat-called in his direction.

He was taken to the infirmary for a routine check-up. The doctor shone a light in Max's eyes and tested his reflexes.

'Are you taking your medication?'

Max nodded, but couldn't remember taking any medication. He felt tired and asked to be returned to his cell.

He lay on his bed and fell into an immediate reverie.

***

Max was driving to his high school 20-year reunion, which he'd seen by chance advertised on Facebook. It was taking place in the school assembly hall. Max initially said he wouldn't go, but he changed his mind for one reason: Claire must surely be there.

Max considered asking Harper to be his date for the evening, but then Juno insisted on coming.

Max pulled into the school car park, hoping someone he knew would see his Bentley, but no one was there. He drove up and down looking, he said, for the best parking bay.

'This car isn't an affirmation of who you are,' said Juno.

'I beg to differ,' replied Max.

They parked and walked to the entrance. Max had taken a lot of care and consideration with his clothes. He dressed to impress in his best suit, a fedora hat and a newly-bought Astrakhan overcoat.

Juno smiled at him and said he looked like a Bronx pimp. He wanted to retaliate by saying her baggy jumper and long skirt (worn to cover up her burgeoning gut) would fool nobody. But he didn't.

In the school foyer, a smiley guy with a clipboard welcomed them.

'Max Hope,' said Max.

The smiley guy looked down the list on the clipboard.

'Sorry. I can't see a Max Hope on here,' he said.

Max craned his neck and looked down the list. He saw some familiar names from his youth, but neither his name nor Claire's were on it.

His heart sank.

'Well,' said smiley guy, 'go through anyway. Probably an oversight.'

Max and Juno went into the assembly hall. It was festooned with balloons. Tables were set out with food and drink. Several nerdy people worth avoiding milled about.

Aggressive hip-hop music played at ear-splitting level.

'Let's go home,' said Max.

'Give it a chance,' said Juno.

Max got some drinks. Juno stacked a paper plate with food.

They saw an open fire escape at the far end of the hall – a group of people had congregated outside to smoke and avoid the music. Max and Juno tentatively went out and joined them.

A large balding man in a Hawaiian shirt (with a tiny grinning

Thai woman clinging to his arm) approached. The man playfully adopted a boxing pose to Max.

'Put 'em up. Put 'em up!' said the man.

Max didn't know who the fuck he was.

'Come here, you little prick,' said the man. 'It's me, Paul Finch.'

Paul gave Max a bear hug, which knocked his fedora off. As Max bent down to pick it up, Paul ruffled his hair, much to his annoyance.

'Dying your hair, I see, you vain wanker. A-HA-HA!' laughed Paul.

'Hello, Paul. Long time no see,' said Max, fixing his hair.

'Look at you, you prick,' grinned Paul. 'You look like a fucking pimp!'

Juno laughed, along with other people who began to gather round. Max glared at Juno.

'Enchanted, mon petit fleur,' said Paul, lecherously to Juno. 'What are you doing with this loser? A-HA-HA-HA-HA!'

Paul then indicated to the Thai woman on his arm.

'This is my wife, Dong. She doesn't speak English good, thankfully. I bought her – I mean I married her – last year. A-HA-HA-HA-HA!'

'Paul very funny man,' said Dong.

'My sides are splitting,' said Max.

Paul turned to Juno.

'Me and your old man were chummy for a while until he tried to shag my sister at a party and we had a punch up.' He turned to Max. 'I gave you a good hiding, didn't I, Maximillian?'

'Just Max, only my—'

'And be fair, you deserved it, you little prick,' said Paul.

'It was a draw, as I remember,' said Max, smiling angrily.

'A draw?' said Paul. 'I punched fuck out of you.' He turned to Juno again. 'Let me tell you something about this degenerate little prick: nobody liked him, but I took him under my wing because I felt sorry for him.' He looked at Max. 'Isn't that right?'

'No,' said Max.

'Mike was there. Remember Mike Barrow? And Edgar Parr? And Steve Glock? Steve's dead, poor bastard.' Paul turned away. 'Mike, Edgar, come over here, look who this pimp is!'

Mike Barrow and Edgar Parr came over and joined in the casual yet hurtful passive-aggressive humiliation of Max. Juno, already tipsy on white wine, giggled along with the barbs.

Max's former friends interrogated him about what he did for a living. He tried to gloss up The Emporium with the usual "objets d'art and curiosity showroom" spiel, but they all saw through it.

'I know The Emporium,' said Edgar Parr. 'It's a shitty little junk shop in Maida Vale!'

Everyone laughed. Max tried to defend himself, but was drowned out.

'Max is also writing a novel,' said Juno, trying to be helpful.

Max squirmed. The vultures could smell blood. They pretended to be interested, and bombarded Max with sarcastic questions about his novel. He tried, and failed, to put an exaggerated positive spin on it, while they grinned behind their hands.

'It's a complex philosophical story about the human condition, which exhibits a high degree of verbal interplay within a framework of technically eclectic shifts of thematic subject development,' said Max.

'Sounds fucking pretentious,' said Mike Barrow.

'I doubt you've ever read a book, you tosser,' Max shot back.

'Ooh, tetchy,' said Mike, Paul and Edgar, in high voices.

'I wouldn't expect you to understand,' said Max.

'We understand. You're an unemployed rag and bone man. A-HA-HA-HA-HA!' laughed Paul, and everyone else.

'Like you arseholes have achieved so much,' seethed Max.

'Hey,' said Paul, chummily putting his arm around Max's shoulders, 'there's no need for that. We're just yanking your chain, Maximillian.'

'My name is Max, okay? Just Max!'

Max shrugged off Paul's arm. The laughter stopped. Tension.

'Why are you being a prick about it?' said Paul.

'You're the prick, mate,' said Max. 'I live in a big house and I drive a Bentley. What do you drive, a ten-year-old fucking Hyundai?'

'What can I say?' said Paul, turning to the others. 'Once a cunt, always a cunt.'

Max picked up a beer bottle and smashed it over Paul's head.

Paul collapsed to the floor, his face laced with blood.

'Who's the cunt now, Paul?' shouted Max.

Dong screamed. Commotion ensued as Mike, Edgar and Dong tried to attack Max. Juno sprayed Mace in their eyes, then dragged Max back into the school assembly hall.

'Are you a fucking psychopath?' said Juno.

'Who takes Mace to a school reunion?' asked Max.

On the way to the exit, Max overturned a table of food.

'I always hated this place. Fuck all of you,' he shouted.

In the car on the way home, Juno laughed bitterly.

'You're a disaster area,' she said. 'A total disaster.'

From then onwards, the two of them grew ever-further apart. They argued over trivial things, and had less and less to say to each other.

Juno gathered a coterie of yummy-mummy girlfriends around her, (Max secretly called them The Coven), and spent more time with Mud and Fud.

Max spent whole afternoons with Harper. It gave him a spring in his step, although work on the novel came to a stop, and his money dwindled due to Harper's new increased rates. He lived two lives – Harper during the day, and Juno at night. Juno didn't bother to ask about his book's progress anymore.

Apart from a couple of regulars, Harper didn't have many clients. She blamed the economic downturn, and her reluctance to do more hard-core stuff. Max was pleased. It meant she had more time (and need) for him.

He enjoyed her affection, and she seemed to enjoy his company.

'If it wasn't for you, I'd be alone most of the time,' she said.

'Same here,' said Max.

Some days, they stayed in bed and watched old romantic movies on TV. Other days, they visited museums, or saw musicals in the West End (Max despised musicals, and they cost him a fortune, but Harper insisted). They chatted about literature and philosophy, and walked around hand in hand. Max became paranoid they'd bump into one of Juno's friends and be found out, but it added to the thrill.

He even began to believe Harper was falling in love with him, but he couldn't be sure how genuine her feelings were. It ate away at him. Did she see him as just another business transaction? A mug punter to exploit? Max often heard her refer to clients as "pay-pigs".

He decided to subtly test her. As he was leaving her flat one afternoon, he pretended to have no cash on him to pay her with. He noted an immediate hardening of her features.

'I accept all major credit cards,' she said, producing a credit card reader.

Max smiled, then "remembered" he did have cash. He handed it to her.

'Maybe one day I won't have to pay to be with you?' he said.

Harper smiled thinly while pocketing the money.

'Maybe, baby,' she said.

It left a nasty taste in his mouth. He didn't contact her for a few days as punishment, but she left him several cute voice messages.

The next time they met, she allowed him to have full penetrative sex, although there was a discernible frostiness about the encounter.

Afterwards, they lay naked.

'I don't know who you are,' said Max. 'You speak with a false accent, and your name is probably false too.'

'Is your real name James?' she shot back. 'Are you single?'

'Touché,' sighed Max.

'You have the indentation of a wedding ring on your finger,' said Harper. 'I'm not stupid. I've never lied to you. Anyway, all human interaction is a pretence to some degree.'

She sat up and stared at the slate grey sky through the window. Max watched the contour of her spine for a moment. He worried at the thought of losing her.

'I'm married. I have three children. I'm not a good husband or father,' he said.

'That isn't my problem,' said Harper.

'I know. I'm sorry,' said Max. 'I just wanted to make a connection with someone. I don't know who I am.'

'We're unknowable to ourselves. Life itself is unknowable,' said Harper.

'Christ, you're very French, aren't you?' said Max.

'Home of the existentialists,' said Harper, smiling.

She lay down beside him and they embraced.

'My name is Max.'

'It suits you,' said Harper.

***

'Hey, knob head, wake up,' said a gruff male voice.

Max opened his eyes. He lay on his cell bed, embracing thin air.

A burly prison guard stood over him.

'What now?' moaned Max.

'You've got visitors.'

Max stood up. The guard handcuffed him.

'Distracted from distractions by distractions,' muttered Max.

He was led down a corridor. Inside a room, Detective Superintendent Lamb, Detective Chief Inspector Hicks, and Ched Hazzard could be heard arguing.

'What do you mean, "diminished responsibility"?' said Hicks.

'He suffered mild brain damage,' said Ched Hazzard.

'Undiagnosed,' said Lamb.

'He's mentally ill and did not receive help,' said Ched Hazzard. 'The system let him down. This point needs to be addressed.'

'We're back to the victimhood angle again,' said Lamb.

'So, it's autism, PTSD, and now bipolar? Bullshit!' snarled Hicks. 'You said you couldn't detect any psychotic behaviour in him?'

'He doesn't betray usual psychotic behaviour, no,' said another voice – Lee. 'Not even schizophrenia. He didn't previously, either. That's why I didn't refer him, or prescribe anti-psychotic medication.'

'And now four people are dead,' said Hicks. 'Pre-meditated murder.'

'Hey,' said Lee. 'I am not responsible for—'

'Why are you trying to protect him?' interrupted Hicks.

'We shouldn't be having this conversation,' said Ched Hazzard. 'It is against legal procedure.'

Max was brought into the room. Everyone fell silent.

Max sat down at a table. A woman in a business suit sat across from him reading legal papers – the lawyer for the opposition.

'Please don't stop the invective on my account,' Max said to Hicks.

'Is it true your memory has returned?' asked the lawyer.

'Don't answer that,' said Ched Hazzard.

'What can you remember?' asked the lawyer.

'Don't answer, Max. You're not obliged to answer anything.'

'Oh, come on!' shouted Hicks, kicking over a chair.

'Someone murdered my family,' said Max. 'You should be looking for them. They're out there, somewhere.'

Lamb, Hicks, Lee, and the lawyer left the room.

Max and Ched Hazzard were alone.

'So I'm autistic and bipolar?' asked Max.

'Speculatively, unless proved otherwise,' said Ched Hazzard. 'How much of your memory has returned?'

'A lot,' said Max. 'But not the… not everything. Not yet. There are gaps. I get vivid remembrances of certain things. It's frustrating.'

'Max,' said Ched Hazzard, leaning closer, 'I'm going to need to know your side of the story, and soon. Otherwise, my only advice is for you to act insane. I mean totally bat-shit crazy.'

'I'm not going to do that,' said Max. 'I'm not crazy. I'm in a crazy world.'

30

Max returned to his cell and lay on the bed, flicking through random TV channels. The sound was fixed. On one channel, a magazine-style show seriously discussed how "aubergine" was this season's colour. Another channel showed a US sitcom in which improbable cliché characters said unfunny things in obvious ways. The studio audience laughed hysterically after every single line. On the next channel, a dull political programme had low-ranking politicians arguing about the state of the economy and immigration and education. They made existence seem such a relentless grind.

Never-ending debates and disagreements. Differences of opinion. Conflicts of interest. Corrupt agendas. Ideological wank. It's always someone else's fault. Incessant change for the sake of change. Some incremental gains and losses. The complex flaws of a system trying to keep a deeply flawed species under control.

Max switched over to the next channel. A dog food commercial, with a chocolate Labrador running across a sunlit lawn.

'Chekhov,' whispered Max.

***

Perdita held a chocolate Labrador puppy called Chekhov in her arms.

Willow cradled a golden Labrador puppy, called Ibsen.

Max (suddenly the best dad in the world) chose their names.

Juno was annoyed with him because he'd bought the dogs as birthday presents without consulting her, and she would be the one who'd have to look after them most of the time. But she did admit they were cute.

'You never bought me any pets,' said Aldous.

'Because you're useless with pets,' said Max. 'Hammy the hamster disappeared because you refused to leave it in its cage.'

'No animal should be caged,' replied Aldous.

They were all in the back garden. A weekend heatwave. Aldous, now fourteen and taller than Max, offered to help his dad dredge a bloom of algae out of the pond which threatened to choke the Koi carp. The pond had greatly increased in size. It dominated the garden. Max and Aldous stood at its edge, sifting out slime with pole nets.

'Do you remember you nearly drowned in here, once?' asked Max.

'No,' said Aldous.

'I saved you.'

'This pond always scared me. Still does.'

'Why?' asked Max.

'The water's so dark.'

'It's full of life.'

'It's full of death, too,' said Aldous. 'You can't have one without the other.'

'You're cheerful,' said Max.

They continued silently dredging for a while, then Aldous said,

'Nanna Mud is always criticising you. I tell her to stop.'

'Oh,' said Max. 'What does she say?'

'She keeps saying you're a loser.'

'She's not in a position to criticise anyone,' said Max. 'She's a silly old cow with a yappy little dog and stupid sunglasses.'

Aldous laughed. Max thought he was laughing at his comment, but he was laughing at Chekhov and Ibsen chasing a delighted Perdita and Willow around the garden.

Shortly, Aldous turned to Max and asked,

'What do you do all day, Dad?'

'You know what I do,' said Max, with slight irritation. 'I work at The Emporium, and I'm writing my novel.'

'Oh yeah,' said Aldous. 'Can't wait to read it.'

'You can, when it's finished.'

'When will it be finished?'

'When I say it is,' said Max. 'Genius takes time. Genius. Takes. Time.'

***

'I think Perdita's gay,' said Juno to Max, one night in bed.

Perdita had shorn her hair into a crew cut. She'd never shown interest in boys. Her twin sister was the opposite, yet they were similar in so many ways. Completely different personalities, but best friends and fiercely protective of each other.

Willow's bedroom was adorned with pictures of pop stars and actors; Perdita's was covered in carefully curated lonely seascape photos by Gustave Le Gray, and Victorian sepia portraits by Julia Margaret Cameron.

Willow rode ponies; Perdita drove go-karts. Willow read Young Adult fiction, Perdita read horror and science-fiction. Willow wore make-up and dresses, Perdita wore army boots, jeans, and T-shirts with political slogans on them.

'Yes, she probably is,' said Max.

'I think it's great,' said Juno. 'Don't you?'

'Why is it great?' asked Max.

'Some of the best people in history have been gay. There's no stigma attached to it anymore, thankfully. Well, there is, and always will be, that's human nature.'

'If she's gay, she's gay,' said Max, carefully. 'I'd rather she wasn't, for her sake. It will bring complications into her life. But I'll support her, if she needs my support.'

'Good,' said Juno. 'I worried you'd get angry, or say something homophobic.'

'I'm not homophobic. My sister's a lesbian,' said Max.

'Yes. Sorry,' said Juno.

They lay in the dark for a while.

'We've been lucky with the kids,' said Max. 'No serious illnesses, or broken bones. They're healthy.'

'Well, you've cursed them now, haven't you?' said Juno.

'Sorry,' said Max. 'Have I alerted the omnipotent omniscient goblins of fortune to punish them for my hubristic observation?'

'They have operatives everywhere, you know,' said Juno, only half-jokingly.

'Then I say a fond "bollocks" to the invisible non-existent entities who control fate and make us mere puppets of their morbid and unjust caprice,' muttered Max, turning over onto his side.

***

The following week, Willow broke her arm during PE at school and Juno wouldn't let Max forget about it.

***

Max enjoyed taking the dogs for a walk when they were puppies, but as they grew, it became a chore. They couldn't be let off their leads in case they ran off and were hit by a car. They dragged him along until eventually Juno paid a professional dog behaviourist to work with them "holistically", but it was a waste of money.

Chekhov was particularly fond of Max. Max sometimes took him to The Emporium for company, and once took him to Harper's flat.

Somehow, the dog (wet with rain) managed to open her bedroom door and jumped excitedly onto the futon while Harper was giving Max oral sex. Harper freaked out about it.

272

Max had a sense the dog understood the concept of his cheating on Juno. Chekhov looked at Max suspiciously for days afterwards.

'Stop judging me,' said Max to the dog. 'You don't understand.'

***

Max sat in the back office of The Emporium one afternoon, jerking off to hard core porn on his computer.

'Yap, yap, yap!' yapped a familiar voice.

Max froze. He turned and saw Mud watching him in the doorway.

'Hard at work, I see,' drawled Mud, behind her large impenetrable sunglasses.

'Yap, yap, yap!' yapped her yappy little dog again.

'I wasn't masturbating,' said Max, tucking his penis away and switching off the porn.

'Then your method of writing a novel is somewhat novel. No wonder it's taking so long,' said Mud.

'What the hell are you doing here?' croaked Max.

'I own the place,' said Mud.

'You've never visited before.'

'You're a disgusting little worm,' said Mud.

Max's instinct was to kill her. His eyes darted around for something to cave her skull in with, but he saw her chauffeur waiting outside.

'I'm conducting important research on the effects of porn,' gabbled Max. 'You know, like Kinsey?'

'I'm closing this shop down forthwith,' said Mud. 'I suggest you find alternative employment. If you were anyone else, I would report you to the authorities. However, as you are my son-in-law, and father of my grandchildren, I will allow you a modicum of dignity and not take this perverted episode further than the two of us, and Binky (the dog). I have never liked you, and I very much doubt that situation will ever change. I am constantly dumbfounded as to what my daughter saw in you. You are nothing more than a lazy no-mark second-rate weak-willed blank of a man. It's time you stepped up your game and made something of yourself, don't you think?'

'I completely agree,' said Max, and he did.

Mud walked towards the shop door, pausing only to notice most of the stock had gone. She ran a gloved finger along a table which highlighted layers of dust, then showed her dusty finger to Max.

'Dis. Gust. Ing,' she said.

'Yap, yap, yap!' yapped Binky, as they disappeared into the street.

Max stood on the spot, suspended in life, watching balletic drifts of glittery dust motes in a shaft of sunlight. The fresh air from outside mingled with the stale air inside. He could feel the machinations of fate drawing the boundaries ever-narrower.

His mobile phone rang, making him jump. Harper's number. She only rang when she needed money.

'What?' said Max into the phone.

Sobbing came from the other end. Great. More problems.

'My boyfriend beat me up and threw me out,' blubbed Harper.

He drove across town and met her at a cafe, where she sat with a black eye and a carrier bag containing her few possessions.

'He turned nasty on me and said he didn't want a whore living in his apartment any longer, the bastard!'

'Does he know about me?' asked Max.

'Yes,' nodded Harper. 'He wants to castrate you.'

'So, what happens now?' asked Max.

'You're the only person I know. You must help. I need somewhere to live, and money.'

Max gave her some cash and found a cheap hotel for her to stay in.

'This is temporary,' he told her.

He went home. Juno anxiously confronted him.

'Mud told me what happened,' was her opening gambit.

Max's blood ran cold.

'I can explain,' he said.

'No, let me explain,' said Juno. 'The thing is, my family have suffered an unexpected heavy financial loss, what with the economy and pension scheme irregularities and investments not returning the yields that were expected, so belts are going to have to be tightened and cutbacks made. The Emporium is the first to go, I'm afraid. I know you love that awful place because it reminds you of Rex, but it's a financial burden. Also, my allowance is being halved, which means the allowance I give you must be halved too. It's a terrible pickle.'

'I see,' said Max.

'Sell the Bentley and get a little run-around,' said Juno.

'No. That car is good for my mental well-being. It gives me status.'

'Well get a bloody job, then,' said Juno.

'Why don't you get a job?' sniped Max.

'I'm painting again,' said Juno. 'I intend to exhibit new stuff soon.'

'What can I do?' said Max, pacing. 'I don't have any qualifications. A minimum-wage job isn't going to solve anything, and it will delay me completing the novel. We're fucked! Everything is fucked!'

Max started to hyperventilate.

'Calm down,' said Juno, shocked at his overreaction.

'We could run away and change our names and start again,' said Max.

'Stop being unusual,' said Juno.

'Let's go to Beachy Head right now and throw ourselves off.'

'Jesus, things aren't that bad,' said Juno.

Max took some deep breaths and calmed down.

'I don't want the kids to know anything, okay?' he said, finally.

***

275

Max spent the next two weeks trying to write another chapter of *Slush Pile*, while shuttling around town with Harper, looking for a small flat she could live in. Max paid for everything.

'Don't you have any savings at all?' he asked her.

'None,' Harper sadly replied. 'Anyway, I thought you were rich?'

'Times are bad,' said Max.

He put a deposit down for a tiny furnished one-bedroom maisonette in a run-down part of Acton. The estate agent said it had potential.

'Potential for what?' asked Max.

'Demolition,' laughed the estate agent.

'It will do,' said Harper, ungratefully. 'But I want it redecorated.'

'I can't keep financing you,' Max told her.

'Then I need to work. Do you want to be my pimp?' asked Harper.

'Don't be crude. But, okay,' said Max.

'Fine,' said Harper. 'Then do me a favour.'

She delved into her bag and pulled out a Taser gun.

'What the hell is that for?' asked Max.

'Get revenge on my ex. Do some damage,' said Harper.

'Does that thing work?' asked Max.

'Yes,' said Harper. 'A client of mine liked having his balls zapped with it. Long story.'

'I'm not sure about this,' said Max.

'I'm not asking you to kill the guy. Just maim him.'

Max took the gun. It felt good in his hand. Powerful. The scumbag deserved punishment. Max had always wanted to be a vigilante.

'Just this once,' he said.

***

A blinding white flash of light happened inside Max's skull. A meteor storm of electricity exploded outwards, then quickly became blanketed in a cloak of total darkness.

Max could feel his face pressed against something cold and hard. His breathing came in short snorts.

He lay on the floor of his cell, unable to move.

The heavy cell door clanked open. Footsteps.

'Get a doctor, and call for an ambulance,' said Walker.

31

I've been here before. It feels familiar. It's a place beyond. It has no horizon. No limits. No day or night. No pain. No time. It isn't a hell or a heaven. It isn't a human construct. It is simply something else.

***

'Is he going to die?' asked Walker.
Movement. Corridors. Doors slamming.
Light. Dark. Light. Dark.

***

Max had been standing across the street from Harper's old apartment for an hour with a baseball cap pulled low over his face and one hand in his coat pocket, gripping the Taser. Like all good assassins, he held a copy of *The Catcher in the Rye* in his other hand.

People came and went through the electric security gate, but none of them were Scott (Harper's ex). Harper had given Max a photo of him.

A delivery man went through the gate. Max ran over and slipped in before it shut, then followed behind as the delivery man was buzzed into the lobby.

Max went straight up to apartment 7 and rang the bell. Bing-bong it chimed. (He'd never rung it before). A place he often associated with pleasure now felt like hostile territory.

There would be no coquettish smile waiting inside for him today.

Max waited. He rang again. Bing-bong. He slipped the Taser out of his pocket and obscured it in his sleeve.

The door opened. Scott stood bleary-eyed in a dressing gown, even though it was early afternoon.

The two looked at each other.

'If you're looking for the whore, she's gone,' said Scott.

'I have a message from Harper,' said Max.

(He'd rehearsed saying 'She says "No hard feelings",' as he pulled the trigger, like a mafia hit, but he suddenly lost his nerve.)

Max aimed the Taser at Scott.

'Is this a fucking joke?' asked Scott.

Max pressed the trigger. Nothing happened. Max's hand trembled. He pressed the trigger again. Nothing.

Scott took a step forwards. Max took a step back.

'Are you the twat she's fleecing now?' asked Scott.

Max remembered the Taser's safety catch was on. A schoolboy error.

He clicked it off and pressed the trigger – thin wires shot out of it and zapped Scott directly in the crotch. Scott jolted, then collapsed to the floor of the landing. He shook violently and foamed at the mouth.

Max released the trigger.

Someone was coming up the communal stairs. If they walked through the landing doors, Max would tell them Scott was having an epileptic fit, then leave saying he'd call for an ambulance. Or he'd Taser them too. Yeah, Max, Taser everyone in the world.

The person passed the frosted landing glass doors, briefly hesitated to blow their nose, then continued up to the next floor.

Movement came from behind the door of apartment 8, no doubt alerted by the gurgles emanating from Scott's throat.

Max stuffed the Taser into his pocket and made his escape, unseen. He walked a few streets back to his car and sat in it for a while.

What if Scott died?

Fuck him. Scott represented all those fucking shit cunt motherfuckers who got away with being fucking shit cunt motherfuckers.

The world was full of them.

Max didn't feel bad. In fact, he felt good. No nausea. No conscience.

He drove to Harper's flat. The porch light was on, signifying she was with a client. When the creep left, Max went inside and found Harper wiping semen off her bedsheets.

'It's done,' said Max.

'Good,' said Harper.

'I fucked him up, big-time,' said Max.

'I need to shower,' said Harper. 'I have another client in ten minutes, so you'd better leave.'

'Has business picked up?'

'The money isn't as good around here,' said Harper. 'I have to do anal to make up the shortfall. Don't worry, you'll get a return by the end of the week.'

'Can I join you in the shower?' asked Max.

Harper rolled her eyes contemptuously and went into the bathroom.

'You're just like all the rest,' she said. 'All men are the same.'

'Hey, I'm not one of your douchebag clients,' said Max.

'All men are inherently violent and full of self-regarding entitlement over women,' said Harper.

'I just committed a crime for you,' said Max indignantly. 'You asked me to do it, and you can't even thank me!'

'Blah, blah, blah,' said Harper, in the shower. 'Blah, blah, blah.'

***

Max returned to consciousness again. He kept his eyes shut. He lay on a bed, encased in tight bedsheets. People were around him, talking.

'How bad is it?' asked Lamb.

'There's a lot of brain activity,' said Doctor Brooke.

'Will he regain consciousness?' asked Ched Hazzard.

'Difficult to say,' said Doctor Brooke.

'The trial will have to be postponed,' said Lee.

'If he dies, there won't be a trial,' said Lamb.

'I think he can hear us,' said the doctor.

Max perceived foetid wet lips close to his right ear.

'If you die,' whispered Hicks, 'I will fucking kill you.'

***

A loud crack of thunder signified the beginning of Armageddon. No life would survive the meteor's impact, or the shockwave. Boz looked to the sky as the first flames shot through the clouds.

'We are all undone by our weaknesses in the end,' he said, smiling.

THE END.

Max, drenched in sweat, lifted his fingers from the laptop keyboard then reclined in his chair in Harper's flat.

'It's finished,' he said.

'What happens now?' asked Harper, looking up from a crossword.

'I want you to read it.'

'Goodness. How privileged I feel,' she said.

'Read it now. I want your honest opinion.'

'Are you sure?' said Harper.

'Positive. This novel is the most important thing I'll ever create.'

'More than your children?'

'More than my children.'

'That's a big statement.'

Max swivelled around and faced Harper.

'This novel will survive,' he said. 'It's my testament. It tries to make sense of all the suffering. It asks, "How can we be?"'

'I'll read it,' sighed Harper.

Max went home. He didn't tell Juno he'd finished the book. He didn't feel the elation he expected either, just emptiness.

He went back to see Harper the next day. They sat opposite each other at her tiny breakfast table, their knees touching.

'Well? Did you read it?' asked Max.

'I read it,' said Harper.

'And?'

'It's Intelligent. It's Erudite. But…'

'But what?' asked Max.

'What is the story?' asked Harper.

'It's about a man trying to find meaning in a meaningless world,' said Max. 'It's ultimately a solipsistic semi-autobiography.'

'Hm,' pondered Harper. 'It's very pleased with itself. And it's unwelcoming. Your writing is too much about a closed world. Boz is cold and misanthropic. It's very jaded. Bleak, too. I mean, everyone dies in the end.'

'But everyone does die in the end,' said Max.

'You have to offer the reader some hope,' said Harper. 'Otherwise it becomes depressing. And Boz needs redemption of some kind.'

'So, you hated it?' asked Max.

Harper reached across the table and held Max's hand.

'I didn't say that.'

'It's a steaming pile of shit, isn't it?' said Max.

'No,' said Harper. 'It's a big achievement. Christ, do you think being a novelist will make you happy? You have a false impression of what success is, and it will only leave you disappointed.'

'Everything leaves me disappointed,' said Max.

He went home. He no longer had The Emporium to use as an excuse to be out of the house during the day. Juno made him turn an upstairs room into a writing den, but he didn't like being under her scrutiny.

He typed 'All work and no play makes Max a dull boy' hundreds of times, just to sound busy. He preferred to write at Harper's flat (he told Juno he was writing at the library), although he kept being interrupted by clients screwing her.

Max realised he was in a tight spot now. If his novel failed, which he secretly knew it would, he had no back-up plans. His percentage of Harper's earnings barely covered his petrol bills. He knew she short-changed him, too. Money was getting tight. Juno sold two paintings, but for much less than expected.

Max's financial advisor called at the house. Max never understood any questions the man asked. He felt stupid.

'Your finances are a mess,' said the financial advisor. 'The tax people are nosing around. They might audit you.'

When not at home or at Harper's flat, Max sat in cafés watching other writers tapping productively at laptops, which made him jealous. They all seemed to know each other, and were no doubt writing posturing issue-based high-minded topics of liberal socio-political moralism.

Max was swimming against the tide. *Slush Pile* needed a complete overhaul to prevent it sliding into one long unfocused rant from Boz, who was developing into a Nietzschean proto-fascist anti-hero.

No publisher would touch it. Max introduced a new female character, called Claire. She was Boz's childhood love, a strong, conscientious and intelligent redemptive figure.

Around this time, Max began to suffer intense migraines again. He went to see Deepak, who now ran a small private medical practice.

'I fell off my bike when I was a kid,' he said to Deepak. 'Knocked myself out. I went to hospital. A blood clot developed.'

'I can prescribe you painkillers,' said Deepak. 'Also, your blood pressure is high. You need to take it easy.'

'I'm under a lot of pressure,' said Max. 'My life is complex.'

'Isn't everyone's?' sighed Deepak.

God, Deepak looked prematurely old. His thinning hair was white, and bags hung under his eyes. Max wondered if he ever slept.

'I don't usually take medication,' said Max.

'Are you allergic?'

'No. A masochist.'

'Try meditation,' said Deepak. 'It works for me.'

Deepak wrote a prescription for painkillers. Max collected them, but didn't take any. He hid them in a cupboard at home.

He tried meditating. It made his migraine worse.

That night, he finished *Slush Pile*, with a new ending:

*Boz lay in a pool of blood. Claire cradled his head in her arms.
'Do you know what mankind's essential quest is?' she asked him.*

'To suffer in ignorance,' said Boz.

'No. It's to accept reality, and find peace and contentedness within its precepts,' said Claire.

'Will you teach me how?' asked Boz.

'Yes. I don't propagate passive or negative outlooks on life, value systems or worldviews. I believe in structuring a narrative in which there is a purely logical path, where life continually moves forward and where our ultimate goal is to reach enlightenment.'

Boz looked at the sun sinking onto the horizon. His eyes then met Claire's. They were the most beautiful pools of blue.

'Show me,' he said.

'Close your eyes,' Claire whispered.

Boz closed his eyes.

Claire quietly hummed "Marble Halls", and stroked his hair.

'Beautiful,' said Boz. 'Beautiful.'

A smile spread across his lips as he slipped away into eternal bliss.

THE END

A tear rolled down Max's cheek. Despite Harper's criticism, it needed to end in death. Facing death and the prospect of oblivion with stoic dignity was the subject at the heart of the story.

Max emailed the first three chapters to literary agents. This time, they were bound to recognise his genius.

He presented a printed manuscript copy of the novel to Juno.

'The holy grail,' she sarcastically said on receiving it.

She kept him waiting for four days while she read it. He found her asleep with it in her lap, twice. When she finally gave it back, every page had notes scribbled in red ink and lots of question marks, and single words like "Illogical", "Motivation?" and "Silly!"

'It's very you,' she said.

'What does that mean?' asked Max.

'It's unclassifiable,' said Juno. 'There's something oddly blinkered about your writing and your mindset in general. Boz is unlikable and too esoteric. And the ending was lachrymose. It felt grafted on. Also, Claire was too wishy-washy. But that's just my opinion.'

'Opinions are like arseholes – everyone has one,' said Max.

'Charming,' said Juno.

Restless dog days followed. Weeks of waiting for literary agent replies.

Max found it difficult to concentrate on anything. Bills went unpaid. So did the follow-up demands. He desperately needed money, but refused to claim benefits out of pride.

One literary rejection came. Then another. Gulp.

He faced the prospect of getting a low-paid job until the writing career took off. The thought kept him awake at night.

***

285

Max opened his eyes. A blurry Room 9 came into focus. Daylight.

Doctor Brooke busily fussed with the window blind, but stopped when he realised Max was awake.

Neither said anything for a short time, then the doctor broke the silence.

'Can you hear me, Max?'

'Yes, I can hear you.'

'I have bad news. You suffered a brain haemorrhage. I'm afraid it resulted in the loss of motor functions in your legs.'

'Permanently?' asked Max.

'Yes,' said the doctor. 'I'm sorry.'

Max tried to move his legs. Nothing. Paraplegia.

He wanted to cry, but no tears came out.

'My life is in pieces,' he said.

32

Max lay on the bed in Room 9. His eyes were half-open, but glazed from a heavy sedative Doctor Brooke administered.

Outside, an evening sky of ragged-shaped clouds tinged with pink gently glided by.

Max surveyed them with pleasure, before his eyelids closed.

***

Juno sat at the kitchen table stuffing an entire chocolate gateau into her mouth.

'For fuck's sake,' said Max on seeing her.

'What?' blushed Juno.

'It's 8am,' said Max.

'Don't judge me,' said Juno, cramming more gateau in.

'You need help,' said Max.

'Ha! That's good coming from you.'

'What's that supposed to mean?' asked Max.

'If anyone needs help around here, it's you,' said Juno.

'Oh really?'

'You need a personality transplant,' scoffed Juno, although her words were muffled by cake.

'Can you stop binging for a moment, please?'

'Leave me alone,' said Juno.

287

'You're a mess,' said Max. 'Figuratively, and literally.'

'You don't have any sympathy for me,' shot back Juno.

'Get a grip on your self-pity,' said Max.

'The worst thing to ever happen to you was,' said Juno, sucking the melted chocolate off her fingers, 'you fell off a fucking bike when you were nine!'

'I was eleven, actually,' said Max.

'Big-fucking deal!' shouted Juno.

'I nearly died,' said Max. 'I still suffer from it. Why are you bringing that subject up now?'

'Is it the seminal moment of your life? Falling off a bike?' said Juno, with glossy brown-smeared lips.

'One of them, yes,' said Max. 'I suppose the most traumatic thing to ever happen to an over-privileged brat like you was, your butler didn't make your hot water bottle warm enough, or your pet pony wasn't the right shade.'

'You're such a prick, do you know that?' spat Juno.

'I'm aware of it,' replied Max.

'I'm embarrassed by you,' said Juno.

Max, about to leave the room, wheeled around.

'Well I'm embarrassed by you,' he said. 'Look at yourself. You're a fucking disgrace!'

Juno threw her plate at Max. It missed his head by inches and smashed against a wall.

'I was raped by my uncle when I was a child!' she screamed.

A long silence followed.

Max began picking up the broken crockery.

'Leave it!' said Juno. 'Get out!'

Max took Ibsen and Chekhov for a walk. Or rather, they dragged him around the surrounding streets and people laughed at Max's lack of control. The dogs strained at their leads so much, they vomited (then ate the vomit).

When he returned home, Juno had shut herself in the bedroom. Max knocked gently and asked if she was okay.

'Fuck off,' she replied from within.

Max went into his writing room and determined to find employment of some kind. He hated the thought of Juno being embarrassed of him.

I'm embarrassed of myself, he thought.

He set about typing a CV. It didn't amount to much; one line about being the proprietor of an objets d'art showroom, and another about being a successful novelist ('My novels are huge in Romania; sales figures upon request,' he wrote.)

He embellished the CV with a few qualifications, then added some more until the page filled up with a colourful and entirely untruthful catalogue of lies. The vast gaps in his work history now included stints as a croupier, diving instructor, botanist, and a whole host of impressive medical qualifications. The rest of the page contained filler about his hobbies (opera, the films of Sergei Eisenstein, glass-blowing, and fundraising for charities).

Max went to a local employment bureau and sat down with a career advisor. (At the next desk, a heavily pregnant woman with six young screaming children told an advisor she wanted a full-time job in 'the adult entertainment industry'.)

The advisor looked at Max's CV.

'What are my prospects?' asked Max.

The advisor tried to disguise a smile.

'Excuse me, I'd like to show this to my colleagues.' she said.

The career advisor took the CV over to other career advisors standing at a water cooler and showed it to them. Max watched as they read the CV, then looked at Max. Each in turn burst out laughing.

Max seethed with anger.

'You people are unprofessional,' he said, as he got up and left.

***

Max opened his eyes. The lids felt gluey and heavy. Room 9 was now bathed in twilight.

A porter, who'd been staring at him, hurriedly cleared the bedside table of food and accumulated rubbish.

They briefly made eye contact, but said nothing. It seemed to freak the porter out. He backed away and rushed out of the door.

High up in the sky, the red lights of an airliner winked on and off.

Max's eyelids shut. He fought against sleep, but lost.

***

Max drove aimlessly for a while, then found himself quite by chance in the vicinity of his high school.

He walked into the park bordering the school and wandered around it for the first time in over twenty years. One summer in his mid-teens he'd hung around here with a cooler than usual crowd. He was only ever a peripheral figure, but for a brief period he flourished amongst them.

I'm nostalgic for a life I didn't particularly enjoy, he thought, as he passed the empty bowling green.

He felt much less streetwise than the others, who, although the same age as him, seemed older and more worldly. They all had part-time jobs, smoked and drank. Max didn't. When offered puffs or cans of beer, he always reluctantly declined. He listened with fascination to their anecdotes about fumbled sex and dabblings with soft drugs.

Thinking back, he realised what morons they all were.

They soon became bored with him and moved to different locations without telling him where, so he spent evenings riding around parks on his own in the twilight without realising the potential danger.

He sat on the bench they always used to sit on. (Wow, they used to sit on a bench in a park! How cool!)

As Max sat ruminating, he noticed the abundance of litter. Plastic bottles and fast food packaging were carelessly strewn about with abandon. He couldn't remember seeing any litter in his youth, but maybe you only start to notice these things when you get older.

Max yearned to return to the summers of his youth. He choked back tears in mourning for the past. (He forgot about the long stretches of boredom, anxiety and unhappiness which consumed him back then.)

He wanted to live his life again, so he could do everything differently and better. He bitterly regretted wasting so much precious time, in the full knowledge it could never be clawed back. Instead of hanging out with idiots, he should have been pursuing Claire and planning a career.

Claire only lived a few streets away (he remembered now).

Where on earth did she go?

Max walked over to the gate in the school perimeter wire fence where, every night, Claire (and he) began their walks home. A rusted padlock now kept it shut. He stood there trying to bid the past to return and conjure up the ghosts of himself and Claire. As he did so, melancholy stole upon him.

'Paedo!' shouted a boy's voice.

A group of school pupils were watching him. They made intimidating gestures and chanted 'Paedo, paedo, paedo!' at him.

The kids were big. They started throwing stones at him. Max backed away and hurriedly left the park.

He drove by Claire's house, but it had been demolished and replaced with a block of flats.

He pulled up in his car and sat thinking about the gradual erasure of the past. The disappearance of people and places and things. Before long, nothing of his childhood would remain. Everything must pass.

A relatively short time ago these suburban streets were remote fields and woods. Humans took it upon themselves to concrete and tarmac it over and carve it up for themselves, a community nest. It happened within living memory.

Before long, this current world and the people and streets and houses would disappear too. Such is the nature of the beast.

Life is aimless, thought Max. *Aimless and futile.*

He observed a man mowing a garden lawn. The man mowed it with great precision, as if it mattered. Max wanted to get out and tell him not to bother, but didn't. The lawn represented something to the man. Enjoyment in the repetitive action of the task; satisfaction in keeping nature at bay for a while. Nature played along with Ozymandias and his folly.

***

Max opened his eyes. Room 9. Darkness. He could hear his heart beating. In the corridor, two police officers chatted.

Max tried to move his legs. They were numb.

'God,' he whispered to himself.

He closed his eyes.

***

Max sat in the living room at home, looking through the job section of his local paper. He didn't understand most of the jobs, or what they entailed. What the fuck did an "Outreach co-ordinator" do? What did "Diversity Inter-Departmental Personnel Management and Inclusion Advisory Officers" do all day? They sounded like made-up job titles, yet they paid well, and every company needed them. Max dismissed them as a scam.

Juno, watching TV, glanced at him. Loathing and pity crept into her opinion of him now. Worst of all, she felt the same about herself.

'Find anything interesting?' she asked.

'Most of these aren't jobs at all.'

'What are they, then?'

'Time fillers.'

'That's a very condescending remark.'

'Absolutely,' said Max, not listening.

He couldn't stop thinking about how he'd sent *Slush Pile* to twenty more literary agents, and also to publishers, but none of them replied, not even with standard rejections. Nothing.

***

He lay on Harper's bed while she gave him oral sex. He didn't really want it, but she offered.

'Urgh!' she said, stopping.

'Sorry, I forgot to wash my prick,' said Max.

'No, look, you have a grey pube,' said Harper.

Max sat up and inspected the pubic area she pointed to. Indeed there was a grey pube. It almost glowed white amongst the bramble patch of darker wiry hairs. Another seminal staging post on his march towards the grave.

'I think it makes my penis look distinguished,' said Max, trying to make light of the matter. 'Like a late-career Cary Grant.'

'Shave it all off,' said Harper.

'Oh? Do I disgust you?' asked Max.

'Let me pluck it out, at least.'

'No,' said Max.

Harper continued blowing him, but she couldn't take her eyes off the grey pube.

***

A school half-term arrived. They seemed to occur every couple of weeks, to Max's growing annoyance. The kids came home in a bad mood, having been told they couldn't go on the school skiing trip. (Max didn't have the money.)

'What would you learn by going skiing anyway?' he reasoned.

To alleviate the bickering, Max, under instruction from Juno, agreed to take them into central London for the day. Juno didn't go, as she couldn't walk far.

Max invited Margot to accompany them to the Victoria and Albert Museum. (And the Science Museum, followed by the Natural History Museum).

Margot was already waiting for them in the foyer. She looked pale and distracted and didn't say much. She spent most of the time on her phone (as did the kids, who also wore headphones spewing out tinny dance music). Questions to Margot were met with yes and no answers.

Max took them to the Cast Court, his favourite room.

'That's Trajan's Column,' he said, to their indifference. 'That's the Puerta de la Gloria Gateway. And that's Michelangelo's *David*.'

'Not the real ones though, are they?' said Perdita.

'No, they're life-size plaster casts,' said Max. 'But that doesn't take away from their magnificence.'

'There's a real Nando's nearby!' said Willow, looking with genuine excitement at a food app on her phone.

'Cool,' said Aldous, Perdita and Willow, suddenly perking up.

'I'm buying,' said Margot, leading her nieces and nephew out.

Perdita looked back and indicated for Max to join them.

'Philistines!' shouted Max in their direction.

He walked away and visited the other museums on his own.

***

Max opened his eyes. Dawn. A single bright twinkly star hung in the firmament. Venus, he guessed.

'One fuck-up after another,' he said to himself, as a brief summation of his life.

33

An hour later. Lee sat by Max's bed.

'I'm sorry about your legs,' she said. 'It will take a while for the full realisation to sink in.'

'Where did you go?' asked Max.

'When?'

'When I needed you. I wanted to book more appointments with you at your house in Fulham, but you disappeared.'

'Oh. Yes,' said Lee. 'I... I was going through problems of my own back then.'

'What problems?'

'Personal problems. It's not important.'

'What problems?' repeated Max.

Lee stared out of the window.

'My father became ill. He lived in America, so I had to go and look after him. I stopped working to do so, but he died after a year. As a result I became ill myself. Chronic fatigue syndrome. It took me a long time to recover. I stayed in America and trained in cognitive psychology.'

'What made you come back?' asked Max.

'You. I heard about the murders. We have unfinished business.'

'Unfinished business?' asked Max.

Lee nodded.

'Has the new haemorrhage affected your memory?' she asked.

'I don't think so.' said Max. 'But it's wrecked me, physically.'

'Care to update me?' asked Lee.

Max, to the best of his ability, recounted the events so far enclosed. It took a while. When he finished, he looked exhausted.

'Sorry I haven't got further. I get distracted,' he said.

'You're very close now,' said Lee.

'I knew nothing of the bipolar and autism aspects of my personality,' said Max. 'They should have been flagged up.'

'There are discrepancies in your diagnoses.' said Lee, her face flushing momentarily. 'Your lawyer is looking into it.'

'My lawyer?' scowled Max. 'That idiot was in here just before you. He tried to get me to sign a contract for some TV movie-of-the-week about my life. He's only interested in the money. My paraplegia is something to be exploited to gain sympathy, he said. It will be great for the plot and character arc. The fucking plot and character arc!'

Max's face contorted with pain.

'He is somewhat idiosyncratic,' said Lee.

Max exhaled a deep sigh and calmed down.

'Did you speak to Claire?' he asked.

Lee's eyes looked down at the floor.

'No,' she said, after a long pause.

'You couldn't find her?' asked Max.

'We can continue this another time,' said Lee.

'No, I'm ready.' said Max. 'We're running out of time. There's much more I need to rediscover.'

'Then proceed when you're ready,' said Lee.

Max concentrated. His breathing slowed. He closed his eyes.

***

Max sat on a bus trying to memorise all of the lies on his fake CV. His hands shook with fear as he looked at the fake qualifications and fake references. He'd applied for a job as editor of a medical journal, never expecting to hear back from them. But they had. Now he headed to his first proper job interview at the age of forty-one. He expected them to quickly realise he was a hopeless imposter. He knew he'd fold under questioning and confess his fraudulent duplicity.

The bus pulled up right outside the medical journal offices in a busy square in central London. Max got out and stood at the entrance, with no intention of going inside. As usual, the ambitious and driven aspect of his nature pulled in the complete opposite direction of his lazy day-dreamer nature. Neither dominated or could be reconciled.

Max feared getting the job as much as not getting the job.

He grabbed a discarded coffee cup, gingerly walked into the building and signed in at the reception desk.

'Everything here is in chaos right now,' apologised the receptionist, who showed him into an empty corridor and told him to wait. Max badly needed to purge all of his bodily fluids at once.

A door was opened by a friendly-faced man with a trimmed beard.

'Max Hope? I'm Tom. Come in and take a pew.'

Max went inside the office. He left the door open so he could make a quick exit, but Tom told him to close it. They sat down. Tom sat behind a desk piled with ignored paperwork. His mobile phone kept buzzing, and he looked harried.

'Sorry, but I'll have to make this quick,' said Tom to Max. 'I've got ten meetings I need to be at right now. Let's hope one day we can harness the multiplicity of quantum physics, eh?'

Tom laughed. Max laughed too, out of politeness.

'The somewhat haphazard unorthodoxy of this interview is in no way a reflection on you, so I do apologise,' said Tom. 'The lowdown is, this company has just been taken over by another company, so it's in flux due to restructuring. I'm the deputy science editor and I'm not qualified to conduct job interviews, but the recruitment department have been fired, irony of ironies.'

'Irony of ironies,' echoed Max.

'Do you have a CV with you?' Tom asked. 'I lost the one you sent.'

Max handed over the CV and fake medical certificates he'd made at home. Tom took cursory glances at them.

His desk phone rang. He ignored it, and waited until it rung off.

'I see you're trained in evidence-based medicine?' said Tom.

'Yes. I'm also a novelist,' said Max. 'My new novel is about—'

Tom's desk phone rang again.

'These people will not leave me alone,' Tom growled. 'Fucking lawyers. My ex-wife is taking me to the cleaners.'

'I have a wife,' said Max, as the phone rang off again.

'And you worked as a health service manager?' asked Tom, typing a text and looking impatiently at his watch.

'Yes,' said Max, getting confident. 'I also trained as a radiographer, and have extensive knowledge in the fields of the effects of glycated haemoglobin and thyroid function.'

'Great. Great,' said Tom, not listening. 'What qualities do you feel make a good medical editor?'

'Well, erm…' Max didn't know the answer. 'Intelligence.'

'Fantastic,' said Tom. 'And you have editorial experience, right?'

The door opened. A woman in a business suit poked her head into the room.

'Tom, you really need to be at that meeting now,' she said.

'I'm on my way,' said Tom, smiling irritably.

The woman retreated and closed the door.

'As I'm sure you will know,' said Tom, 'the job basically involves ensuring methodological quality in the new medical articles. You'll be overseeing the substantive editing, the copyediting, proofreading, formatting, stuff like that. For someone like you, it'll be pretty easy, won't it?'

'Very.' laughed Max.

'Are there any questions you'd like to ask?' asked Tom.

'Erm…' said Max.

Someone knocked on the door.

'I'm on my bloody way!' shouted Tom.

Tom handed Max his CV back, then stared at him for a moment. Max didn't know if this was a good or bad sign.

'You know what?' said Tom. 'I've got a good instinct for people, and I like you, Max. You've got a nice energy about you. You would not believe some of the jokers I've met today. When can you start?'

Max tingled slightly. His right eyelid fluttered.

'Monday?' he heard himself say.

'Fantastic,' said Tom. 'We've got three weeks until the next journal comes out, so we can ease you in gently. The week before publication is when things get manic.'

Tom leaned across the desk and offered his hand.

'Welcome aboard,' he said.

Max was about to ask if he could have three weeks' salary in advance, but someone else knocked on the door and Tom had to go.

Minutes later, Max sat on another bus, still holding the empty cup of coffee. He was now a medical journal editor; an adult with a job, and a wife and a family. He'd become one of the millions of people Rex used to rail against. A commuter. A worker drone. It felt good.

'Keep overestimating them, Max,' he smiled to himself.

The initial euphoria wore off quickly. He'd made a commitment and would have to go through with it.

'Don't you need qualifications for that sort of job?' asked Juno, when he got home.

'I dazzled them with brilliance,' he said.

'You bludgeoned them with bullshit, more like,' she replied.

'Ye of little faith,' said Max.

Two standard rejections from literary agents appeared in his email box later that day. He lay in bed all Saturday afternoon with Harper, brooding about the negative responses.

'You should self-publish,' suggested Harper.

'Self-publishing is for failed writers.'

'No, it's very popular now,' she said, handing some sheets of paper to him. 'I printed off all the information you need.'

'So you pre-empted the rejections?' asked Max.

'I'm just trying to help.'

All weekend, Max worried about the person he'd be on Monday. He needed to make a good first impression and hoped he wouldn't be the apologetic vulnerable little boy he was at heart. The potential for awkwardness troubled him. *Why did I get into this predicament?* he thought. *I don't want to be a journal editor.* He felt hemmed-in by life. The wrong life. Waylaid.

If this attempt at normality failed, he vowed to commit suicide.

On Sunday, he drank himself into a stupor, but it didn't stop Monday morning from happening. He woke with a hangover and a feeling of utter dread. He vomited vast quantities and considered himself unfit for work, but Juno told him to 'man up'.

As he left the house, Juno said, 'Be good,' as if it was Max's first day at school. 'I'm going to be here on my own in this empty nest,' she continued sadly.

Max wanted to get the day over with as quickly as possible.

He drove to the nearest station and took an overcrowded commuter train packed with people who all looked like they wished they were somewhere else.

On the journey into the city, Max imagined worst-case scenarios of how his day could go. Would he last the entire day without being fired? Would someone discover his subterfuge? Was such deception an arrestable crime? He wasn't even sure what the job entailed.

'I'm way out of my depth,' Max muttered to himself.

The woman next to him glanced in his direction.

No, thought Max. *I'm approaching this wrong. It's merely a trivial moment. An obscure, brief chapter. Life amounts to nothing more than a series of meaningless activities. Everything is nothing.*

Max wanted to be sick again as he arrived outside the journal offices. He went next door to buy a coffee. The abundance of choice baffled him, and the staff made him feel like a moron.

'I just want a coffee with milk!' he kept repeating.

When he went into the medical journal reception (holding undrinkable soya sludge in a cup), the receptionist could find no record of him.

Fired even before I began, thought Max. *Another humiliation.*

As he turned to leave, Tom appeared, friendly-faced, but still harassed.

'Max, come and meet the team,' he said.

He led Max upstairs to a large central disorganised office. People were introduced to him. They all looked unimpressed by their new colleague. Max felt like he belonged to a different species.

'Max is a doctor and novelist, among other things,' Tom told them.

Max blushed. It did feel like the first day at school. His shoulders tightened in anticipation of being asked awkward questions about qualifications and training, but no one even feigned interest.

'Cool,' and 'Nice to meet you,' they said, more interested in their mobile phones.

Tom showed Max into a small side office with a desk, chair, phone, computer, half-dead pot plant and filing cabinets. A dirty window looked down into a cobbled courtyard.

'This is your new home,' said Tom without enthusiasm. 'As soon as things settle down, we'll get you an assistant. The editorial meeting is on Wednesday morning, so you can meet the team then. In the meantime, get yourself familiarised and let me know if you need anything.'

Max wanted to ask if he needed to sign a contract, and how much the salary was, and when did he get paid, but Tom rushed off.

Max sat down and switched the ancient computer on. While it booted, he looked out of the window. Down in the courtyard, the workers from neighbouring offices were already skiving off in small groups; drinking coffee, smoking and looking at their phones.

A woman called Jenny knocked on the open office door, then entered with a cup of coffee and a security lanyard.

'These are for you,' she said, putting the coffee next to his soya sludge.

She gave him a log in code for the computer, his new email address, and a flash drive with the latest articles he needed to read on it, then she smiled wanly and left, closing the door behind her.

Max checked his new email box. It was empty. He checked his home email address. Another standard rejection from a publisher. As usual, they 'couldn't connect with the material.'

He slotted the flash drive into the USB. Seventy-nine pages of writing appeared. The first article was headed: *Studies of Mitochondrial DNA in a Population of Drosophila melanogaster.*

Max scrolled down unending densely-written paragraphs.

'What the fuck?' said Max.

***

'You're bleeding,' said Lee.

Max was back in Room 9. Blood gushed out of his nose, soaking the bed sheets in deep crimson. Lee held some tissues to Max's nostrils.

'I fail to see where this is going,' said Max.

Lee pressed a button for assistance.

'We're closer now,' she said. 'Much closer.'

34

Nurses changed the sheets and cleaned Max up. Doctor Brooke could do little except stem the haemorrhaging.

'How do you feel about the upcoming trial?' he asked, when they were alone.

'I won't make it to trial,' said Max. 'I'll be dead by then. I can feel my body shutting down.'

The doctor went to the window and unnecessarily adjusted the blind.

***

Towards evening, Lee returned to Room 9, with Ched Hazzard in tow.

'It's about time your lawyer was included in this,' she said. 'Are you ready to continue?'

Max nodded.

'Make yourselves comfortable,' he said.

***

Max sat in his office at the medical journal, attempting for the third time to read the first paragraph of *Studies of Mitochondrial DNA in a Population of Drosophila melanogaster.* It was the most boring thing he'd ever read.

Jenny knocked, then came in with more articles in hard copy for him to read and edit.

'Everything okay?' she asked.

She had a lazy left eye. Max hadn't noticed it before.

'What exactly, in a roundabout way, and with regard to this particular article am I supposed to do?' asked Max, carefully.

Jenny narrowed her eye(s).

'First and foremost,' she said, humouring him, 'you have to ensure it fulfils the inclusion criteria in the review plan.'

Max nodded. He didn't know what the review plan was.

'Yes, I know that, but then what?'

'Then,' continued Jenny, 'you rigorously check it for accuracy and identify issues for clarification.'

'Of course. Then?'

'You return the edited review to the contributor for further revision until both parties are happy, then you sign off on it and put it forward for the next edition.'

'Exactly right,' said Max. 'Well done. What time is lunch?'

Jenny smiled thinly and put the new articles on his desk.

'Whenever you want,' she said.

Jenny left.

Good start, thought Max. *She already thinks I'm a total arsehole.*

He contemplated joining the skivers down in the courtyard; maybe make some new friends. Then he decided against it. They'd ask too many questions. He didn't belong there. Or anywhere. He realised how lonely and friendless his path was, at a remove from normal life. Isolation. Disconnect. He could only observe, but not join in.

Max sat alone on a bench in the square and ate a sandwich.

How many other people are imposters across the world? he mulled over to himself. *There must be hundreds of thousands, all looking over their shoulders every day. It's all pretence, like Harper said.*

He returned to the office and continued trying to understand the first article. An internet search informed him *Drosophila melanogaster* was the common fruit fly.

No one else bothered him that afternoon. At five o'clock he asked Jenny if it was okay to go home.

She looked at her watch.

'I guess so. But 5.30 is the usual end of day.'

Max hung around for ten minutes more, then sneaked out.

He went over to Harper's flat, but she was busy being spit roasted by two men.

Max went home.

'How did your day go?' asked Juno. She was in her studio painting a large triptych of Jesus undergoing a sex-change operation.

'It went,' said Max.

The next morning when he arrived at work, Tom said,

'Remember the editorial meeting tomorrow morning at 9.30.'

'Looking forward to it,' lied Max. 'I have lots of ideas.'

Max shut himself in his office and skim-read two new articles on his desk; one about bone density, one about intraocular lenses. Then he watched the skivers in the courtyard and twirled around in his swivel chair until he became dizzy.

He lunched alone in the square. Checked emails. Two unread. One from Tom reminding him of the editorial meeting tomorrow morning at 9.30 (again); the other, a literary agent rejection.

Max spent the whole afternoon spell-checking *Slush Pile,* then emailed the novel to a few self-publishing companies. He went home at 5pm. He considered calling in sick in the morning to avoid the editorial meeting.

But he didn't.

The next morning, Max sat on the bus contemplating different methods of suicide. He arrived at his office and nervously paced.

'Ready to meet the team?' asked Tom, poking his head in.

Tom led Max to a meeting room at the front of the building. (Max felt like he was being led to the guillotine). Its large windows looked out onto the square. One window was open, letting in exhaust fumes and noise. Seven people sat around a conference table. Tom briefly introduced each one. Max now felt incredibly gauche and out of place. Helpless. Hopeless. The meeting started with someone talking about fracture prevention as a possible lead article.

Someone else talked passionately about statins.

All of his life, Max had passed office buildings and seen people sitting around conference tables discussing stuff. He always wondered what they were talking about. Now here he sat, being one of those people (albeit pretending).

'As it's Max's first issue,' said Tom, 'I think he should contribute an article on his specialist subject, the effects of glycated haemoglobin in diabetes.'

Everyone turned and looked at Max.

'Oh, I think the fracture prevention review might be a better idea,' said Max. (The statin person scowled at him.)

'Don't be modest, Max,' said Tom. 'Tell us everything you know about the effects of glycated haemoglobin in diabetes.'

A bus noisily pulled up outside. Max figured if he ran out now, he might catch it.

What are you going to do, Max? Run away? Hide? Feign a heart attack? Confess to being an imposter?

'It's noisy in here,' he said, as a delaying tactic. 'Can the window be shut, please?'

A man got up and went to the window.

Max squirmed in his chair. He became hot and light-headed.

Think, Max. Think. Confess. Faint. Lie. Run.

All the people at the table were still looking at him expectantly. The whole universe stopped to look at him. He opened his mouth without knowing what he was going to say.

A sudden huge explosion outside shattered the windows. The entire building shook. The room went dark for a moment, then light again.

Max was thrown to the floor. His eardrums throbbed. Silence. Then screaming began in the street.

Max looked up. Broken glass and soot covered the conference table. The people around it were cowering. Apart from some cuts, they all seemed okay. Smoke drifted by the smashed windows.

The man by the window bled from multiple glass lacerations.

'The bus… it blew up,' the man gasped in shock.

'We need to get out of here!' shouted Tom.

A strange muted panic ensued. Everyone in the building began filing out into the square. Max followed.

Outside, a scene of devastation confronted them. The bus had been blown in half. Its roof peeled back like an open sardine tin.

Alarms made a cacophony of discordant noise. Glass and debris were scattered all along the street.

Then Max noticed the splattered blood everywhere, and body parts – a torso impaled on railings. A decapitated head on the pavement. The lower intestines on the bonnet of a parked van. An arm here. A leg.

Someone sobbed hysterically. Another person vomited.

Walking wounded staggered around in a daze.

'We need doctors.' said an approaching policeman.

'I have medical training, so do my colleagues,' said Tom, who then pointed at Max. 'This man is a doctor.'

'Come with me,' said the policeman.

The policeman, Tom, Max and four others picked their way towards the shattered bus. Inside it, survivors groaned for help.

All except Tom and Max climbed into the bus. Tom knelt down in the road to help a woman lying on the ground. Her legs had been ripped off. Her eyes stared wildly, as if unbelieving, then they rolled up into her head.

Tom started ripping clothing into strips to fashion a tourniquet as he recited the Lord's Prayer.

Max, watching Tom, stepped into something slippery. He looked down and saw he was standing in steaming human viscera.

He stumbled around to the other side of the bus to retch. Splinters of glass crunched underfoot. Emergency sirens could be heard approaching in every direction.

The bus driver sat at the wheel, covered in blood. He begged Max to help him, then fell out of the cab and into his arms. Max carried him over to where ambulances were arriving and handed the bus driver to paramedics. Ranks of deafening police cars and fire engines also raced into the square.

Max turned around and walked into the park at the square's centre. He sat on the bench where he'd eaten lunch the previous two days. The sun shone in the clear blue sky above. He looked up and saw a leg hanging listlessly from the branch of a tree. The leg was clad in blue denim and a black Converse high-top. Max gaped at the sight of such a surreal incongruity.

He sat there for a while, feeling the bus driver's blood congeal on his hands, then turn crusty. Claire entered his mind. Blood. Claire. Snow.

His phone rang in his pocket. He took it out – Juno's number.

'It says on the news that a terrorist bomb has blown up in the square where you work. Are you okay?' she asked, sounding concerned.

'I'm fine,' he said, with surprising calmness. 'See you later.'

He walked back to his office building. Police were cordoning off the square. Max showed them his lanyard and they allowed him through.

TV reporters jostled to speak to witnesses, but he bypassed them all.

Tom and the rest of the staff were gathered in the central journal office.

'Max, thank God, are you okay?' asked Tom.

'I'm fine,' said Max.

One of the office girls, who Max didn't even know, hugged him and sobbed on his shoulder.

'You saved lives,' she said, seeing the blood on his hands.

'It was nothing,' said Max.

Tom addressed the room.

'We've done all we can here today. Go home, take a couple of days off and regroup. If anyone needs counselling, we'll arrange it.'

The staff dispersed. Max extracted himself from the office girl. Tom patted Max on the back.

'What a day, mate. What a day,' said Tom.

Max went into his office to get his coat. In the courtyard, medics were setting up a temporary triage centre. Max watched a badly-burned woman on a stretcher convulsing with a cardiac arrest. A doctor attempted to save her, but it was too late. They pulled a sheet over her body.

Max managed to hail a cab and went home.

When Juno saw the blood on him, she looked shocked.

'I'm fine,' Max said. 'Don't cause a fuss,'

He showered, then watched the TV news. Twelve dead, it said. More expected to follow.

Max went into the garden at sunset and stared at the pond. The water had a menacing black sheen to it, which fascinated and scared him in a way he couldn't explain.

Am I supposed to have some kind of nervous breakdown to fulfil the act of being normal? he thought.

Max went to bed and slept soundly.

The next day, the death toll had risen to fifteen. Max felt remarkably unfazed. Too unfazed. It unnerved him.

He spent most of the day emailing an online publishing company. For an express service price of only £8000 (a bargain), an editor and proof-reader would knock *Slush Pile* into shape, then it would be available to download on their website (the writer receives 70% royalties), and printed copies could be ordered. *Remember – the cost is an investment!* proclaimed their advert.

'The price seems steep,' warned Juno. 'It's vanity publishing. You'll never make a profit back on it. Where will you get the money from?'

'I'll find a way,' said Max.

He went out that afternoon and pawned lots of Juno's jewellery without telling her. The pawnbroker sensed his desperation and gave him much less than it was worth, but Max didn't care; he now had funds to unleash *Slush Pile* onto the world. He vowed to buy the jewellery back when the book made a profit.

The next morning (Friday), Max paid the online publishing company.

As a conciliatory gesture, he spent the rest on a holiday to the coast for himself, Juno, and the three children that weekend.

Max pondered how he could exploit the trauma he witnessed as a way of making extra money. He set up an anonymous email account, then wrote the following letter to the local paper.

I thought you would like to know one of the heroes from the bus bombing is a local novelist and doctor. He works at the medical journal where the explosion happened, and was the first to rush out to help people. After saving several lives, he joined other emergency services in the triage area and treated casualties for around three hours. When asked, he modestly said that he wasn't brave, it was just the moral and ethical thing to do. He won't accept any praise or awards, but I feel the community should be proud of someone as courageous as Max Hope.

Max's finger wavered for the briefest of moments, then he pressed "send".

That afternoon, the kids came home from school. Aldous sported dreadlocks, and stank of marijuana.

'I've got a taste for the herb,' he said, when questioned about it.

Perdita had a military-style buzz cut and wore army fatigues, while Willow displayed a tongue piercing and nose rings.

'What have I reared?' said Max on first sight of them.

'Don't judge,' said Juno. 'Embrace change.'

After cursory initial enquiries about the bombing, the kids made for their rooms.

'Wait, I've got a surprise,' said Max. 'We're all going on holiday together to the coast for the weekend.'

A loud collective groan greeted him.

'Include me out,' said Aldous.

'We leave in T-minus thirty minutes,' said Max.

'Can I bring my boyfriend?' asked Willow.

'Can I bring my girlfriend?' asked Perdita.

'Can I bring my weed?' asked Aldous.

'No to all of the above,' said Max.

The kids looked to their mother. Juno shrugged with resignation.

Willow packed four suitcases just for herself. Perdita only needed one. Aldous stuffed a carrier bag with t-shirts.

They crammed into the Bentley and set off. The kids sat grumpily in the back listening to music on headphones. Juno sat in the passenger seat wearing huge black sunglasses like her mother. No one spoke.

Traffic jams plagued them all the way.

Max put Wagner's *Gotterdammerung* on the stereo at full volume.

When they arrived at the coast, a hurricane was blowing in. The sea crashed in torrents onto the beach and rain pelted down. The hotel Max had booked stood on a cliff, bearing the full brunt of the storm.

Wind howled through the casements. Floorboards creaked. The Hope family were the only guests.

'I'm scared,' said Willow, as they checked in.

'Well, I'm going down to the beach for a bracing walk,' said Max.

'Are you deranged?' asked Juno.

'You lot have no sense of adventure,' said Max.

He went outside (instantly regretting it) and made his way down many slippery flights of steps carved into a steep rock face leading to the beach, which stretched far into the distance in both directions.

He then strode onto the deserted sand and stood looking out to sea.

Black clouds scowled angrily overhead, but along the horizon a beautiful sunlight transfixed his eyes. He wanted to swim out to it.

The wind gusted around him. Sand stung his eyes. His hair flailed wildly. Max drew his coat closer to his body.

'Claire,' he whispered. 'Where are you?'

He walked further along the beach, stopping every now and then and turning around with the feeling of being followed.

What am I doing here? Where am I going? he thought. *I should go back. I should be with my family.*

The wind suddenly dropped. An eerie silence fell.

Max turned to go back, but the wind resumed with extra force, as if trying to attack him. It screamed and wailed in his ears:

'KILL THEM, MAX! KILL THEM ALL!'

Max ran in terror, lost in swirls of sand which pinched at his skin and clawed at his hair.

'KILL THEM, MAX! KILL THEM ALL!' it repeated.

Max ran up the steps and staggered into the hotel lounge, where Juno sat alone, reading a book and sipping a Martini.

'You look like a drowned rat,' she said.

Max took to his bed with a fever and stayed there until the next day.

The storm passed.

'The kids are bored,' said Juno. 'And so am I. We're going out to explore the town. You coming?'

'No,' said Max, wincing. 'I have a terrible migraine.'

'You shouldn't go out into storms then, you tool,' said Juno.

Max went down to the deserted bar and sat nursing a beer.

'I think I'm possessed,' he said to the barman.

The barman didn't speak English, but offered him some nuts.

Max's phone pinged, alerting him to a new email.

'Hey mate, hope ur OK. See u back at work on Monday; we have a trauma counsellor coming in. Tom xx.'

'Oh God,' Max groaned.

That evening in the empty hotel restaurant, Max sat at a

table with Juno, Aldous, Perdita and Willow. The three kids wore earphones and watched videos on iPads.

'Can you take those earphones out and switch those things off at the table, please?' said Max.

They reluctantly did so.

'Thank you,' continued Max. 'Now let's have a conversation like normal families do.'

No one said anything. Max got the ball rolling.

'Aldous, what have you done to your hair? You look stupid.'

'I like it,' shrugged Aldous. 'At least it's not dyed.'

Willow and Juno suppressed laughter.

'I think it's cultural appropriation,' said Perdita, snootily.

Silence descended once more.

'That was a good conversation,' said Aldous, to more suppressed laughter.

Max ground his teeth angrily.

'You have partners now, is that correct?' he asked the two girls.

Both nodded.

'Don't worry, I use protection,' said Willow.

Max tensed up. Juno blushed and looked away.

'What do you mean?' asked Max. 'Protection from what?'

'What do you think she means? Protection from the mafia?' laughed Aldous, before belching loudly.

'We're sexually active, Dad,' said Perdita. 'We have been for quite a while. It's normal.'

Max looked at Juno.

'Did you know about this?' he asked.

'They're not children anymore,' replied Juno.

'Yes they are!' said Max.

'I've shagged loads of girls,' boasted Aldous. 'It doesn't mean anything. It's just sex.'

'That's a typical misogynist comment,' said Perdita.

'Yeah, right,' said Aldous to Perdita. 'I hear you like your girlfriend to butt-fuck you with a strap-on.'

'Ick! Disgusting,' said Willow.

'Hypocrite,' said Aldous, to Willow. 'You're bisexual, like all girls are now, which is cool, but you've blown every boy in your year.'

'No, I haven't,' said Willow. 'Not every single one.'

'They call you "The Cream Queen",' laughed Aldous.

'That's enough!' barked Max.

He felt like stabbing everyone. Everyone, everywhere.

'Seeing as it's confession time – I've got a tattoo,' said Perdita.

'So have I,' said Willow.

'I've got loads,' said Aldous.

'Ooh, let's see!' said Juno, excited.

Aldous rolled up his sleeve – his upper arm was covered in a badly-rendered portrait of Bob Marley, marijuana leaves, a Jamaican flag and a spliff.

'Jesus Christ,' said Max.

'No, it's Bob Marley,' said Aldous. 'I'm gonna absolutely cover my whole body in this shit, man.'

'I think it has a certain artistic merit,' beamed Juno.

'I've also got elephant ears on either side of my dick,' said Aldous.

'Ick!' grimaced Willow.

Perdita rolled up her sleeve to reveal a tattoo of barbed wire around her upper arm.

'It symbolises the plight of refugees, and those of us in the LGBTQ community who are marginalised by bigotry and intolerance.'

'I've got exactly the same,' said Willow. 'Mine represents solidarity with Perdita's causes, but also with Black Lives Matter, which I'm passionate about—'

'Me too,' interrupted Perdita, eagerly trying to out-virtue her sister.

'Yes, and #MeToo,' added Willow.

A waiter brought the main meals to the table.

'Is this gluten-free?' Perdita asked.

'We're gluten-free and proud,' confirmed Willow, taking a photo of her food. 'Anyone who isn't is a fascist.'

'It is food, no?' said the Lithuanian waiter.

'I'm a vegan,' huffed Aldous. 'This risotto has chicken in it.'

Max sat silently watching his children complain about every aspect of the food. They fussed and dissected it until there was only a few vegetables left, which they reluctantly ate.

Juno ordered another bottle of wine (her second) for herself. She hardly ate anything anymore in an attempt to lose weight, but the drink bloated her all the same.

Willow continually took photos of herself pulling a 'duck face'.

'Why do you keep doing that?' Max asked her.

'I post them on social media. People are obsessed with me.'

Max gripped the arms of his chair. The vein in his temple throbbed. He didn't recognise the creatures around the table. They were not people he would willingly associate with, but it was like Stockholm Syndrome – he'd developed feelings for them.

'In other news,' he said to stop himself turning the table over, 'my novel is being published next week.'

'Cool,' said Aldous, as if genuinely interested. 'What's it about?'

'Fundamentally, it's about the complex nature of humankind and our capacity to accept the tyranny of unknowingness,' said Max.

'Not a comedy, then?' said Aldous.

'It sounds conceptually abstract,' said Perdita. 'How does it reflect the issues affecting a modern diverse society?'

'It reflects the fragile randomness of existence,' said Max, shifting uncomfortably in his chair. 'It transcends the tragic futility of the id.'

'That's some heavy shit, man,' said Aldous.

'Your father is paying an exorbitant fee to have it vanity published,' scoffed Juno. 'Everyone else rejected it. Everyone. Fifteen years in the making, that novel.'

An awkward silence.

'Oh God!' said Willow, rolling her eyes. 'Aldous is taking pictures of his knob under the table to sex-text to his girlfriends.'

Aldous giggled.

'Supply and demand,' he said. 'Supply and demand.'

Max stood up and walked out.

A few minutes later, he found himself standing alone on the empty beach, lit by the glow of a bright white full moon. Clouds scudded across it, creating ghostly penumbras. A breeze cooled Max's blood temperature.

'Max,' whispered a voice close to his ear.

Max looked around. The beach was deserted.

'They're laughing at you, Max,' said the voice. 'You know what you have to do. Kill them. Kill them all.'

'Shut up!' shouted Max.

'They'll laugh even more when your novel fails,' said the voice.

'I'm not listening,' said Max, covering his ears.

'They'll keep laughing, Max,' continued the voice. 'You must teach them the ultimate lesson. It is your destiny.'

Max turned and ran back up the steps to the hotel. When he got there, everything was in darkness. The restaurant and lounge were closed.

Max looked at his watch: 2am.

He knocked on his room door. After a while, Juno opened it, bleary-eyed and in pyjamas.

'Where the fuck have you been?' she said, going back to bed.

'I was only gone ten minutes,' he said.

'Five hours,' said Juno. 'I suppose you got drunk somewhere. Is this where we are now?'

'I'm stone-cold sober,' said Max.

He slid the glass balcony door open.

'We need to talk,' said Juno.

'I was only gone ten minutes,' he repeated.

Max stepped out onto the balcony and sat in a chair.

'I don't feel involved in your life anymore,' said Juno. 'You don't let me in.'

'There's nothing to be let into,' yawned Max.

He stared at the cold bone of moon. It refracted stabbing shards of light across the glassy black rippled waves.

'I can't do this anymore,' said Juno.

'Do what?' asked Max.

'Whatever it is we're doing,' said Juno, adding, 'You're a selfish, un-communicative, miserable and arrogant man.'

'You make it sound like a bad thing,' said Max.

He closed his eyes. Within seconds he fell asleep.

Max was woken by a seagull squawking on the balcony railing right in front of him. He shooed it away. Bright sunlight hurt his eyes.

Behind him in the room, Juno was ready to leave.

'We've had breakfast and the car is packed. I tried to wake you, but you didn't respond,' she said.

Max looked at his watch: 10am. His head felt like it was about to split open.

'What the hell is happening to me?' he mumbled.

They drove home in silence.

Once back, Max went over to see Harper, but she didn't let him in.

'I'm busy, honey,' she said.

'Do you have my money?' asked Max.

'It's all about the money with you, isn't it?' said Harper, suddenly turning angry and slamming the door in his face.

He tried to open it with his key, but the locks were changed.

'I own this fucking property!' he shouted through the letter box.

***

'He needs to rest now,' said Doctor Brooke, to Lee.

Max's eyes returned to Room 9. He lay still and tense. It was dark outside now.

Lee stood up.

'Good, Max,' she said. 'We're almost there.'

'I have a bad feeling about where my memories are going to take me,' said Max.

'We'll continue in the morning,' said Lee.

Ched Hazzard and Doctor Brooke both concurred.

Lee and Ched Hazzard left.

Doctor Brooke checked Max's temperature.

'I can arrange physiotherapy for you, if you like?' said the doctor.

'It may have escaped your notice, but I'm fucked,' said Max. 'Rutger is little use to me now.'

'Rutger got fired,' said the doctor. 'He was caught exposing himself to children in the swimming pool.'

'Really? You can't trust anyone these days,' said Max. 'Everyone's in it for themselves, for instant gratification.'

'On that we agree,' said the doctor, turning to leave. 'Do you want the light left on?'

'No,' said Max. 'Leave me in the dark where I belong.'

The doctor turned off the bedside lamp, then exited.

A thin oblong of light from the corridor fell across the bed. The hard-faced policewoman from before glanced through the door glass from time to time. Max tried to rest. He needed to preserve his energy for the big memory push the next day.

'Maybe I did kill them after all,' he said to himself.

35

A murky morning. Thin light penetrated patchy grey clouds. Max sat up in bed picking at a stodgy hospital breakfast. He left most of it. His appetite had gone.

Ched Hazzard and Lee arrived in Room 9. They were more business-like than before. No small talk. A sense of urgency.

'Shortly after the bus bomb, you started hearing a voice telling you to kill your family. Correct?' asked Ched Hazzard.

Max nodded.

'How did you feel about that?' Lee asked Max.

'Afraid.' shrugged Max.

'Please elaborate,' said Ched Hazzard.

'Remember, we're here to help you,' said Lee. 'We need as much detail as possible. Can you continue?'

Max nodded.

The three of them sat in silence for a while. Max stared at the wall.

***

By the following Monday morning, most of the windows in the square had been replaced, although some were still boarded up. The bus had been removed and taken to a warehouse to be examined by forensic experts. Just a scorch mark in the road remained.

All the cars were removed too, replaced by police bollards and traffic cones. The road and pavement had been hosed clean. The leg in the tree was gone, along with all the other body parts. What a horrible job to do. Somewhere, people were matching jumbled arms and legs and heads and torsos back together like broken mannequins.

The final death toll reached seventeen, which included the religious fanatic who blew himself up on the bus. At the maniac's flat, police found the walls covered in misinterpreted twisted slogans advocating the murderous teachings of a false prophet.

Amid the square's muted atmosphere, tourists were taking jaunty photos of themselves at the crime scene.

The facade of the medical journal building still bore scars of flying objects. Max went inside.

In the central office, Tom assembled the whole staff.

'We need healing, people,' he said. 'I've hired a self-help guru to get us back in the zone. Throughout the day, we'll each have one-on-one sessions with Guru Judy. Starting with Max.'

Tom led Max to an office requisitioned for Guru Judy.

'Is she a trained trauma counsellor?' asked Max.

'Guru Judy is a friend of mine,' said Tom. 'In you go, mate.'

Max opened the door and went inside. The unmistakable sickly-sweet aroma of joss sticks. The walls were draped in silk hangings. Mystical music combined with whale-song played on an iPod.

Guru Judy, a frumpy middle-aged suburban woman, sat cross-legged on a rug. She wore a caftan and headscarf.

'Oh fudge,' groaned Max.

At Guru Judy's suggestion, Max sat opposite her and uncomfortably assumed the lotus position.

'Closer,' she said. 'Feel my cleansing love. Consider your earth.'

Their knees were now touching.

Guru Judy talked about chakras and energy fields and connecting to ancient minerals and assorted mumbo-jumbo. All Max could think about was his legs were numb and his back ached.

Guru Judy waved her hands around Max to cleanse his aura.

'Honour your resistance,' she said, sensing his scepticism. 'Use it to allow your thoughts to be right here and now. Whenever your mind tries to take control, I want you to clap your hands and shout out, "I surrender".'

'Why?' asked Max.

'To connect with your heart,' said Guru Judy.

'But that's a meaningless statement,' said Max.

'Honour your resistance,' replied Guru Judy, forcefully.

Max tried to connect with his heart and honour his resistance, but all he could think about was slicing Guru Judy's stomach open, ripping out her innards and skeleton, then climbing inside and dancing around the room while wearing her hollowed-out epidermis.

Having failed to break Max, Guru Judy suggested they maintain eye contact while she talked about mental and physical blocks. Max was creatively and emotionally frigid, she diagnosed. She swayed gently from side to side, humming, and encouraged Max to do the same.

Max resisted at first, then gave in. They soon became synchronised. He felt woozy, then overwhelmed with emotion.

'Your aura is cleansing itself of negative poison,' said Guru Judy.

Max wanted to burst into tears, but he didn't know why. He clapped his hands and shouted, 'I surrender!', then he crawled into a corner, curled into the foetal position and sobbed uncontrollably.

Tom entered the room and looked at Max.

'Take the rest of the day off, mate,' he said.

Max went straight home. In the living room, Juno lay on the sofa in a dressing gown watching *The Exorcist* with the sound at full volume.

Ibsen and Chekhov greeted Max. Juno barely acknowledged him. The house smelled of teenagers.

'Where are the kids?' shouted Max above the movie noise.

'Out. Friends,' replied Juno.

'You okay?' asked Max.

Juno lifted her head up and looked at him.

'That's the first time you've ever asked me that,' she said.

She resumed watching the film.

'I had a headache,' shouted Max. 'They told me to come home.'

'You've only been in that job for a week,' Juno shouted back. 'You should be trying to impress them by putting in some effort.'

The doorbell rang. Max answered it.

'Yeah, what?' he said to a casually dressed man in his late forties.

'Max Hope?' asked the man.

'Depends who's asking,' said Max.

'I'm Bob Thrush, reporter for the *Chronicle*,' said the man, showing Max his ID card. 'We received an anonymous email last week telling us about your heroics in the bus bombing.'

'Oh?' said Max, feigning ignorance.

'I'd like to interview you,' said Bob. 'The *Chronicle* is considering you for a local hero award.'

'Well, you'd better come in,' said Max.

Bob stepped into the entrance hall.

'Your mother sucks cocks in hell!' screamed a demonic voice from the living room.

'Sorry, that's my wife,' said Max. 'I mean, the demon in the film she's watching. The Exorcist.'

'A classic of the genre,' said Bob.

'Let's go upstairs,' said Max, wishing he hadn't let the reporter in.

They went up and sat in Max's writing room.

'You have a lovely house,' said Bob. 'Must cost a fortune?'

'Mm,' said Max, guardedly.

He hadn't offered tea or coffee. He didn't want to leave the reporter alone for a second.

'I was lucky to find you at home during the day,' said Bob.

'I'm suffering flashbacks,' said Max. 'They let me come home.'

'So, you were one of the first on the scene, is that correct?'

'The very first,' lied Max. 'But I don't want any praise. I simply did the moral and ethical thing. There was no room for hesitation. I'm a doctor, so my medical training kicked in.'

'Yes, I want to talk about your medical training,' said Bob.

'Why?' asked Max.

'Well, I couldn't find any trace of you on the *Medical Register*,' said Bob. 'Or anywhere else, in fact.'

'I'm ex-directory,' blurted Max, immediately aware of the faux pas.

'Ex-directory?' asked Bob, narrowing his eyes.

'I don't want to talk about my medical training,' said Max.

'Where did you train, just out of interest?' asked Bob.

'Do you want to hear about how I saved several lives last week, or not?' asked Max, with a frosty stare.

'You don't display any of your medical degrees,' said Bob, looking at the empty walls. 'Nothing suggests you're a doctor at all.'

'You want to see my medical degrees?' said Max, getting up and rifling through a drawer with irritation. He pulled out the fakes he'd used at the job interview and held them up for Bob to see. 'Happy?'

Bob leaned forward to look at them better, but Max snatched them away and shoved them back into the drawer.

'Mr Hope, I was only asking—'

'I'm not feeling very well,' interrupted Max, wincing with pretend pain. He indicated that he wished to usher the reporter out. 'We'll have to do this another time.'

'Do you know who might have sent that email to us?' asked Bob.

'Not a clue. Now please leave,' said Max.

'You've been through a traumatic event,' said Bob. 'I'm sorry if I've upset you in any way.'

'You haven't,' said Max. 'I simply don't like the insinuating tone of your questions. It's unprofessional.'

'Who was that?' asked Juno, when the reporter had gone.

'No one,' said Max.

Max considered sending an email to the *Chronicle* to complain about Bob Thrush, but decided not to in case it drew more attention.

Later, the online publisher emailed Max to say *Slush Pile* was ready to go on sale on their website.

Max watched eagerly as it appeared on their list of many new novels. He immediately ordered twenty hardback copies to give to everyone at work.

'I am now a published author,' he announced to Juno and the children at dinner. They reacted with general indifference.

He obsessively checked sales on an app through the evening. It stayed at twenty (his twenty). He checked again first thing the next morning: twenty-two.

Max tingled with excitement. He'd sold two copies. Two!

He walked into work buzzing. In the central office, staff were talking animatedly, but as Max entered they went silent.

Max smiled at them, then went into his office. He looked out of the window into the courtyard. Office workers were smoking, drinking coffee and checking their phones as normal. People had died down there only a few days earlier.

He checked his phone for *Slush Pile* sales updates. Still twenty-two.

Never mind. Early days. Plenty of time. Word of mouth.

Without knocking, his office door opened and Tom, followed by two people Max didn't know, entered. Max thought it rude, but he smiled nevertheless.

'Good morning,' said Max. 'I'm feeling a bit better, thanks. My debut novel was published yesterday, and I've already sold many hundreds of copies. I'll bring some in tomorrow, and—'

'This is him,' interrupted Tom, chewing his lip.

Max registered the negative body language of the three people.

'Is something wrong?' asked Max.

'It's been brought to attention,' said Tom, 'that your medical degrees and certificates are...'

'Fakes,' said one of the other two.

'Your qualifications are a pack of lies,' said the second.

'Who are these two?' Max asked Tom, assuming a vestige of authority.

'We're legal representatives of this publication,' one of them replied.

'This is very embarrassing for me,' said Tom. 'I took him on in good faith. I had no reason to think he was an imposter.'

'An internal inquiry is in process about this deception,' said the first legal representative. 'We will—'

'I resign with immediate effect,' interrupted Max.

Silence.

'Is that all you have to say?' asked the second legal representative.

'No one needs to know about this, do they?' asked Max.

'Are you serious?' asked the first legal representative.

Max walked to the door.

'Where do you think you're going?' asked the second legal rep.

Max walked into the central office. Everyone watched him.

'Hey, come back here!' said the first legal rep.

Max walked out into the square and continued in a random direction for several streets. He passed swathes of people. People who, unlike him, belonged. People with places to go. People with careers and real qualifications. People who didn't have to pretend. Did they notice the pariah in their midst? The fake. The liar. The imposter. Something was missing in Max that they all had.

He chanced upon a railway bridge and decided to kill himself.

An Overground train thundered past below, making the bridge vibrate.

When the next one comes, I'll jump, he thought.

He waited, preparing himself for violent destruction. And he waited. And waited. No more trains came.

Max went to the station office and asked where all the trains were.

'A suicide down the tracks,' said a ticket guard. 'All trains have now been suspended on this line.'

'Well, isn't that just typical?' said Max.

Max walked on until he found himself in a park. He sat on a bench and watched the day go by while contemplating his situation.

His phone rang. He answered it.

'You bastard!' shouted Tom. 'They're now saying you took no part in saving anyone's life at all! You fucked off! I could lose my job for this, you cunt! I'm going to make sure you never—'

Max hung up.

This is all Bob Thrush's fault, thought Max. *He's behind this.*

Max drew up a plan: he'd borrow Harper's Taser, then go and maim that piece of shit reporter. He took a train over to Acton.

When he knocked on Harper's door, she wouldn't let him in, again.

'What's going on?' he shouted through the letterbox.

The door suddenly opened and out stepped Harper's ex-boyfriend, Scott, pointing the Taser at him.

'You want some of this, big man?' he said to Max.

Max backed away, into a fence. Scott, crazy-eyed, came at him and pressed the Taser hard to Max's face.

'Don't hurt him too much,' said Harper in the doorway, enjoying two men fighting over her.

'Do you wanna fuck with me?' Scott screamed at Max.

'No,' said Max. 'No, I don't.'

'Then why the fuck are you shouting through my letterbox?' said Scott.

'This is my property,' said Max.

Scott kneed Max in the balls. Max crumpled to the ground.

'This is Harper's property,' snarled Scott. 'That means it's now my property. And if you ever come here again, you're dead. You hear me? You're a fucking dead man!'

Scott went back into the flat.

Max looked at Harper.

'It's just business, baby,' shrugged Harper, shutting the door.

Max wandered aimlessly around the streets for a few hours, before going home at 6pm.

Juno was cooking dinner. The kids were in their rooms.

'Any calls for me?' asked Max, cautiously.

'Nope,' said Juno.

'Anyone at the door asking for me?'

'No. Why?'

'No reason,' said Max.

'When do you get paid?' asked Juno.

'Soon,' he lied. 'Why?'

'This place is a mess,' said Juno. 'We need to hire a new cleaner.'

The house was grubby. Dog shit stains were on the carpet.

'What happened to the old cleaner?' asked Max.

'You fired her to save money.'

'Why can't you do the cleaning?'

'I'm not a domestic slave!' shouted Juno. 'I'm an artist!'

Max checked his phone for book sales. Still twenty-two.

'I sold two books,' he said.

'Whoop-de-do,' said Juno.

Max went upstairs and stood under a steaming hot shower. His balls ached. He had a knot of fear in his stomach from the threat of exposure and humiliation. He wanted to run far away.

'Kill them, Max. Kill them all,' whispered the same voice as before.

'How?' asked Max.

'You figure it out,' said the voice.

Shortly, Max and Juno sat in front of the TV eating dinner on trays.

A repeat of one of her documentaries on art was being shown on an obscure satellite channel. Juno looked so young and vibrant as she walked around a Moroccan temple talking about ancient mosaics.

Max looked at the bovine woman at the opposite end of the sofa, and noticed a tear rolling down her cheek.

327

Max spent most of the evening in his writing room staring at his computer screen for *Slush Pile* sales updates. No matter how many times he kept refreshing the page, the figure remained the same.

He went backwards and forwards to an upstairs window and peered through a crack in the curtain at the street, looking for signs of police, reporters, or Tom.

The only cars that pulled onto the drive were hatchbacks with monotonous beats pumping from them. Teenager cars. Aldous, Perdita and Willow went out separately with different groups of friends to God-knows-where. Max heard Juno asking them as they left if they were going to be having sex and doing drugs.

'Hopefully,' they replied, with contemptuous entitlement.

'Drink plenty of water and use condoms,' she advised.

He and Juno both lay awake in bed that night, in the dark. He could not bring himself to reveal his sacking. He planned to leave in the morning as usual, and... and what?

The train suicide was a sign, thought Max. *I'm supposed to live. Destiny is telling me I have a purpose to fulfil, and it will allow me to fulfil it. It wants me to kill. It's ordering me to. It's justified.*

'I want a divorce,' said Juno, suddenly.

A long tense stillness followed. Max's mind raced.

'We'll talk about it in the morning,' he said.

Nothing more was spoken. Neither of them slept.

In the early hours, Aldous, Perdita and Willow slunk home one by one. Max heard them stumbling up to their rooms, paralytic, before they passed out on their beds. Willow was violently sick.

Max got up at dawn and left at 7.30 while Juno and the kids were still in bed. He wasn't sure where he was going, or how he would fill the day. He caught a commuter train into the city and flicked through the job section of a newspaper. Nothing appealed to Max. The jobs baffled him. Everything needed qualifications, or years of training. All were oversubscribed. Hundreds of applicants for every position.

Desperation. Nowhere to run. Nowhere to hide.

Fuck it. Fuck this bullshit. Fuck ambition, he thought. *Fuck adult responsibility. Fuck the system.*

Max didn't want to do anything.

He watched his fellow commuters. How many of them were faking their way through life? What subterfuge lay behind their carefully constructed facades?

'What have I done with my life?' Max said aloud. 'I'm a liar and a fraud. Now I'm snared in a trap of my own making.'

Two commuters glanced in his direction, the rest ignored him.

He alighted at Earls Court Tube on a whim, then bought a bottle of brandy in an off-licence and wandered the streets.

Prostitutes emerged from cheap hotels and rundown flats in once-grand Georgian terraces, wearing cheap tarty clothes and sad looks on their faces. They tottered off to appointments in high heels with defiant acceptance.

Lone shifty-looking men hung around doorways, staring at phones, impatiently waiting for anonymous sex in grubby bedrooms within, like drug addicts restless for their next fix.

If Max had the cash, he would have joined them.

He went into Old Brompton Cemetery feeling morbidly upset, then opened the brandy bottle and took a few swigs, guiltily looking to see if anyone was watching. As if it mattered. The first gulp almost made him retch, but then a mellow warm glow filled him. He walked amongst elaborate decaying monuments of dead God-fearing people, now turned into mud and slime by their benevolent creator.

Each one of these people had hopes and dreams, but to what end? he thought. *They loved. They were loved. They were generous and kind. They experienced happiness and success. So? Who cared now? Such empty bourgeois values we place on arbitrary things in our obscure temporary lives. No one's watching. There's no punishment or reward. The brutal fact is we're nothing more than material substance; mere receptacles of external sensations, nerve endings and complex chemical compounds. Our perceptions of this vale of tears are fictions of necessary delusion; a series of elaborate and compelling guesswork. What outrageous lies we allow ourselves to believe. All are invented constructs to save us from the unacceptable bleakness of reality.*

Max sat on a tomb, consumed by his own insignificance.

Culture? Religion? Commerce? Politics? Love? It's all bullshit, he thought. *A time will come when all life in this galaxy will be snuffed out. Colonising the moon or Mars won't save us.*

It began to rain.

Max took shelter under one of the long colonnades in the centre of the cemetery. Beneath it, steps led down to gated vaults where you could see shelves of Victorian lead-lined coffins. Rich Victorians made a grandiose theatrical display of death, unlike modern times of bland industrial disposal and identikit memorial. The society of dead lay inside those air-tight sarcophagi perfectly preserved, like hideous dolls awaiting resurrection.

Max checked *Slush Pile* sales on his phone. It had decreased by one, because someone had returned their order. They'd also added a one-line review, which read:

Slush Pile? Shit pile, more like.

'Kill them, Max. Kill them all,' whispered the voice.

'Yes, I will,' said Max, between more swigs of brandy. 'They leave me no choice. The end game is in motion.'

Max envisioned setting fire to the medical journal building, and then to Harper's flat, and his own house. And the *Chronicle* offices too.

Yes, burn them all to death. Blitzkrieg everything. Scorch the earth.

Cleanse the wounds of the past with flames of revenge. Leave no trace of this carnival of humiliation. Let death and destruction have dominion over all.

Juno was going to leave him. The kids would go with her. Everyone would know of his employment misdemeanour, and of the lies he'd told about his supposed bravery after the bus bomb. He'd swiftly become a homeless, penniless outcast.

His blood burned with shame. The brandy felt like hot mercury in his stomach, but he drank even more.

'KILL THEM ALL!' screamed the voice.

The clouds were turning black and the sky a strange mauve colour. A flash of lightning. A crack of thunder rolled overhead. Hailstones fell.

Max ran out into the storm and climbed onto a mausoleum roof. He raised his arms to the storm.

'Kill me! Kill me!' he shouted.

More lightning flashed. Thunder growled, but as quickly as the storm had arrived, it dispersed and faded away. The sun came out.

Max needed to talk to someone. Anyone. He needed to confess his evil designs. He took out his phone and called Margot. When she answered, there was lots of noise at her end of the line. People were shouting and chanting slogans of protest.

'I can't talk right now, Max,' said Margot. 'I'm at a demonstration rally. We're causing a public nuisance and making a lot of noise in the name of peace. All we want is peace, and we won't be quiet until we get it.'

'*Vegan peace!*' chanted the protestors. '*Queer peace! Black peace! Transgender peace! Feminist peace! Islamophobia peace!*'

'Margot, I have been ordained to fulfil a horrible destiny,' said Max.

'Sorry, what?' said Margot.

'I'm going to kill lots of people,' said Max.

'I can't hear you,' shouted Margot. 'Are you okay? Have you been blown up again?'

'I am a demonic god. I am invincible,' said Max.

'I can't understand a word you're saying,' said Margot.

'This is the last time you'll ever hear from me,' said Max.

'It's all kicking off here. I have to go,' said Margot.

'Fate wants me to kill them. It's inevitable,' said Max.

'It's turning into a riot. A peace riot. It's beautiful,' said Margot.

'*Nuclear peace! Abortion peace! Refugee peace!*'

Margot hung up.

Max's phone immediately rang again.

'Margot, I want to be stopped!' he said, on answering it.

'It's Bob Thrush,' said the reporter at the other end. 'We're going to run a front-page story about your employment deceit and your false claims of heroism in our next edition. I was wondering if you'd like to say anything about it?'

'Let's meet face to face,' said Max.

'Where?' asked the reporter.

'Old Brompton Cemetery, under the colonnade.'

'Why there?'

'Why not?' asked Max.

'I'd prefer a pub or cafe,'

'Take it or leave it. I'll be waiting,' said Max, hanging up.

He hunted around for a sharp object to bludgeon Bob Thrush with.

Finding nothing suitable, he smashed the brandy bottle and left the serrated neck of it in a strategic place along the colonnade, where he intended to stab the reporter to death.

Max hid behind a mausoleum and waited. A migraine throbbed, as though his brain was trying to kick its way out of his skull.

Thirty minutes later, he watched a car pull up by the colonnade. Bob Thrush got out of it with a photographer. Fucking cockroach. Max cancelled his murderous plan. He couldn't kill them both.

Max sneaked out of the cemetery, then caught a Tube to Deepak's surgery to obtain painkillers.

'I want the strongest stuff you've got,' he said, sitting in Deepak's consultation room. 'Horse tranquillisers, if you have them.'

'I can see you're in pain,' said Deepak. 'I'll write a prescription for a very powerful painkiller. They're new on the market, but you must be careful with them. They cause extreme drowsiness. Don't drive or operate heavy machinery within twenty-four hours of taking them.'

'I'll lock away the keys of my combine harvester,' said Max.

Deepak wrote out a prescription for four tablets only. Max doctored it to read fourteen. When he presented it to a pharmacist in the local chemists, she looked surprised.

'Fourteen?' she said, behind the counter. 'Those tablets are potent. I don't think we have the authority to issue that many to one person.'

'It's all right, I'm a doctor,' said Max.

After consulting a colleague, she gave him the tablets.

Max swallowed one on the Tube. It had an immediate effect.

A station master woke him in an empty carriage an hour later when the train reached the end of the line.

Max took the next train back into the city, but fell asleep again.

He woke up sitting on the poop deck of the Golden Hinde sailing ship tourist attraction docked next to Borough Market. An actor dressed as Captain Cook was making fun of him.

'This sailor's had too much grog!' the actor said, to the amusement of other visitors. Then he whispered close to Max's ear, 'Fuck off, you piss-head. There are children here.'

Somehow, Max found his way to the park in the square across from the medical journal. Up in the conference room, he saw Tom holding an editorial meeting.

'I… kill… you,' slurred Max, to himself.

A police officer woke Max on the park bench and threatened to arrest him for vagrancy. Night had fallen.

Max took a train over to Harper's flat, fully intending to pour petrol through her letterbox and set it alight. But he forgot to bring petrol, then he fell asleep on her doorstep. A voice woke him.

'You again?' said Scott, standing in the doorway. 'I said I'd kill you if you came here again. Here comes the pain!'

Max jumped up and ran down the street.

Scott chased after him, naked except for a flimsy bath robe.

Max soon lost him at a busy junction.

When Max arrived home, Bob Thrush was waiting in a car outside, by the driveway. The reporter got out and confronted him.

'You're proving to be elusive, aren't you?' said Bob, cockily.

Max, with strength he didn't know he had, grabbed Bob by the neck then lifted him up and pinned him against a tree.

'I lost my job because of you,' growled Max. 'Do you have any idea of the consequences of your actions?'

Bob looked terrified. There was something about the quiet power and fury burning in Max's eyes.

'Please don't kill me,' gasped Bob.

'Do not come here again,' said Max.

Max dropped him. Bob scuttled back to his car and sped off.

Max went into the house. Twenty hardback copies of *Slush Pile* sat in the hallway, delivered earlier in the day. None of his family had bothered to take one. Juno and the three kids were in the living room watching a noisy reality TV show.

Max took the books up to his writing room and threw them into a drawer.

'I have a new plan for you,' whispered the voice, close to his ear.

'I think I know what you have in mind,' said Max.

***

Max took a sharp intake of breath. He was back in Room 9.

'I can't go on,' he said, with tears streaming down his face.

'Let's take a short break,' said Lee.

36

Max stared at the yellowish-black bruises on his arms from all the new injections and insertions he'd received. The tracks of his veins underscored them in an unpleasant purplish blue. He regarded them with detachment.

'The voices-in-the-head stuff is going to be very divisive,' said Ched Hazzard, standing at the window.

'It was only one voice,' said Max.

'Even so,' said Ched Hazzard.

Lee entered the room. In the corridor, Detective Superintendent Lamb and Detective Chief Inspector Hicks paced impatiently.

'They're desperate to come in here and listen to Max's recollections,' said Lee.

'Well, they can't,' said Ched Hazzard, closing the door firmly. 'My client is on the verge of revealing potentially damaging information relating to his case.'

'But it's a foregone conclusion,' whispered Lee.

They both sat down next to the bed.

'It's not looking good for me, is it?' sighed Max. 'My whole life was a catalogue of disasters. I handled everything badly.'

'Tell me about it,' said Ched Hazzard.

'Shall we move on?' said Lee.

Max nodded slowly.

'I'm not looking forward to this,' he said.

***

Max sat at the desk in his writing room at home. He arranged the thirteen strong painkillers into a smiley face.

'Time is of the essence,' said the voice. 'Strike while the iron is hot.'

'Stop bombarding with well-known phrases,' said Max.

On a piece of paper he wrote: 1 x saw; 1 x hammer; 1 x tarpaulin; 1 x wheelbarrow; cleaning fluid; gaffer tape; lime.

He looked out of the window into the back garden. The black pond twinkled with moonlight. Max crossed out lime.

He went down to the living room, where Juno, Perdita and Willow's eyes were glued to a violent TV fantasy drama about dragons; Aldous stared at porn on his iPad.

Max watched the four of them, which they found uncomfortable.

'What do you want?' asked Juno.

'I'm glad you asked,' said Max, in an unusually warm way. 'I'd like us all to have dinner together tomorrow night. I'll cook.'

Max registered glances of discontent.

'Why?' asked Aldous.

'Two reasons,' said Max. '*Slush Pile* is selling phenomenally well, and I got promoted at work today.'

'You only started there last week, how could you get a promotion that quickly?' scoffed Juno.

'I have been touched by genius,' said Max.

'But you can't cook for shit,' asked Aldous.

'It will be a gesture of love and goodwill,' said Max.

The three children began to make lame excuses to get out of it; they all suddenly had important non-existent social engagements, but Max was having none of it.

'Can we invite friends?' asked Willow.

'No. Just us five,' said Max. 'Attendance is compulsory.'

The three kids looked at their mother for confirmation.

Juno sighed, then nodded.

'Thank you for your co-operation,' said Max.

Shortly, the doorbell rang. Max rushed to answer it. A hoodie-wearing monosyllabic teenage boy (bigger than Max) stood at the threshold. He wanted to see Willow. Willow took the boy up to her room. Max heard them having muffled sex.

Max complained to Juno about it.

'They're horny teenagers,' replied Juno.

Max slept alone that night. Juno used the spare bedroom. Max was glad. Disturbing dreams plagued him. The bedsheets lay in a twisted heap on the floor when he woke the next morning.

He breathed in the crisp early-morning air as he took Chekhov and Ibsen for a walk. Today was going to be a momentous day. The end of Max's old life, and the beginning of Year Zero.

'There is no punishment or reward,' he reminded himself when the frequent waves of doubt beset him. 'Destiny compels me.'

But what would his new life consist of? And where?

Max scaled back his plans for mass murder. The logistics of killing his mother, father, Mud, Fud, Harper, Scott, Bob Thrush and Tom seemed wrought with complications. His immediate family came first, then he'd deal with the rest.

When he returned home, Juno sat alone at the breakfast table.

'What should I cook tonight?' Max asked, brightly.

'When are we going to talk about the divorce?' asked Juno.

'Are you sure it's what you want?' asked Max.

'Absolutely. One hundred percent,' said Juno.

'We'll discuss it tonight,' said Max.

He left the house on the pretence of going to work. First though, he went into the garage. A wheelbarrow and a hammer were in there, so he crossed those off his list. He unhooked the garden hose, removed the nozzle from one end, and the other end from the tap in readiness for later, then he drove away.

At a cash machine, he withdrew the last money in his account. He went to a hardware store on the edge of town and bought a saw, industrial-strength cleaning fluids, gaffer tape and black tarpaulin.

'Planning a murder, are we?' laughed the cashier.

'Guilty as charged,' said Max, playfully.

He put the items in the car boot, then got a Tube into central London, where he killed a few hours sauntering around Covent Garden, then Trafalgar Square, Whitehall, Horse Guard's Parade and Downing Street, before mingling with tourists outside Buckingham Palace.

Time moved agonisingly slowly. Every step he took was a step closer to the point of no return.

He went to the South Bank and looked at the antiquarian book stalls, then he queued for the giant Ferris wheel (the London Eye) before climbing into one of its glass observation bubbles. As it reached its highest point, Max looked down at the Thames and the surrounding vast metropolis beyond. His phone rang.

'It's me, Bob Thrush,' said the reporter on the other end of the line.

'What do you want?' asked Max.

'I want money. Ten thousand quid, in cash.'

'Why?'

'Why? Because I'm blackmailing you, dickhead, that's why.'

'Why ten thousand pounds?' asked Max.

'I've got gambling debts, and… it's none of your fucking business!'

'I haven't got ten thousand pounds,' said Max.

'Don't lie, you liar,' said Bob. 'You're loaded. Bring the money in a briefcase to the main concourse at Waterloo station in one hour.'

'What would be the point of me doing that?' asked Max.

'Because maybe, just maybe, I can make that little story about your deception disappear.'

'I don't give a fuck about that,' said Max. 'Sorry, no deal.'

'No deal?' shouted Bob. 'You're not in a position to say no deal! I've got you by the bollocks!'

'On the contrary, this conversation is being recorded,' bluffed Max.

There was a long pause from Bob Thrush.

'You're bluffing,' he said eventually.

'I work for MI5, you prick,' said Max. 'You blew my cover, and now a big operation is in jeopardy because of you.'

He could hear Bob's breathing increase.

'This isn't me,' said Bob, panicking. 'I'm not Bob Thrush.'

The line went dead. Max smiled.

He continued gazing at the sunlit river winding into the distance.

I won't use the hammer on the kids, he thought.

On the Tube home, he checked his phone for sales updates of *Slush Pile*. The novelty had worn off. Still only one sale. A brief review by the anonymous buyer read: *Worst. Novel. Ever.*

Max recognised his family's grisly deaths would be symbolic, akin to a sacrifice; a howl of alienated discontent in a world of cold hard indifference.

Max Hope would also die tonight. The old Max Hope.

He stopped off at a vegan food store and bought the ingredients he needed. Vegan sausages. Vegan lasagne. Vegan everything. Then he drove home.

'Any messages for me?' he asked Juno.

'No,' she said.

'Are you going to help me cook?'

'Do I have a choice?' asked Juno.

Max went up to his room and set about crushing the painkillers (and some of Juno's sleeping pills) into fine powder using the hammer as a pestle. He collected it all into a cellophane pouch and sealed it.

Max went back down to the kitchen and helped (hindered) Juno, who did most of the preparation and cooking. Max pointed at things and made suggestions, most of which she ignored.

The kids wandered down every so often to inspect what their parents were doing, and gave snarky remarks about Max's cooking ability.

'Don't knock it till you try it,' said Max.

He opened an expensive bottle of red wine and placed it on the dining table, which he'd clothed in a pristine calico cloth along with their best cutlery and crystal glasses. He lit candles and put a Chopin album on, then poured himself a small glass of wine, before cutting up a line of powder and pouring it into the wine bottle.

After shutting Ibsen and Chekhov in the lounge, he stood at the dining room window and stared at the setting sun as it bathed the back garden in a bucolic red glow.

'The horror,' he whispered. 'The horror.'

When the food was ready, he called the kids down and told Juno to sit at one end of the dining table. The kids slunk down one by one with earphones on. Max made them remove the earphones and confiscated their mobile phones. ('It's like being in Auschwitz!' moaned Aldous.)

Max ushered them into the dining room.

He then went into the kitchen and sprinkled the rest of the powder over everyone's food, except his own.

'Voila,' he said, bringing in each meal.

Vegan pizza and sausages for Aldous. Tofu lasagne for Perdita. Vegan mushroom risotto for Willow and Juno. A bloody steak for himself.

Max poured everyone wine, then he took his place at the head of the table. No one spoke.

'Commence shovelling,' he said.

He had no appetite, but forced himself to eat so as not to arouse any suspicion. His armpits dripped with sweat. His foot tapped nervously with anticipation. He assumed the powdered pills would knock them out with quick effect, but what if they didn't? He really didn't want to use the hammer unless necessary.

Juno nibbled at her food and stared directly at Max behind her black sunglasses, all vestige of affection gone. She had turned into an obese version of her mother. No resemblance to Claire remained.

'This is surprisingly tasty,' said Perdita, after a few initial tastes.
The others gave similar murmurs of approval.

'I might not even throw this up,' said Willow, who looked gaunt and thin. Her clothes hung on her.

'Let's have a nice conversation,' said Max, fighting the urge to scream.

He looked at Perdita to start. Perdita tried to think of something to say.

'Um. Who can name all of Jupiter's moons?' she asked.

'I said a conversation, not a pub quiz,' said Max.

'Ganymede, Calisto, Io and Europa,' said Willow.

'You're in the same classes as me,' said Perdita, to her sister.

'Tell us about your job, Dad,' said Aldous, eating with his fingers.

'I edit medical articles for a prestigious journal.'

'Don't you need medical qualifications to do that?' asked Perdita.

'I have many hidden talents,' said Max.

'Very hidden,' muttered Juno.

Juno hardly ate anything, which concerned Max, but she was already on her second large glass of wine.

'So how did you get the job?' asked Aldous.

'By intuition,' replied Max, testily.

'I don't know what that means, but cool,' said Aldous.

'What are you girls studying at school at the moment?' asked Max, changing the subject.

'Wittgenstein and Kierkegaard in philosophy, Mahler in music, and Solzhenitsyn in literature,' said Willow.

'In other words, dead white men, as usual,' said Perdita. 'I don't see the relevance of such casually racist and sexist pseudo-intellectual patriarchal taxonomy. We're campaigning to wipe out the traditional curriculum and replace it with a progressive liberal, female, minority and gender-neutral consensus.'

'Have you applied for university yet?' Juno asked Aldous.

'Screw university,' said Aldous. 'I'm dropping out and going to my spiritual home – Jamaica. I'm gonna chill in the sun and get out of my head on rum and skunk all day.'

'How lame,' said Perdita.

'I'm going to be a veterinarian,' said Willow. 'As well as a fashion and make-up vlogger.'

'Because there aren't enough of them!' laughed Aldous.

'Oh, and your plans are so ambitious,' shot back Willow.

'Now, now,' said Juno.

'I'm going to be a campaigner against injustice, like Auntie Margot,' said Perdita.

'Auntie Margot was arrested yesterday,' said Willow. 'The cops beat her up. Nan and Granddad bailed her out.'

'One day, I'm going to make a public nuisance of myself in the name of a useful cause,' said Perdita.

'Cops, man. Feds. Fucking pigs,' said Aldous, yawning loudly.

'That's the wrong attitude to have,' said Juno. 'The police do a tough and unforgiving job. We should be grateful for them. To me, gratitude is one of the most ecstatic emotions. That, and forgiveness. I believe in the innate goodness in people.'

Then Juno dropped her fork. She attempted to pick it up, but dropped it again.

'First signs of Parkinson's,' joked Aldous.

'I sort of agree with you, Mummy,' said Perdita, with glazed eyes. 'I worry about my generation's cynical mistrust of politicians and the media, and the police and religion. We need to pull together to create a better society, rather than turn against each other because of our petty differences.'

'But it's the politicians and the media and the police and religion that create those divisions,' said Aldous, beginning to slur.

'Then it's up to us to correct the mistakes of the past, otherwise what sort of world are we going to inherit?' said Perdita.

'True dat,' said Aldous, trying to keep his eyes open. 'True dat.'

Willow giggled. Strings of drool hung from her mouth.

Max watched silently.

Juno attempted to pick up her cutlery again, but she'd lost the motor coordination skills to do so.

Aldous's head nodded as he blearily forced himself to stay awake.

Willow sank down in her chair.

'Meat… is… murder,' said Perdita, pointing at her father's steak and blinking her heavy-lidded eyes.

'It would have died anyway,' said Max.

'Not… in my… name,' said Perdita.

She lost consciousness and fell forward into her plate of food.

'Cool,' said Aldous, doing likewise.

Willow began snoring. Juno stopped moving.

Max's favourite Chopin nocturne, number 2 in E Flat, began. He sat humming along to it.

'What… have… you… done?' slurred Juno.

Max froze. Juno was still watching him behind her sunglasses. She then slid slowly off her chair and onto the floor, out cold.

Max jumped up, collected the remaining food, put it into Chekhov and Ibsen's bowls and let the dogs into the dining room to eat it. Although the dogs showed concern for Juno and the kids, their first priority was to gulp down the food as quickly as possible.

While they did so, Max cracked open a dining room window, closed the kitchen and dining room doors, and sealed them with towels.

He went out to the Bentley and attached the garden hose to the exhaust pipe, before feeding the hose through the window into the dining room.

Then he started the car engine. Exhaust fumes pumped into the dining room. Max could hear Chekhov and Ibsen whining and scratching at the doors with growing distress.

Max wandered down the drive to check no one was snooping around.

All was twilit and still.

He went back to the car and stepped on the accelerator.

'This is the most humane way,' Max told himself.

(Aldous's Auschwitz comment crossed his mind).

After ten minutes, he switched off the engine, removed the hose from the exhaust, then wound it up and put it back in the garage. He took the tarpaulin out of the boot, grabbed the wheelbarrow and the saw and took them into the living room.

The dogs were silent now – but someone coughed. Juno.

'Fuck,' said Max.

He put a handkerchief over his mouth and nose and looked into the dining room. Through the toxic fog, he saw the three teenagers were dead. All colour had gone from their faces, their lips were blue and their eyes were slightly open, but sightless. The dogs were dead too.

But Juno was crawling across the floor, purple-lipped, gasping for air.

Max went inside and knelt by her.

'Why?' she gasped.

'Believe me, I wish it hadn't come to this.' said Max.

He put his hands around her neck and strangled her. She writhed.

'Don't fight it,' he told her. 'You'll die quicker this way.'

Juno shuddered. Max stared deep into her eyes as her body stiffened, then went limp. Juno was dead.

He cradled her head for a short while. The fumes started to make him woozy, so he stood up and opened wide all the windows and wafted it out, pausing only to listen to Nocturne number 8 in D Flat.

'Now I am become death, the destroyer of worlds,' he said.

The house phone rang. Max hesitated before answering, 'Hello?'

'Oh, it's you,' sneered Mud. 'I want to talk to my daughter.'

'She's not here,' said Max. 'She's gone away.'

'Where?' asked Mud.

'She's on a plane right now heading to Australia. Didn't she tell you? She's got a new job out there. All very last minute, you know how these TV things happen. The kids and I are joining her for several weeks. It's in a very remote part of the country, so it will be difficult to get hold of us, but don't worry, everything is fine. Oh, the taxi has just arrived to take us to the airport. Got to go. I'll let Juno know you called. Bye-bye.'

Max hung up, then searched around for Juno's phone and switched it off. The kids' phones constantly pinged with messages from various friends and sex partners. It took Max twenty minutes to text them all the same lie about how they were just boarding a plane at short notice and would be out of reach for a few weeks, then he switched every phone off.

Running on pure adrenaline, Max sent emails to family, friends, and the kids' school explaining the sudden departure of the family on the fact that he was a secret agent, and they had to move to Canada so he could testify at a drugs trafficking trial.

To obfuscate things even more, he claimed he was also on a witness protection programme, so it was important that no contact be made until a safe period had elapsed.

Max shut the windows, drew the curtains, turned some lamps on, then dragged the four corpses, already stiffening from rigor mortis, into the living room and propped them up on the sofa.

'I know I haven't been the greatest husband or father,' he said, to the gruesome tableau, 'but I'm not entirely to blame for this situation. I would, however, like you to know that I forgive you.'

Max changed the music on the stereo – "Mon Coeur S'ouvre a ta Voix", from Saint-Saens' *Samson and Delilah*. It played on a loop at full volume.

Now came the tricky bit: how to dispose of the bodies. Max hadn't thought this problem through properly and began to see the potential difficulties, namely of cutting up and disposing of them in the pond.

Draining the blood alone would be a logistical nightmare.

He awkwardly dragged Juno into the ground floor shower room. Piss, shit and trapped methane seeped out of her.

With great difficulty, he hung her upside down in the shower cubicle and slit her throat with a kitchen knife. Blood gushed out in a torrent of angry redness that threatened to overflow the shower basin. Max had to unclog pubic hair from the plughole, before the drain greedily glugged the liquid down.

Each time the flow slowed, Max sliced the neck incision more, to the point where Juno's head stayed attached by only a flap of nape skin.

He stripped to his underwear and diligently carried out the same procedure on Perdita, Willow and Aldous, in the bigger upstairs walk-in shower, where all three could be drained at once.

'Blood of my blood,' he said, letting the warm crimson pour through his fingers. 'Flesh of my flesh. I give life, and I take it away.'

He washed his hands, then put on a coat and shoes and went out to the side alley where there was a pile of unused bricks. He loaded some into the wheelbarrow and deposited them at the edge of the pond, before pushing the empty wheelbarrow to the back door. In the dining room, he cut up some tarpaulin and wrapped Chekhov and Ibsen in it, sealed with gaffer tape. He put the dogs into the wheelbarrow, wheeled them to the pond, weighed them down with bricks and tipped them into the water.

A splash, a pop of bubbles, then nothing.

Returning to Juno, now sufficiently drained, Max sawed off her limbs. He parcelled her remains up in tarpaulin, sealed it, then put her in the wheelbarrow. Weighed down with bricks, he dumped her in the pond.

After dismembering the other bodies upstairs, he looked at the heap of viscera, tendon, cartilage and bone and the wet raw meat that used to constitute his children. Their flesh had sliced like tender tuna steak.

He bundled it all up in tarpaulin. Wheelbarrow. Bricks. Pond. Splash.

Max watched the batch of body parts sink into the murky depths. He waited until the last few bubbles popped.

A twig snapped in the dark nearby. Max looked up. Two gold eyes were watching him. A fox. It scrambled out of sight. Max exhaled.

He spent the following hours in a frenzy of cleaning, not stopping until the shower rooms, the dining room, and kitchen were spick and span, and everything returned to its rightful place (the unused bricks, the now-clean wheelbarrow, the unused hammer and the kitchen knife). Carpets were scrubbed of any leaked bodily fluids, and his clothes laundered.

Next, he gathered up every mobile phone and tablet computer, put them all in a black bin liner, and threw them in the pond too, along with the saw and gaffer tape.

He showered, dressed, then went around examining for anything he might have missed. No trace of the night's horror remained.

Finally, he rifled through Juno's wardrobe, certain she had a stash of emergency cash hidden in there. And lo, he found a shoebox with £5000 in it.

Max collapsed onto the bed and fell asleep.

He woke at dawn. His whole body ached. For several blissful seconds he couldn't recall why. Then it all came flooding back to him. He sat up, covered in cold sweat. Had it been a horrible nightmare? Max ran from room to room, hoping Juno and the kids were still alive.

The house was empty.

Max went out to the pond. Everything appeared normal, apart from a single blob of blood floating on the surface. As he watched, a koi carp rose up out of the murk and swallowed it.

Max walked around the pond, peering into the water. From certain angles, if you squinted, the tarpaulins could be seen at the bottom.

However, silt was already forming a layer on them. Soon they would be totally obscured.

Max packed a suitcase and put it in the boot of his car. He held no sentimentality for the house or its belongings, only taking some of Juno's remaining jewellery to pawn, if necessary.

He looked everywhere for his passport, but couldn't find it. A quick escape to the continent was out of the question. The hidden places of the United Kingdom would suffice.

Max drove away without looking back. First stop – his parents' house.

'What the hell are you doing here?' his dad asked.

Max hugged him, then he kissed his mum.

I forgive you, he thought. *I condemn you both to life.*

'I've been promoted to set up a new branch of business in Australia.' said Max in reply to his dad's welcome. 'I'll be there for a long time overseeing the operation. Juno and the kids are joining me. We fly out in a few hours. I thought you'd like to know.'

'That's all rather sudden,' said Mum.

'It's the nature of the beast,' said Max. 'I'll give you more details as and when I know them.'

'Max, what's going on?' asked Mum, with genuine concern. 'You don't look well. You're not making sense.'

'It's that stuck-up bitch wife of his,' said Dad. 'She's always worn the trousers in his house.'

'Don't talk about my wife like that,' retorted Max. 'Why couldn't you have been a nice father? I might have been happy and fulfilled.'

'Oh, boo-hoo, Max,' sniped Dad, 'Blame me for your inadequacies, and defer responsibility, as usual. You're always the victim.'

'Shut up,' hissed Mum to Dad.

'I'd better be off,' said Max, looking at his watch. 'Time for me to start a new life far away from here.'

'I gave you the best of everything,' said Dad. 'You're an ungrateful, spoilt, and emotionally stunted little bastard.'

'All you've ever done is criticise and belittle me,' said Max. 'You never gave me a word of encouragement.'

'It's called "tough love",' said Dad, almost swallowing his words. A well of anger boiled up in Max, then subsided.

'The truth is, me, Juno and the kids are emigrating to Australia. We never want to come back. There's nothing here for us,' said Max.

'Don't say that,' said Mum. 'We're here.'

Max looked around at the living room – there were no photos of him or Margot on display.

'Why did you abandon me and Margot in the park?' he asked.

'What?' asked Mum.

'You and Dad got in the car and left us in the park. You went home without telling us. Who does that to their kids?'

'I don't remember that happening,' said Mum.

'It didn't happen, that's why,' said Dad.

Max stared at both of them and shook his head.

'I wish I could forget so easily,' he said. 'I wish I could forget all of it.'

As he walked back to his car, his mum called out, 'Maximillian,' but he didn't stop.

He climbed into the Bentley and drove away.

Tears flooded his eyes. The familiar streets and houses of his youth passed by for the last time. A primal yearning churned deep inside. He cried for his lost youth. He sobbed for his lost family. He wept with regret for the unfixable disaster his life had become.

***

The memory faded and blurred into Room 9. Tears ran down Max's cheeks.

Lee, and Ched Hazzard remained in their chairs.

'How do you feel, Max?' asked Lee.

'I'm a cold-blooded murderer,' said Max. 'I did it all along. You knew. Everyone was right about me. I clinically killed my family. They didn't deserve it. I can't bring them back.'

'Remorse is good,' said Ched Hazzard. 'It plays well in court.'

'I don't need a trial. I'm guilty.' said Max.

349

'But we have lots to play with here,' said his lawyer. 'I'm talking about borderline personality, bipolar disorder, post-traumatic stress, possible autism, as well as drug addiction, depression and—'

'No,' interrupted Max. 'No excuses. I'm guilty.'

'But, Max, we—'

'Leave me alone!' shouted Max to Ched Hazzard.

'We'll give you some space,' said Lee, getting up and prompting the lawyer to do the same.

'I need to stretch my legs,' concurred Ched Hazzard.

He left, but Lee lingered at the door.

'The question at the heart of this will continue to be, "Why did you do it?"' she said.

Max lay silently for nearly half a minute.

'Why does anyone do anything?' he finally said. 'Who knows what true motivations lie at the heart of man? I'm in the dark. We all are.'

Lee left, dissatisfied.

Max tried to hold his breath for as long as possible in a vain attempt to bring on heart failure. It didn't work. It just gave him acid reflux and a full colostomy bag.

'I'm sorry, Juno,' he gasped. 'I'm sorry, Aldous, Perdita, Willow, Mum, Dad, and Margot. I am so, so sorry.'

37

Over the course of the evening and through the night, Max was left alone, save for occasional visits by nurses (accompanied by a police officer) to check on him. Max barely noticed them. He lay quite still, pursuing his fugitive self across the canyons of his mind.

***

After driving away from his parents' house, Max dried his eyes and went to a bank to withdraw all the money in a joint account Juno had denied existed. He found the cash card and PIN number amidst her belongings, but expected there to only be a few thousand pounds in it, at most.

At the bank counter, a dead-eyed clerk looked at a computer screen and said, 'Twenty-five,' in response to Max's request for an account statement.

'There's only twenty-five pounds in the account?' huffed Max.

'Twenty-five thousand,' said the clerk.

Juno had been pleading poverty, the fucking liar.

'I'd like to withdraw it all, please,' said Max.

'Not possible, sir,' yawned the clerk. 'We have an anti-fraud policy maximum £2000 limit on counter cash withdrawals.'

'But I have ID with me,' said Max.

'We need twenty-four hours' notice for big amounts.' said the clerk.

Max was about to go ballistic and demand his money, when a branch manager invited him into her office.

Max reluctantly agreed, although those private side offices intimidated him. Important transactions took place inside them; serious, grown-up responsible stuff.

She offered him tea or coffee, but he could tell she didn't want him to say yes. He almost said yes to piss her off, but declined. She was very polite, yet seemed harassed and overworked. Max just wanted to get out of there.

It must be horrible having to be professionally nice every day when you don't feel like it, thought Max. *But fuck her, and fuck the crooks who run the banks. Fuck all those corrupt bastards.*

She tapped (sometimes jabbed) at the keys of her computer, and kept apologising for the system being slow, even though it wasn't. Clearly under pressure, she kept up the polite pretence.

Max smiled at the possibility of her being a fake too, but a better fake than himself, obviously.

Finding her to be attractive, he attempted to flirt. She didn't respond.

Women no longer paid him any attention. They didn't even bother casually flirting with him anymore. He'd become an early middle-aged ghost, a stealth bomber of total male irrelevance to women. He figured it could work in his favour, as a cloak of anonymity.

'Can I ask what the money is for?' she asked.

'A grand piano,' lied Max. 'I'm a concert pianist.'

She glanced at his hands.

'I used to play the cello,' she said, absently.

The transaction was quickly and painlessly completed, and the branch manager asked him if he wanted anything else. Max felt like saying, 'My wife and children are lying at the bottom of the pond in my back garden in a state of dismemberment. This time yesterday, they were alive and well and blissfully unaware of the horrible fate that awaited them. Isn't life pitiless?'

But Max simply said, 'No.'

He left the bank with £2000 in cash, and the best wishes of the branch manager. Stepping outside, Max breathed deeply of the exhaust fumes which greeted his lungs in the busy high street. It was a mild sunny day, but everyone walked fast. No one dawdled, not even the old people. Life moved faster now than ever before. No one had any patience. No one wanted to chat or listen. They all stared at their phones for instant hits of media content. The great connected disconnectedness. Stay up-to-date. Stay relevant. Consume. I want. I need. Me, me, me. What about me?

'I'm out,' said Max, to himself.

He crossed the road and sat in a café nursing a coffee. He emailed the online publishing company asking why *Slush Pile* had sold so badly.

A prompt reply came, *'We are not liable for advertising and publicity of the books. You didn't promote it on social media as far as we are aware. Plus, your novel tested badly with our editorial staff. They considered it to be bleak and lacking plot and dramatic tension.'*

Max replied, *Yet you still took my fucking money, didn't you, you cunts. Fuck you!'*

When he next checked their website, *Slush Pile* had been withdrawn from sale.

Max drove the Bentley to a car dealership on the edge of town and part-exchanged it for a bland second-hand modern hatchback. The salesman sensed Max's impatience for a quick sale and gave him a terrible deal. Max knew it was a terrible deal, but let the dealer fuck him over just to get away from the place. He desperately wanted to start his new life and disappear.

He sat in the salesman's office waiting for the paperwork to go through, contemplating his next move.

Okay, he thought to himself. *I drive away from here and just keep going. Cornwall? Isle of Wight? No, I'll head north. Find a seaside town. Stay in a bed and breakfast. Lie low and bide my time. Change my name. To what?* The salesman's name was Dickie Daws. Max smiled. *I like that*, he thought.

'What's the reason for selling such a nice car?' asked Dickie Daws.

'Practical reasons,' said Max. 'I have kids.'

'Kids are great, aren't they?' said Dickie Daws.

He got his phone out and showed Max photos of his small children.

Max inwardly groaned and thought of saying, 'Don't show me photos of your ugly children, you apron-stringed pussy-whipped emasculated piece of shit.'

But he realised how unsympathetic it sounded, so he simply nodded and said, 'Cute kids.'

Max drove away in the Honda (or Hyundai, or whatever it was; it stank of sickly-sweet pine air freshener). His suitcases were in the boot and the open road was at his mercy. Free at last.

Continuous suburban sprawl glided past. Lots of people were out doing humdrum stuff, keeping themselves occupied and useful in the human formicary.

Max soon found himself on the M25 London orbital road. The M1 North came into view. Yes, he would head north. To York, maybe. Somewhere. Anywhere.

His car was one of hundreds of thousands of others snaking their way across the landscape. What were they all doing? Where were they going? To what end?

He drove non-stop for three hours, then stopped at a motorway rest area. Petrol. Coffee. Food.

A mass of people in transit. Organised chaos. All of them unaware of the serial killer in plain sight.

Police officers were on patrol. Max wondered if they were looking for him. Had his dark deeds already been discovered? Surely not. He looked for potential escape routes, then got up and left.

This is my new life, he thought as he got back into his car. *Running and hiding. Vigilant at all times. So be it.*

It was early evening when he reached York. In an elegant residential outskirt of the city, he randomly picked a small hotel in an Edwardian villa, and booked in for the night using the Dickie Daws pseudonym.

He ate dinner in his chintzy room, then fell asleep in a chair.

The next morning, Max woke early and looked at a road map of the UK. His eyes fell upon the coastal town of Whitby.

That's where Dracula came ashore, he thought to himself. *Perfect. Me and Count Dracula – both outcasts and fugitives.*

At breakfast, he tried to make flirtatious small talk with the pretty waitress, but she wasn't interested.

Max told the hotel receptionist he wanted to visit York Minster. He was informed it was in walking distance and given directions. When he finally reached it (after getting lost), he was hot and exhausted, so he turned around and got a cab back to the hotel, in a bad mood.

He watched the TV news in his room, but nothing interesting seemed to be happening in the world. He briefly switched on his phone. No emails.

He stared at himself in a mirror for three whole hours.

After taking a shower, he towelled himself dry. Then he took another shower, scrubbing his skin, and towelling it again until raw.

A distant police siren prompted him to check out. He drove on, stopping at a pharmacy to buy a hat, sunglasses and hair dye.

A hazy afternoon sun hung in the sky when Max arrived in Whitby.

He chose a hotel on the West Cliff, and specified a room overlooking the beach, which he was duly given. An over-friendly staff member let him into the room. It was chintzy (again), but had a nice en-suite bathroom and a large bay window. If you craned your neck enough to the right, Whitby Abbey became visible.

'Are you here for a reason?' asked the staff member.

'Is anyone?' replied Max.

Max used the hotel free Wi-Fi to check the internet, but he found no news regarding himself. He also checked the latest online edition of the *Chronicle*, but it also contained no mention of his name.

Bob Thrush must have been scared off by my MI5 bluff, he thought, but he knew the prick would soon be sniffing around again. It was only a matter of when.

Max put on his new hat and sunglasses and looked in a mirror.

If I passed myself in the street, I would think I was someone who had their shit together, he thought. *How wrong I would be. How little we know of each other. We remain unknown, even to ourselves. Didn't Harper say that?*

He went down to the beach. The weather was turning. A strong wind blew in from the choppy sea. Dark clouds scowled. He watched as a young family hurriedly packed away their belongings, and a sense of envy stole over him. They were normal, with friends and schedules and places to be. Max had nowhere to go and nothing to do.

'I had that life once,' he reminded himself. 'It didn't make me happy, did it? I am now where I wanted to be all along. Nowhere. Free.'

But it was freedom at a great cost. A despicable freedom.

He thought of Tom and his ex-colleagues at the medical journal; they were working at their desks right now. But for circumstance, Max would be there too, in that crappy little office, editing articles about haemorrhoid cream and diarrhoea treatments, or staring down at the people in the courtyard. But he wasn't there, he was here on a windswept beach with seagulls wheeling and squawking overhead.

The beach stretched out wide and long. Max walked to the deserted far end and skimmed pebbles across the surf.

I'm glad to be out of that life, he thought. *All those wankers with their cups of coffee, and their parochial pay-grade obsessed career ambitions.* Then he added as an afterthought, *I can't imagine myself being alive this time next year.*

He picked up interesting shells and examined them.

I didn't need to kill my family. I should have killed myself instead.

Early evening rapidly approached. In the far distance, the outline of Whitby Abbey loomed. An impulse urged Max to go there now.

No time to lose. Time waits for no one. The opium of time.

His family were dead in the pond at home. Rex lay decomposing in a mausoleum. Zoe was a skeleton in a wicker coffin. Bus bomb victims' bodies were being pieced back together. Broken people in boxes. You always think there's going to be more time. But time for what?

Max walked back along the beach.

Spots of rain began falling as he climbed the 199 steps to the abbey.

He reached the top, stopping twice to catch his breath.

Old age creeping up on me, he thought. *The day will soon come when I won't physically be capable of doing this anymore. I'll kill myself when it happens. An ideological martyrdom, equal to Socrates.*

Max walked alone and lonely around the ruins, under the bruised sky. Trapped in life. The social contract no longer applied to him. A great fear suddenly engulfed his senses. He tried to contain it, but the dark beauty of the abbey's romantic decay encouraged the feeling.

A scream tried to prise his lips apart.

On the sea's horizon, the sun ran red with blood.

Max stumbled into the graveyard of Saint Mary's. There, amongst its gnarled tombstones, furious tears ran down his cheeks.

'What was the point of your lives?' he said aloud. 'Where are you now? Where do we go?'

Max could remember less and less of his own life. Entire years were becoming blank. He wanted death to cleanse him of the burdensome memories.

The doors to the church were locked. Max banged desperately on them for admittance, certain that something was coming for him, something menacing and full of vengeance.

He ran to the cliff top. Wide-eyed with terror, he screamed long and loud at the sunset until he passed out.

When he woke, a hiker dressed in waterproof clothes was standing over him in the dusk.

'You okay, mate?' asked the hiker. 'Shall I call an ambulance?'

Max jumped up and backed away from the hiker, then he ran all the way back to the hotel. He got into bed shivering with a fever and hid under the covers until overcome by restless sleep.

The next morning, he sat in the bay window of his room, looking out at the grey sky. Sea mist rolled in. Max's bones ached. His stomach rumbled and his head throbbed with a migraine.

He switched on his phone. It immediately pinged with messages. An email from Margot read: *'Where r u?'*

An email from the school headmaster read: *'I would like you to explain your rather bizarre previous email. The education of your children is of paramount importance.'*

An email from Bob Thrush read: *'You can run, but you can't hide.'*

The phone began to ring. Max waited until it rang off.

Had his crime been discovered already? And why did Margot want to know his location? Danger signals.

A helicopter flew along the coast. Max stood behind the curtain and watched it pass. Movement in the corridor. Max went to the door and listened. His throat went dry. His heart beat fast. He cracked open the door and peered into the corridor, but it was empty.

His phone pinged with a voice message. He played it: Harper, crying. Scott had kicked her out again, and she wanted to be with Max now, she said. She realised what a terrible mistake she'd made and pleaded forgiveness. Max switched the phone off.

He went out to a chemist and bought packs of paracetamol. Back in his room he hatched a plan to head straight for the Highlands, like Richard Hannay in *The Thirty-Nine Steps*.

Then he immediately changed his mind.

I've spent my whole life running and hiding, he thought, *If these are my last hours or days, I want to spend them in style.*

He looked online for the most expensive hotel within a reasonable distance, and found a stately home hotel an hour's drive away. The perfect place for a final stand.

Leaving Whitby behind, the mist cleared. Max passed lots of places he would otherwise have loved to explore. Quaint villages and old market towns. Moorlands and hills. Tiny hamlets with strange names tucked away in the folds of forests. Roads veined off in all directions, pointing to destinations and attractions never to be arrived at. Parks and pubs. Museums. Vast multitudes of houses full of unused rooms and unwanted furniture and wounded people going through motions of existence; voiceless masses of individuals looking for connections amongst the fragments of modern discordance, hopeful for a better tomorrow; maybe a lottery win or a sudden change of fortune.

Cancerous scabs of ugly new utility housing developments dotted the landscape. Incessant change. Irreversible damage. Every village was earmarked for huge expansion, and every field a potential new building plot; every stretch of countryside a future town. Before long the whole country would be an unending characterless suburb.

I don't want to see the future, thought Max. *The myopic march of parasitic human conquest will overstretch its limits. A devastating collapse will occur. A die-back. Good riddance.*

The shadow of his iniquity hung over each second now. It nudged Max like the shark in the sea (if indeed it had been a shark), filling him with a sick, exhausted adrenalin rush. A one-way journey to annihilation beckoned; he knew it.

I'm complicit in my fate, thought Max, driving along an A road. *I could have tried to get more help for myself. I could have been more understanding. Too late now.*

He arrived at the hotel in the early afternoon. It was approached by a long winding road through parkland. The main building, a Victorian gothic edifice, impressed on initial sight, but it dismayed Max to see modern wings grafted on to each side, with a hideous spa complex stuck on the back.

Max went into the reception in a pretty palm court with a sweeping staircase and a huge chandelier. The main public rooms were nice; a grand saloon, a cocktail bar in an atrium, and a restaurant set in a neo-gothic library designed by Pugin. But beyond this, it was all corporate chain-hotel bland. The website said the building had been restored to its former glory, but it didn't say it had been raped of its soul.

A snooty receptionist told Max the only available suites were in the new wings. Max reluctantly agreed and took a key card for room 237.

An equally snooty desk clerk asked for lots of unnecessary personal information, which irritated Max.

'I want a room, not life insurance,' said Max.

He found room 237 at the end of a confusing labyrinth of identical peach-coloured corridors. The room disappointed, considering its exorbitant price. The only window looked out on the kitchens and the rear car park.

Max fell onto the bed and tried to sleep, but heartburn crippled him.

Then his phone pinged. An email from his mum. It read:

A reporter from the Chronicle was just here asking about you. Are you in some sort of trouble?'

Max went for a walk in the hotel parkland. There were huge redwoods and ancient cedar trees. He lingered for a while in a wood and listened to birdsong. A gentle breeze rustled through the leaves.

I might kill myself here tonight, he thought. *Use all the paracetamol, and just fade away. Let the insects eat me.*

Shortly, Max chanced upon a chapel in a clearing and went

inside. It had that familiar pleasant damp smell and the chill air of absence. He was quite alone. Sunlight shone through the stained-glass windows, creating abstract patterns on ribbed stonework and creepy memorials commemorating centuries-dead local nobility.

The day grew dark. Heavy rain fell.

One hundred years from now, thought Max, *all the things I fear will have happened. They're inevitable. That time in the distant future will come. It too will pass. That future is as unreal to me as "now" is to the people in these tombs. I'm alive at this precise moment, experiencing these thoughts and feelings and emotions. Yet so did they, once, long ago. Everything is temporary. Everything must die.*

Max felt eyes looking at him. He turned around, but was still alone.

His mobile phone rang. Harper again. She begged Max to take her back. Against his better judgement, he agreed.

He went to the hotel reception and made enquiries about the nearest railway station, then he called Harper and told her he would meet her there (and reimburse her ticket). She said she'd come right away.

Max didn't care that she was using him.

He ate lunch in his room, then dyed his hair. A few hours later he drove to a nearby branch line station surrounded by moorland.

Harper's train arrived as the sun set over the hills. She was the only passenger to get out. She sported a black eye.

'Did that scumbag do that to you?' asked Max.

'He did,' said Harper. 'But don't worry, I kicked him so hard in the balls, he'll be shitting blood for a week.'

The train departed, leaving them on the deserted platform.

'It's hardly *Brief Encounter*, is it?' said Max.

Harper smiled sadly and lifted up a limp carrier bag in her hand.

'These are all my possessions in the world,' she said.

The last rays of light lit up a calligraphy of clouds in a parchment sky. Both paused for a moment to acknowledge it.

It was dark when they got back to the hotel. Harper didn't say much. Neither did Max. He already regretted her presence. They showered, then went down to dinner. Most guests ate in a large brasserie in one of the new wings, but Max wanted to impress.

He and Harper dined in the Pugin room. The food was hideously expensive, and the service abysmal; the atmosphere oppressive with condescension. The only other patrons were three silent geriatrics in tweed.

The room, lit entirely by black candles (suitably complimenting the gothic carved gargoyles and plasterwork), sucked all the oxygen out of the room, making Max feel nauseous.

Max and Harper made unmemorable small talk.

At one point, they were served some kind of weird squid risotto as a pretentious amuse-bouche, and supplied with chopsticks to eat it with.

Max tried and failed to get any of it into his mouth.

'Squid gives me diarrhoea,' he said, giving up.

'Do you do pizza and chips?' Harper asked the waiter.

Max ordered their most expensive bottle of champagne, but it gave him a terrible bout of acid reflux.

'So, what are you doing here, darling?' Harper eventually asked.

'I killed my wife and children, then chopped them up and threw them in a pond in the garden,' said Max. 'Now I'm on the run.'

'That's not funny,' said Harper, giggling.

She rubbed his groin with her foot under the table. They went back to the room (miles away) intending to have sex. Max didn't really want sex, but Harper considered it necessary. He'd go through the motions for her sake. In the event, Max was unable to achieve an erection, so he watched Harper masturbate herself to climax. He found it mildly erotic, but the acid reflux returned and ruined any vestige of pleasure for him. He secretly hoped a fatal heart attack was imminent.

They watched TV for a while. When Harper fell asleep, Max

362

went for another walk in the grounds, taking the paracetamol with him, not intending to return.

In the woods, a full moon illuminated the smooth beech trees. An owl hooted. Max stripped naked and stood still. It felt natural and primal.

He breathed deeply of the night air.

A twig snapped in the near-distance. Max panicked. He quickly got dressed and went back to his room where he checked the internet for news of himself, but found nothing.

Again, he questioned if his family were actually dead, or if he dreamt it. Nothing seemed real to him anymore.

He rang Juno's number, expecting (and hoping) for her to answer. It went to voicemail. He tried Aldous, Perdita and Willow's numbers, with the same result, and left the same message on each one:

'Sorry. You didn't deserve it.'

The weight of their absence began to drag him down.

He went to bed thinking about Claire. Beautiful Claire. Those eyes. That enigmatic smile.

He lay awake for hours, before silently crying himself to sleep.

The following morning, he woke to the sound of Harper whispering in the bathroom. The shower was on. When Max went to investigate, he found her sitting fully clothed on the toilet with the lid down.

She froze when she saw him, and almost dropped the mobile phone she held in her trembling hand.

'I wasn't doing anything,' she said to Max, as she abruptly hung up.

'Who were you talking to?' he asked.

Harper pushed past him and went to the bedroom door. She looked frightened of Max.

'I'm going to look at the spa facilities, and maybe have a treatment,' she lied, ashen-faced.

'You haven't got any money,' said Max.

'I took some from your wallet,' said Harper, rushing out.

Max watched her as she went down the corridor. She glanced back at him a couple of times, but didn't stop. Her phone began ringing as she disappeared around a corner.

Max shut the door and switched on his own phone. It immediately began pinging with multiple messages.

He switched it off, sensing danger, then threw on some clothes and grabbed his car keys.

He went to open the door to make a quick exit, but paused with his hand on the handle. Something didn't feel right.

A deafening uneasy silence.

Max looked through the security spy hole. A squad of heavily-armed police officers were edging their way towards his room.

He calmly jammed a chair under the door handle, then backed away to the window. All looked calm outside. He opened the window and stepped out onto a spiral fire escape.

A knock came from the door.

'Room service,' said an unconvincing voice.

Max closed the window behind him and went down the steps, then he casually walked through the car park, expecting violent confrontation.

The thought crossed his mind that a sniper might shoot him dead at any second. He braced himself. Do bullets hurt? Would death be instantaneous? His sphincter puckered.

The world was now his enemy. Yes, Mrs McCabe had been right all along.

In the periphery of his vision, he saw police vehicles parked in front of the hotel. Max's car was in the side car park. He ducked behind a row of cars and made his way to his Honda (or Hyundai). Unlocked it. Climbed in. Started the engine. Pulled away.

A service road for deliveries led off from the hotel. Max serenely drove through parkland for a mile or so and began to feel smug at such an easy evasion of capture.

But when he reached a high perimeter gate, it was locked.

Option 1: Abandon car and run. (Where to? In his haste to leave, he'd left behind his wallet and cards).

Option 2: Turn car around and escape through main hotel entrance. (Based on the premise they wouldn't believe such boldness).

Option 3: Surrender. (No, not without a fight).

Max made a U-turn back towards the hotel and switched the stereo on.

A CD of Bach's *St. Matthew Passion* played. He whacked the volume up and gunned the car forward.

The hotel soon came into view once more. A police car sped past in the opposite direction. It braked into an emergency stop and reversed. Max continued on into the car park. Police were swarming around the hotel.

The blue lights of the police car flashed in his rear-view mirror and a siren blared. A pursuit was now in progress. Max raced down the hotel gravel drive.

At the main entrance gate a squad car tried to block his way, but Max rammed it aside and drove into a country lane. A helicopter appeared overhead. Max kept going, swerving past slower vehicles.

Smoke came from under the bonnet – damage from the collision. Max increased his speed. In his rear-view mirror, he saw more squad cars chasing him in a convoy. He'd watched these car chases on TV real-life crime shows. They never ended well.

Is this random, or pre-ordained? thought Max. *Has every step of my life been leading me here? Was it inevitable? The whole silly dance of my life seems like a trivial prelude, building up to this. I've merely gone through the motions, waiting for it, anticipating this unfortunate inevitability, dragged and manipulated through years of humiliations and failures of an existence I never asked for.*

Countryside gave way to an urban area. Max glanced at himself in the rear-view mirror. The eyes of a cold-blooded murderer stared back at him. He barely recognised himself. What masks we wear to disguise our mercenary corruption.

At the last split second he saw a child running across the road ahead.

Max swerved and avoided the kid, but lost control of the car. Tyres squealed.

The car clipped a curb and lifted up in the air, rolling.

Light, dark, light, dark.

Impact. A shattering of glass. A grind of compacting metal. The airbag exploded. The music stopped. Time stopped. The world held its breath. Max didn't even feel any pain.

***

Max opened his eyes. Room 9 blurred back into view once more. He lay still for a while, listening to his own laboured breathing.

A strange rattling sound emanated from him. Not a good sign. He listened. Perhaps an infection, or pneumonia. The desperate need to exist which he felt at that moment came as a shock. All notions of reason and rationality in death's embrace evaporated into panic. He waited, poised in anticipation.

The machines attached to him pinged and beeped warnings.

The sky outside began to noticeably lighten. Dawn.

Max became aware of someone sitting close by, silently watching him in silhouette – Lee.

'Claire?' croaked Max weakly. 'What happened to her?'

He slipped in and out of consciousness.

'You know what happened,' said Lee. 'You were there. You blamed yourself, but it wasn't your fault. You suppressed the memory deep within. There are no answers, I'm afraid, just questions.'

'But that explains… nothing… It's not good enough.' said Max.

'No, Max,' said Lee. 'It never is.'

The machines beeped and pinged erratically. Alarms rang.

People ran into the room.

A wave of euphoria enveloped Max. Liberation. Terror. Billions of people coalesced into one single identity. The events of his life now seemed like an obscure distant dream.

He saw vast geometric forms stretching off to infinity, and kaleidoscopic shapes similar to a complex structural formula.

A whispery sigh escaped from his lips as he suddenly, unexpectedly, slipped away.

38

The weather forecast predicted a light sprinkling of snow, but by late afternoon it blanketed the landscape. Large flakes continued to fall in gentle fluffy drifts. The naked trees were washed pewter with frost.

Max saw Claire walking home alone through the park. He caught up with her, pushing his unwieldy bike.

'Hey,' said Max.

'Hey,' said Claire.

Her nose and cheeks were red from cold, which matched the colour of her woolly bobble hat.

'What did you think of the lesson on metaphysics?' asked Max.

'I thought I imagined it,' said Claire, with a smile.

'All that we see or seem is but a dream within a dream,' said Max.

'I like abstruse philosophical principles,' said Claire.

Butterflies fluttered in Max's stomach. He desperately wanted to kiss her and spend the rest of his life at her side.

'I thought it was interesting when Mr Grant talked about how life is a constant battle for self-knowledge, but it's a battle that can never be won,' said Max.

'I liked the bit about how our memories are unstable and changeable imaginative constructs,' said Claire.

'Yes,' said Max. 'Our memories have a tendency to cling to random meaningless details, yet it lets treasures vanish.'

Claire glanced at Max.

'It's to do with amygdala activation affecting protein synthesis in the hippocampus,' she said.

'That's not a sentence you hear every day,' said Max.

They reached the perimeter of the park. Claire always turned left to go home and Max always turned right at this spot. Claire stopped, as if to say goodbye, but Max turned left.

'Don't you live in the opposite direction?' asked Claire.

'I want to take the scenic route on such a lovely warm afternoon,' he said.

Claire smiled. A puff of vapour obscured her face for a second. Max wished he could bottle the vapour and keep it.

They crossed the road and walked down a residential street.

The snow crunched underfoot in a satisfying way, but they kept to a careful pace because of the sheet of ice underneath.

'What are you planning to do for a career?' asked Claire.

'Become a novelist,' said Max.

'You are the best in English,' said Claire.

'Words are, like, the sort of thing I'm good at and stuff,' said Max, trying to be funny. 'I'll probably be a world-famous award-winning actor, too,' he added.

'Wow,' said Claire. 'A multi-hyphenate, no less.'

'What are you going to do?' asked Max.

'I'm going to travel, initially,' said Claire.

'Where to?' asked Max with a sinking heart. 'For how long?'

He immediately wanted to change his career plans to travel with her.

'Not sure,' said Claire. 'I'll do charity voluntary work in Africa, then go to college to study philosophy in America.'

'Yeah, I'm thinking of doing exactly the same,' said Max.

'What kind of novels will you write?' asked Claire.

'Deep stuff about the human condition,' said Max. 'About how we are helpless in the hands of destiny. We're fated to die, but don't know when or how, yet we endure living under such cruel terms.'

'Is fatalistic fiction commercial?' asked Claire.

'Yeah,' said Max. 'I'd like to write something about how our genes endow us with the mental programmes for developing a conscious identity that grows to see itself existing as an end in its own right; a self that, besides doing all it can to ensure its own basic comfort and security, typically strives for self-development. It aspires to not only be itself, through continually affirming its presence in the world, but to make more of itself through learning, creativity, love, spiritual growth, social influence and symbolic expression.'

Max had learnt it by rote to impress her.

'Sounds interesting.' said Claire. 'I look forward to reading it.'

A car passed by. A parent was driving some boys home. One of them threw a snowball at Max. It hit him directly in the face.

'Wanker!' the boys shouted in unison. The car drove onwards into the slippery distance with the sound of the boys' howls of laughter.

'Idiots,' said Claire. 'Are you okay?'

'It's an old joke we have,' lied Max, wiping painful snow out of his eyes. 'I'm actually very good friends with them.'

Max saw Claire's hands were red with cold. He took his gloves off and offered them to her. She politely refused, but he insisted.

'Thanks,' she said, putting them on. 'I was about to take my clothes off.'

'Huh?' said Max, as they continued walking.

'People who develop hypothermia often take all their clothes off at the last moment before they die,' said Claire. 'It's something to do with the brain going haywire and confusing extreme cold with extreme heat. That's why people who freeze to death are often found undressed, which makes it look like they were assaulted.'

'Really?' said Max. 'Is that true?'

'I read it somewhere.'

Max shoved his shivering hands into his pockets.

A large snowflake managed to find its way down the collar of his coat. It landed on the nape of his neck, then melted and trickled down his back.

They passed a bungalow. In the living room, an old man and an old woman were slow-dancing. Max and Claire noticed them at the same time and stopped to watch.

'Aw. Sweet,' said Claire.

'It must be great being old,' said Max. 'You don't have to worry about exams and careers anymore. There's nothing to prove.'

'I'm sure they worry about many things,' said Claire. 'Just different stuff, like ill-health, and money and infirmity.'

Max put his bike to one side and gestured for Claire to slow-dance with him. She laughed, but took up the offer.

Max held her in his arms, smitten.

The elderly couple saw Max and Claire. The man came over to the window, scowled at them, then drew the curtains shut.

Max and Claire stopped dancing.

'He thought we were making fun of them,' said Claire.

They continued walking.

'Maybe they were having one last dance before committing joint suicide,' said Max.

'Don't say that,' said Claire.

'It's romantic,' said Max. 'You dance beautifully, by the way.'

Claire chuckled, which pleased Max. He stuck out his tongue and let snowflakes land on it.

'Do they taste good?' asked Claire.

Max pretended to be a pretentious food critic.

'I'm getting gooseberries and a hint of walnut,' he said.

Claire stuck out her tongue, then grimaced.

'Mine tasted of used sanitary towels,' she said.

They crossed a road. Usually it was busy with traffic, but today there were only a few tyre tracks in the snow. Parked cars and bushes wore icing sugar blankets. Max wondered how long the pure whiteness on the ground would last until it thawed into dirty slush.

Before they reached the other side, Max slipped over.

'Oh!' said Claire. 'Are you okay?'

'Just a broken rib or two,' joked Max, although he did feel pain in his ankle.

Claire helped him to stand up. She almost slipped over too, emitting a squeal as she did so. They both laughed.

Max wanted to kiss Claire. The moment felt so right. But he didn't do it. He didn't want to ruin the moment. He held her gloved hand for a little bit too long.

She didn't tell him to let go, but he did anyway.

He picked up his bike. They scrunched along a bit further in silence.

Max swallowed and prepared to ask Claire to go out with him, but he became distracted. Ahead of them, a man furtively approached a house with no lights on and knocked on the front door. A woman in a robe answered and ushered the man inside.

'What's going on there?' asked Max.

'He's an electrician come to fix the electricity?' ventured Claire.

'He didn't have any tools,' said Max, as they passed the house. 'It's getting dark and he looked quite nervous. What are they doing in there?'

'You, sir, are a nosey parker,' smiled Claire.

'Something sinister is occurring,' said Max, darkly.

'Vampires, you mean?' said Claire, playing along.

'Who truly knows what happens behind the net curtains of suburbia,' said Max in a movie trailer voice.

'Maybe they make macramé dollies in the dark while wearing night vision goggles,' said Claire.

'Yes, Watson, that can be the only rational answer,' said Max.

Claire stopped.

'I'm worrying about that old couple now,' she said. 'Do you think we should go back and see if they're all right?'

'Why?'

'Compassion,' said Claire. 'It's the cornerstone of humanity.'

'I watch the news,' said Max. 'Compassion is a luxury of humanity, not the cornerstone.'

'That's a very misanthropic statement,' said Claire.

'Misanthropic, but true,' replied Max. 'An essential facet of being a serious writer is seeing life as painful and meaningless.'

'So you have no compassion?' asked Claire.

'I'm a very compassionate person,' said Max. 'In fact, I have way too much compassion, to the point of inertia. I'm selective in the things I'm compassionate about.'

'Such as?'

'Animals,' said Max.

'Which animals?' asked Claire.

'My goldfish, Trumpet, mainly,' said Max.

'What about people?'

'I prefer animals to people,' said Max. 'Okay, I agree, that does sound misanthropic.'

'A little bit,' said Claire with a shake of her head.

They continued walking.

'I told the careers advisor I wanted to be either a veterinarian, or a human rights lawyer, and he laughed at me,' said Max. 'He said I should lower my expectations. So I told him, in fifty years, all the oceans will be as acidic as a can of cola. New York will be in the hurricane belt. London will be hotter than the Sahara. Bangladesh will be under water. My career prospects are meaningless in the scheme of things.'

'You said that to him?' asked Claire.

'I'm a nihilistic realist,' said Max. 'Hope by name, but not by nature.'

Claire was quiet for a moment.

'I choose optimism,' she said. 'It's easy to be cynical. It's the default position of too many people. Cynicism is lazy thinking, and also an intellectual cul de sac.'

'I totally agree,' said Max, backtracking on everything he'd just said.

'Positivity is life-affirming,' said Claire. 'Negativity bores me.'

'My sentiments exactly,' said Max.

They continued in silence again.

No one he knew spoke with the same intelligence as Claire. All the boys fancied her, but only because she was the prettiest girl by far.

Her eyes. Her smile. Max opened his mouth to declare his undying love for her, but nothing came out.

They stopped at the corner of the main road. Claire looked at him.

Max became anxious. This felt like a seminal moment; a parting of ways. He didn't want Claire to go, ever.

A welt of red spread across the horizon, the last vestige of sunlight.

Claire saw it first, then Max followed her gaze.

'See,' she said, pointing into the distance. 'There's so much beauty in this world. It's up to us to recognise and appreciate it. We take it for granted. People walk around like they're just awake.'

'But that's exactly how I feel – like I've just woken up,' said Max.

'That isn't what I meant,' said Claire.

'No, I do know what you mean,' insisted Max.

There were a thousand things he wanted to say to her. He was no closer to knowing Claire, and he felt he'd misrepresented himself.

It was the last day of school term. It may as well have been the last day of Time itself.

'I have to go,' said Claire.

She took off Max's gloves and gave them back to him.

'Keep them,' said Max.

'I'll survive,' said Claire, smiling.

She looked in his eyes with something resembling love, then kissed him on the cheek.

'Finally woken.' she said.

'What?' asked Max.

Claire began crossing the road. She didn't look back, or wave. Max watched her vanishing within the flurry of snow which fell in ever-thicker swirls. He felt compelled to run after her, but as he moved, an articulated lorry silently skidded into view out of nowhere. It hit Claire full on. The impact created a dull thud, followed by a crack.

The lorry continued sliding for another hundred yards before finally coming to a halt.

Max stepped forward, dumping his bike at the kerb, and looked at the spot where Claire had just been. A few dots of blood marked the snow, then a long smear of red followed the path of the lorry.

Small fragments of skull lay nearby, like broken eggshell.

The only sound came from the back wheel of Max's bike, which clicked round and round.

A woman ran out of a shop and screamed.

Max put on the gloves. They were still warm.

He bent down and scrunched up a snowball, then realised he had no one to throw it at. He let it drop from his hand and felt tears on his cheeks, but he made no attempt to wipe them away.

It was getting dark now. Lights were being switched on.

Max stood alone in the twilight. His and Claire's footprints were already fading away beneath fresh snowfall. Within minutes they would disappear completely.